To my copycat

THE CUTE PSYCHO

MORALLY AMBIGUOUS DUET
BOOK ONE

VERONICA LANCET

PREFACE

Dear brave reader,

You must be truly courageous to open the pages of this book.

THIS BOOK IS DARK. And by that I mean, it's super dark (but it's also cute and romantic). There is gore, lots of gore, some questionable romantic cannibalism, obsessive love interests and **VERY** disturbing scenes.

This book isn't your regular dark romance either. It has sci-fi and PNR influences and treads the line between contemporary and speculative fiction. So you must be able to suspend your disbelief at times. (Not when it comes to the love story, though, because who doesn't want a sickeningly sweet love story like Vlad and Sisi's?)

SO KIDS, DON'T TRY ANY OF THESE SCENARIOS AT HOME, ALL RIGHT?

This is your warning to turn back, or you will not be able to unread the things you read next. You will be grossed out. You will probably have nightmares. Not worth it if you ask me. So close the book and save yourself the trauma.

But if those warnings only made you more curious, then welcome to the dark side, friend.

Enjoy the mayhem!

FULL TRIGGER WARNINGS
animal abuse

blood (gore)

blood play

cannibalism

consensual non-consent

death

derogatory terms

descriptive CSA

descriptive rape

drugs

guns

human experiments

extreme graphic violence

extreme graphic sexual situations

extreme depictions of torture

grooming

kidnapping

knife play

miscarriage

murder

non-con/dubcon

primal play

self-harm

substance abuse

suicide

uncomfortable religious situations

1

VLAD

AGE EIGHT

"You're sure there's nothing wrong with him?" My father paces around the small office, glaring at the doctor.

"We've run tests. Considering his condition..." The doctor looks me up and down, pursing his lips as his eyes focus on my naked chest. "He's in spectacular health. It's quite extraordinary, actually." His hand goes up to stroke his chin.

I tilt my head, returning his scrutiny with my own, my eyes meeting his gaze and holding the contact. Unnerved, he quickly looks away.

"Look at him and tell me he's normal," Father continues, pointing his finger at me.

I don't react, since I don't care about *his* opinion. And as I glance around the room, my eyes zone in on a sparkly glint of metal. Mentally, I do an estimation of the time and amount of movements it would take me to reach it.

"There's something wrong with his eyes, I tell you," my father says, and my attention switches to him momentarily.

He comes closer, but still keeps a distance. I can see it in his expression and the way his lip curls slightly at the corner as he looks at me. I disgust him.

I have since I came back.

I don't react when he suddenly brings his fingers in front of my face, snapping them twice. Unblinking, I turn my eyes toward him, regarding him curiously.

"See? He's fucking soulless. Whatever they did to him..." he trails off, shaking his head. The doctor is quick to assure my father that I am perfectly healthy and that it may be residual trauma.

"Trauma, my ass. He doesn't talk! All he does is stare at me like a fucking mute!" my father exclaims, throwing his hands in the air and pacing around the room again.

The doctor comes closer, his eyes narrowing at me as he prompts me to say something.

I watch in annoyance as he slows his speech and uses oversimplified words as if I were mentally challenged.

A small frown appears on his face as he brings his hand up to check my neck. His fingers don't reach their destination, as I catch them mid-air, folding them backwards until he's yelping in pain.

One swift movement and the sharp, steely object is in my hand. The doctor doesn't even get to react as the blade makes contact with his skin. A clean line from ear to ear appears just beneath his jaw and blood comes out in spurts like a jet spray, painting me red from head to toe. The doctor's body falls to the ground with a thud, and my father snaps his head around, his eyes widening in horror.

One hand goes to his forehead as he's massaging his temples, all the while cursing out all kinds of obscenities.

Me?

I only have eyes for the redness of the blood, the mesmer-izing color that seems to remind me of something.

The liquid is dripping down my face, the feel of it on my skin intoxicating and liberating.

I close my eyes, honing in on that feeling. My tongue sneaks out to lick my lips, tasting the forbidden substance and reveling in the metallic taste.

So familiar...

"You're a fucking monster," my father spits at me. I open my eyes to regard him with a bored expression and it seems to fuel his anger further, as he starts throwing stuff at me.

One mug hits the side of my head.

What should have been a blinding pain is muted by my already dead pain receptors. My skin breaks and opens to let out even more red liquid. It flows down my face, coating my lashes and blinding my right eye.

Father is breathing harshly, his gaze fixed on the gash next to my hairline. Slowly, his eyes find mine, and we stare at each other in a contained battle of wills.

"*Bozhe!*" he whispers, three fingers going to his forehead before descending to his torso, to make the sign of the cross. Finally, one hand settles on the handle of his gun, and he seems to debate whether to kill me or not.

I make his decision easier as I hop off the bed, advancing toward him while still holding his gaze. Wrapping my fingers over his, I take out the gun and point it toward my head, the cold butt of the pistol making contact with my flesh.

"*Davai!*" I bark, my voice groggy and ragged from disuse. My eyebrows are drawn together in consternation as I urge him to do it. *Kill me.*

"*Ubei menya,*" I utter again, and his eyes widen in shock

before his hand tightens on the handle, wrenching the gun away from me.

"Clean yourself," he mutters before leaving the room.

Taking a deep breath, I allow myself to feel disappointment for a moment before I turn back to the doctor's corpse.

Father may not know it, but he just left me with a gift. And I plan to take advantage of it to the fullest.

Hours later, my father's guards show up, and they find me elbows deep in the doctor's chest cavity as I reorganize his organs.

Bummer...

* * *

"We can't let him stay here, Dima," my mother whispers to my father, thinking I can't hear them. I turn my head to the side, my gaze fixed on the bird hopping around the windowsill.

I know I'm not wanted in the house, and everyone has made it clear that they don't wish to share a space with me. Not that I blame them, since I've noticed the fear in their eyes as they look at me. They are all afraid I'm going to snap somehow, but even that fear is not enough to make them kill me.

I am a child after all, and even seasoned killers frown upon killing the young. If only they knew what's in my mind... they would certainly *not* hesitate.

"Are you my brother?" I look down into the curious eyes of a little girl. Her hair is parted in the middle, two pink ribbons holding the strands together. It looks oddly reminiscent of something.

"Hey," she pokes my side, frowning when I don't answer.

"You're my brother. I know you are," she says with more confidence, folding her hands across her chest.

I shrug at her, and my gaze returns to the bird. Foreign information starts flooding my brain. I seem to have read somewhere that birds have hollow bones, their structures different to allow for flight. I wonder how they would look on the inside...

My hand shoots out, my fingers wrapping around the slim body of the bird. I'm quick enough that she doesn't have time to spread her wings.

Bringing her toward me, I study the way her eyes close, the membrane serving as her lid inciting my interest. Sharp... I need something sharp.

I'm about to reach for a knife when the little girl's hand covers my own. She looks terrified as she glances between me and the bird.

"What... don't..." she stammers, her lower lip quivering.

I tilt my head to look at her, my eyes narrowing slightly.

She tries to pry my fingers off the bird, her efforts futile. When it finally dawns on her that she won't be able to do it, tears gather at the corners of her eyes.

I still, the sight shocking and foreign. It awakens something uncomfortable in my chest. For the first time, as I weigh the options, I find myself leaning toward making her stop crying, even if it means passing up on satisfying my curiosity.

"Katya!" my mother exclaims in outrage, tugging her away from me. My eyes follow the trail of her tears, already entranced by them. My fingers become unwittingly loose until the bird flies away, unharmed.

"Never do this again, you hear me? Never approach your brother alone. He's dangerous!"

My mother continues to scold Katya, telling her just how

awful I am, but as I look into her eyes, I see some type of understanding.

My parents decide to place me in the attic, as far away from their other children as possible. It's funny because for as much as my past before a couple of months ago is a void, I don't think I've ever felt particularly close to my family — even *before*.

There's only ever been one person who's been by my side through thick and thin—my twin, Vanya. And she's the only one who is not afraid to interact with me, even risking our parents' anger if they found out.

To everyone else, I'm just a necessary evil.

What they don't seem to understand is that my behavior isn't intentional. I don't just set out to do harm. It just... happens.

Like a haze covering my mind, I forget about my surroundings and I focus on one object only—my prey. I hone in on my target and everything else falls away. It suddenly becomes only about the unanswered questions.

How many pumps of blood does the heart have left after death? How do organs look from the inside of the body? So many questions, and so many situations to explore.

"Like that, cut through the stomach too," Vanya advises and I take heed, slicing the blade and making a straight cut from sternum to pubis. The fat under the skin is making it hard for me to get to the inside, but as Vanya urges me on, I can only dig the edge of the knife deeper, a sharp sound signaling I've hit bone — the ribs.

One of my father's men had come to bring me food. But just at that time, Vanya had a different idea. While I don't always indulge her, this time she'd pouted at me and I couldn't find it in me to say no to her.

"Why didn't you ask when I killed the first man?" I

mutter under my breath. I'd already accidentally killed one man in the morning. It would have been easy enough to perform an experiment then. But when Vanya gets something in her head, it's hard to dissuade her.

"He wasn't interesting." She shrugs, going around me to plop herself on a chair. She's looking curiously at the body, her black eyes focused on the blood pooling on the floor.

It's a condition we both share... this thirst for blood.

I get to work, opening up the chest, the flaps of flesh folded on either side of the body.

"What now?" I look up briefly and Vanya purses her lips, regarding the open cavity with interest.

"The stomach. Let's see what he had for lunch!" She jumps up, her feet connecting with the wood floor and making a harsh sound. Her lips stretch into a wide smile, signaling the excitement is getting to her.

I shake my head slowly, but a smile plays on my own lips.

I tug the stomach out, severing the connective tissue until I can remove it. Placing it on the floor, I take the knife and I make a few incisions, the pouch immediately giving way to the sharpness of the blade, the contents spilling out.

Digestive fluid and bits of undigested food inundate the floor. I move slightly to the right to avoid getting anything on my shoes. Vanya too scrunches her nose once the smell hits, but still, her eyes are glued to the barely recognizable pieces of food.

"Whoever gets the most right wins." She crouches next to me to move the pieces around, trying to make out what they are.

"Sure," I agree, even though we both know she *will* win. When have I ever *not* let her win?

We spend the next hour debating what each crumb could be, a green particle proving to be particularly elusive.

"Broccoli," she leans back, confident in her answer.

I shake my head, but I don't say what I'm thinking—broccolini. Instead, I use the knife to move a piece of the stem toward her, knowing she will put two and two together.

Her eyes widen and she smirks at me.

"Broccolini! I win!" She springs up, jumping around the room and gloating about her small victory.

My eyes swing back to the mess next to me, and I drop the utensils. Using my bare hands, I cup the heart, ripping it from the chest. My thumbs are in position and I start pumping, curious how much blood is left inside and how it will react to an outside force.

Blood comes out in spurts, a squeaky sound permeating the air. Vanya and I stare at the poor, abused heart for a moment, before we both start laughing.

"It sounded like a fart." Vanya crouches on the floor, holding onto her belly with one hand and wiping tears from her eyes with the other.

I can't help but join in.

Our jolly time, however, is cut short as we hear the floor creaking.

"Someone's coming!" Vanya immediately composes herself, rising to look around for a hiding place.

She spares me a glance, her finger going to her lips to tell me to keep my mouth shut.

No one can know she's been with me—least of all our parents.

Eyeing the big closet, she opens the door and sneaks inside, leaving me in the middle of a bloody mess.

When my father opens the door, his expression is already resigned as he takes in the disaster.

He doesn't waste any time grabbing me by the nape and dragging me out. I don't react, not even when his fingers dig painfully into my skin.

We make it to the basement, and father flings me to the ground in front of him.

"If you're such a fucking psycho, better put those urges of yours to some good use." He nods to the man strapped to a chair. His face is already busted, purple swelling taking away any semblance of humanity from him.

"Let's see what you've got." My father folds his hands over his chest, taking a step back and looking at me expectantly.

Gazing around, I note a variety of tools on one side, so I take my time to pick one that would suit my needs.

I don't know what Father expects to see, but I'm not about to waste this chance trying to please him. Not when my mind is already focused on my next experiment.

A few steps and I'm in front of the prisoner, a pair of pliers in my hand. I'm quick to open his jaw and take his tongue out, the pliers settling nicely against the piece of muscle. The man barely has time to react before I pull—hard. My strength may not be that of an adult, but with a good gauge of angles, the tongue gives way.

The man writhes in pain as I tighten my fingers on the handle of the pliers and give one last pull, the tongue slipping from the cavity.

Long and with striations of pink and red, the muscle doesn't seem as interesting as I'd first thought.

With a low curse, I fling it to the floor, approaching the prisoner again and forcing his mouth open, curious about the damage.

He's bleeding, the blood pooling in his throat as he's trying his hardest not to choke on it.

The way clear, I'm suddenly curious about the inside of his throat. Grabbing some metal, I prop his jaw open so his teeth won't come clamping down on my skin. Then, folding my hand nicely around a tiny blade, I insert my arm into his mouth, feeling around the warm channel, before going down his throat. My arm is small enough that it fits down his esophagus.

His mouth is almost touching my shoulder, and I give a last push before I feel the edge of the stomach. Releasing the blade from my hand, I maneuver it around and penetrate the wall from the inside, pushing until the tip of the knife reaches the surface.

The man can't even yell in agony, and it must be quite the pain, because I start lifting the knife, continuing to cut through his tissue.

By the time my arm is out of his body, he's dead, his torso a bloody mess of uncoordinated cuts.

Damn!

It's not pretty. Maybe next time I'll do better. I study my mistakes carefully, already forgetting about my father's presence.

I'm startled by a slap on my back, Father's body next to my own as he stares at my work.

"I'll be damned..." he whispers, almost in awe.

2

VLAD

AGE TWELVE

Sharpening my knife, I look at Marcello's work of art from the corner of my eye. Begrudgingly, I have to admit that he has a knack for this sort of thing. Whereas my end product is often messy, his is neat, every detail in place, as if it had been thought out well in advance. And it had. Marcello is not one for impulsivity — he leaves that to me. No, his work is exquisitely minute.

"You're done?"

His tools fall to the ground with a thud. He nods, bringing his sleeve up to wipe some of the blood from his face.

Only a couple of years older than me, Marcello is the son of an Italian capo—our family's associates.

Since our very first assignment together some years back, the adults had decided that we worked best together and they'd repeatedly paired us, so we could do the most *unsavory* work.

With a bored expression on my face, I examine Marcello's

handiwork. The dead man had been a rat that my father had caught feeding information to the Albanians.

I'd observed enough to know that ours was the most strategic position. With access to all the major ports, we were the first to know when a special shipment would arrive. Of course, everyone vied for that type of information, which made our organization the perfect target for infiltration.

My father had been the one doling out punishments in the past. But since he'd witnessed the damage Marcello and I could do to a prisoner, he'd decided to leave the rats to us.

A cut runs down from his neck to his pubis, splitting the man in two. His arms and legs had been nicely broken and folded inside in a grotesque manner. This was all about the show, since his body will spend at least a couple of days in the grand hall.

A reminder never to cross the Pakhan again. After all, no man wanted his body desecrated and exposed in a sick spectacle.

I know I will enjoy my own time when the exposition is done, since I get to do a thorough examination of his remains.

Vanya is already restless thinking of the opportunity.

In the last few years I'd learned to control myself better, and I'd made a promise to my father that the only men to die by my hand would be the ones with a death warrant over their heads.

In return, he'd offer me any bodies he could spare to satisfy my morbid curiosity.

He doesn't realize though, that it's not only *my* curiosity, but Vanya's too. We share the same obsession with how things work... what makes humans tick. And we enjoy our time dissecting and discussing the insides of a corpse.

Vanya's not only my twin. She's my partner in crime.

And however much my parents may be against my sisters coming near me for fear of their safety, Vanya's never been one to let others dissuade her when she's made up her mind. And we've already been inseparable since birth.

But while she may be just as deviant as I, she's also the more humane of the two. The only one who can ground me when I feel my control slipping.

I may have promised my father not to kill his men, but that doesn't mean it's easy for me. It's not a conscious decision when it happens. It's more like a compunction. One word from Vanya, though, and I comply.

I move out of my chair to assess Marcello's work from up close, noting some marks of hesitation.

"What's gotten into you?" I narrow my eyes as I survey the jagged lines. Lines that any other time would be perfectly straight.

Marcello's not looking at me. He's staring into the pool of blood on the ground, his expression a mix of regret and melancholy.

"Don't tell me you've gone all soft." I tilt my head to study him.

The messier the work, the harder it's going to be for me to salvage something out of the body. And it's completely unlike Marcello.

He grumbles something under his breath, taking a step back and heading toward the makeshift bathroom. Turning the faucet on, he splashes some water onto his face.

I'm getting impatient, and Vanya will, too, if we don't end this soon. I'd already promised her the afternoon, and she always throws a fit when I don't fulfill my promises.

Marcello quietly steps back into the room, his head hung low. I stifle the urge to roll my eyes at him.

"My sister," he starts, and I turn to face him, surprised at his words. "It's my sister's birthday. She'll be three today."

"I didn't know you had a sister," I simply state. I've never seen Marcello like this... full of unknown emotions.

It's a state I can't deal with.

"Had... that's a good way of putting it," he says with a bitter laugh.

I frown, confused.

"I don't even know her name," he continues, sighing deeply before plopping himself on a chair.

I move closer. Marcello threads his fingers through his hair, suddenly looking tired and much older than his age.

I may not empathize with his feelings, but I do know what Vanya means to me, and a world without her would be completely bleak.

"What happened to her?" I don't know what prompts me to ask him that, since I should just ignore him and go about my day. Somehow, though, my curiosity gets the best of me.

"She's in a convent... she's better off there. I still wish..." He shakes his head, getting up and moving toward the door.

I purse my lips, trying to identify what's happening with Marcello and how I can help him get back to his normal working capacity. We are a team after all, and one half doing a poor job will affect the entire whole.

Just as I'm going through all the possibilities, the door to the basement opens to reveal my father. He's dragging in two battered bodies with him.

"Your lucky day, son," my father says and winks at me as he throws the bodies to the ground.

Lucky indeed.

Marcello's issue is firmly forgotten as I look at the newest additions to the torture room.

"Permission?" I ask, needing to know what I *can* and *cannot* do.

My eyes on the bodies, I wet my lips in excitement, all types of punishments going through my mind.

"They're all yours. We caught them stealing from the depot. We already have one for the hall."

Father regards Marcello's work, his lips tugging upwards at the abomination currently residing in the torture chair. It doesn't look human anymore, and as the new prisoners also glance upon the horror show, they realize their turn isn't far off.

Bringing some of his men in, he removes the work of art meant for display, and I take advantage of the brute force of the soldiers to ask for a few favors of my own. Seeing that Marcello isn't going to take the lead on this one, I might as well take advantage and fulfill one of my own fantasies.

Vanya will be so giddy when I tell her, since we'd developed this particular hypothesis together.

"Hang the prisoners to the ceiling," I start, pointing at the men on the ground. "Feet down."

Soon, father and his men are gone. I'm left with a melancholic Marcello, and I decide it's high time he stopped moping around.

And what could be more fun than the two Ms—murder and mutilation?

"Marcello," I call out to him, as I proceed to lay out my plans. I explain to him that this is a competition, and the aim is to cut as much of the body without killing them.

"They are most likely to die from blood loss, so we need to be careful with our slices. The one who cuts the most of the body and whose prisoner still lives is the winner," I say, satisfied with the game and excited to be on the winning side.

Maybe I am taking advantage of Marcello's tumultuous state to gain some leverage in this competition, since his cuts won't be as precise as always. But *maybe* this will be what he needs to get his head in the game.

After I've finished explaining the rules, he nods thoughtfully, agreeing with my terms.

We each build our own stash of knives, blades, saws, and other tools before proceeding to the prisoners' side.

"Start!"

We take a blade each, and we begin cutting. True to his work ethic, Marcello starts out small—he saws the ankles off.

Assessing my own project, I try to think strategically. Every single piece I cut will increase the bleeding.

Closing my eyes, I picture an anatomy book I'd read, looking for the major arteries and how they traverse the bodies. My best bet is to be mindful of the femoral artery and cut as high up as I can. As I mentally run through all the scenarios, I get another idea.

Smiling, I look at my stash, pleased to see a small flamethrower. It seems I'd anticipated it before even thinking it through.

I take one of the saws and I start cutting, centering my incision right where the hip socket meets the femur. I need to be as fast as possible to ensure minimal bleeding.

But while I have my entire plan accounted for, there is one thing that Marcello has over me—strength. Puberty has given him the advantage of stature and strength, so I'll have to find ways to bypass that.

Taking a small chair, I climb on top of it, so I'm at eye level with the prisoner's stomach. I stoop slightly for better access and I continue cutting.

When I reach the artery, the blood comes out in spurts,

bathing my clothes. I barely avoid the stream to my face as I'm quick to use the flamethrower to cauterize the wound.

Marcello narrows his eyes at me when he sees my trick, and I just smirk.

"Not against the rules," I smirk.

He shakes his head, but doesn't comment further, using his own method to slow down the blood flow.

Smart.

He's switched positions, bringing up the man's legs closer to his chest and securing them there with a rope. The position ensures that the blood won't flow as fast due to gravity.

Finishing one thigh, I turn to the other. Every now and then I check to make sure the prisoner is still alive.

The sounds of steel against bone and the muffled cries behind the men's gags reverberate in the room.

When I'm done with the second thigh, the artery cauterized, the blood flow minimal, I stop to think of my next steps.

Marcello sighs as he watches the blood from his own prisoner pool down. He'd tried to go the faster route too, aiming for the thighs. But without fire to close the artery, the blood is simply flowing freely.

"You win." He shakes his head, taking a step back and untying the man's legs, so that the body is once again in a vertical position.

Blood rushes out in spurts, just like a fountain, pouring down and flooding the ground.

I lick my lips, the sight tantalizing enough to make me forget my own project.

But not quite.

"What now?" Marcello comes around to survey my work.

I'd already gotten rid of his legs, but now it's even trickier. Any higher and the organs will spill out.

A devious smile stretches across my face. Ah, too bad Vanya won't be here to witness this.

"Help me out, will you?" I say, stepping off the chair. "I am the winner after all." I wink at him, taking the chainsaw and plugging it in.

"You don't mean to...." Marcello's eyes widen slightly.

"I don't have much use for him now. I've won, and statistically speaking, the chances of me cutting more without killing him are very low. This way we can enjoy the show." I grin at him.

Starting the chainsaw, I climb back on the chair, aiming for the man's midriff and pushing the revolving blade into his side.

I should have used goggles.

I realize that belatedly as pieces of flesh and bits of organs jump into my face. I shake them off, continuing to cut through.

Marcello looks done with me, and I'm not even halfway through.

"You could help me, you know," I add drily. He's the one with the extra strength.

"Really?" he retorts ironically, but does end up taking the chainsaw from my hands, cutting the last part of the man's torso.

He barely takes a step back before the man's entire chest cavity falls to the ground, the intestines slowly unwinding in a serpentine, blood, bile and stomach juice all mixing in a foul combination.

Marcello scrunches up his nose, quickly putting some distance between him and the half-body still hung to the ceiling.

I raise my gaze, taking in the eyes stuck in perpetual horror, the ugliness of life and death combined to both enthrall and disgust. My feet take me closer, and I can't help but be mesmerized by the sight of red—of mayhem and destruction.

It's like a long-forgotten memory is trying to surface, a need to hurt and be hurt swallowing me whole as I remain rooted to the spot.

It's much later that I realize I must have lost track of time. Marcello's already gone. My father's cleaners are at work.

There's also my older brother, Misha, watching me from a corner, his lip curled up in disgust.

"Freak," is all he says as I meet his gaze with mine.

I don't reply. I don't have to. I merely let my mouth open up widely into a full smile. His composure is immediately shaken off, and he scurries away, muttering something to himself.

For all his bullying tendencies, Misha is nothing but a coward. And no matter how much he picks on me, I know he fears what I'd do to him.

After all, I'd told him in great detail one time, when I'd seen him pick on Katya and Elena. He's almost sixteen now, yet his fascination with Elena, our youngest sister, hasn't escaped me. Mother and father prohibit *me* from associating with my sisters, yet they turn a blind eye to Misha.

Maybe I should just kill him and be done with it. But Vanya won't let me. Every time I try to tell her my plan of getting rid of him, she has to lecture me that family is where I should draw the line.

"We don't kill family, Vlad," she'd pouted at me, her arms crossed over her chest. And I'd reluctantly agreed with her. But she'd had to take it one step further and make me vow I'd never lift a hand against family.

My word is probably the only thing that makes me *human*, since I'd long resolved to make it binding. I can't behave like normal people, and I can't empathize with their situations. *That*, I'd learned, makes me extremely dangerous. But Vanya had made me see that I could still function in society—be in control somehow—by having a set of personal boundaries I'd make myself accountable for.

Who would have guessed that someone like me would end up having principles? But they are the only thing that keeps me from succumbing to a pure animalistic rage.

* * *

"D o you want to go there too?" Vanya comes to my side, laying a hand on my shoulder.

Staring out the window and into the garden, I can only nod as I watch Katya and Elena run around, playing with a kite. Their laughs are so foreign, but at the same time so fascinating, that I can't help but look on—as an outsider.

Vanya is the only one crafty enough to sneak in to visit me. But she's also the only one who truly knows me—the only one that sees *me*. We've been together since the very beginning. It would have been strange if she *hadn't* sought me out.

Katya and Elena, though, are too young to understand why they aren't allowed to interact with their older brother. I've exchanged a few words with them in passing, but I've never been part of their little world.

And I want to.

Why, I can't say. I know I'm not like other kids my age. I know there's something wrong with me. But when I see them smiling without a care in the world, I wish, just for one moment, to be normal too. To play with others and enjoy their company. Because as it stands, I'm either feared or tolerated.

Never desired.

"I'd never leave you, brother." Vanya's arms sneak across my waist as she lays her head on my shoulder. "You know that, don't you?"

"Yes," I reply, almost absentmindedly.

Because she's the only one who cares about me, who sees more than a freak or a killing machine.

She sees *me.*

"Forever," she whispers, her little finger wrapping around mine in a solemn promise.

"Forever," I vow.

3
VLAD

AGE FIFTEEN

Staring down at the tattoo artist, I watch as he traces the contour of his design on my arm, the needle of the gun penetrating my skin in what should have been a mildly painful jab. Given my already deteriorated pain receptors, the only thing I can feel is a ticklish sensation as he moves the gun across my skin.

"It's so pretty!" Vanya gushes from my side, craning her neck to get a better look at the emerging design.

I grunt in agreement.

In just a short week, I'd gone from bare skin to almost full body armor. I'd long wanted to erase the ugliness of my skin and bathe it in something meaningful, yet pleasing to the eyes.

Misha's preferred nickname for me—freak—isn't just related to my less than normal behavior, but also to the marks that run across my body. So many cuts, he'd called me a Frankensteinian abomination when he'd seen me without my shirt off.

Cuts and ridges of healed flesh run all around my torso, arms, and legs. Although my back had not been spared, my chest is the worst, with a thick scar running from my sternum to my belly button. Like a tree, it branches out in smaller lines, some more prominent, others shallow.

My face is the only unblemished thing—a wonder.

To avoid people's questioning eyes, as well as the condemnation or pity in their expressions, I'd decided to cover everything up in ink.

Although I'd wanted to do this for a while, the tattoo artist had advised against doing it before I reached puberty, since the designs might get distorted with my growth spurt. And so the moment I'd seen a change in my body, I'd made the appointment.

It's been a week since we'd started the process, and it had taken a lot of convincing that I could take the successive pain. Luckily, he's one of the Bratva's go-to artists and he must have heard about my not-so-stellar reputation, because the minute I'd looked a little contrite, he'd ended up accepting the job.

Vanya's been at my side throughout, marveling at the designs and trying to convince me to let her get her own. Of course, that would never happen, since our father would have my balls if anything happened to his little girl.

So far, the tattooist had finished my legs, chest, and back, as well as my right arm. The left arm is the only one still needing some more ink.

I'd spent sleepless nights with Vanya choosing the designs, and we'd discussed at length the cohesion of the entire picture. She, more than anyone else, knows what it means to me.

The bodysuit is split into three events—before, during, and after.

On my chest, right under my navel, a wooden chest with intricate designs sits half-opened—Pandora's box. Black inked smoke erupts from the confines of the chest, slowly turning into skulls, each painted with an expression of malice, despair, and desolation—evil unleashed upon this earth.

The corrupt spirits take up most of the space on my chest, their rotten faces reaching my shoulder blades and dissolving into a calming mist. From my shoulders to my wrists, Buddhist runes run all along my arms—all meant to contain the evil, keep it from spreading like a disease.

In a similar fashion, my back is a mosaic of warriors in different fighting stances, all tasked with the protection of the box. Alternatively, they are also meant to offer a buffer between the forces of evil and the outside world, should the box be unwittingly opened. Vanya had come up with that small detail.

"Sometimes, little cracks become holes of astounding magnitudes," she'd said, hinting at the possibility that no matter how hard one may try *not* to open the box, it will snap open regardless. So she'd suggested a safety mechanism. Something to keep the *bad* from spilling out.

"The warriors will protect you, but they will also protect the world—from you," she'd thoughtfully commented, taking a pen and outlining her idea on paper.

Her words had struck a chord in me. She knows me so well she's aware that there's a high chance I may snap at some point in the future.

Then the last piece—the legs—portrays what will happen when the last remnant of good will be vanquished. The descent into Tartarus. The place where evil makes its playground, and the last stop.

The final destination.

But should everything else fail, the wretched spirits unleashed from Pandora's box would not only venture into hell by themselves. No, they'd drag any innocent soul they could find.

And that... should be avoided at all costs.

"I can't believe it doesn't hurt," Vanya notes as the needle goes deeper into my arm.

"It hurts sooo much!" I pretend to complain, winking at her.

The tattoo artist raises his gaze, looking between me and Vanya, his eyebrows knitting together before he shrugs, his attention back at his work.

"He's weird," Vanya complains, getting up from her chair and stretching a little around the room.

"Vanya!" I let my voice boom a little, worried she might be up to some type of mischief. She can do whatever she wants, but only after my tattoo is done.

"Chill, I won't do anything," she sighs, her shoulders slumping as she comes back.

"Good. If you behave, I might put in a word with Father to let you get your own," I mention, and her face immediately lights up.

"Promise?" She's quick to interject, and I shake my head in amusement.

"Promise," I chuckle.

Vanya's body has similar markings to mine, and I know she's self-conscious about them, too. Worse than me, there's a scar bisecting her right eye. Over time, it's healed, so that now there's only a faint line above and below her lashes.

Still, she's at an age where her appearance is very important to her. While I'd promised I would talk to our father on her behalf, it will not be easy, since she's not allowed to interact with me in any way.

Even now, I'm scared that the tattoo artist will tell Father about her presence here. But when Vanya gets something in her head, there's nothing I can do about it. I couldn't tell her no when she'd asked to come with me.

When can I say no to her?

She's the only one I have. The only person I can freely talk to.

Over time, things have only gotten worse. I've managed to get my impulses under control, and I've tried my best to assume a more friendly disposition. All in the hopes that people wouldn't run away from me.

It hadn't helped.

Now, more than ever, people seem to be more terrified of me when I try to smile or crack a joke. For all my efforts to assimilate with other people, I've become even more ostracized.

There's Marcello, but he's different. Although we do get along, I can tell he hates what he does. He does his part of the job, but his eyes are dead inside when that happens.

He's not like me... He doesn't get the thrill of cutting inside of the human body, the fascination with what hides inside—a million unanswered questions, yet the answers are staring us right in the face.

He doesn't understand.

Yet for all his disgust toward our extracurricular activities, he's the only one aside from Vanya that doesn't revile me. He can stare me in the eye and challenge me, without fearing I'd slit his throat in a moment of fickleness. He can talk and argue with me, about nothing and everything.

He doesn't realize just how much those little things matter to me. Not when people run away from me the moment I try to open my mouth to talk.

"This should be it," the tattoo artist sighs, leaning back to examine his work. "You need to be careful now." He proceeds to instruct me on how to take care of them.

Soon, Vanya and I are out the door and heading back home. The tattoo shop isn't too far from our house, but we take a detour as we sneak down some of the more populated streets of Brighton Beach.

"Wait!" Vanya exclaims as she hurries toward one of the shop windows, looking quite awestruck as she gazes at the dresses on the mannequins.

"You know Father will *never* let you wear something like that," I say, amused, as I nod toward the length of the dress. It barely reaches above the knee, and Father has a steadfast rule for all his daughters. Nothing that shows too much skin.

Vanya sighs in frustration, her eyes darting between her drab mid-thigh dress and the one in the shop's window.

"Do you think he'll ever let me wear something like that?" she asks in a rather hopeless tone.

"I doubt it," I answer honestly.

Being the Pakhan of the Brighton Beach Bratva means that Father's image must be impeccable. That extends to his own family—especially his daughters. The standards are different, of course, for his sons.

The women of the family must be demure, with a shy disposition and malleable enough to their male counterparts.

The men, on the other hand, show their strength through the amount of violence they can wreak on their enemies, the ruthlessness with which they lead.

As far as that goes, I'm Father's model child, even though I know that deep down he's terrified of me. Vanya, on the other hand, is the opposite of everything they stand for, and so far she's managed to hide her dark side well. No one besides me knows what she's truly capable of.

Luckily, my father has my other two sisters, who are the epitome of decorum—sweet and demure.

"Damn it," she curses softly, her eyes still focused on that piece of fabric.

Without even thinking, I grab her hand, going inside the shop and filling her arms with stacks of clothes.

"Go on, try them," I urge her when her eyes widen in question.

"Really?" Her voice is small as she asks and I just nod. "But we don't have money..."

"We do. I do, so don't worry," I assure her, leading her toward the changing rooms.

Her lips tremble slightly and she launches herself at me, her arms going around my neck in a hug.

I close my eyes, relishing the small gesture.

No one touches me.

No one dares, anyway. It's little moments like these that remind me I'm human, with human needs.

When was the last time someone hugged me?

I... don't remember.

Has anyone ever hugged me?

"Go!" I say again, shaking myself from my musings, happy I'd decided to do this for her.

She dashes into the changing room, and the sound of hangers crashing to the floor tells me that she's beyond excited.

A smile plays at my lips as I absorb some of her infectious delight.

Vanya proceeds to show me every single dress, and I give my approval, letting her know she can buy whatever she wants.

I have some money stashed away, and since I don't need it for myself, I can at least spend it on her.

When she's done trying them on, we pay for the dresses and head out. Before going home, though, I also take her to a drugstore, so she can choose something for her face.

Since she's so bothered by her scar, maybe there are ways to cover it up without resorting to tattoos. Stopping in front of the makeup aisle, I help her decide on a shade of powder closer to her skin tone.

When we've also paid for the makeup, the smile she gives me could light up the entire world. So satisfied am I with the turn of events, that I start thinking of what jobs I could do to make more money.

Vanya deserves everything and more.

Hand in hand, we finally go home.

* * *

My eyes linger on the piece of the puzzle, trying to visualize the entire picture. It takes me a couple of seconds to imagine all of the possibilities and soon the entire puzzle forms itself in my mind. With a sigh, I start putting the pieces in place.

Sometimes I don't even know why I bother with puzzles, since it always takes me the same amount of time to finish them—regardless of the difficulty level.

Since my father had decreed that I'm only allowed to kill with his permission, my spare time has nearly doubled. At first I'd tried reading some textbooks to get my diploma, but even that had been too easy.

Having an eidetic memory means I only need to read something once to remember it forever. A bit ironic, considering my own memories are almost non-existent before the age of eight.

I move to the next puzzle, and I study the picture for a

second, hoping this one would prove slightly more difficult than the previous one.

I'm focused on solving the puzzle when a bundle of clothes drops in front of me, the already laid out pieces scrambling around.

I frown, slowly raising my gaze to meet Father's angry one.

"Why do you have these?" is all I ask, noting it's the same clothes I'd bought Vanya a couple of days ago.

"Why..." Father sputters, shaking his head and taking a step back. "Imagine my surprise when your brother told me he saw you carrying a bag full of clothes. Girl's clothes, no less," he says, assessing me shrewdly.

Misha... Of course he'd go running to Father.

"So what?" I shrug, unperturbed.

"Son," he starts, clearly uncomfortable, "maybe we should have a talk."

I tilt my head, narrowing my eyes at him.

A talk?

When he sees me silently watching him, he releases a fake cough, his eyes darting around suspiciously before speaking again.

"I know you're at an age where..." More fake coughing occurs. I almost want to roll my eyes at him and tell him to spit it out already. "Where you're noticing girls," he finally says, and the corner of my mouth quirks up.

So that is the crux of the issue.

My brother's conquests are legendary, if one is to believe the street rumors. There's not a girl he hasn't fucked. Of course, according to the rumors. One look at Misha and you could tell he probably paid people to spread them. And considering the coward he is, I bet he even has performance anxiety.

"Indeed," I drawl, leaning back on the palms of my hands and waiting for whatever Father *clearly* has to tell me.

"Maybe I should ask your brother to have a talk with you," he adds thoughtfully after a while, and my face immediately scrunches up in disgust.

"Don't worry about it, Father. I am perfectly fine as I am. And I have no interest in..." I pause, choosing my words carefully, "*that*, at least not yet," I say honestly.

Does he really think any girl would want to associate with me? Grown men go out of their way to avoid me. Girls react the way girls do—they take one look at me and they run off screaming.

Apparently Misha is not the only one with a reputation in the neighborhood.

"Oh." He frowns slightly, eyeing the clothes on the floor.

"Son... are you..." he stammers, and I want to groan out loud. Surely he's not about to ask me about my sexual orientation? "Gay?"

I blink once, slowly.

"No," I answer, staring him in the eye. "I'm not gay. Nor am I a transvestite," I add, knowing that's the next thing he'd ask.

"I see," he replies, strengthening his spine. He is, no doubt, happy he won't be shamed by a gay or gender nonconforming son.

In our culture, admitting to such a thing would be like signing my death warrant, and I know Father would be sad to let his favorite weapon go.

Not that I hadn't thought about it too. He's right that I am at an age where I should notice girls, or boys or... someone. But I can't muster the interest for anyone or anything. My thoughts are centered only on my next kill—when, who, and how.

Besides, even if I were, who would dare approach me?

I give him a nod, carefully lifting the clothes off my puzzle and depositing them next to me.

"Vanya's going to kill me," I mutter under my breath, knowing she'll be pissed if anything were to happen to her new clothes.

Father stops dead in his tracks. Half turned, his profile is bathed in shadows as he looks at me strangely.

"What did you just say?" he asks, his words slow and measured.

"Nothing," I lie. I'm not about to throw Vanya under the bus. Not when her presence is the only thing keeping me sane.

"Yes, you did," he continues, coming toward me. His eyes darken, and I'm having a hard time identifying the emotion on his face.

Is he angry? Shocked? Afraid?

His features are drawn up in a combination of all three, and for a moment I find myself unable to react.

"No, I did not," I repeat, keeping up the ruse. For good measure, I even let my lips widen in a small smile.

"Yes, you did. You said your sister's name. I heard you clearly." His hand reaches for my shirt, lifting me up.

Stunned, I look at him confused. This is the first time in years he's willingly touched me. Never mind that it's also the first time he's dared to go against me.

"I don't know what you're talking about," I reply, feigning ignorance.

"You think Ilya didn't tell me about your little adventure at the tattoo shop?" he asks, and I have to keep myself from reacting. It won't do anything but provoke his ire, and it's the last thing I need right now.

I can't afford for him to lock Vanya away or prohibit her from ever visiting me again. That would be unbearable.

"It's not her fault," I immediately start talking. "I convinced her to come with me there. She was worried about upsetting you, but I forced her." I look Father in the eye as I say this, wanting him to believe my words.

"Her... your sister," he continues, his face the same mix of unrecognizable emotions from before.

"Yes. Vanya didn't want to, but I convinced her," I repeat, and watch, almost in slow motion, as his eyes widen, his hands releasing my shirt.

I get myself together and put some distance between us. I wouldn't want to hurt him, even by accident. I'd made a promise that I'd never harm my family and I will hold myself to that.

"Vanya... you spoke with Vanya?" Father repeats, almost as if in a daze. I nod.

"It's not her fault. Please don't punish her, Father."

He raises his eyes toward me, the corners sloped downward. His face suddenly looks old and weary.

"How long have you been talking to Vanya, son?" His tone is gentler, and my eyebrows knit together in confusion.

"It's not her fault," is all I say, but Father is quick to assure me no harm will come to her.

"I know she... that she's your twin," he amends, and that gives me a little hope. Maybe he will see how important Vanya is to me, and that she should stay by my side.

She is, after all, my better half.

"From the beginning. She's been sneaking to see me. Please let us hang out. She calms me," I say, hoping he'd understand.

"She calms you?" he asks.

"Yes, she does."

"Son..." he starts, shaking his head, and taking a step back, "Your sister's dead."

"What?" I blink rapidly, afraid I misunderstood him. "What did you say?"

"Your sister's dead. She's been dead for the last seven years," he explains, but I stop listening.

My ears are ringing, a deafening sound pulsating in my eardrums. My hands go to cover them, hoping to lessen the impact of the noise, but nothing works.

I fall to my knees, eyes wide, limbs shaking.

No... he's lying.

"Vanya's alive," I state, full of confidence. Why, I'd seen her just a few hours ago.

"Son, look at me," Father says, and numbly, I do. "Valentino Lastra found you and your sister in a cage. You'd been taken by a madman and..." He pauses, taking a deep breath. "Your sister was already dead when they found you two, and you weren't far behind. I... the doctor told me you'd likely blocked the information because it was a traumatic event, but this... *Bozhe*, you've been seeing her from the beginning..." He shakes his head, "This isn't normal."

"Dead?" I ask, my mind honing in on that one word. "Vanya's dead?"

She's been dead this whole time?

No! All this time, she's been here with me.

"She's not dead," I state again, and out of the corner of one eye I see her. But before my very eyes, the fifteen-year-old Vanya that had grown alongside me suddenly morphs into a child, her clothing torn and dirty, blood pouring from every orifice.

"No..." I mutter, and my feet start moving, chasing whatever phantasm resides in my head. "She's not dead," I say again, running after her.

* * *

I don't know where I am or where I'm going. Time ceased to exist the moment Father dared to imply my sister is dead.

She's not.

How can she be dead when she's been by my side all these years?

I've seen, heard and touched her. We spent days and nights talking, debating, and sharing our most personal thoughts.

She can't be dead!

I stare at the empty subway seats, my mind a mess of thoughts. I'd followed Vanya's form all around the city, hopping from stop to stop in hopes she'd talk to me.

Confirm she's not dead.

Even now, my senses are on alert, looking for any sign of her.

I can't help but think back to all the moments we shared, looking for clues it might have been all a lie. But as I examine each interaction, I'm left with a sense of terrifying loss. Because to me, it all seemed so real.

But if it's not...

My vision falters, and images start to get jumbled in front of me, everything fuzzy and unclear. I bring my hands up to rub my eyes, willing the fog away from my sight.

"Vanya," I whisper as I see her in the next wagon, leaning into the door. She's smiling mischievously, her head tilted to the side as she's studying me.

I jump up, getting to my feet and following her.

The door pings as the train reaches the station and Vanya quickly runs out. I follow, hot on her trail.

She dashes out of the subway and toward the park across

the street. It's already night out, and I find that I'm having an increasingly hard time focusing on her form.

Her giggles fill my ears as she runs across the green expanse of the park.

"Vanya!" I call out her name. She turns slightly, raising an eyebrow at me before changing direction.

It's only when I start panting, already out of breath, that she stops, tentatively stepping in front of me.

She looks ethereal in her long cream dress, her face pale in the moonlight, the scar on her face even more prominent.

"Vanya," I breathe out, the need to touch her—making sure she's real and alive—eating at me.

I take a step further. When I see she's not running anymore, I take another step.

"Brother," she replies, her voice a soft melody to my ears.

But as I lift my hand, reaching out to touch her, my fingers pass through her form. Like a hologram, her smile never falters as my hands claw at her non-existent shape.

I keep touching her, hoping at some point my hands would meet solid flesh.

"Why... how?" I'm stunned as realization starts to flood my brain.

She's not... real. She *truly* isn't real.

I stare at her in wonder, her sweet face forever frozen in a welcoming smile.

"No," I shake my head, taking a step back. "This can't be..."

My mind is going crazy, thousands of scenarios forming in my head, and none of them pleasant.

My sister, my twin... my everything.

She's dead.

She'd been dead for seven years.

While my brain starts rationalizing this information, my

heart—that pitiful organ in my body, useless except for pumping blood—can't bear to let her go.

So entranced am I by the illusion in front of me that I don't even hear the steps behind. I only feel the blow to my head as I'm pushed to the ground by the intensity of the attack.

Voices... I hear voices. But somehow I can't translate them into meaningful phrases. I know people are talking around me, but to me it's only incoherent sounds.

Lifting my gaze up, I see around ten people, some my age, some older, all crowding up on me.

A few of them remove switchblades from their pockets, brandishing the weapons in front of me, all the while saying something. Their lips are moving, sounds are coming out of their mouths, but for the life of me, I can't understand a thing.

Dazed, I bring my hand to the back of my head, not surprised when it comes back coated in a sticky substance. As I bring the bloodied hand into my field of vision, I can't help but become entranced by the blood flowing freely down my palm.

For a moment, the people surrounding me are forgotten. It's just me and the red substance. My senses seem to react to it in such a familiar way, my pupils dilating, my nostrils flaring as they inhale the metallic scent.

I bring one finger to my lips, smearing the blood and tasting its essence. On a sigh, my eyes close, my temples throbbing.

Suddenly, I open my eyes and there she is.

Vanya.

She's small... smaller than any child her age should have been. Her clothes are torn at the knees and all around her torso, blood gushing out from open wounds.

Her eyes are bleak as she looks at me, her small lips parted on a silent word.

I freeze as I take a better look at her face, her scar deep and gnarly, her eye almost hanging out of its socket.

"Vanya," I whisper.

She takes a step toward me before falling to her knees, more blood pooling on the floor.

Somehow, *that* blood is all I can see or think of. And as one of the people around charges me with a knife, my entire consciousness collapses.

I snap.

I don't know exactly what's happening. It's like I am, but I am *not*.

My hand reaches out to grasp the sharp end of the blade. I feel it cutting into my flesh, yet I feel *naught*.

I stand up, my eyes glazed with whatever's come over me. It's like there's no more room for logical thought. Everything is sensation... primal instinct.

Twisting the blade around, I wrench it free from his hand, using my fist to send it flying into his neck.

His eyes widen for a moment, but I don't give him any opening. I grab the handle of the knife, pushing it down his torso and cutting into his flesh, relishing the way the skin gives way to the sharpness of the blade, more and more blood pooling down.

It's like I'm an addict and I've finally found my drug, because as I see the red liquid accumulate in buckets on the ground, I can only whisper.

"More."

Two more men charge at me, and I quickly disarm them, using their own knives to end their lives.

Guts, intestines, and organs spill on the ground. And blood... so much blood.

I start laughing maniacally as I gaze upon the flooded asphalt, my only thought to cause a deluge of biblical proportions.

Blood... more blood.

The other guys are quick to flee, but they missed their chance. No, they never had a chance to begin with, because they chose the wrong target... at the wrong time.

Licking my lips, I smirk as I invite them to make a run for it, the need for chase already simmering in my veins, almost as much as the need to draw blood. Like a predator, the desire to *earn* my prey is almost as satisfying as finally getting the prey.

My eyes are quick to follow their retreating figures, and then I just run.

Thirst like I'd never known before claws at me, making my heart drum with the intensity of a thousand beats per minute. And in that moment, I know, deep down, that I'm not human anymore.

There's no more reason left behind. Just an all-encompassing urge to kill, maim, and destroy. Bathe in a river of blood.

The guys never stood a chance. One after another, they fall. My hands are haphazardly cutting through their flesh, and when the frustration becomes unbearable, I abandon the weapons in favor of my own hands.

Digging deep into the already wide open body, I wrap my fingers around the ribs, enjoying the way they snap under my strength. The way the organs turn to mush as I push into them, ripping everything apart to shreds.

More...

I don't know who I am anymore as I chase one man after another, turning their bodies into an unrecognizable mess of flesh, blood and bile. But the color is, oh, so alluring, that I can't seem to stop myself.

Even when the last one is down, this intense craving inside of me blooms even more, the need to continue killing almost overwhelming.

My eyes move rapidly around me, gazing past the park and into the streets, where unwitting passersby are walking around. I can almost feel the pulse beneath their skin, and my desire for more blood intensifies.

I take a step forward. And two. By the third one my legs feel heavy, my entire body falling under a strange lethargy.

From the corner of my eyes, I glimpse my father, a tranquilizer gun in his hand as he's aiming at me. He's not alone, and soon I realize I'm cornered from all parts.

Still, no matter how much I want to stay and fight, my body stops obeying me.

And I fall.

4

VLAD

AGE TWENTY

S tepping under the warm water jet, I watch as some blood pools at my feet. I feel for the knife wound, my fingers measuring its depth. Satisfied it's not too deep, I get out of the shower and take out the first aid kit.

I force my brain to shut off all the noise around me, focusing only on getting this damned wound fixed.

I place myself in front of the mirror to get a better look at my body. Then, taking some gauze and soaking it in disinfectant, I douse it all over the affected area. The pain is minimal, almost like a ticklish feeling. I can't even remember the last time my body had ached, or any wound had pained me.

Now, they're simply there. I know I have to be careful, so that they don't become septic, but other than that they don't interfere with my other activities.

I'd gotten this specific one because of Bianca, my new partner. I grit my teeth as I think about that, because most of the time she simply annoys me with her presence.

This time it had been no different. She'd goaded me into

a fight and when we'd reached our target I'd snapped, losing control and slaughtering an entire room of people. It was during that bloodbath that someone must have jabbed me in the ribs, although I have no recollection of it.

If only Marcello were still here.

I sigh as I continue the ministration, taking a Band-Aid and placing it on top of the wound.

Marcello and I had had a quiet understanding and we'd worked in one of those rare partnerships where one didn't even have to speak for the other to follow. We were evenly matched in most things, his intellect sharp, his skills unparalleled. But *certain* issues had made him abandon his place in the famiglia.

I still keep tabs on him, but something's changed. He's... broken.

That doesn't mean I forgive him for leaving me partnerless, since my father had needed to find a replacement as he doesn't trust me to do a job on my own.

Hell, I don't trust myself either.

After my break-down in Harlem, a few years ago, he'd placed me under strict supervision, knowing that my grasp on my sanity had dimmed considerably, once I'd found out my sister was, in fact, dead.

Although I don't appreciate the constant attention, even I have to admit that I'm too dangerous to be left alone.

My fascination with blood had only increased after that incident. But the same substance that once brought me joy has now become my main trigger. If before I lived for the sight of blood pouring out of my victims, now I avoided it like the plague, knowing that if I became too enthralled by it, my mind would slip from me.

Usually I can feel a crisis coming, and I do my best to

calm down. But sometimes, the bloodlust becomes so strong, I'm simply no longer human.

A killing machine. A monster. A berserker.

People have given me many nicknames over the years, but only one has stuck: Berserker. Ironically also my code-name, I'd been given the nickname after the Norse mindless warriors. Those fighting in a fury-like trance with no recognition of what goes around them except destruction.

Because that's exactly what I become when I lose myself.

A mindless monster.

Of course my father couldn't rid himself of his perfect weapon, so he'd sought to control me in the least intrusive way—a new partner.

Bianca is three years younger than me, and while her age would put her firmly into an inoffensive category, she's also a born killer. Clinically diagnosed with Antisocial Personality Disorder, Bianca is brash, reckless and a major pain in the ass.

We do complement each other well on the battlefield though, since guns are her weapons of choice while mine are knives. This way, I engage in close combat, and she has my back from a distance.

Theoretically, it's not a bad arrangement, since we work pretty well together. But she's also an immature brat and her carelessness sometimes endangers our missions.

My wound bandaged and ready to go, I put on some clothes and head to the gym, thinking I'd spend what time I have left before the next mission training.

I start humming a soft melody, still forcing myself to tune everything out.

But as I cross the backyard to get to the gym, I hear my brother's leering voice.

"Come on, Lenochka, drop the towel," he says, and I turn my head slightly, noting they are all by the pool.

Misha is sitting by the pool, leaning on his elbows as he looks suggestively at Elena.

Both Katya and Elena are sitting timidly in a corner, their hands tightly gripping the towels covering their bodies.

They look a little apprehensive as they spot Misha, and I can see Elena's eyes darting between the pool and the house.

They're almost teenagers now, and while my father keeps Misha under control, there's no denying the lascivious way he looks upon our sisters, especially Elena.

I'd mentioned this obsession of his to Father and he'd grunted, assuring me Misha would never overstep his boundaries. But I have to wonder. Does Father not see the pest he has in his own house? Is he so blinded by the fact that Misha is his eldest that he's willing to overlook his cowardly behavior and decidedly dishonorable reputation?

Elena takes a step back, cowering behind Katya. Born only a year apart, Katya's always been the stronger of the two. Sometimes their relationship reminds me of Vanya and me...

Shaking myself from that line of thought, I turn to leave.

Misha chooses that exact moment to be the asshole he is, rising from the pool and going to where the girls are. I watch from the corner of my eye how his fingers circle Elena's wrist, jerking her toward him.

"Let her go," Katya's voice booms, but even that isn't enough to stop Misha as he rips the towel off Elena's body.

"Look at you, Lenochka," he whistles, his eyes roving down her body with interest, "who knew you were packing a punch," he continues, one hand going for her breast.

I don't know exactly when I move, but before Misha can

touch Elena, I wrap my hand around his neck, squeezing painfully.

We might be years apart in age, but I've long surpassed him, both in height and body mass.

His feet aren't touching the ground as I tighten my hold, looking him in the eyes and enjoying the fear reflected. His lids move rapidly, and he tries to blink away the terror I know is coursing through his body.

"What have I said about those wandering hands, Misha?" I ask him, as I lean in, my face millimeters away from his. "Don't tell me you don't remember what I told you?"

I watch the emotions play on his face—terror, outrage, arrogance. Even with my fingers suffocating the life out of him, he dares to have a smug expression on his face.

"Fuck you, freak," he spits, his saliva hitting my cheek.

I close my eyes for a second, willing myself to calm down. I'm not surprised at his pathetic attempts. After all, when has Misha done anything noteworthy?

Bringing my other hand up, I wipe my face with the back of it.

"You seem to have forgotten. Don't worry, I have not." I give him my most brilliant smile as my finger traces his features, settling just above his eye.

"Freak," he scoffs, fake bravado on his face, "you can't do anything to me. Father will kill you before he lets you harm a..."

He trails off, his words becoming a scream as my fingers dig into his eye socket. I grasp his eye and I pull. It doesn't take long for it to pop right out of the orbit.

The girls are screaming in horror behind me, scurrying away.

I only have eyes for my dear brother. Pun intended. My lips quirk up as I pull on his eyeball. I push forward, my fingers curling inside his orbit, digging in, his screams music to my ears.

I'd done this plenty of times before, so I know what to expect when my fingertips meet bone. I just have to break the sphenoid and I'll have easy access to his brain.

Just as I'm about to give him what he deserves, I hear another screech in my ear. I do my best to ignore it, but her voice breaks through my defenses.

"You promised, brother. You promised you'd never kill family," she speaks, her form materializing next to me. She wraps her ghostly hand around my arm, urging me to let go.

My eyes widen as I watch her... so little, so powerless. She's dressed in the same bloody rags, her entire body a mess of cuts and wounds, her own eye hanging out of its socket.

My entire body starts trembling, and I let go. Misha crumbles to the ground and I take a step back.

"No," I whisper to myself.

She's not real. She's never real.

You'd think that years of seeing one's dead sister would make it easier on the eyes. But every time I see her small, feeble body racked with pain, I just lose it.

I try to regulate my breath, almost losing sight of what's happening around me. How Father's guards are storming in, taking Misha away to give him medical assistance.

Or how someone jabs a needle in my skin, the entire world starting to sway with me.

"Not again," is the last thing I say as I pass out.

I come around much later and realize I'm in my room. A cold rag is on my forehead, and small hands are tending to me.

I don't think. I just react, grabbing the arm of the

intruder. A small gasp escapes her lips, and I realize I'm staring at my sister.

Katya.

"What are you doing here?" I croak, looking around for any guards.

Her lips are trembling as her eyes move between me and my painful hold. I quickly release her, expecting her to move.

She doesn't.

"Thank you," she starts, a little unsure, "for what you did back there. Misha is always picking on Elena and..." she trails off, looking away, suddenly embarrassed.

"What?" I ask, my voice a bit brusque.

"He makes her uncomfortable," she eventually says. "He always tries to corner her alone, and I can't always be with her. Maybe now..."

"He won't bother her again. I'll make sure of it," I declare.

I don't know where this came from, but as she smiles at me, I find myself happy at my decision to intervene.

"Thank you," she says again, surprising me anew when she leans forward to kiss my cheek.

I'm staring at her, dazed. She... touched me.

Everyone is afraid to even come close to me, and yet she, of her own volition, touched me.

My eyes must give away my bewilderment, because she confesses, "You're not so bad, you know."

Standing up, she leaves the room. And I'm still pondering her words... and her kindness toward me.

* * *

"**M**otherfucker! What do you think you're doing?" Bianca yells at me from behind.

I turn my head slightly toward her, holding up a piece of meat. "Barbecue?" I ask jokingly.

Well, she doesn't take it very well, because she quickly takes out her pistol, pointing it toward me and shooting.

The bullet whizzes past my ear in a deafening sound, lodging itself firmly in the head of the man next to me.

I don't react, although Vanya, sitting right by me, quickly places her palms over her ears, her eyes squeezed shut.

"Now, that was just mean." I pout at her, half annoyed.

"Dude, you've been skinning him *alive*. For hours! What's wrong with you?" She shakes her head at me, coming around to glance at my work of art.

"It was supposed to be a quick job. In and out. And to think I'm usually the troublemaker," she mutters under her breath, scrunching up her nose in disgust when she leans in to look at what's left of the man.

Yes, it should have been a quick job. But once I'd realized who our target was—an Armenian human trafficker in charge of some questionable trafficking rings in Maine—my interest had been piqued.

It's not often that we're sent after human traffickers. Might be because my father is the one choosing our targets, and he doesn't want me to get too hot-headed on a job, since he knows I'd vowed to make Vanya's killer pay.

But just like this skinless fellow in front of me, I don't know much about the circumstances of Vanya's death.

My memory of the years before I'd returned to my family is fuzzy. I've only managed to piece together some things. Like the fact that Vanya and I had been abducted when we were three and we'd been held captive by some sort of madman for almost five years. Although my father and his associates had relentlessly looked for us, it was only by chance that the Italians got to us first.

Marcello's brother, Valentino, had been leading a team inquiring into a human trafficking ring led by some dangerous people when they'd found us—or rather a dead Vanya and her half-dead brother. Even he hadn't been able to offer me more insight, citing pure luck behind their sudden discovery of the location.

We'd both been found in a cage. The details are, even now, hard to stomach. Vanya had been well on her way to putrefaction, and me? Starved to the extreme, I'd already had one foot in the grave.

Because of the circumstances of Vanya's death, as well as my own rather morbid state, a doctor had told me it's normal for the brain to block some memories—particularly traumatic ones. He'd also said that Vanya's presence in my mind might be explained by the residual trauma of living with her corpse for days on end.

Well, certainly that's one way of looking at it.

But there's also my way. Vanya is here with me to ensure I find her killer and I punish him or her accordingly.

An eye for an eye.

Even now, as if knowing the direction of my thoughts, she preens, her lips spreading into a languid smile.

I shake my head at her, returning my attention to Bianca.

"Maybe I could have gotten some information out of him," I mumble, "eventually."

Looking down at all the stripes of flesh I'd taken from his thighs and his back, I'm suddenly bummed that I didn't get to do the entire body. It had been going great too, since the bleeding had been minimal and my mental state never better.

"Sure," she mocks, raising an eyebrow at me.

"Now where's the fun in taking the rest of the skin if he's

dead?" I sigh, returning to task and continuing with his chest.

"Wait," B says, her fingers going to her temples. "Let me get this straight. You're going to continue skinning him? *He's dead!*"

"Of course he's dead," I add drily, "you killed him."

I resist the urge to roll my eyes at her. But seeing that I'm in such a good mood, I refuse to engage further.

"You'll thank me when you get your Christmas present. I'll make you a shiny new leather holster. One hundred percent *man*-made too." I wink at her.

When she gets my meaning, she backs away, her hands up, her eyes half-shut in disgust.

"Ew, no thank you. You can keep it for yourself." She waves me off, going to an empty chair and opening her laptop.

"Stalking again?" I ask, amused.

Her face immediately lights up and she turns the screen around to show me the latest pictures of the subject of her obsession.

"I don't get it." I shake my head, turning back to my work. Might as well finish this now.

"Of course you don't get it," Bianca mutters, "we've established you don't know what love is," she says with a dreamy sigh, staring at the computer and no doubt imagining herself with that suit of hers.

I don't even deign a reply, because she's not too far off the mark. I *don't* know what love is. At least not the type of love she's implying. I know loyalty and family ties. I know my connection with Vanya, the type that not even death can sever.

But the type of love she's talking about? The butterflies

mixed with bodily fluids and eternal devotion? I mentally groan at the picture, firmly depositing it out of my mind.

That type of love isn't for me, and likely won't ever be. After all, I have but one purpose.

Find my sister's killer and return the favor. When that's done... I'll have to see if I'll stick around.

* * *

After the confrontation with Misha, things get progressively worse at home. My father sends me on mission after mission just to ensure Misha and I are not in the same location at the same time. At any other point, I would have been thrilled to perform sanctioned killings twenty-four seven. After a while, though, even the prospect of blood fails to rouse my interest.

My mind, my biggest enemy, won't leave me alone. And it's not only in the form of little Vanya hanging around me at all times. No, this time I'm getting increasingly paranoid about Misha and his intentions.

He'd had a doctor see to his eye and put it back in place, so the damage had not been too bad. But his behavior afterwards had been deeply concerning. He'd been... nice. Or as nice as Misha can be. Still, it had been entirely too disturbing to be on the receiving end of such non-assholery.

He'd even apologized to Elena.

Extremely unlike Misha.

The more I became suspicious about my brother, the more I started doing unnecessary things. Like hacking into the live feed of our compound. Or the mainframe. Or everyone associated with Misha.

When you're as antisocial as I am, you tend to develop

hobbies that don't involve... socialization. Or humans. Or anything that lives, breathes and talks back. Except for Vanya, but she's not really alive, anyway. Computers are heavenly manna for someone like me. Not only are they extremely interesting, but they also provide constant challenges for me, since my impatience might be my winning quality.

My time is split between a computer screen and corpses, so you could say I've become an expert. In both.

"Are you going to keep on doing that?" Bianca asks, yawning and stretching back.

We'd been assigned to supervise an out-of-state shipment of drugs. A little unusual, since our missions in the past always finished with someone dead, but still within normal parameters, considering my father's plan to keep Misha and me separated.

I shrug, closing the laptop and placing it aside. I *might* have been doing it ad nauseam, since my curiosity won't let me rest until I get to the bottom of everything that's happening, but I'm not about to let Bianca know about my suspicions.

Not when there's little evidence to support my theory. I only have my intuition and my not-so-stellar people-reading skills — which no self-respecting scientist would take as anything but bogus.

"I'm bored," I reply.

She sighs, almost exasperated.

"You've been bored for the last three missions," she continues, and I stifle the urge to roll my eyes at her.

We may be a team, but we still get on each other's nerves... most times.

To pass the time, I switch to reading at some point, exchanging more jabs with Bianca in between.

It's not until the truck carrying our asses and the

merchandise comes to a sudden stop, throwing off our balance, that we realize something *may* be off.

Both Bianca and I react to the potential threat — her hands on her guns, my fingers wrapped around my *shashkas*.

It didn't take long for us to realize we'd been sent into an ambush, with people coming at us from all directions.

But they hadn't banked on one thing. For all our bickering, Bianca and I are top-class assassins, and forced proximity has only enhanced our work compatibility. We killed fast and in sync. Whoever sent these guys clearly hadn't done their homework.

When all the corpses lay on the ground, it became clear this wasn't just a simple attack.

"Bratva," I grimace as I note their tattoos.

Suddenly, my previous concerns become urgent, and I can barely contain my ire, getting behind the wheel and yelling for Bianca to get in the car.

"It's a coup," I add, eventually, my eyes fixed on the road as I break all speed limits.

"A coup? But who?" She frowns.

"My stupid ass of a brother, that's who. Fuck! I should have seen it coming. Misha's always been power-hungry, but I didn't think he had it in him." The words pour out of me.

I should have trusted my instincts.

"But..."

"No one else could have ordered those Bratva soldiers to come after us. Think about it, B," I say when she seems unconvinced.

Misha must have promised them something in return for helping him overthrow my father. He's always been dissatisfied with his role within the organization, mostly because he knew Father didn't trust him as much as he should have, being the firstborn and the heir.

Our ongoing conflicts, though, must have only strength-ened his resolve to take matters into his own hands.

I should have known that someone like him would never be satisfied with not being *important*. But regardless of what he's doing to take over the Bratva, my utmost worry is for Elena and Katya.

Fuck!

If he's gotten rid of Father and his loyal soldiers, then there's nothing standing between him and doing whatever he wants to them.

The thought of that, coupled with Vanya's cries in my ears, only serves to make me hit the accelerator harder, speeding down the highway in hopes I might make it in time.

"He'll kill them," Vanya keeps chanting next to me, her words not helping my already tense headspace.

I barely take my eyes off the road for a moment to get Bianca to load the camera feed from the compound.

The moment the screens flare to life, I'm not surprised when I see blood everywhere, my father slain by his own son, his body lying in the middle of the great hall.

Misha has his men move Father's corpse to the exhibition area—the place reserved for traitors and enemies of the Bratva.

"Fuck," I mutter, realizing I may have underestimated Misha. He's not *as* dumb as he's led me to believe.

And the fact that he's displaying Father's body in such a manner in the great hall is a warning for everyone thinking of going against him.

We reach the compound in record time, and Bianca offers to use her skills as a sniper to have my back and get Misha.

Once we split, her heading toward a good vantage point and me moving toward the hall, I turn to Vanya.

"See, it won't be by my hand," I joke, and she gives me a brilliant smile. Knowing that *I* won't be the one to put the bastard out of his misery seems to be doing wonders for Vanya's mood.

A few guards get in my way, but I'm quick to split them in half, my blades running smoothly across their stomachs.

The alarm goes off, and I know it's only a matter of time before I'm surrounded. Smiling to myself, I just wait.

Sure enough, quite a few soldiers come out of the great hall, all surrounding me. I let myself be caught because I know Bianca should be almost at the south tower now, which should give me a few uninterrupted minutes of conversation with my dear brother.

A couple of kicks and the men think I'm down, holding me by my arms and dragging me inside the room.

Misha is standing in the middle of the hall, his hands behind his back as he gazes at Father's corpse.

A quick glance around the room and I don't see anyone else here - not Mother and not my sisters either.

"Brother," he spits at me when the guards stop in front of him.

"Such a welcome," I drawl.

"You should have been dead already," he continues, clearly put off by my sudden presence.

"And you should have learned by now that I'm not that easy to kill," I retort.

"Ah, but don't worry. This time you will, and by my hand too," he says, pacing around in front of me.

Jittery. A little too jittery.

"Where are the women?"

He stops, raising his eyes to find me. He holds my gaze for a moment before he starts laughing.

"The women?" he asks, his arms wide open in wonder.

"No more women," he replies sneakily, and I narrow my eyes at him.

"What did you do, Misha?"

"What did I do?" he repeats, looking unhinged as he continues to pace around. "I'm finally where I belong. At the top."

From the corner of my eye, I see Vanya plant herself in front of Father, an inscrutable expression on her face. Her eyes are downcast, the corners of her mouth sloped downwards. She's... sad.

Turning back to Misha, I'm surprised to see him blabbering on about how he's going to turn the Bratva around and the deal he's already made on Father's behalf.

"You should have stayed gone, freak. Then Father wouldn't have been so against human trafficking. Drugs don't bring in the money they used to, but humans..." he whistles.

Ah, so this was his aim.

"Really? And how are you going to do that?" I keep track of his movements so that his form is lined up with the opening in the window. "You know Agosti has a monopoly on that," I add, curious to see who he's been talking to.

"My contact is even more powerful," he snorts, "and once we join forces, we'll take the city by storm." He continues to prattle on about his grand plan, but there are no details about this mysterious partner of his.

"I doubt anyone would ally themselves with you," I start, trying to rile him up into disclosing who he's working with. "Doesn't he know you've got a track record of making dumb decisions?"

He stops for a second, coming closer to me.

"They trust me, brother. Unlike others, they see my potential."

They... Interesting.

I'm about to open my mouth to ask more when I hear a sharp sound and a circle appears on Misha's forehead. Blood leaks out of it, his eyes rolling to the back of his head. And then he falls.

I take advantage of the slight disorientation of the men holding me and I pry my hands loose, immediately going for the blades hidden in my boots.

The men stand no chance as I throw the knives. They lodge deep in their throats, hitting the perfect spot.

And they're down.

I turn toward the window where Bianca is likely still looking at me through her rifle, and I wink at her.

Now...

Vanya is hopping around with glee, looking at Misha's dead body with a delight I hadn't seen in a while.

Shaking my head, I go back to the main living quarters, needing to make sure Katya and Elena are safe.

The hallway is empty, and as I make my way toward the second floor, I get increasingly worried.

I can't hear anything...

I barge inside the girls' room and I blink twice, before averting my eyes. Vanya runs from my side, and I close the door softly.

Elena's naked body is on the floor, an angry cut at her neck. The entire carpet is soaked in her blood.

I take another step, and my worst suspicion is confirmed.

Bruising around her thighs and blood between her legs tells me exactly what happened here. Or who.

I sigh deeply, disappointed at this turn of events. I'd hoped they would be fine...

Vanya, on the other hand, is on her knees in front of Elena. She's bawling her eyes out, her hands touching her face, her hair. She's crying for the sister that met the same fate she had.

Taking a blanket from the bed, I cover Elena's body, hoping to offer her some modesty, at least in death.

Vanya is inconsolable as she keeps trying to rouse her sister. Everything to no avail.

Shaking my head, I look around for Katya, confused that she's not here.

A small hope flares inside of me as I think that she might have been spared. I search every single room of the house, finding Mother's dead body and that of those loyal to my father.

No Katya...

By chance, I stumble upon someone who moans in pain. Realizing he still lives, I crouch next to him, thinking I might get some answers.

He's face down on the carpet, and as I turn him around, I note it's the family doctor—Sasha.

"Sasha," I say, slapping his face to get his attention.

His eyes are unfocused, but eventually he finds his words.

"Vlad..."

"Where is Katya?" I ask, getting straight to the topic.

"Katya..." he croaks, grimacing in pain, "He gave her to him," he finally says.

"Him? Who?"

Sasha shakes his head.

"Misha's partner." Is all he says before his eyes close.

Still feeling a pulse, I put him over my shoulder and I meet up with Bianca back in the great hall. Vanya is sluggishly trailing behind, her face one of desolation at losing both her sisters.

Placing Sasha on a table, I realize I'm the one in charge now. So I just shoot orders, taking out my phone and dialing contact after contact, knowing that the entire place is due for a cleaning.

"Your sisters?" Bianca eventually asks, and I just shake my head.

Elena may be dead, but Katya isn't.

I just have to find the man who took her.

"You'll make them pay, brother. Promise me." Vanya comes around me, her eyes misted with tears.

I look down at her and I feel my heart jerk a little in my chest.

"Promise," I say, taking her small hand in mine.

It seems I have my work cut out for me.

Two sisters. Two faceless enemies.

A smile pulls at my lips.

* * *

"Shh, it's starting," Vanya shushes me, directing her gaze toward the stage, her big eyes full of curiosity.

Somehow, her bad eye doesn't hang out of its socket as much today.

Leaning back into my seat, I chug some champagne, knowing it's going to take a while until they get to the interesting part.

With a bored expression on my face, I watch as a man in a dog mask saunters on the stage, calling out a number and inviting a man and a woman to join him.

The man in the mask commands them both on their knees before lowering his zipper and taking his cock out, dipping it in and out of the man's and woman's mouths.

I glance warily at Vanya, thinking she's too young to be

seeing something like this. But then I remember she's *not* real.

Her attention is wholly focused on the people on the stage. In just a short while, their positions change. The woman is on her knees, getting railed from behind by her partner, while the masked guy is fucking the man in the ass.

The show becomes even more interesting when they call out yet another number, and another man joins them on the stage. The masked man takes a step back, making the newcomer join the fucking train before taking his dick in his hand once more and riding his ass.

It's like a never-ending chain, especially when they keep calling out names, more people joining in, the masked man always in control at the end of the line. Men and women are arranged alternately, so there's always a cock fucking a hole.

Weirdly enough, the stage is the least problematic aspect of this entire place. And ghost or not, I ask Vanya not to look around, especially not up.

Like an opera house, the entire room is sectioned in boxes on different levels, all looking down at the stage.

But the boxes belong to the richest and most depraved. The ones who crave the anonymity the crowd cannot give them.

I let my eyes wander around briefly, but the images are too much, even for me.

Men in their late fifties are getting their dicks sucked by teenage boys. Some have shunned all morality and are actively fucking children. But then probably the worst box is the one that has a few people *watching children* fucking each other.

I'd known I'd see sick people in here; I just hadn't realized *how* sick.

"Do you think we'll find her?" Vanya speaks again, her voice hopeful.

I try to put the things I'd seen out of my mind as I turn my attention to her.

"I don't know," I answer honestly.

It's been months since Katya's disappearance, and I'd used all the resources at my disposal to dig into human trafficking rings in the area, thinking she'd show up in an auction.

She is, after all, the virgin daughter of a Pakhan. That's bound to get a pretty penny anywhere. So I'd listened to the chatter in the underground world, knowing I'd find something, eventually. And I had. I'd found out about *this*.

The Block, aptly named after its famous auctions, is one of the most exclusive human trafficking rings on the East Coast. Run by an elusive drug lord, it caters to the elite and the most debauched of the bunch.

It had proven a little harder to get myself an invitation, and I'd had to put all my experience with computers into making an entirely new persona for myself on the Dark Web.

A bait here and there, and I'd somehow managed to snag myself an invitation. A *VIP* invite.

But tackling the Block had not proven that easy. They had regular auctions, and with time, the chances of me finding Katya slimmed considerably.

I've been coming here for a while now, and still no trace of her.

"We're not giving up, though," I quickly assure her.

After the mass orgy ends, the second event of the evening involves cooking a live man. Well, I can stomach this better than *that*.

A few times here and I'd learned that I can excuse myself from certain events that don't... tickle my fancy.

I'd certainly excused myself from the sexfest. Even now I shudder to think about being close to so many bodily fluids... so not appealing.

It's enough that I bathe in human entrails when I lose my mind, often waking up in pools of blood, with organs hanging off my clothes. I'm not about to engage in that while I am lucid too.

A man needs to maintain some dignity.

But my first trip here I'd won myself a taste of human flesh. Not too bad, but I'd overcooked it. I blame Vanya for that since she'd kept distracting me until the meat had burned.

After that, as a regular member, I'd been able to make my preferences known.

Vanya is yawning by the time the auction opens, and I borrow the binoculars from the table to carefully study every girl that fits Katya's age and coloring.

Hours later, though, we're back to where we started.

"What if..." Vanya starts as we make our way out of the club.

I look down at her, but a man in a black suit comes crashing down into me. I frown as I watch him fumble with some sheets of paper fallen to the ground, helping him pick them up.

"Thank you," he says, looking intently at me, his eyes oddly familiar. Yet I can't say I've seen him before.

His hand lingers a little too much on my own until I shake him off, moving forward and ignoring the way my temples throb with pain.

Odd.

"Hm?" I turn to my sister, briefly distracted.

"What if that man didn't sell her? What if... he kept her?" Vanya asks, and I still, my eyes widening at the realization.

Shit!

I'd focused all my resources to find hotspots of human trafficking, thinking she might end up for sale. But this... Vanya is completely right.

What if he kept her?

"Then we need to double our efforts and find out just who Misha's partner was."

Partners... He'd mentioned plural.

"We can do this." Vanya nods at me confidently.

"Indeed," I reply.

We'll find everyone involved. And when Katya's safe and back home, I'll refocus on getting Vanya's killer.

Who would have known, though, that the clock was ticking?

And not in my favor...

5

SISI

"**W**here exactly does it hurt?" Sister Magdalene asks me, and I lower my head slightly, feigning pain in my stomach.

She makes me stretch on the infirmary bed while she pats around my abdomen.

"Here?" she asks, and I give a low moan of pain. Her brows knit together in concentration. "What about here?" She moves her hand lower, and I react to the motion by squeezing my eyes shut.

Stepping away from me, she shakes her head, pursing her lips and regarding me pensively.

"I think we got a new shipment of painkillers in the back. Let me go look for them," she eventually says, propping me against the pillows and leaving the room.

I almost feel sorry for what I'm about to do, since Sister Magdalene is a sweet lady. She can be a little grumpy, but she's never been anything but nice to me.

How I wish she would have been in charge of the infirmary when I was younger.

All the injuries I'd collected over the years have created a mosaic of scars on my body. Maybe things would not have been so dire if she'd been...

I shake myself from my musings. I came here with a purpose, so I can't linger.

Swinging my legs off the bed, I move toward the medicine cabinet, opening it and browsing the labels.

I'd borrowed Catalina's phone and researched on the internet exactly what I needed to do. After my last confrontation with Mother Superior, I'd decided to give them a taste of their own medicine.

Besides a few warranted jokes here and there, I'd mostly kept out of trouble. Keeping to myself and doing my chores, I'd tried to avoid a conflict with *another* Cressida. But somehow I'd still come under Mother Superior's scrutiny, and out of nowhere she'd decided to double my workload.

I'd never been one to scoff at my chores, since I know that everyone does their part to benefit the entire community. Be it kitchen or cleaning duty, I'd always done my best to do my job properly.

This time, however, the amount of chores that Mother Superior had assigned to me has been too much. Her reasoning? I'm done with my education, so now I can dedicate my entire time to the community.

For a week, daily, I'd been assigned to help prepare the food for breakfast and lunch, and then clean the classrooms in the afternoon when the lessons were over. It had worked fine in the beginning.

But as more work accumulated, I started operating on automatic pilot like a robot. I didn't even realize how one day slowly turned into another, my focus dimming, my strength fading.

Until the moment of reckoning, when Mother Superior had sent me to clean her office. Slightly sleep-deprived and with my muscles strained from all the effort, I'd been a little absentminded as I'd tried to clean everything thoroughly.

When I was cleaning her desk, though, I must have bumped into one of her vases because one moment I was focused on dusting the surface, the next I'd been scared out of my mind by the sound of something falling on the floor.

When Mother Superior had come to check on my progress, she'd taken one look at me cleaning the pieces from the floor and she'd gone off in a tirade.

I'd taken it all, since it had been my fault the vase had broken. But she'd had to hit below the belt.

"I don't know why we took you in when not even your parents wanted you," she'd said smugly, and I'd tried my best to not show how much those words affected me.

She'd continued to spew more insults, and the entire time I could only think about how this is supposed to be a place to worship God and do good deeds. The entire mission of Sacre Coeur is to help others, yet Mother Superior and her army of nuns have only shown me that if you don't fit a specific mold of *helpless*, then you're not worth anything to them.

They are always invoking a higher moral standing, criticizing me and Lina for the circumstances that had brought us to Sacre Coeur, often forgetting to look at themselves and how their own behavior toward us doesn't make them any better.

Well, let's see how high and mighty they are in a less ethical situation.

My eyes roam around the rows full of medicine until I find what I'm looking for.

Pocketing the entire thing, I quickly scribble down a note for Sister Magdalene implying I'm all better, and then I dash out of the infirmary.

It's already dark outside, so I try to blend in the shadows, going straight for the church and entering it without anyone seeing me.

It takes me a while as I ransack the altar area, but I eventually find the container with wine. Unscrewing the lid of the bottle of pills, I read the instructions, measuring what dosage I should add for the intended effect. I calculate the grams against the perceived volume of the container and then I get to work.

Taking a knife from the altar table, I start crushing the pills into as fine a powder as I can. When I've done that to the recommended dose, I add the powder to the container and I stir it well.

Putting the wine back in its place, I leave for the dorm.

The following day, we all go to mass. The priest starts his sermon, and I can't help the giddiness inside my chest at the thought that those women are finally going to get what they deserve.

I barely pay attention to the prayers around me, my thoughts focused on the result of my plan. Too bad, though, that it will not be immediate.

"Sisi, what's wrong?" Lina asks me when we return to our room.

"Nothing." I give her a smile, even though inside I'm a little too impatient. I take a book and sit down on my bed, attempting to distract myself for a while.

It's only a few hours later when we go pick up some fruit that we hear of the wondrous thing that's come to pass.

All the senior nuns, including Mother Superior, had developed a rather nasty stomach ache, after which they'd promptly closed themselves in the bathroom.

There was one problem, however, in that there were not enough bathrooms available for the nuns, and some of them had to relieve themselves in nature.

"Good God, are they alright?" Lina asks the sister who'd relayed the news.

"Not all." She shakes her head, her lips pursed with worry.

"But... how could this have happened?" Lina stammers, looking concerned.

"Indeed," I feign surprise. "How could this have happened? And all at once?" I shake my head, trying to emulate their expressions of consternation.

"We don't know. The few that didn't make it to the bathroom were mortified. Poor souls," she says before glancing around suspiciously, "they used the bushes in the grove," she whispers conspiratorially.

Both Lina and I gasp at this piece of news.

"How terrible," Lina adds sincerely. Of course she'd feel bad for those nuns, even though they are the same ones who'd terrorized her before.

It's not a surprise, however, when Mother Superior, once she'd gotten her bowels under control, asks everyone for an emergency meeting.

I'm still chuckling on the inside, especially when I see all the *victims* in one corner, looking rather worse for wear.

My upper lip is constantly twitching as Mother Superior proceeds to talk about the *incident* as if it had been a sacrilege.

"Whoever did this *will* be punished." Her voice booms in the room. Everyone is quiet as she stares us down. But then, in the silence of the room, the growly sounds of a stomach reverberate in the air.

One of the senior nuns looks up guiltily, before dashing out of the room and presumably in search of a toilet.

I can't hold my laughter anymore, and a tiny giggle escapes me. Lina's elbow makes contact with my side as she gives me a look.

Luckily, it's promptly masked by Mother Superior's voice as she continues her speech.

"We've investigated the infirmary, the *only* place someone could have gotten the laxatives from," Mother Superior continues, removing the bottle of laxatives from her habit and holding it up. "It's missing half its contents. We know someone among you did this. If no one admits to it, then we will have to make Sister Magdalene bear the punishment, since the pills were under *her* care," Mother Superior says smugly and Sister Magdalene pales.

"But," Sister Magdalene starts, but Mother Superior is not having it.

Placing a hand up to stop her, she addresses the room once more.

"You have five minutes to reveal yourself. If not," she nods at Sister Magdalene, who is immediately resigned to her fate.

Damn! I didn't think it would get this far. Certainly, I didn't think Mother Superior would put the blame on Sister Magdalene.

Sister Magdalene's eyes meet mine from across the room, and I know I can't let her take the blame for something that's entirely my doing. Besides, I can add a little something extra to my revenge.

Taking a step forward, I exit the formation and address Mother Superior directly.

"I did it," I admit. "I put the laxatives in the wine."

Mother Superior's eyes sharpen on me.

"I should have known it could have only been *you*." She spits the words, but I'm not deterred.

"But," I start, dragging my gaze around the room, "why is everyone else fine, then? Everyone partook in the communion wine. How come only a select few developed issues?"

At my words, she looks like she's been struck.

People start whispering, asking the same question I did. Why were they fine when the senior nuns were not?

"If you look on the box, you'll find the instructions as to how to consume the pills for them to be effective. Yes, they were in the wine. But *only* if you drank a certain amount of wine would the laxatives have worked," I point out, almost proud of myself for not faltering.

"How much wine did you drink, Mother Superior?" I ask, a little cheekily.

"How... What... You," she sputters, her eyes bulging in her head.

"What, it's true. You must have imbibed quite a lot... I wonder, isn't that a sin too? Succumbing to vice... tsk, tsk."

Her face becomes a mottled mass of red as my words sink in, and everyone gasps when they realize that I might be right.

"Assisi! You're grounded!" she yells, stalking toward me.

I move back, but I'm already one step in the grave, might as well jump all in.

"What about you? Or the other nuns? Shouldn't someone punish you for getting drunk on communion wine?" I know I'm overstepping a lot of boundaries and breaking a lot of rules in this moment, but as everyone stares at me, stupefied, I can only smile.

"Shut up, Assisi!" Mother Superior catches up with me, her hand circling my wrist as she tries to drag me out of the room. Lina looks at me with worry in her eyes, but I shake my head at her. This is *my* mess.

"Why? You're not so high and mighty now, are you?" I speak louder, addressing the other nuns, too. Mother Superior is dragging me by the hand until we're out the door.

"You've really done it this time, Assisi," Mother Superior continues to chastise me, but I can't find it in myself to care.

Not when she throws me into the dark, barren room I'd come to associate with all my punishments, not even when she tells me I'm going to spend all my time here until I repent.

When she locks the door behind her and I'm left in the chilly chamber, I take a seat on the floor, bringing my knees to my chest for some heat.

"Ah, but how can I regret it?" I mutter to myself, a smile playing on my lips. Just the sight of the senior nuns looking embarrassed in front of everyone had been enough. Because I'd proven my point.

Not even *they* are above reproach.

6

SISI

C losing my eyes, I let the warm water pour over me, hoping to remove the cold that had seeped deep into my bones. I should have known Mother Superior would not let me out without a good reason. She'd let me stew in that dark room for close to three days until she'd come to get me, ordering me to get dressed and make myself presentable.

I'd been confused about her behavior, but when I'd found out my brother, Marcello, had come to visit, it had all made sense. She didn't want Sacre Coeur to get in trouble for abuse.

Tired and chilled to my core, I'd tried to put on my best performance, even though I'm sure I must have stressed my happiness a little too much, my smile strained as I'd tried to convince him my life was perfect.

I hadn't seen Marcello in almost a decade, Valentino being the only one visiting every couple of years or so. But this time, Marcello had a good reason for dropping by.

Valentino's dead.

I'd been shocked when I heard that he'd taken his own

life. But I couldn't muster any other feelings aside from pity, since we'd never been close.

He would come by every few years to make sure I was doing fine, but it had always seemed more like a duty than his own desire to see his sister.

Marcello, though, had managed to surprise me this time. He'd implied he might bring my younger sister, Venezia, to visit.

I sigh deeply at the thought.

I've never even met Venezia. All I know about her is from Valentino, but even that isn't much.

It's funny how most girls brought up here are orphans, with no one to turn to. And while my own parents are dead, I do have family out there. They just don't want me...

When I finish washing, I go back to the room, once more putting on a mask and pretending everything is fine. Lina's curiosity about my brother is not helping either, since she can't seem to stop herself from asking questions.

A smile plastered on my face, I recount everything we'd talked about. I try to ignore the way my heart contracts when I think about the family I have behind the walls of Sacre Coeur. Because in the end, do I really have them if I can't count on them?

Time passes, and a new priest arrives at Sacre Coeur. Father Guerra's entire persona is shrouded in mystery, the rumors about his affiliation with the mob proving to be the most interesting thing Sacre Coeur has seen since Cressida's disappearance years ago.

Regardless of his potentially dangerous reputation, everyone is taken with the guy, including Lina. She'd had her reservations in the beginning, but seeing how he'd been kind to her and Claudia, she'd decided to put aside her prejudice against him.

Well, I'm still on the fence.

He's tried numerous times to talk to me and invite me to confession, but I'd declined each time. There's something entirely too fishy about the man. It's in the way his eyes move around the room, as if he's cataloging everyone. His gaze is more that of a predator than a man of God.

But while my instinct tells me not to trust him, the fact that he hasn't been outwardly nasty to me like others before him has earned him the benefit of the doubt. I may not like him, but that doesn't mean I will be rude.

It all comes crashing down one late afternoon when Claudia goes missing. Lina and I both split to look for her around, but it's like she's simply vanished.

After looking everywhere, I return to our room to find Claudia huddled in her bed, her eyes red from crying.

"Claudia?" I gasp, going to her side at once. "What happened?" I take her in my arms, hugging her to my chest.

She's sobbing uncontrollably, and I do my best to calm her down.

"Did someone bully you again? You promised you'd tell me," I say gently.

She shakes her head, burying her face deeper in my chest.

I just hold her, letting her cry until her tears dry out. But when she starts talking... I feel like my entire world is being shaken.

"Father Guerra," she starts, her voice strained, "he touched..." she trails off, swallowing deeply before raising her eyes to look at me. "*Mamma* caught him..."

Her eyes tell me everything I need to know, and the reason why Lina is not back yet.

My hands ball into fists at the thought of that man raising a hand against Claudia. I just hope Lina's okay too...

While waiting for Lina, I do my best to calm Claudia down, once again assuring her that she's done nothing wrong.

A while later, Lina slowly opens the door, sneaking her head inside.

"Lina?" I ask, my brows furrowing when I see her pale features and her eyes full of fear.

"Can you come out for a second? And bring me a dress." I frown, but comply.

I leave Claudia on the bed and I quickly rummage for a dress. Exiting the room, I'm greeted by a sight I never thought I'd see.

"What is going on?" I ask as my eyes rove over her blood-stained clothes.

Is she hurt?

"Something bad happened. Like terrible." She gives me a slight smile, her entire body trembling.

"Lina... you're scaring me."

"Did Claudia tell you anything?"

"No... she only mentioned you were with Father Guerra." I don't say that I gathered what must have happened. Instead, I just wait for her to tell me.

"He was touching her..." Her voice comes out as a whisper as she breaks down, her entire body convulsing with sobs.

"What do you mean?" I ask, holding my breath.

"He was touching her under her clothes..."

"No!" My hand goes to my mouth. I'd imagined some-thing bad must have happened, but I would have thought Father Guerra hit her or punished her... not this. "Where is he? What happened?" I continue, my mind already working on a plan. That scourge needs to pay for this.

"I... I killed him," Lina says in a small voice, and I still.

"You're kidding." I look at her for any sign that this is a joke. But it's not.

"No... I really killed him. I didn't mean to, but..."

She starts telling me all the particulars and I listen attentively. She is already in shock, so I know I must tread carefully. Still, I would have never expected this of Lina. She'd struck at Father Guerra in self-defense, and the knife she'd used had caused him to bleed out and die.

In her shocked state, she'd tried to hide the body by placing it in the confessional booth. The more she's talking, the more I'm shuddering, thinking what a close call this had been — for both her and Claudia. But I'm proud of her for defending herself and her daughter.

"We need to do something about that," I start, steering the discussion toward a more logical course of action.

"You... I killed a man." She looks at me in confusion. I don't want to tell her I have *some* experience dealing with murder, so I just react as naturally as I can.

"Yes, and I would have killed him, too. That wastrel! Now, about the confessional booth," I say, thinking how to best get rid of Father Guerra's body. Since she's stuffed him in the confessional booth, we need to act fast before someone finds him.

"That's why I came back. I can't do it alone. I know this is too much to ask but..."

"No buts!" I immediately interject. "Come on, dress, and we'll figure it out."

I leave her to talk to Claudia while I try to think of a way to get rid of the body. In my case, it had been rather easy since the coffin had been right next to us. But this... we'd have to transport Father Guerra somehow and bury him in the cemetery. It's the only way.

When Lina comes back, I tell her my idea, as well as the

fact that we could use her empty suitcase to transport the body. It might get a little messy, but at this point, it's our best shot.

"Sisi, are you sure you want to do this? It's my fault... I can just tell them what happened," Lina stops to ask me when we're closer to the church.

"And who'd believe you? You already said he's from a prominent family. They probably have enough influence to make sure you get blamed for everything. Think about Claudia. What would happen to her without her mother?"

While I'd been perfectly fine with going to prison, since I wouldn't be leaving anything behind, it's completely different for Lina. She has Claudia, and I would do whatever is necessary to make sure mother and daughter are not separated.

Including, should the time come, take the blame myself.

We discuss the circumstances more in depth, realizing that Father Guerra's opportunity to get Claudia alone might not have been a fluke. Usually, Lina and I take turns watching Claudia, but since Mother Superior had been adamant about increasing my workload even more, I'd had less and less time to spend with them.

I don't want to think that anyone, not even Mother Superior, would sanction such an action, but knowing what I know about the woman and her hate toward us, it's entirely too possible.

When we reach the church, Lina shows me where she'd stuffed Father Guerra. Opening the door to the confessional, I see his puny body drenched in blood, and I feel a small degree of satisfaction at knowing he can't harm anyone anymore.

He should have suffered more.

Forcing myself to focus, I assess the situation and comment. "He's too big."

"We just need to fold him a little," Lina says, and I try to visualize how it could fit.

"How about we try a fetal position?" I suggest, going around the suitcase and finding the best position to lay him in.

"Let's try," Lina agrees, and we start stuffing his body in the suitcase, folding his limbs in different positions until we manage to get all of him inside. Then, pressing on the flap of the suitcase, we try our best to close the zippers and lock the luggage.

"Damn," I breathe out, a little tired from the exertion.

The journey to the cemetery is rather easy since the wheels of the luggage make it easy to carry it. The hard part will be digging a hole so we can bury it.

Since I'm *extremely* familiar with the cemetery, I know the exact spot that should pass undetected. This specific parcel is unmarked and situated under the shade of the tree, which should mask the freshly turned earth.

Going in the back to procure some shovels, both Lina and I start digging.

"Honestly, this wasn't that bad," I comment when we've finished digging. "I think I'd rather dig up graves than wash dishes. Do you think I can apply for the position?" I say half-joking. Honestly, I wouldn't mind it that much. Dead people can't hurt you. The living, however,...

"Sisi..." Lina starts laughing. "You really want to trade dishes for graves?"

"It's still work." I shrug, but my lip is twitching.

Days pass and we try to put the Father Guerra incident out of our minds, convinced that the worst has passed.

We were wrong.

And we get to find that out the worst possible way. By coming face to face with Father Guerra's rotting body on display in the convent's grotto. All the nuns are kneeling in a prayer to be delivered from evil, some fainting at the sight and odor of the desecrated body.

Lina, on the other hand, is horrified. Because whoever's done this must know she killed Father Guerra. In fact, a message written in blood confirms it.

We don't linger outside more than we have to, and once we're back in the room, Lina starts talking.

"They know... and they're coming for me," she says, terrified. She proceeds to recount that both our families are in fact deeply involved with the mob. I listen in shock as she tells me about the five families and how they are all involved in illegal businesses, a fact which makes them extremely dangerous.

"I may have limited knowledge about the mob," she takes a deep breath, "but I know most live by one principle—retribution. His family will want justice for what I've done to him."

I don't speak for a long time. Mostly because I'm having a hard time wrapping my head around everything.

That means Valentino... and now Marcello are mafia bosses.

"I need to call Enzo, tell him everything," Lina says suddenly, getting up and taking out her phone.

While she's talking to her brother, I take a moment to digest everything she's just told me.

It's in my veins... this evil.

7
SISI

Fearing for her safety and that of her daughter, Lina decides to leave the convent and move in with her brother.

"I'm so sorry, Sisi," she whispers in my ear as she gives me one last hug.

"Don't! You need to think about Claudia." I try to reassure her, even though I have no idea how I'm going to survive this place without her.

I'd known from the beginning that she would leave at some point. But now that the moment has come, I find myself terrified at the prospect of being alone.

"Take this," she hands me her phone. "It has data, and you can call me any time."

"Lina..." I trail off, blinking rapidly to avoid crying.

"We'll see each other soon. I'm sure of that." She gives me one last smile before turning to go.

I say goodbye to Claudia too, and I can see the confusion in her eyes. Poor baby, she has no idea what's happening.

"We'll meet again," I whisper in her hair as I squeeze her in my arms.

Then... they're gone.

It takes me a while to get back to my previous rhythm, but their absence is like a gaping wound. During the day, I go about my work, but during the night, it's the worst. The deafening silence of the room is stifling, and I can barely fall asleep.

I miss hearing them breathe.

Even if we didn't talk, I knew they were there.

Now... It's just me.

The convent is trying to move past the Father Guerra incident, even though the nuns have become more and more inclined to believe in the occult. The number of ghost stories circulating around, or the fact that Father Guerra may have been the undead, would be funny if not for the fact that I have to return to an empty room at night.

I pride myself on being the type of person who doesn't have those sorts of fanciful notions. But late at night, even the smallest sounds, like the floor creaking, make me alert and on my guard.

"Damn it," I mutter to myself as I trudge my way back to the room after a full day of work. My muscles are aching, and my eyes are closing.

Already paranoid, I make sure to lock the door before changing my clothes and getting in bed. I'm fading in and out of sleep when the phone buzzes next to me.

Thinking it might be Lina, I quickly grab it and open it. There's one unread message. Frowning, I squint at the text, confused.

> Congratulations! You've won a brand new iPhone. Follow the link to redeem the prize.

Did Lina sign up for something? I keep rereading the message, trying to think what to answer. I can't in good faith redeem the prize, since I could not have it shipped to Sacre Coeur anyway. Instead, I decide to craft a message advising them to choose another winner.

> Thank you for your consideration. I, however, cannot accept such a gift. Another lucky person may benefit more from it. Please forward it to someone else.

Hitting send, I snuggle back under the pillow.

I barely get to close my eyes, though, when my phone buzzes again.

> Congratulations! You've won a brand new iPad. Follow the link to redeem the prize.

I scroll up and realize this is a different number than before. Surely, Lina hadn't participated in so many contests.

I type up the same message and hit send.

When the next text comes, however, I'm not surprised. Instead, I'm starting to become suspicious.

> Congratulations! You've won a brand new car. Follow the link to redeem the prize.

Different number, but the same text. The only difference is the prize. Annoyed at whoever is messaging me out of the blue, I decide to play their game.

> The link does not work.

The screen immediately blinks to life with another text. This time, an answer.

> My apologies. Please try this one.

My paranoia is through the roof at this point. They can't reply to my previous messages, but they promptly replace the link? Something isn't right. No one even knows this number aside from Lina and her brother. Unless...

My eyes widen at the possibility that it may be Father Guerra's relatives. What if they think Lina is on the receiving end?

The phone immediately drops from my hands, and I back away from it. But the more I think about it, the less it makes sense. Why would the mob send these ridiculous texts? Maybe it's simply a prank. To test my theory, I type up another text.

> I'm sorry, but I am a nun and I have renounced all earthly possessions. I cannot claim such a prize.

I hit send and wait. Sure enough, another text. This time, from the same number.

> Congratulations! You've won two gallons of Holy water from the Vatican. Follow the link to redeem the prize.

I stare at the screen with open-mouthed shock before suddenly bursting out laughing. They are mocking me now. Whoever is on the other end is definitely making fun of me. Well, game on.

> Only two? How is that the same price as an iPhone? I feel cheated.

I smile cheekily at my reply, especially when I see that the stranger has texted back, finally ditching the format.

> How many do you want?

> You, Sir, are making fun of a poor nun. Don't you know it is a sin? You'll end up in Hell.

> You don't seem too nunly to me. I hear communion wine is quite dangerous these days...

My smile dies on my lips as I read the message. This person knows... that can only mean one thing. Whoever is texting me knows I am not Lina. Dear Lord, maybe it is the mob. And maybe they know I helped Lina bury Father Guerra.

> Did they send you to kill me?

Apprehensively, I hit send.

> Kill you? No, too morbid. But you could click that link. No deaths involved. Promise.

Who could it be? If it's not someone Guerra sent, then who else?

> Send me the Holy water with a Vatican certification and I may click the link.

Pushing my chin up, I feel a little proud of myself for not giving in. Instead, I power off the phone and I place it back in its hiding place.

If they don't plan on killing me, that's all the assurance I need.

Well, imagine my surprise when I open the door to leave for work the following morning.

Holy water. Two gallons of it.

Hanging from the neck of the bottle is a ribbon and a small note.

With love from Vatican City.

Incredulously, I look back and forth between the note and the water. Is it someone from the inside? It has to be; otherwise, no one would have been able to place the water here. The security at Sacre Coeur is tighter than a prison, so no outsider could have done this.

I do the only thing I can think of. I grab the phone, turn it on, and send another message.

> Who are you?

Despite my initial reservations, the unknown number and I establish a routine of texting back and forth. I'm a little embarrassed to admit, even to myself, that I started craving the interactions simply because I'm lonely. It's funny how when Lina and Claudia had been around, I'd considered myself such a strong person and I'd confidently declared that I didn't need anyone. Yet the moment they disappeared from my life, I started leaning on a stranger...

Not my best moment.

Our interactions are not constant and consist mostly of him trying novel ways of getting me to click that damned link, and me not clicking it. But somehow they've become the highlight of my day.

I mean, when all I do is work and sleep, a little non-spiteful human interaction can do wonders. I'd even become a little reckless in that I'd started carrying my phone with me outside my room.

> Congratulations! You've won a brand new cow. Follow the link to redeem your prize!

I shake my head at the message, quickly typing my reply and attaching a picture. When he'd seen that the regular prizes did not work, he'd started coming up with the craziest ideas, like the one at hand.

> No thank you. I already have a cow.

I send a picture I'd snapped of Lizzy, my favorite cow, when I was milking her. The reply, though, doesn't surprise me in the least.

> Congratulations! You've won a brand new ox to mate with your cow. Follow the link to redeem your prize!

A slight giggle escapes me, but I quickly compose myself when I see some nuns heading my way. Afraid of getting caught with the phone on me, I quickly dash toward the cemetery, since no one should be there today.

But just as I cross by the church, I hear a blood-curdling scream. I still, frowning. Before I know it, I'm dashing inside, opening the door and stepping toward the altar.

One of the younger sisters is on the floor, staring in front of her with shock. Her entire body is trembling as she tries to find her voice to scream again. When I turn my eyes to the source of her terror, my eyes widen.

"Lord," I whisper, almost dropping my phone.

Behind the altar, Sister Elizabeth's body is nailed to the wall, her habit wide open to reveal an empty chest cavity.

I take a step forward and note that her organs and everything that *should* have been inside of her are laid on the altar table.

I move closer, and the most striking feature jumps out at me.

The letter C is branded on her forehead.

"Lina..." My thoughts immediately lead me to Lina.

Because this looks entirely too similar to how Father Guerra's body had been treated, the organs on display, the body ravaged by some type of wild beast.

I don't even think as I dial her number, afraid that this could have been intended for her.

"Lina," I start when she answers. "Something bad happened..."

8

SISI

Staying away from the crowd that's already formed in front of the church, I keep pacing around waiting for Lina and Marcello to arrive.

I must admit that I've missed her so much that when I get her phone call that she's arrived, I'm over the moon. It's been too long since I've seen her, and I can't help the happiness that blooms inside my chest.

"Lina?" I spot her in the distance and I run toward her. "Oh, Lina! I missed you!" She takes me in her arms, her hand caressing my back affectionately.

"Sisi, are you okay?" she asks, and for a moment I just close my eyes, simply soaking in her presence.

I nod, but taking a step back, I realize she's not alone.

"Marcello? And..." I swing my gaze at the newcomer, struck by his lethal aura.

He's big, just as tall as Marcello, and with a physique to rival my brother's. It's all well hidden beneath his immaculate suit, but there's no mistaking the way his shoulders bulge under the material. There's tension radiating off him in spite of the mask of cordiality that seems to be in place.

Rehearsed. Too rehearsed.

I should know, I've done it too many times.

"Vlad," he introduces himself, his voice deep and raspy. As he talks, his smile is a little too wide and not quite reaching his eyes. I raise my gaze to his, and like two bottomless pits, his dark eyes seem to engulf me whole.

Dangerous.

I don't know what makes me think that, but his entire body language speaks of a predator ready to pounce on its prey. Even now, he's boldly assessing me under the guise of civility, but as our eyes meet, something passes between us.

A tremor goes down my body, and my temples throb under the assault of his scrutiny. A soft pressure courses through my limbs, settling in my fingertips as they suddenly become numb.

Hand outstretched, he's waiting for me to grasp it—as politeness dictates. But somehow, the hairs on my body stand up straight just at the thought of being in proximity to him.

I finally wrench my eyes from his, and I blink twice. "Right, so," I say, realizing his presence had made me slightly disoriented.

Who is he and what is he to Marcello?

His features don't change, and there's no reaction given that I've just ignored him. In fact, his lips twitch a little, stretching even further, as if he's trying to overcompensate.

I turn to Lina, but I still see him from the corner of my eyes. I don't know why, but I have the urge to run in both directions at once — away and towards.

"Tell us what happened," Lina urges, and I try to seek comfort in the topic at hand. Certainly, I try to ignore the humming inside my body or the way all my senses seem to be on alert.

"I don't know all the details either, but I was close to the chapel when one nun started screaming. I went inside and... You should see it for yourself if Mother Superior will allow it. It's just..." I shake my head, trying to act as perturbed by what I've seen as possible.

"She'll allow it," Vlad interjects with confidence, and I'm sorely tempted to sneak a peek at him. What makes him so sure? Does he know Mother Superior? All types of questions are going through my mind when I realize my body had instinctively turned toward his, my eyes stuck to him.

He's returning my bold stare, and for a moment his mask drops, the polite grin turning into a languid one of inquiry. His eyes glint in the sunlight as he focuses on me, a small frown appearing on his face.

I don't get to dwell on that, since his expression suddenly changes again, his affable smile back in place.

"Easy," his hand steadies my arm, his touch searing against my skin. I immediately jerk away, clarity returning to my mind.

What the...

Marcello and Lina are ahead of us, so I just quietly turn to follow them, using my fingers to rub at the spot he'd touched. I may not have been around men much, but I don't think this is normal...

When we reach the church, tens of nuns are outside, some praying, some sobbing, and Mother Superior seems to have a hard time assuaging everyone's fears.

True to his word, Vlad approaches Mother Superior and has a word with her, returning to confirm she'd allowed them at the crime scene.

Not surprisingly, Marcello tries to make us wait outside while they investigate, presumably wanting to preserve our delicate sensibilities. Lina and I, however, are having none of it and eventually he relents and lets us join them.

All throughout this, Vlad is silently trailing behind, just watching. Every time those eyes of his settle on me, though, I feel like I'm on a bed of needles, all of them pricking at my skin.

Stepping inside the church, Sister Elizabeth's corpse is fully displayed behind the altar. Her entire body had been desecrated in such a manner that even I'd had a hard time recognizing her.

While my initial reaction had been one of shock, since the first thing that had greeted my eyes had been her displayed womb, empty of her organs, her ribs flaring out into the open, I'd quickly become entranced by the sight.

I'd spent a little time studying her form and how she'd been laid out like an offering, the entire spectacle intriguing and a little... alluring. There had been brutality in her death, but the way in which everything had been arranged spoke of someone highly organized.

More than that, the fact that the organs had been carefully placed on the altar table in a symbolic manner was even more captivating. Because even with my novice mind, I could recognize that this wasn't the work of a mere killer.

Even now, as we step inside, I can't help but be drawn to the entire ensemble, a certain beauty creeping from death.

"Who would do this...?" Lina gasps, her eyes wide with horror as she glances at the body.

I try not to show just how fascinating I find this entire scene, but my own body betrays me as my eyes focus on Sister Elizabeth's open carcass.

"This looks eerily similar to what happened to Father Guerra," I point out, almost absentmindedly. "His insides had also been tampered with. Well, not in *this* manner, but quite similar."

Both bodies had been dealt with the same type of care... It may not seem like it with how grotesque everything looks, but there had been a great deal of consideration for every piece of the scene.

"But who would do that? We still don't know who dug up Father Guerra and put him in the grave..." Lina intervenes, shaking her head. "And why? Why the C?" I can see the way her lips tremble ever so slightly as she looks upon Sister Elizabeth's face, the C angrily glaring at us.

Vlad moves behind us, and his presence is like a thick smoke infiltrating the entire room; you feel it in your every atom. Even now, the awareness is unnatural as I feel his slightest movements, or the way his eyes seem to bore into my back.

Taking a deep breath, I try to focus on the body, something deep within catching my eye.

"Wait..." I say, frowning. My feet move of their own accord until I stop in front of the body, my eyes roving over her form.

"Assisi, what are you doing?" Marcello asks, almost exasperated.

"I think I saw something glint in there..." I trail off, catching sight of something inside her body. I don't even think as I stick my hand into her chest cavity, squinting to get a better look as my fingers move around.

To my surprise, whoever's done this did a marvelous job. The organs have been smoothly removed.

"Assisi," Marcello calls out again, but I don't mind it.

Then, I hear *him*. A sound resembling a pained groan escapes his lips, and my eyes are immediately drawn to the back. He's looking at me with a strange expression on his face, his black eyes unfeeling, yet exuding a strange warmth.

Shaking myself, I return my attention to the body, trying to ignore Lina's cry of outrage, or the way Marcello keeps calling out my name.

"Damnation!" I mutter when my fingers finally grasp at whatever's inside the body.

Holding tightly, I take out my fist and dump the contents on the altar table.

"What...?" Marcello exclaims, his gaze unwavering from the bloody teeth on the table.

Vlad, on the other hand, seems a little perturbed as he removes a handkerchief, wiping the sweat off his forehead.

Odd. He doesn't strike me as the squeamish type.

"Now, this is an interesting turn of events. Wouldn't you say so, Marcello?" He bends low to study the teeth. His voice has an added charm to it. It's in his lilt as he pretends to be wholly unbothered.

Once again, I find my attention entirely focused on him, and I don't like it. Scowling, I return to the body.

"There's something else. I couldn't grasp it before." I take out the other bit, trying my hardest not to look back at Vlad.

I don't know what it is about him, but he scares and intrigues me at the same time.

It's his smile. His very fake smile.

"Here!" I grab onto the material, taking it out and placing it on the table.

"It's vellum... mayhap human vellum." Vlad speaks first, procuring a knife from the inside of his blazer and using it to turn the piece of flesh around. Frowning, he takes out his handkerchief and removes the blood.

"*Paying for the sins of others,*" Marcello reads, and Lina reacts with a sudden intake of breath.

"It's because of me, isn't it? Whoever is doing this, it's because of what I did..." she says, and Marcello is quick to comfort her.

I lean in to take a closer look at the piece of skin.

"Whose skin is this?" I ask. "Is it hers?"

"Probably not," Marcello replies with a grimace.

"How are you so sure?" I continue. As I move my gaze from Marcello to Vlad, it's obvious they know more than they are telling.

"Because whoever did this," he starts, giving Lina a sad look, "is not targeting you."

"What do you mean?"

"This," Vlad intervenes, swinging his knife around and pointing towards the C on Sister Elizabeth's forehead, "is the mark of a serial killer. The C by itself could have pointed to you," he turns to Catalina, "but the teeth confirm it's a serial killer we've been looking for."

"What...?" I narrow my eyes at him. Why do I get the feeling they are not telling us everything?

The conspiratorial looks that pass between Vlad and Marcello make it clear that they are familiar with this.

And it's only making me more intrigued.

"Let me get this," I place my hands on my hips, tilting my head to the side as I address them, "you're saying that the person who killed our Sister is a serial killer? Then what about Father Guerra? I don't believe it's a coincidence these things happened almost within a week of each other." Closing my eyes, I bring my hand to massage my forehead, trying to think about the connection between Father Guerra and Sister Elizabeth.

It's when I open my eyes again that I find myself face to face with Vlad. He's getting increasingly closer to me until we're mere breaths apart.

What...

My breath hitches in my throat as his presence over-whelms me. He's so close I can smell him. His scent is unlike anything I've ever encountered, a hint of burned sandal-wood mixed with musk all over a faint layer of vanilla. It's fairly intoxicating, like darkness wrapped in silk, caressing my senses into overload.

I blink rapidly as I realize his gaze is focused on my fore-head, right where my birthmark is.

"Vlad!" Marcello calls out, but it's like he can't hear him.

His features are taut, his smile completely gone and replaced with a pure predatorial look. We're not touching, yet I can sense the dangerous tension radiating from him.

Suddenly, I feel like a gazelle in a savannah, my only focus is survival as I will my limbs to stay still, hoping to avoid the detection of the predator.

"Don't move!" Marcello surprises me by whispering from the side, and I nod.

Vlad's nostrils flare slightly as his eyes caress my face in a slow perusal. He leans closer, inhaling.

"Vlad!" I hear Marcello's voice again, but it's like every-thing falls away. Everything becomes muted as Vlad turns his blank eyes toward me, his breath on my lips.

His hand moves slowly, gently, completely at odds with the big hulking man threatening me with his closeness. Then he does the most unexpected thing. He swipes his fingers over my forehead, taking some of the blood I'd smeared before with my hand and bringing it to his lips.

"What...?" I whisper, stunned.

His lips open to welcome the red liquid, his gaze still set on my face. My limbs feel heavy and warm next to his, his mouth shockingly alluring. I take a deep breath, my palms sweating.

"Assisi, come here, but slowly. He might be dangerous," Marcello says.

It's weird, because I can feel the danger he emanates. It's pure and raw and not unlike a lion stalking his next meal. Yet I can also feel something else. An emptiness that silently calls out, and once again my instincts tell me to both stay and run.

Seeing how worried Lina and Marcello are, though, I slowly move away from him.

"What's wrong with him?" I ask, seeing that Vlad is still in the same position. I doubt he's even noticed my absence.

"He's not... normal," Marcello relays.

"Not... normal?" I repeat numbly, my disturbed mind finding this entirely too fascinating. I watch as Marcello goes to Vlad's side, snapping his fingers in front of him as if he's trying to wake him up from a trance.

"More..." I think I hear Vlad speak, but I can't be sure.

"Marcello, what are you...?" I take a step back when I see my brother folding his sleeves, his features taut as he's surveying the situation.

Don't hurt him!

I don't know where this comes from, but my only thought is making sure Marcello doesn't do anything to Vlad.

I move forward, swiping Lina's arm aside and ignoring Marcello yelling at me to stay back.

Vlad moves too, rather too swiftly as he meets me in the middle. I don't even get to react as his hand shoots out, wrapping itself around my throat and pushing me into the wall.

I hear Lina's cry of alarm, and Marcello as he tries to stop her from intervening, but I can't seem to care.

His fingers wrapped around my pulse point, his warmth

transferring from his skin to mine makes me lose all reason. I try to blink some sense into myself, but it's like my body's stopped obeying, giving in to sensation instead.

His grip is firm, and yet gentle. Our entangled position aside, his hold isn't painful. If anything, it's almost tender in the way his fingers play with my skin, almost like a soft caress enveloped in violence.

Nothing about this man makes sense. From the moment I'd met him until now, he's never once acted as I expected him to. And that... intrigues me.

I raise my eyes to his, finding those striking black orbs against pale skin, and I try to understand.

Who are you?

There's a strange dichotomy to him—carnage that leaves way to calm, aggression tempered by civility. The thirst for blood reflected in his gaze should make me afraid. But it only does the opposite.

It calls to my own.

Good Lord, but my entire body starts shaking, small tremors coursing through me and accumulating deep in my lower belly.

The more he stares at me like that, as if he'd kill me and kiss me at the same time, the more my body reacts.

"Assisi, are you okay?" Marcello asks, worried.

"I'm fine... he's not hurting me." I manage the words out, my eyes still fixed on Vlad.

"Vlad, I need you to focus, okay? You're hurting my sister right now." My brother starts as he tries to reach a side of Vlad that isn't gone yet.

Marcello keeps talking to Vlad, and I notice a small shift, his arms flexing slightly, his eyes gaining a hint of recognition.

"Sister?" A rough sound escapes his lips.

His hand tightens over my throat, his eyes moving wildly over my face.

"Yes, she is my sister. And you are hurting her right now."

"Sister?" He repeats, the word seemingly striking a reaction. "Sister..."

One moment I'm up in the air, the next my feet touch the ground. Even more surprising, Vlad staggers to his knees, his features drawn in pain, his mouth open on a sound that won't come out.

I look into his eyes and I see only one thing.

Suffering.

His arms come around my midriff, bringing his face flush against my belly. Heat emanates from where his body meets mine, and a deep sense of comfort settles in my bones.

"Sister," Vlad whispers again, and I get the sudden urge to thread my fingers through his hair, lull him into a sense of security where he can finally relax, away from whatever demons seem to have possessed him.

His arms tighten around me as he continues to repeat the word sister, each time more urgently than before.

I don't know how to react. I only know that I want to help him overcome whatever he's going through.

Lowering my hand to his back, I pat him slowly, trying to offer him some comfort. He immediately reacts to my touch, purring like a big cat the more I stroke him.

"It's okay. You're safe here." I feel compelled to add, and his shoulders slump slightly, his head moving on top of my habit as if he's seeking something. Then, out of nowhere, his breathing regulates, his chest rising and falling softly.

"I think he's sleeping," I say after a while. Somehow I wish for nothing more than to continue to hold him, but I know it's not my place.

Likely will never be.

So I slowly take his arms off me, a lump forming in my throat as I watch him fall to the ground.

"What was *that*?" I ask Marcello once I'm next to him.

"He..." He frowns, trying to find the right words to explain Vlad's condition. "Has some trauma. This must have triggered him."

I nod absentmindedly, even though my gaze keeps on straying to his form on the floor.

"Before we leave, I want to ask you something," Marcello surprises me by saying.

"What?" I frown.

"Do you really want to take your vows? If you feel in any way that this life isn't for you, you can tell me. I'm worried about your safety here, and Mother Superior won't let me hire a guard for you."

My eyes widen, and I don't know how to answer.

"You... you're saying..." I breathe out slowly, afraid I'm misconstruing his meaning. "You're saying I can leave the convent? But where would I go... I...."

"You can come live with us," Catalina interjects, coming toward me, "we'd love to have you, isn't that so, Marcello?"

My brother nods.

"It's your home too. And you'd be safer there."

"I..." I don't know what to say. I'd never in my wildest dreams dared to believe I would leave this convent. "Yes, yes, please," I answer promptly, happiness bursting in my chest at the thought. "Thank you! I... you do not understand what that means to me."

"Did you not like it here?" he asks, studying me in confusion.

"It's not that," I start, not wanting to sound ungrateful. "I don't think I'm fit to be a nun," I admit, lowering my gaze.

If only they knew just *how* unfit I am to be a nun....

"I think this is the best option. I've always known Sisi wasn't meant for this life," Catalina agrees, taking my hand in hers.

I'm so happy at the prospect of leaving this dratted place that I barely hear Vlad moving about.

Lina and Marcello gaze back at him, and I turn too, watching as he's slowly rousing from his sleep.

"Damn," he curses. He looks disheveled, yet entirely too appealing. "What happened?"

"I think you've had your fill of blood for today," Marcello adds, and a conspiratorial glance passes between the two of them.

"Sorry about that," he says, looking around the room. His eyes find me and he frowns, tilting his head to the side as if he's seeing something he can't quite explain. Then it's over.

One moment his entire persona seems to be enveloped in darkness and pain, the next his mouth stretches into another fake smile, erasing all traces of his *real* self.

"I'm glad you're fine," Lina tells him, but I just narrow my eyes at him.

What is his deal exactly?

"So what did I miss?" He smirks, as if he hadn't just endangered my life.

I raise an eyebrow at him, but his smile only widens when he sees my contrite expression.

We finish our business in the church, and Marcello lets me know he'll speak to Mother Superior on my behalf and that I can return home with them.

I just plaster on a pleasant smile, not daring to dream about it until it happens.

But it seems this time, the fates are actually on my side.

9
SISI

I try not to show how affected I am by everything that's happening. How the simple fact that I am in a car, driving away from that wretched place, is making me feel like I'm on cloud nine. Or how looking out the window at all the passing buildings that are *not* Sacre Coeur gets me incredibly giddy.

Marcello doesn't know, but he's just given me the gift of a lifetime. I don't know if he really wants me around, or if he thinks I will be an inconvenience, but I plan on doing my best not to cause any problems that might make him regret taking me in.

When we reach his home, I'm blown away by the size of it. More so, the beauty of the architecture inside. Sacre Coeur hadn't lacked in that, but it had been a clinical beauty. It had been a house, not a home.

Suddenly I can see Lina's touches throughout the rooms, and a warmth envelops me.

"I didn't tell you," I lean over to whisper in her ear. "But I'm happy you married my brother," I tell her sincerely.

"Me too," she replies, blushing slightly.

I've always considered Lina and Claudia my family, but now they truly are. And to know we are going to live in the same place again... I can't help but feel a dizzying amount of happiness at the thought.

With a nod, Marcello leaves us to our devices, asking Lina to show me my room.

"Is he always like that?" I frown when we're alone.

"He's..." She purses her lips. "More reserved. But he's been wonderful to me."

"I'm glad." I squeeze her hand in comfort.

She'd told me the circumstances of their marriage and the fact that the Guerras are still a danger to her and Claudia.

To be entirely truthful, I still have a hard time reconciling the fact that our families are involved in organized crime. And that makes me slightly curious about Vlad's connection to the mob, since he seemed to be Marcello's good friend.

Not for the first time since we've left Sacre Coeur, my thoughts stray to that man. Maybe it's because I'm not used to strangers, but his presence had impacted me. I can vividly picture his dark eyes staring at me, his hands on my body...

Shaking my head at the intrusive thoughts, I ground myself in the present.

Lina takes me to a guest room on the second floor, telling me we'd have time to go shopping and decorate it in the future.

I can only nod, since anything is perfect for me. And the room she shows me is bigger than I would have imagined. It's a simple bedroom, with a double bed, a vanity, a wardrobe and a small ensuite. But it's *mine*.

I'm still rooted to the spot, admiring the room, when Lina taps me on the shoulder, handing me a few clothes.

"We're a similar size, so this should do until we get you

more clothes. You can finally get rid of the habit," she says, looking me up and down and scrunching her nose.

I don't even know how to reply as I take the clothes from her. I've never worn anything other than the clothes provided at Sacre Coeur, so this is a new experience for me.

Impatient, I put the clothes on the bed and start pulling at my habit, ready to be rid of it. Lina's lip curls up as she sees my excitement, and she closes the door, so I can have some privacy.

Looking through the clothes, I choose a green dress that's not too short nor too long.

"I don't have any bras that would fit you, but we can buy some tomorrow," Lina comments, and I nod, pink staining my cheeks. That's the one area where Lina and I don't match since I've been cursed with huge breasts. Still, it's not like I've worn anything other than a bustier before. Although, looking in the mirror after I've donned the dress, I can see how the form would be more flattering with a bra.

"Wow, I can barely recognize you," she breathes when she sees me. My hair, too, is unbound and flowing down my back.

"It certainly feels different." I keep on looking in the mirror as if I'm seeing myself for the first time.

"You have no idea how happy I am that you're here." Lina leans her head on my shoulder, smiling at me.

"Me too," I reply.

Too happy.

And that makes me slightly afraid. Because now that I've tasted happiness, if it's wrenched away from me, it *will* kill me.

The day has even more surprises in store as I get to meet my sister, Venezia. My first impression is that we look nothing alike. While Marcello and I may have our coloring in common, since both of us have blonde hair, Venezia's is a soft brown color. Her eyes, too, are a hazel shade compared to my light brown ones.

I keep staring at her, trying to find some commonality, but there's none.

"You're so pretty," I say at some point, overwhelmed by the fact that she looks exactly like a doll.

She blinks twice before a blush creeps up her neck, and she lowers her eyes.

From what Lina had told me, I would have expected her to be bolder and more outspoken, but the Venezia in front of me is shy, second-guessing her every word.

"Thank you," she eventually whispers.

Our conversation is a little stunted, as neither of us can come up with a topic. But we'll have enough time to get to know each other.

"Can I... " She starts, rather nervously, "Give you a hug?"

"Of course!" I answer immediately, wasting no time in tugging her into my open arms.

Saying good night to Lina and Claudia, I head to my own room, still in awe that I get to have a space all mine.

How many times have I dreamed about this very thing? Before Lina had come along at Sacre Coeur, I'd been rooming with dozens of other girls. The notion of having something to myself when everything had been shared has always been hard to understand.

Laying my hand on the bed, I trace the contour of the silky sheets, excitement forming inside of me at the thought of sleeping in such luxury.

I quickly shower, drying my skin properly before sliding between the sheets. I sigh deeply, the coolness of the material against my naked skin feeling divine.

His hand wrapped around my throat; he pushes me roughly on the altar. My back hits the cold table, my eyes wide with terror. Swiping aside all the religious paraphernalia, I see a cross falling to the ground, the sound reverberating in the church.

He surveys me from head to toe, his molten gaze sweet yet biting, like a Pagan God waiting for his sacrifice, my demise the fuel for his very essence.

"Stop," I whisper as his fingers tighten around my flesh, stopping my airflow. For a moment my breath hitches, and I can only stare at those dark eyes that aim to consume me — body and soul.

His other hand is roaming freely on my body, goosebumps appearing as he trails his fingers up my thigh, until he stops at the curve of my hip, his palm splaying over my waist.

His lips widen in a wicked smile, the first genuine one I'd seen from him. He looks indomitable as he looms over me, my life and death in his control.

I try to struggle against his hold, my hands pushing at his shoulders, but everything I do is in vain. He's too strong, as he has me pinned down with his massive body, and I have to admit that I'm at his mercy.

His mouth moves to my ear as he whispers some indiscernible sounds, his chokehold slowly becoming a tender caress.

Suddenly his hand is gone. My eyes widen when he starts kissing his way up my neck, my body shuddering with a mixture of fear and curiosity.

"What are you doing?" My voice quivers as I ask.

He doesn't reply. He merely smiles against my skin before his mouth opens up, his teeth lodging into my flesh.

I scream, the pain surreal as he breaks the skin, blood flowing freely from the wound. He laps at it, smearing it all over my neck and up my cheek, his devilish tongue swirling circles on the surface of my skin.

Briefly, he raises his head, a wide smile showing blood-stained teeth.

"You're mine. To kill and to..."

I jolt awake, disoriented and covered in sweat. Finding myself in my bed, I look around the empty room, breathing a sigh of relief when I see there's no one around. My hands immediately go around my body, trying to make sure I'm still in one piece. My fingers linger on my neck, finding the skin intact.

A soft tremor goes through my body as I remember the vivid way in which his teeth had felt on me, the sharp pain that had racked my entire being as he'd relentlessly pushed against me.

I'd tried so hard to forget the incident from the church, and now he's haunting my dreams. I must have been more affected by his presence than I'd let myself believe, because there's no other explanation for this.

The wind is blowing outside, the curtain swaying around, in and out of the room. Frowning, I get out of bed to check it.

I'm sure I closed the window before falling asleep.

Feeling slightly paranoid, I lower the window, pulling on the latch so that it's locked in place. Glancing outside, I only see the green expanse of the backyard. No sign of anything or anyone.

Relieved it's only my overactive imagination, I go back to bed. But as I slide between the sheets again, I realize something else. There's a wetness between my legs that wasn't there before. It's accompanied by a low hum in my loins, a tingling almost like an itch.

My hand dips low, and I'm shocked to find my fingers coated in a viscous substance. My first thought is that I must have been so scared that I wet the bed. But the texture is entirely different, and for a moment I'm afraid something is wrong with me.

Quickly grabbing my phone, I open the web browser and search what it means.

The answer, however, doesn't help.

Arousal. Sexual desire.

"Oh, hell no," I mutter to myself as I read through article after article. I can't have been aroused by that... man trying to kill me. I'm almost disgusted with myself for allowing myself to think that, so I power off the phone, placing it on the table.

"It's just residual fear." I try to convince myself.

Sleep barely comes to me, and when I have to wake up in the morning I'm rather cranky. I still have this nagging feeling that Vlad is near and that he *will* kill me. I know it's such an irrational fear, but somehow I'm convinced that I'll meet my end at his hands.

There's something terrifying about him, just as it is fascinating.

* * *

Once again, as I meet up with the girls to go shopping, I can't stop him from taking over my thoughts. It's like everything I do reminds me in a way of him, and of that dream.

His black, bottomless eyes and his searing touch are ingrained in my mind. I only have to close my eyes, and it's like his breath is on my neck, his mouth close to my skin.

"That one looks so good on you, Sisi," Lina says sincerely, and I snap out of it. I blink twice, trying to gain some focus.

"I think so too," I reply, a little too late.

If she notices how distracted I am, she doesn't mention it. We continue shopping, getting everything from clothes to phones and laptops.

Passing by a hair salon, though, an idea comes to me.

"I want to get a fringe," I tell Lina, explaining that having something to cover my forehead would make it easier for me, since people wouldn't be staring so much.

She nods thoughtfully. "If that's what you want, then of course."

Lina and Claudia go to get some sweets while I endure the ministrations of the hair stylist. Already, I feel bad as I see my hair gathering on the floor, flashbacks of Cressida's punishments flashing through my head.

It takes everything in me not to bolt. Luckily, the entire thing is over in minutes, and the new look seems to suit me perfectly.

I thank the technician and move to pay.

All the while, my skin prickles with awareness, as if someone's watching me from behind.

Turning rapidly, I see a shadowy shape take refuge behind one of the columns.

I don't even wait for the change, telling them to keep the rest as I run, chasing after whatever's following me.

No one.

There's no one behind the column, or anywhere around it. I stand in the middle of the shopping mall, disoriented as I look around, attempting to pick out whatever phantasm I'd seen.

I'm going crazy.

I didn't lose my mind during my twenty years in that wretched place, but I am now. For God's sake, I used to hang out in a cemetery, and I'd never been scared of ghosts or any other supernatural creature. It seems rather ludicrous to become so paranoid now.

It's all his fault.

"Aunt Sisi," Claudia calls out my name, dashing toward

me. Plastering a smile on my face, I pretend that everything is okay.

Once we have what we came for, we're ready to head back.

I'm already tired, both physically and mentally, and as soon as we get home, I excuse myself to my room.

I need a nap.

Hopefully, this time I won't have an uninvited guest in my dreams.

Opening the door to my room, I place the bags on the floor, my hands already on the zipper of my dress.

All of a sudden, a hand covers my mouth, an arm sneaking around my waist and bringing me into a hard chest.

What?

My first instinct is to try to scream, regardless of the palm pressing against my lips. My limbs start struggling, and I move my head around, trying to kick at whoever is behind me.

"Shhh," a chilling voice whispers in my ear, "we wouldn't want your brother to find me here."

My heart in my throat, I can only stop moving. My entire body is stiff as I realize just who is behind me, holding me hostage.

Oh, hell. I may die after all.

10
VLAD

Humming to myself, I open the door to the basement, depositing the tools I'd brought with me on a table.

Vanya is sulking in a corner, and she only gives me one hostile look before turning her head and proceeding to ignore me. She's been doing this for the past few hours, and I have yet to find what caused her displeasure.

Although, I *may* have one idea.

Focusing on the task at hand, instead, I put that particular topic out of my mind.

"I trust the condition of your lodgings has been to your satisfaction?" I smile at the man currently tied to a chair in the middle of the room. "Wait." I frown. "I forgot you can't talk." I shake my head and in two steps I'm in front of him, taking his gag off and letting him exercise his mouth for a while.

And if he knows what's best for him, he will exercise it *right*.

"What the hell... Where am I..." he stammers, his eyes

wildly assessing the chamber, before settling on me, "And who are you?"

"Mr. Petrovic, I am profoundly offended that you don't know who I am," I drawl, settling on the floor in front of him.

The first round is going to be easy. The next... depending on him.

"How am I supposed to know?" he spits at me.

Shaking my head, I make a tsk sound, gathering the end of my sleeve and folding it up my arm. Holding my hand out for him to see my tattoo, I watch as the entire previous bravado drains from his face.

My reputation, so to speak, is more through word of mouth than solid evidence. I have, after all, retired from the more unsavory part of the business years ago, when I'd realized that my reaction to blood had worsened, making me become too unstable. Instead, I'd taken to polishing a classier image that nonetheless strikes fear in my adversaries.

Although most people don't know what I look like, they do know something—my name and my tattoo that identifies me as the current Pakhan.

Mr. Petrovic should feel honored, indeed, that I am personally tending to him, since my forays into murder or torture are rather limited these days, a fact that I'm deeply mourning, since both are the best cure in satisfying my boredom.

As it stands, even my science experiments have been put on hold, the chances of me ruining the bloodier steps higher than me completing the project.

But him...

I smile just thinking about it.

It's been years since I'd last found a solid lead into the person who'd taken Katya. And I'd only been able to do that by scouring through all of Misha's connections and hidden communications. A lot of the people I'd found had ended up dead, but a few had changed identities over the years, trying to run away.

From me, or from someone else, I can't say.

Case in point, Mr. Petrovic had changed his identity ten times in the last decade, each time choosing a different nationality, and moving to a different part of the country.

I guess he'd thought himself safe with all those security measures. But he hadn't counted on my commitment to finding him.

A few years ago, I'd ended up enhancing a face recognition software that could now take old footage and analyze it for behavioral patterns and tics. You can hide from the world, but you can't hide from yourself.

And Mr. Petrovic might have changed his name, and his appearance to a degree. But some things never change. Like his slight limp, an old injury to his distal tibia making the connection to the talus quite shaky.

His gait analysis had presented a ninety percent accuracy, and in my desperation, I'd overlooked the ten that were not conclusive.

My software, though, had done its job.

"Now that the introductions are over, let's focus on today's topic, shall we?" I grin at him, opening my little pouch and removing a knife and an apple. "Here's how things are going to go. I am going to ask questions and you are going to answer. If I like your answers, then no pain. If I don't." I wiggle my eyebrows at him, "Well, you shall see."

His head moves around the room, probably searching for a way out.

"We're at a subterranean level. There's no way out, Mr. Petrovic. Not even if you manage to get past me, which, let's face it," I purse my lips, "is not happening. So your best bet is to be as cooperative as possible."

I start peeling the apple, my eyes firmly set on his terrified expression.

"Why don't we start with your connection to Misha," I say, taking a bite from the apple.

I already know that Mr. Petrovic used to act as a broker between the US and Europe, bringing people over with the promise of a job and then selling them further. Which begs the question. Why would he be involved with Misha?

"I don't know who that is," he says, rather too quickly.

"Mr. Petrovic." I sigh, a little bummed it's not going to be as fast as I'd wanted it. "I'm a busy man. *Very busy*. Think about it, instead of interrogating you for hours, I could be out enjoying the sun, killing a dozen people, and getting my daily dose of vitamin D. Instead, I have to be cooped up inside, with the prospect of killing just *one* person." His shoulders slump, his eyes widening a little.

Good.

"How is that fair for me?" I take another bite, keeping my eyes on him.

"Please..." The cry for help is barely audible, but I guess he finally realized the situation he finds himself in.

"I didn't hear you." I put one hand to my ear, waiting for him to repeat himself.

"I can't tell you," he says, almost resigned to his fate. "They'll kill my family," he continues, his eyes pleading with me.

Well, this is one of those situations that I usually dread, because if someone's family is in danger, the chances of them talking are... slim. Not zero, though. It's just a matter of adjusting the torture accordingly so they break.

"I guess we'll talk in a few days, Mr. Petrovic." I stand up to leave, and I hear his sigh of relief. I guess he doesn't realize what those few days will entail.

A quick message to one of my men, Maxim, and he's already here.

"V sadu?" he asks, eyeing the prisoner.

Oh, Maxim, how well you know me.

"Indeed, in the garden," I reply, mischief twinkling in my eyes.

Maxim nods, going over to Mr. Petrovic and grabbing him by the chair. He easily lifts him in the air, and I follow behind as he takes him to the garden.

Like the entire level of this place, the garden is subterranean too. It's more of a greenhouse, if I'm being honest, but I've built it in such a way to emulate outside conditions.

We reach the garden and Maxim goes in the back, to a pair of suspenders. Maneuvering the chair around, he hitches the legs of the chair through the suspenders, ensuring the chair is about two feet off the ground.

"What... what's happening?" Mr. Petrovic keeps talking, his eyes bulging in his head.

"This is my attempt at convincing you to talk. We'll see if it works. In a few days." I give him a brilliant smile, after which Maxim promptly gags him again.

Then, he removes the bottom of the chair, so that Mr. Petrovic's ass is slowly molding through the hole.

Under the suspended chair, there are about five bamboo sprouts, all newly planted and ready to grow tall and beautiful. Mr. Petrovic is about to get up close and personal with a few of them, and very soon. If he's lucky, one might even penetrate him in the ass, and stimulate his prostate. A little pleasure amid all the pain.

Alas, I don't think he's that lucky.

Leaving the greenhouse, I check the time, knowing I have another matter to tend to.

Vanya is trailing behind me, her attitude much improved.

"We'll find her," she says confidently, jumping up and down in a dance of happiness.

How I wish I could share her outlook.

But it's been nine years since Katya was taken. Nine years that I failed her, and if she's still alive, she's likely lived through countless terrors.

Sometimes I have to ask myself if I'd rather find her alive but broken, or dead and at peace.

* * *

A ssisi Lastra.

I let the name roll on my tongue as I remember the tiny girl with fiery eyes. It is my duty to test a theory when it arises, and she'd just handed me a challenge.

Meeting her had been... interesting. To say the least.

She'd certainly not been what I expected, given that she grew up in a convent. Hell, she hadn't even been on my radar until a short while back when Father Guerra had turned up dead at Sacre Coeur.

I pride myself on having eyes and ears in all places, but Agosti's sister had been a blind spot. Not that she'd been of any interest until Guerra ended up disemboweled in public. And so I'd decided to get a little more insight into that particular event.

She might be just a small player, but in the big scheme of things, it's the small players that decide the outcome of a game. In their insignificance, they are the best pawns, going about undetected, with people sparing them the least attention.

So I'd set about hacking her phone. It hadn't even been hard to find out her number, since Agosti isn't the best at keeping his communication with his sister a secret. One phishing message and I'd been sure she'd bite, after all, a naïve miss like her is the best target for such things.

But she hadn't. Instead, she'd replied with the most outrageous thing. She'd renounced her *prize* in favor of someone else. Only after a few, slightly embarrassing attempts, did I realize I was not in fact speaking with Catalina Agosti, but with her close friend, Assisi — Marcello's sister.

I'd been even more befuddled when her retorts had taken a humorous route, and I'd found myself compelled to continue the banter.

I certainly hadn't expected to enjoy sparring with her so much, or for so long. Given my limited interaction with the outside world, it had been just a way to get rid of my boredom.

But then I met her in the flesh... Well, that had been unexpected. For such a little thing, steeped in ignorance from those dogmatic teachings at Sacre Coeur, she'd certainly been intriguing. Her reaction to the mutilated nun had been simply astonishing.

I should have realized from her caustic replies to my messages that she wouldn't be just a regular miss. Where I would have expected her to run screaming at the sight of blood and organs, she'd taken it one step further by getting her hands dirty.

My lips twitch as I remember her elbows deep in the nun's guts. Considering it's one of the last things I remember from that particular encounter, it had definitely made an impression on me.

The last thing I can recall had been zoning in on her face,

admittedly a very handsome face. But her birthmark, that red spot just above her eyebrows, had caught my attention and held it.

It had been like becoming hypnotized by that red. Then she'd had to actually smear blood on it, and I'd simply lost it.

When I'd woken up, though, something extraordinary had happened. I'd set my sight on her, and out of nowhere, Vanya had simply vanished.

I'd been dumbstruck by her sudden disappearance. I've lived with her by my side for the last twenty-two years. Not once had she just vanished into thin air. One way or another, she's always been with me. She may not always talk or interact with me, but she's never out of my vantage point.

Until Assisi.

I frown as I think about the crux of the problem. The moment Assisi had disappeared from my sight, Vanya had returned—in full force.

It wasn't until that moment that I'd realized just how refreshing it had been to have a moment of peace, without my sister constantly haunting me.

As soon as I'd made that observation, I'd sneakily made sure to see Assisi again before she left Sacre Coeur. And once more, Vanya had gone missing.

I have no idea how, or even why, such a thing would happen, but I need to test it one more time. Just to make sure it hadn't been a fluke.

I've tried to think what could have caused this mental break, since Vanya is, and has always been, part of my mind. I'd even asked Marcello what had happened while I'd been out. Everything to figure out what could have possibly triggered this connection between Assisi and Vanya.

Still... nothing.

The brain works in mysterious ways. Of that I am sure.

But years of consultations with professionals, and not once has Vanya disappeared from my side. Then suddenly, one meeting with an inconsequential female and she's gone?

I must study this phenomenon in depth to get to the bottom of this. Because if I can permanently get rid of Vanya...

Not that I don't like having my sister around, but I've had decades with her by my side, and that can get tedious.

Parking my car just off the road, I take out a laptop to check the situation. Knowing Marcello, he would have upped security the moment he moved in. Still, that won't stop me. I bypass his cybersecurity, getting myself inside his framework. From there, it's easy to access the security cameras throughout the house.

I fast-forward through today's events until I catch sight of Assisi, seeing exactly which one is her room. Once confirmed, a brief calculation of angles and I spot the window to her room.

Second floor.

Luckily, I've had enough experience climbing buildings to make this a piece of cake.

Leaving my things behind, I skirt through the bushes until I'm at the back of Marcello's house. Identifying the window, I climb up using the relief of the building for support. As usual, Vanya is by my side, climbing at her own pace. When I reach her room, I use a small screwdriver to open the window, effortlessly swinging myself inside.

Marcello would have my head if he knew I'm spying on his sister.

A smile pulls at my lips at the hilarity of the situation. Still, I'm selfish enough that if I see an opportunity to get rid of my sister's ghost, I'll take it, regardless of whom I have to use to achieve my purpose.

The room is shrouded in darkness save for a beam of light from the moon. I carefully step inside, walking toward the bed in the center.

A small form is huddled in the middle of the bed, the sheet covering her entire body as she sleeps peacefully.

My eyes are intent on her for a moment before I look around, mentally calling Vanya.

She's gone.

I quietly walk around the room, noting she's nowhere in sight.

Interesting.

Propping myself against the wall in front of the bed, I study Assisi's sleeping form, wondering just what exactly it is about her that's making Vanya disappear.

Maybe it's her holiness.

But just as the thought arises, a chuckle escapes me. According to what I've learned of her, that's definitely not the case.

Curiosity brimming inside of me, I take a step closer, carefully taking a seat on the bed so I can inspect her better.

With her eyes closed, her lips slightly parted, she looks almost angelic. Her hair, unbound, with strands scattered on the pillow, resembles a halo around her head. I don't think I've ever seen a lighter shade of blonde. Her heart-shaped face is objectively exquisite, the red mark on her forehead only enhancing its uniqueness.

Just at that moment she moves, shuffling around in bed, the sheet slowly sliding down her body.

Fuck!

My eyes widen as I realize she's not wearing anything underneath. It had been easy to refer to her as a girl until now, but as her ample tits pop free, her nipples puckered and standing to attention, I realize my mistake.

She's *not* a girl.

Fuck, but I didn't realize little miss nun would have the body of a porn star.

I also note another thing. Just above her breast, there is a gnarly scar in the shape of a cross. I frown, but as my eyes move over her chest, I see more scars, some smaller, some bigger, as if she'd been tortured for years.

Where did she get those?

A small sound escapes her lips. Her features drawn up in a frown, she continues moving around, the sheet sliding even lower.

I blink twice at the unexpected strip tease show in front of me. Unwittingly, my eyes rove over her naked flesh, down her small waist, taut stomach and...

"Christ, she might still make a believer out of me," I mutter low, unable to believe what I'm seeing.

Rolling around in bed, she ends up closer to me, the curve of her ass in the air as she moans deep in her throat.

I stand up, suddenly uncomfortable with the direction of my thoughts. I feel heat creep up my cheeks, and I have to shake myself.

Think about murder, or mutilation, or breaking someone's bones.

Scaphoid, trapezium, capitate...

I hum to myself the bones I enjoy breaking, slowly finding some modicum of control.

This was only supposed to be a test. A way to rationally explain to myself why Vanya would disappear in Assisi's presence.

Not an exercise in how fast I can lose my mind.

Cursing under my breath, I avert my gaze, focusing on an empty corner to gather my thoughts.

There has to be a logical explanation to it.

But the more I think about it, the more I realize there has to be *more* to this. I can't possibly solve a twenty-two-year-old problem in one night. And so I must come up with something else.

Assisi is restless in her sleep, the rustling of sheets only serving to distract me from my mental exercises, tempting me to sneak a peek at her rather enchanting backside.

Alas, this is not what I came here for.

But Vanya's not watching...

I firmly shut that thought down, trying instead to come up with a plan to study this phenomenon more in depth. But for that, I'd need Assisi's assistance. And I must admit I haven't made the best first impression.

Well, if she's not willing, then I'll have to *make* her willing.

Now it's only a matter of finding out what she wants most, and giving it to her.

Avoiding looking at her more than necessary, I leave the room, a plan already forming in my head.

* * *

"Why are you so interested in her?" Vanya asks from my side. I only spare her a glance, my eyes fixed on the computer as I comb through footage from Sacre Coeur, all in an attempt to understand Assisi better. If I can find out what she most desires, I can give it to her in exchange for her cooperation.

"She's pretty," I half-lie. I don't know why I'm hiding the truth from Vanya, since it's not like she's actually a sentient being that can get upset.

"She is," she agrees, coming closer to study Assisi's face. "But you've never been interested in a girl before. Not even a pretty one," she says, pinning me down with her inquisitive gaze.

"There's a first time for everything, right?" I mutter.

She shrugs, turning her head to watch the footage with me.

Sacre Coeur only has cameras in strategic locations, so the video doesn't give me much to go off.

By chance, though, I spot Assisi leaving the house with Catalina and her daughter, taking a car to go somewhere. My lips curl up as I congratulate myself for setting up a screen to track movement in and out of Marcello's house.

It takes me a while to track down the car, but I find it parked at a shopping mall.

Well, this should be interesting.

I end up spending an entire afternoon watching the women prance from store to store, trying to keep my focus as I file in every relevant piece of information.

Like the fact that she likes blue.

I'd never realized just how tedious women's shopping could be, but for the sake of data gathering, I must suffer through it.

In the end, the only noteworthy thing is Assisi's excitement about every single store. Even the most uninteresting thing seems to get her attention. The fact that she stops to marvel at *furniture* — boring, commonplace furniture— makes me want to groan out loud.

She even stops at a toy store, browsing the shelves and looking at dolls and stuffed animals. Why, she can't seem to tear her eyes from a human-sized teddy bear. She keeps walking around the store, but she always ends up in front of the teddy bear, staring at it until she eventually musters up the courage to touch it.

Wait a moment. Could that be what she desires the most?

Well, that wasn't so hard.

Waiting until she's gone, I go to the store and buy the teddy bear, convinced this will get me into her good graces and make her cooperative.

As I struggle to carry the enormous bear to my car, Vanya decides to make an appearance, frowning as she takes in the stuffed animal in my arms.

"Why do you have *that?*" she asks, a look of incredulity on her face.

I quickly explain to her that I'm trying to impress a lady, leaving out the reason *why* I'm trying to do it.

"I can't believe you're my brother." Vanya shakes her head, pursing her lips and crossing her arms over her chest. "You think *that* is what she desires the most?"

"Yes. She kept admiring it at the store," I explain myself, a bit taken aback by the vehemence in her voice.

She narrows her eyes at me, a look of disbelief on her face.

"And because she was admiring it, you think this is what she desires the most?"

"Exactly," I reply, pushing the teddy bear into the back seat of the car.

"Idiot," she mutters under her breath, and I turn to her, confused. "She doesn't want the bear, you idiot," she continues, "she wants what the bear represents."

"What do you mean?" Now it's my turn to frown.

"She's never lived outside that convent, right? So she's never had a normal life. She wants to experience the outside world," Vanya says, and with a huffed breath, she gets in the passenger seat of the car.

As I ponder her words, it slowly dawns on me that she might be right. She was fascinated by everything, including that weird furniture.

Maybe Vanya's on to something.

I make quick time back to Marcello's house, all the while ruminating on the issue Vanya had raised and how to best proceed in this case.

Then, like the night before, I just sneak into her room and wait for her to come back. After that, I'll have to convince her that I can give her the world if she gives me back my peace.

I don't have to wait long, as the door to the room opens, Assisi strutting inside and placing her bags on the floor. I don't give her an opportunity to scream, or bolt, or both. Grabbing her by the waist, I put my hand over her mouth, whispering in her ear.

"Shhh, we wouldn't want your brother to find me here."

11

VLAD

Marcello would probably shoot first and ask questions later. He certainly would not appreciate my being in the same room as his sister, alone. His concern isn't wholly unwarranted, since I *am* a ticking bomb. And while I normally would not endanger an innocent, I find that this time I cannot stay away.

She struggles in my arms, her body tantalizingly close to mine as she tries to find an opening to kick me.

"Stop moving," I whisper, tightening my hold on her waist. My palm moves over her stomach, and I can't stop the vision of her naked body from entering my mind.

Fuck! I need to stay focused.

"If you promise not to scream, I'll let you go," I say, immediately chastising myself for taking the risk.

Her head slowly bobs up and down in a nod, and I release her.

She doesn't waste any time in putting distance between us, going as far as the other end of the room.

"What in God's name are you doing in my room?" she asks, her eyes shooting daggers at me.

"Aghh," I groan out loud, putting a hand up, "don't bring *him* up! We're not on good terms."

She raises an eyebrow at me.

"You do realize you're talking to a novitiate."

"Former. It seems to me you've shed your habit. Was it too constricting?" I wiggle my eyebrows at her suggestively.

"I don't know what you're talking about," she says, her eyes flashing as she takes a step back.

"Do I scare you?" I ask her bluntly, moving closer to her, caging her in. My eyes roam over her chest—her generous chest, since I would have to be blind not to notice those magnificent mounds hidden by her odiously conservative dress. I note the quickening of her pulse. "I do, don't I?"

I wouldn't fault her for being scared of me. She's not the first and certainly not the last. Although it will make our conversation harder.

"Of course not! But you're in my room, uninvited. It's not proper."

"Don't tell me you fear for your virtue," I drawl, using one finger to caress her cheek.

Her eyes widen, but she doesn't put distance between us. If anything, she raises her gaze to meet mine, challenging me directly.

"I fear no such thing! I can defend myself." She crosses her hands over her chest, pushing her voluptuous breasts up.

I groan out loud, taking my eyes off her chest. Even I am but a man, and breasts like hers are prime material for getting a man in trouble—even those of the monk variety.

"Can you?" I raise an eyebrow at her.

"Of course!" She barely gets the words out when my hand shoots out, pushing her onto her bed, my body on top of hers.

"Please, do," I say, amused.

She narrows her eyes at me, but she doesn't lose her calm. If anything, she seems to be even more composed than before.

"Nothing?" My eyebrows shoot up questioningly. "I could do a lot of things to you from this position. Say, hike up your dress..."

She doesn't react to my taunt. Instead, she turns her eyes to me, her gaze softening.

"You could," she says in a breathy tone, her hand coming up to my face.

I frown, not understanding what she's trying to do.

She smiles briefly before leaning forward and pressing her lips to my cheek.

To say I'm stunned would be an understatement. I'm frozen to the spot as my skin soaks in that small gesture.

Hell, I can count on one hand the times someone's willingly kissed my cheek.

But I don't have more time to wonder about this unusual situation, as her knee lodges between my legs, kicking me in the balls with a force that makes me see stars.

"Fuck," I rasp in pain, moving off her and praying to all deities that my balls are still intact.

"See, not helpless." She smirks at me, swinging her legs off the bed and getting up.

"What are you, some ninja nun?" I mumble, my vision doubling from pain.

"I don't know what that word means, but you need to leave," she says, tapping her foot on the floor impatiently.

I take a deep breath, fighting against the pain.

That's one region where my pain receptors are not dulled.

Bringing myself under control, I get up, putting on my

most charming smile. Instead of making her soften towards me, it does the complete opposite.

"Wipe that smile off your face," she fires at me, and I'm momentarily stunned by her reaction. But I quickly recover.

"Afraid you'll fall for me?" I ask playfully, trying to bring the conversation into silly yet comfortable territory.

"As if," she snorts. "Get to the point. Why are you here?"

"Why, Assisi, didn't those nuns teach you how to give such a warm welcome?" I lay back on the bed, resting on my elbows and watching annoyance appear on her face.

"No, they taught me not to take any bullshit," she tilts her head at me, "especially of the male kind," she says, looking down at me.

My mouth curls up. "Ah, the age-old misandry. You know, I have a theory about nuns and why they are so bitter," I say slowly, and I note a hint of interest in her features.

"Really?" she asks, her tone suspicious.

"They just need a good fuck." I shrug carelessly, but my eyes are honed in on her expression, watching for any slight change. When I see none, I add another thing, just to rile her up, "But you probably don't know what that means."

The reaction is delayed, as her brows knit together in confusion before her eyes widen in realization.

"You cad!" she exclaims, outraged, taking one of her bags and throwing it at me.

"Why?" I put my hands up in defense. "You know I'm right!"

She plays the scandalized maiden very well, but I can see the slight trembling of her upper lip and the way she's trying very hard not to smile.

"You might be right, but you're a cad for pointing it out

nonetheless," she continues, still holding on to that cheeky smile.

"Why? Because that would mean you need a good fuck too?" I add before I can think it through. Her mouth drops open in shock, her lids moving rapidly up and down as if she can't quite believe what I've said.

Even I can't believe what I've said.

It must be her tits. They're distracting and making me think dirty thoughts. There's no other explanation for it. And as my eyes drift lower to the rise and fall of her chest, I have to swallow deeply.

Her eyes rage at me, and before I know it, she tackles me, her hands moving up and down in an attempt to grab me.

I play her game, easily immobilizing her, but as she struggles in my hold, we roll over the edge of the bed.

Assisi on top of me, my back hits the floor, and I stifle a groan at the impact.

She raises her head slightly, watching me with a frown.

"Are you okay?" she asks, worried. I bite back a smile as I file away another piece of information about her.

For all her bark, she's got a soft core.

That might actually come in handy.

"Aghh," I fake grunt in pain, closing my eyes and pretending I've been injured.

"My God! I'm so sorry." She scrambles into a sitting position, her hands going to my shoulders as she's inspecting for damage. "Where does it hurt? I swear I didn't mean to harm you like that," she continues blabbering, her eyes roving over my upper body. I keep fake moaning, somehow enjoying being the object of her concern.

Belatedly, though, I realize that this new position does not help at all. Somehow, she ended up straddling me, her legs on either side of my legs, her pelvis grinding on top of mine.

Ah, she's got a soft core indeed.

"Oh no, you're all red," she continues, using her hands to fan some air into my face.

"I'm fine," I mumble, torn between keeping her where she is, or moving her and getting myself under control.

She frowns at me, but eventually nods, moving aside.

I breathe out, relieved, and I turn to adjust my pants before I can face her again.

"Why are you here?" she asks once more, her tone softer this time. She turns her inquisitive gaze toward me, and I detect a hint of interest.

"I have an offer for you," I say, mentally reminding myself to stop antagonizing her. I need to befriend her, not make her wary of me.

"An offer?"

"Your brother is my friend, and I would be remiss if I didn't offer my services."

"What sort of services?" She arches a brow, quickly going back to her suspicious self.

"Since your brother is fairly busy fighting some unknown enemy, I've decided to take care of your introduction into society myself," I add with a smile.

She doesn't seem convinced as she looks at me askance.

"And does my brother know of this... endeavor of yours?"

"Of course not," I say, racking my brain for a good reason.

Why didn't I think this through beforehand?

Somehow my brain cells leave the conversation when it comes to her.

"You don't know Marcello like I do. He can be extremely overprotective. I'm sure you wouldn't like to walk away from one prison only to find yourself in another." I pause, searching her features for a reaction.

"Go on."

"I have sisters too," *had* "so I can understand the struggle, which is why I've decided to help you familiarize yourself with the world."

"And what's in it for you?"

"I may need a favor or two in the future." She looks at me skeptically, so I amend my words, "Nothing too hard. Accompany me at an event or two," I quickly add, explaining that my position may call for my attendance with a date.

She nods thoughtfully, not entirely convinced.

"I see. But why me?"

"Why not you?" I fire back, this time allowing for some honesty, "You're not scared of me, as we've established. Not even after what happened at Sacre Coeur. Most people would *not* try to tackle me to the ground, as you already have. That just confirms to me you're the perfect person for the job."

As I say the words, I gain a new respect for her, because few people would take me head on like she did, or even dare look me in the eye. For that alone, she is indeed the only one fit for the job.

"There's something you're not telling me." She narrows her eyes at me and I just shrug.

"You can accept, or you can refuse," I lie, her refusal being completely out of the question. But it seems I may need to push her further. "I can always find someone else. You, on the other hand..." I trail off.

When her expression doesn't budge, I stand up, ready to leave.

"Wait," she says, and my lips stretch in a languid smile.

"If we do this..." she waves her hand around, "then we do it my way. We do the things that *I* want to do."

"Agreed." I nod.

"Good," she replies awkwardly, teetering on the heels of her feet, suddenly out of words.

We quickly exchange phone numbers, and I tell her I'll be in touch.

Just as I'm about to jump out the window, she taps my back.

"If we're going to be friends, then you can call me Sisi," she adds, suddenly not meeting my eyes.

"Sisi," I say the word out loud, and a small smile appears on her face. "I'll see you soon, Sisi."

12

SISI

Family dinner had been an interesting affair, but I'd found it hard to concentrate on what was being said around me. Not when all I could think about was Vlad and his weird yet oddly appealing offer.

His presence in my room had taken me by surprise, and for a moment I *had* been afraid of him. Not for long, though. Certainly not after he'd opened his mouth. How he'd managed to both insult and amuse me in the same sentence, I have no clue.

But he'd proven even more intriguing than I'd originally thought.

Slowly letting go of my fear of him, I'd become curious as to why he'd try to get to my room so sneakily. Being friends with Marcello, you'd think he would use the front door, not the window.

None of his actions make sense, which, in theory, should make me more wary. In practice, however, this is just making me more interested in him.

It's also probably the reason why I'd accepted his offer in

the first place. Not that I wouldn't mind living a little, but his persona seems to intrigue me more than the outside world.

I'm not dumb, though. I could tell that there was something he was hiding from me. I hadn't really bought his flimsy excuse that he wants to do a favor for his friend, or that he may need my help in the future. And even to his ears it must have sounded too phony.

Still, with him occupying my mind for so long, I'd just jumped at the opportunity to know more about him. Especially considering that duality of him, the way he'd seemed more beast than man at Sacre Coeur, or the way he'd felt too much of a man under me.

A blush envelops my features as I remember just how good that had felt or how he'd seemed embarrassed by his own body's response.

The internet has a wealth of information, and from what I've read, he's anything but indifferent to me.

It should scare me, this foreign feeling that seems to have made its home in my body. But while I feel some apprehension since I *don't* know Vlad that well, I want to remedy that.

Tapping the screen of my phone, I anxiously wait for his message, since he'd promised to take me somewhere tonight.

My phone buzzes and I'm quick to open the text.

Open the window.

I do, looking down onto the lawn where Vlad is waving at me. Frowning, I glance around, since I'm sure Marcello had increased the number of guards around the house recently.

"Down," he mouths to me, using his fingers to point toward the ground.

"How?" I mouth back, watching as he takes his phone out to text something.

Jump! I'll catch you.

I read the message twice, looking between my phone and Vlad, then raise an eyebrow at the outrageous idea.

Seeing the skepticism written on my face, he shoots me another text.

Promise to catch you. Trust me?

I tilt my head to the side, looking at him for a moment. He has an inviting smile on his face, as if he's daring me to jump, ready to mock me if I don't.

Taking a deep breath, I hike up my skirt and climb out the window, my head already spinning as I look at the distance between my room and the ground.

"Come on," he says, his arms open, his hands motioning toward him.

I guess it's now or never.

Without dwelling too much on it, I close my eyes and take my hands off the windowsill, flinging myself forward and into Vlad's waiting arms.

My landing is not what I expected. True to his word, Vlad's arms come around me, locking me tight into his embrace.

Our faces are millimeters apart, and as I stare into those black eyes of his, everything else fades away.

"Oops," he whispers, wobbling a little before tilting back and falling, with me on top of him.

"I shouldn't make a habit of falling on top of you," I whisper, my pulse speeding up as I feel the heat emanating from his body.

"Next time you can fall under me." He winks at me, and it takes me a moment to realize what he means.

"You..." I clench my fist, ready to wipe the grin off his face, when I hear a sudden noise.

Vlad does too, because his features change immediately, his playful expression gone and replaced with a serious one.

Quickly helping me to my feet, he wastes no time in throwing me over his shoulder and running in the opposite direction of the noise.

He stops in front of a car, placing me on the hood. His arms braced on either side of me, he gives me a droopy smile.

"That was a close call," I say, almost breathless. "I hope I won't have to jump out the window every single time."

"And miss falling in my arms? Why ever not?" he replies, amused.

I shake my head, pushing at his shoulder and jumping down.

He opens the door for me, inviting me inside.

"I'm surprised you have manners," I observe dryly as he gets behind the wheel, buckling his seatbelt.

Head tilted to the side, he gives me a dangerous look.

"The moment I forget my manners," he starts, his tone bleak, "you run."

I blink twice, surprised at the quick change in his disposition.

"Is that what happened at Sacre Coeur?" I ask, curious.

He purses his lips, and for a moment he doesn't seem

inclined to answer my question. But then I see an almost imperceptible nod.

"If that happens again, you need to run as far away from me as you can," he eventually says, and a chuckle escapes me. He doesn't share my sentiment, his features still grave.

He's not joking.

I immediately sober up, and a million questions go through my head.

"Are you... ill?" I muster the courage to ask.

A dry laugh escapes him, his eyes still focused on the road.

"Ill... I wish. At least an illness has a cause... and a cure. What I have has neither."

"I don't understand," I reply, frowning at his cryptic words.

"It's not for you to understand, Sisi. Most days I don't understand myself either." He smiles ruefully. "But I've had enough time to come to grips with the fact that I may never be okay."

"How long have you had this... condition?"

"Condition... That's an interesting way to put it. Who knows, maybe I've always had it. I don't remember a time when I was different. It just got progressively worse over the years."

"Does it hurt?"

He spares me a glance.

"Not for me," he states, and I remember the way his eyes had been glazed over, how his hands had been ready to end my life. Except he hadn't.

"You were going to kill me, weren't you?" I push, seeing this as an opening to learn more about him.

"Yet I did not," he replies ambiguously.

"Why?"

He doesn't answer for a moment. He slowly turns toward me, his eyes clear, his gaze shrewd.

"That's what I'm trying to find out."

We don't speak for the longest time. I try to come to grips with what he's just told me, and a chill envelops my body.

Isn't that what captivated you in the first place? The pure savagery hiding behind the expensive suit.

If I'm honest with myself, that's exactly what had drawn me to him. The fact that he's both man and beast, human yet not entirely humane. There's something deep within him that could crush me in a second.

As I sneak glances at him, I'm once more struck by the way his muscles coil, as if he's trying to keep himself from snapping at any moment. Even when his playfulness is at its best, there's still a tension that radiates off of him.

It's also becoming clearer that I am courting danger by being with him. Yet, why can't I find it in me to care?

Maybe because I see in him what I've tried very hard to surpass in myself; violence that's asking to be let out, blood demanding to be spilled.

I'm at a point where I have to wonder if I am what I am because I've been conditioned, by being called evil my whole life. Or, I've simply always been this way, and some people have astutely noticed before my wickedness manifested.

I wonder... What would he say if he knew I'm a murderer?

Somehow, I think *he* would not bat an eye.

"Have you ever killed someone?" I ask, my eyes on his profile. The more I look at his face, the more engrossed I find myself in his micro-expressions–the rehearsed and the spontaneous.

His lip pulls up in amusement, and he chuckles.

"Someone? Define someone."

"One person? Two?" If he's in the mob like my brother, then he may have committed crimes.

I almost laugh to myself as I realize that not too long ago I was worshiping God in his very house, and now I'm condoning all types of crimes.

"One?" He turns to me, his expression one of disbelief. "Sisi, you wound me." He feigns a hurt expression.

"Then how many?"

"Are you sure you want to know? You might run for the hills," he says, but I persist, thinking it can't possibly be that bad.

"Tell me."

"I can't say I've counted," he turns to me slightly, as if waiting to see my reaction, "but it must be somewhere in the thousands." He shrugs.

I stare. Open-mouthed. I just continue to stare at him, waiting for him to say it was a joke.

When he sees I'm not reacting, he pulls over.

Turning fully toward me, his lips are drawn in a tight line.

"Don't try to make excuses for me, or even make me into something I'm not, Sisi," he says, his fingers going under my chin and pushing it up, forcing me to stare into his eyes. "It's better if we go into this with some degree of transparency. I'm a cold-blooded killer. I don't need a reason to kill. I just do. So next time you see me in a rage, you run. Because I can't promise you won't be next."

"You're trying to scare me," I whisper, my upper lip quivering.

"Is it working?"

I shake my head. I don't know why. The rational side of me *knows* I should be terrified. I should have been scared the moment he'd had me by the throat, my feet in the air, his eyes emotionless as he'd looked at me. He could have easily snapped my neck.

"It should." He comes closer, and I feel his breath as my own. My pulse quickens, my eyes dropping from his eyes to his lips. "I should scare you, Sisi. I should fucking terrify you," he rasps, but I'm not paying attention to his words. I can only see the way his lips move, his tongue sneaking out to wet the lower one, his teeth white and straight, the dream from the other night making me clench my thighs in discomfort, as I remember his painful bite on my skin.

"How... would you kill me?" I raise my gaze to his, swallowing hard as I see exactly what he wants me to—an emotionless killer.

"Why?" His voice is thick, his gaze unflinching.

"Tell me," I urge him, a sick desire forming inside of me.

Too much time spent in the cemetery must have addled my brain.

His hand comes up to my face, brushing the bangs from my forehead.

"I like to bathe in human entrails," he says with a straight face. "The bloodier, the better. But for you, I'd make an exception," he comments, and I frown. His fingers caress my birthmark before going lower, down my cheek and neck. "I wouldn't put a single mark on your body."

Confused, I'm about to open my mouth and ask him what he means. But just as my lips part on a question, one finger shushes me, his mouth brushing past my ear.

"Lethal injection. You would be dead in minutes. Then I'd embalm your body and keep you for my eyes only." His low hum makes the hairs on my body stand up.

He's talking about killing me and keeping my corpse, and the only thing I'm feeling is an intense tingling in my tummy.

"And what would you do with my body?" I ask with a breathless tone.

The corner of his mouth pulls up, but he doesn't answer. Instead, he parries with a question of his own. "What would I do indeed? Tell me, Sisi, what do you think I'd do?"

I can't answer, even though deep down I know. I can only stare into those wicked eyes, intoxicated by the depravity I see in there.

I was never meant to be a nun.

Not when I'm getting aroused thinking this dangerous man would kill me... and keep me.

"Still not scared?" he asks, his eyebrows raised expectantly.

I shake my head, the briefest movement as a smile spreads on his face.

"You surprise me, Hell Girl," he whispers. "You almost look like you mean it."

"Hell Girl?"

"The only saintly thing about you, Sisi, is your name. The rest..." he trails off, his eyes drifting to my chest.

A breath catches in my throat at his perusal. I have the sudden urge to take his hand and press it to my skin.

"You're wicked," I manage to say instead.

"Good that you believe that," he drawls, taking my hand and spreading my fingers out. He lowers his lips to the tips, the warmth of his mouth sending a shiver down my body. "Do let me know when you're scared."

"Why?"

"Fear tastes best," he purrs, giving me a roguish smile, his teeth gleaming, and I have a sudden flashback to my dream and to his blood-stained teeth.

13
SISI

Vlad parks the car, coming around to open the door for me. Placing my hand in his, I let him lead me down the dimly lit streets, the loud sounds of the city contributing to a boisterous atmosphere.

Even now, at night, people are walking around, enjoying the freedom of being lost in the crowd.

"Wow," I breathe out when I see the flashing lights.

"I assume this is past your regular curfew," he jokes as we continue down the street, simply enjoying the night air.

"Oh yes," I readily agree, "but I never minded it before. When you're working from dawn to sunset, all you want to do is crawl into bed and sleep."

He frowns, turning slightly toward me.

"I didn't realize nuns worked so hard," he says, taking my hand and lacing it through his elbow.

"One in particular did," I mutter under my breath, since I'm fairly sure I was the only one who had to work almost double the hours.

He raises an eyebrow, but I just shrug.

"I don't think Sacre Coeur is known for its fair working

conditions," I add briefly, before commenting, "I'm surprised you have no guards with you," all in an attempt to switch the focus from me.

The last thing I need is for someone to pity me for everything that happened there. It's already happened and it's not like I can change the past. And certainly, I would never want to be seen as a victim.

"Why would I need any guards?"

"My brother requires Lina to have at least five guards with her at all times. I assumed that with you guys," I look around before leaning in to whisper, "being in this mob business it wouldn't be safe to just wander around unattended."

"And yet here you are," he smiles, "walking around with me unattended."

"It's different," I say before I can think it through.

"Different how?" He tilts his head to the side, awaiting my answer.

You make me feel safe.

But I don't say that.

"You said you're a cold-blooded killer," I reply with half a smile, "I'm willing to bet that people rarely cross you?" I look up to find him watching me amused, the corner of his mouth curling up.

"You would be correct. People would be fools to attack me," he agrees. "But, unlike the rest of the," he emulates my actions, leaning to whisper in my ear, "mob," before straightening his back again, "I have a certain reputation that keeps people away from me."

"Is that so?" I ask, although what I actually mean is *tell me more.*

"I have a guard I use sometimes to keep up appearances, although if you are in the know." He smirks, unbuttoning the sleeve of his shirt to show me his wrist, and the design that's etched in his skin.

Surprised, I lean closer, my fingers tracing the ink. In the middle is a human skull impaled on a cross. There's only one eye in the socket, wide open and staring at me. A scale of justice is balanced on either side of the cross, one side white, the other black.

His muscles tense as the tips of my fingers move slowly over the surface, and I look up to find him studying me too, a frown on his face.

"What does it mean?"

"Retribution," he says curtly, "an eye for an eye."

"How does that work?" I ask, curious.

"Action and reaction." He covers my hand with his. "In this world, no good deed goes unpunished."

"And people recognize the tattoo?" He nods, tugging my hand into the crook of his elbow once more.

"People spread tales. It's easy to distort the truth when your name is on everyone's lips. Certainly, I've earned my reputation. But there are some things that even I find distasteful." He scrunches up his face in disgust.

"Really? Like what?" My voice comes out a little breathy, and I'm unable to keep the excitement from my voice.

Vlad comes across as this larger-than-life person, and his enigmatic personality is only making me want to know more about him.

A smile plays on his lips. "There's one rumor that I collect my victims' organs, and that I have a collection of them hidden in my basement."

"Let me guess, not true?"

"Not exactly. I'd need a hell of a lot of formol. I may have kept some, on occasion, but only for scientific purposes," he says, looking as if he's reminiscing about a fond memory.

"What else?"

"Hmm," he glances up pensively, "there's one rumor that I only eat human flesh."

"You do?" I squeak, the answer unexpected.

"I'm not particular to it, no. But I can't say I haven't tried it before."

"Wow," I breathe out, stunned. "So you're saying that no matter how crazy the rumors are, there's still some truth to them."

"Isn't that the nature of rumors? There's always some truth, but you never know just *how* much."

"I see." I nod thoughtfully.

"Scared yet?" His breath fans my face as he whispers in my ear.

"No." I turn to him, so close I can almost touch him, "But all this talk of human flesh made me hungry. Now, unless you plan on catching me dinner, I'd suggest you take me somewhere to eat," I say softly, watching his pupils dilate, his lips tugging upward.

"Now, we can't have you hungry, can we?" he drawls, amused, leading me down a lively boulevard.

"Any preference?" he asks when restaurants appear on both sides of the street.

Since I'm not too familiar with restaurant food, I let him decide for me. He settles on a burger place, telling me it's something I *must* try. We go inside, and because everything sounds good to me, I let him order for me, too.

"Oh my," I say, my mouth full, when I finally dive in. This burger thing is positively divine. "Great choice," I add, closing my eyes and enjoying the taste.

There's so much meat and the flavor is bursting on my tongue. I don't even realize when a moan escapes me.

My eyes widen, and I quickly look around, embarrassed.

"No one heard." Vlad's hand comes up to my mouth, wiping some sauce off, "But me that is," he says, giving me a mischievous grin.

"It's too good," I counter, swiping his hand aside.

"I agree." He brings his finger to his mouth, his tongue sneaking out and tasting the sauce. His gaze on mine, I feel hypnotized by the gesture.

So lost am I in his black eyes that I'm startled by my throat contracting in a hiccup.

My hand flies to my mouth, my embarrassment mounting. Seeing as my hiccups won't stop, Vlad pushes a glass of water in front of me. Grabbing it, I gulp it down in one go.

"Easy," he drawls, a languid smile on his face.

His eyes are sharp as his gaze swings from me to the rest of the restaurant, and for the first time, I note that he'd seated us in the back, in full view of the entrance.

His smile doesn't falter as he half-turns to me, his voice low and grave.

"At my signal, you get behind the table."

I stare at him, curious, but I nod.

A man walks toward the back, and Vlad slowly orients himself to the right, stretching his long legs down the aisle to block the man's path.

Everything happens in slow motion, but as I see a hint of steel glinting from the man's trousers, Vlad taps me, swiftly pushing the table down. I realize this is my signal, so I stoop down, hiding behind the table.

From the corner of my eye, I see Vlad kick at the man's leg, promptly tripping him. The man tries to struggle, but Vlad is too fast as his hand grips the gun, taking it out of the man's pants and throwing it to me.

"Just in case." He winks at me, using the back of his palm

to kick at the man's jaw until he's writhing in pain on the ground.

More noise from the front of the store, and as I turn to see what's going on, the other customers are running out of the restaurant, all but four men. They rise from their seats, all aiming their guns at Vlad.

"Petrovic," one man speaks. "We know you have him, and we'll need him back." His words are stilted, his accent foreign.

"Well, come and get him," Vlad says, opening his arms in invitation.

I turn to him, stupefied that he'd do something like this, especially since he's in an open field with men aiming their guns at him—directly.

Suddenly afraid for his life, I close my hand over the gun, feeling the cold silver under my palm. A shudder of excitement goes through me as I examine it.

"The safety's off." Vlad's voice rings in my ear. "Just press the trigger. But not at me, please." He has the gall to joke, even now as the men are coming toward him.

My mouth opens on a warning as I see movement, one aiming for Vlad with his gun. But he's not in the least concerned.

Instead, swiping a silver platter from a nearby table, he holds it up, the bullet connecting with the metal and denting it in its attempt to break the material.

What?

More bullets fly, and I watch in awe as Vlad uses the platter as a shield, thwarting all of their shots.

A brief pause, and I see them try to reload their weapons. It's enough for Vlad to ditch the shield, using it as a throwing disk to aim it at one man's throat. He moves faster than anyone I've ever seen, as he kicks at a table, breaking the legs, and sending them flying toward the men.

It's a cacophony of sounds as they keep firing more shots, and Vlad defends himself with nothing but his bare hands and whatever he finds around.

Tightening my grip on the gun, I lift my head slightly, watching for the closest man. Raising the barrel, I pray that my aim isn't off, and I squeeze the trigger. My shot hits him in his gut, his hand going to his stomach and clutching at the open wound.

While my endeavor to help proves to be successful, now the others fix their gazes at me, switching focus from Vlad to my hiding place.

Vlad makes a tsk sound, sounding almost bored, before grabbing my hand and effortlessly tugging me to my feet and into his arms.

"Bloodthirsty." He smiles. "I like it," he comments before whirling me around, his front fitted to my back, his arm embracing mine, as he caresses the hand holding the gun, firmly placing his finger on top of my own.

One twirl, and he squeezes the trigger, hitting the target square in the face. Another twirl and he avoids an incoming bullet, leaning back to shoot another man.

Three down, two more to go.

The others, seeing as their guns are useless, ditch them in favor of their fists.

"Hold on tight," he whispers into my ear as one man tackles us. Placing his hand under my butt, he swoops me up, aiming my spread out legs at the man in front of us.

"Kick," he says, and I can only oblige, pushing my feet into the man's face until he staggers backwards. One more push and he's out, his head colliding with the edge of a table.

Vlad spins me around, one hand around my waist, the other grabbing a knife from a nearby table. Effortlessly, he swings it forward and it gets embedded into the last man's eye.

As the man writhes in pain, his hand going to his injured eye, blood starts pooling down his face. Letting go of me, Vlad takes another knife, plunging it into the man's neck, cutting open the flesh and watching as more blood flows freely from his body.

Vlad's upper lip twitches, and his pupils dilate as his eyes hone in on the blood. He's in a trance as he brings his hand to the man's throat, coating his palm in red and staring at it reverently.

Sensing the change in him and remembering the incident at Sacre Coeur, I move fast. Grabbing his arm, I turn him around, my hands framing his face so that he looks me in the eye.

I note the paleness of his pallor and the way his black gaze resembles a tar pit. He blinks twice, staring at me with no hint of recognition.

Am I too late?

I'm not even afraid as I continue to plead with him with my eyes. Even knowing what he's capable of, I have no desire to run or hide.

"Come back," I whisper, "come back to me."

He tilts his head to the side, studying me like a predator, his ears pricking at the sound of my words. Still, he doesn't seem to understand me or realize what's happening around him.

Unable to shake him off, I do the only thing I can think of.

I lift myself on the tips of my toes and at the same time I

bring his face closer to mine. Still holding on to his cheeks, I pucker my lips and press them to his.

He doesn't react.

Undeterred, I apply more pressure, pushing into him until my lips are flush against his. His mouth is soft, a contrast to the hardness of him, especially now that he seems to be heading into murderous rage territory.

Holding my breath, I keep my lips on his for as long as I can before I realize I'm out of oxygen. Gasping as I fill my lungs with air, my mouth opens slightly on top of his, and for the first time I get a reaction.

His upper lip trembles faintly, but he responds to my kiss, brushing his mouth ever so slightly over mine.

It's surreal as I open my eyes and note the changes in his demeanor. Life flows back into his face, color infusing his cheeks as they immediately turn red.

Out of nowhere, his hands grab my shoulders, pushing me off of him, his eyebrows pinched together in a frown.

"What are you doing?" he asks, his voice rough.

"Trying to help you?" I give him a sheepish smile that he returns, even in his shocked state.

"Ahh, the kiss of life," he purrs, suddenly back to his old self. "As much as I'd love more of that, we should make our exit before the cops get here," he notes just as we hear the sirens in the distance.

"You did well, Hell Girl," he praises once we get into the car. "You did very well indeed."

I preen at his words, hiding a satisfied smile.

"You said people wouldn't attack you," I add, unusually composed considering we've just been shot at and Vlad probably killed some of the men.

"They were fools," he chuckles, "but I can't say I didn't

enjoy the exercise." He stretches in his seat, and my eyes fall to his biceps.

From the first time I saw him, Vlad's only been dressed in a black business suit. Now that his blazer is off, I get a better view of his bulging muscles, and I remind myself how easily he'd dispatched those men. Even with me by his side, he'd effortlessly waltzed around, everything more of a game than what it actually was—a life and death situation.

Not for the first time, I tell myself that I should feel differently about this... about him. There's just so much violence and brutality under his polished facade, all of it waiting to be unleashed. Yet, I can't help myself.

Like a moth to a flame, that volatility of his is only drawing me in, making me want to know *everything* about him.

If before my place in Hell had been secured, with Vlad by my side, it will be personalized into a true inferno.

"What would have happened if... if you'd lost your manners?" I ask, using the euphemism he'd suggested.

He purses his lips, his eyes on the road as he speeds into the night.

"I would have ripped everyone apart," he states bluntly.

I'm silent for a moment.

"Including me?"

He spares me a glance, his expression closed off, yet there's a hint of curiosity as he regards me.

"I don't know," he admits. "No one's ever escaped with their lives intact when I've... ahm, lost my manners," he says half-amused.

"I did. Twice," I note.

"You did," he narrows his eyes at me, "and I'm looking forward to finding out *why*."

"Maybe it was my magical kiss," I joke, chuckling.

"Then maybe you should do it again." He wiggles his eyebrows at me, and I elbow him in the arm.

"Is that how you thank me for helping you? By taking advantage of my kindness?"

"Is that what it was back there?" he asks, his deep voice making me tremble. "Just kindness?"

Put on the spot, I turn my gaze to the road, unable to think of an appropriate reply.

Because it hadn't been just kindness. It had been so much more.

14

VLAD

I wait for her to answer, wanting her, no, needing her to tell me it wasn't just *kindness*.

Imagine my shock when I'd come around, only to feel soft lips pressed to mine, the intoxicating scent of her body invading my nostrils.

It's never happened before. Never have I snapped out of one of my rages like today, and it's all because of her.

I sneak a glance at Sisi, and for the thousandth time, I have to wonder what it is about *her*. I've only been around her for a few hours now, and already, I feel more at peace than I have in ages.

Maybe it's because Vanya is not around, invading my space and holding me accountable for everything that happens around me. For the first time, it's just me.

And her.

Fuck, and that kiss that wasn't really a kiss but more of a peck... Even now, thinking about it, I just want to close my eyes and embed it into my memory.

She doesn't realize that being this near to her has been the closest I've been to another human being in... forever.

She's bold and open with her touch, sometimes her hand reaching for mine without her realizing it.

It shocks me.

It delights me.

I don't think I've ever felt the absence of touch until she decided to strut into my life and turn it upside down. What is a man to do when he's suddenly faced with all the things he's never had, all within reach?

Take. Take and selfishly take.

But the most bizarre thing is her easy acceptance of me. She'd neither been shocked nor scared, when so many before her have shunned and ostracized me, fear being the ultimate impetus for their actions.

Not in her case.

So accustomed I've grown with others being terrified of me that I have to continually ask her if she's scared yet, worried there may come a moment when I'd be too much for her and she'd just... disappear.

No, that's out of the question.

I'll keep her by my side even if I have to fight her, or Marcello and an entire army. I'd already pretty much decided that when I'd been in her room, but tonight just solidified my decision.

Besides, if she's there to stop my blackouts, then she's also helping other people, since I won't be killing as many anymore. The way I see it, it's a win-win situation.

Satisfied with my line of thought, a smile pulls at my lips.

"What are you smiling at?" she asks, looking all suspicious, her arms crossed over her chest... Already my eyes are following another path, and I have to shake myself to focus on the road.

"Me?" I feign innocence, but seeing her pout at me, those full lips demanding my whole attention, I can't help myself.

"When I lose my manners next time, will you kiss me again?"

Her eyes widen, and she blinks rapidly, looking at me as if she didn't hear me.

"If I must," she murmurs, a little too low, but it's all the incentive I need to pull over.

"What..." She trails off as she sees me open a small compartment, taking a set of knives and testing each blade before settling on one. Just as I'm about to cut my arm open, she stops me, her hand covering my own as she's trying to snatch the knife from me.

"You're crazy," she mutters, forcefully dislodging my fingers from the knife. "Why would you do that to yourself?"

"So you can kiss me again," I answer honestly.

She regards me curiously, all the while taking all sharp objects from my proximity and stuffing them back in the compartment.

"You liked it that much?" she asks, lowering her gaze as a blush envelops her cheeks.

"It was nice." I shrug.

Her eyes immediately flash at me, and for some reason, I know I've said something wrong.

"Nice?" she asks, her eyebrows shooting up. "Nice," she repeats numbly.

I nod. Maybe it hadn't been nice for her? I didn't think about that. What if she'd done it in the spur of the moment and then she'd regretted it? What if she didn't like it? I know I'm not that bad looking. Bianca used to tell me that I could *get it* if I weren't such a psycho. I don't know exactly what she'd meant, but I assume she was complimenting me.

"Just nice?" She inquires in disbelief, emphasizing the word *nice* as if it has a negative connotation.

Ahh, I see.

I must have offended her feminine sensibilities.

"Well," I start, and for the first time, I find myself a little unsure, "I don't have anything to compare it to, but I know kisses involve a little... more." I give her one of my charming smiles. "We can try better next time," I quickly reassure her.

I may not have direct experience, but I've witnessed enough kisses to know they involve more than just lips touching.

For a moment she doesn't speak. She just regards me wide-eyed, and I'm afraid I've said something wrong. *Again.*

"You've never kissed anyone before?" she asks, confused.

I tilt my head to the side, studying her. Since this is foreign territory, I don't want to say something that will offend her or make her not want to kiss me again. The feel of her lips on mine had been unlike anything before, and I'd like to recreate it. Just to ensure it wasn't my erroneous perception at the time.

Science. Yes, it's just science.

"Is that bad?" I speak slowly. I've never in my life felt this uncertain about something, and it's like my entire being hinges on her next words.

She notices my perplexity, so she immediately replies. "No, not at all. Just surprising." Her lips stretch widely across her face in a blinding smile.

I still, staring at her, my mouth emulating hers as I return the smile.

Her eyes soften as she looks at me, and she touches her hand to mine.

"Since we're in the same boat, why don't you show me what you meant by more," she says, a blush staining her cheeks.

I look at her in wonder, mostly because I can't believe she's willing to do it again. Even though I hadn't wanted to believe it, deep down I'd been sure that the first kiss had been a fluke, and that she hadn't really intended to do it.

Because who would want to kiss me?

Over the years, I might have let my mind briefly wonder what it would be like to be with someone, mostly out of my intrinsic curiosity. But even then I'd been more than aware that I had too many things going against me to get closer to another human being, all of which include a ghostly sister, a not-so-pleasant reputation and a lack of self-control. Not to mention the fact that I don't think I've ever found anyone attractive before.

And yet, this woman in front of me seems to cancel everything out.

She's peering at me from beneath her lashes, and I note a sudden shyness in her demeanor. Not one to miss an opportunity when it presents itself, I act—fast.

Leaning toward her, I undo her seatbelt, my hands firmly gripping her waist as I slide her toward me.

She's watching me intently, her legs coming on either side of my seat as she straddles me. Steadying herself against the sudden movement, she spreads her palms all over my chest, their warmth passing through the material of my shirt and into my skin.

Her eyes are wide with wonder as she studies my face, one hand creeping up to caress my cheek.

"You're dangerous," she whispers, her fingers leaving a trail of fire in their wake until they settle on my mouth.

I part my lips, sucking the tips of her fingers in. "Are you scared yet?" I ask, and her eyes crinkle with amusement.

She shakes her head. "No, not yet."

I tug her closer, her chest flush to mine, my hands moving up her waist until I'm circling her ribcage.

The urge to move even further up is maddening, but I don't want to rush her. Not yet.

"What now?" she whispers, staring into my eyes. We're standing so close our breaths are mingling together, and I can feel her warmth on my skin.

"Now," I say, dipping my head and brushing my lips to hers. Just like before, she puckers hers, holding herself still at the contact. "Relax," I speak against her mouth, my tongue sneaking out to part her lips. She stiffens, and I feel her frown in confusion, but she doesn't move away.

"Let me in," I whisper, moving one hand to her face and cupping her cheek.

Soft.

I never realized just how soft a woman's skin is. And like a curious child, I keep circling my thumb around her face. It must please her, because she becomes boneless in my arms, slightly parting her lips and sighing deeply.

I take advantage and fit my mouth to hers, letting my tongue probe inside.

This is it... theory vs practice.

She's hesitant as she strokes her tongue to mine, a moan escaping her at the contact. I swallow the sound, opening my mouth wider and devouring her.

Sisi starts returning the kiss, and soon our mouths are tangled in a slow dance, a give and take that tantalizes the senses.

The feel of her soft mouth opening under mine, the intensity of her kiss as she matches my tempo are driving me crazy as I bring her even closer to me.

Christ, but she wouldn't just make me a believer. She would make me a disciple worshiping *her* as my religion.

She winds her arms around my neck, willingly offering me her embrace as she slowly rocks herself against me. I feel lightheaded as I give in to this wondrous temptation, all the blood rushing down to my cock.

I'm a dead man.

I know she can feel it too because she's grinding up and down my erect cock, the movement coming to her so naturally.

It would be so easy... lower my zipper and push her panties to the side. I would slide right inside her welcoming heat and...

I groan against her lips.

Fuck! Never in my life have I been this aroused, and it's doing things to my brain. The power to think rationally completely leaves me, and for a moment, I have to wonder if the damage will be permanent.

Our mouths are ravenously devouring each other at this point, the tentative exploration from before gone and replaced with pure wild abandon.

Sisi is just as mindless as I am, her hands clawing at my back as she's trying to bring me even closer to her. Her pussy's fitted right on top of my cock as she moves, her lips rubbing against me through my pants.

Ah, fuck, she's soaking wet.

For all my destructive tendencies, I've never been a fan of exchanging bodily fluids. Yet I can't help but wonder how Sisi would taste, her flavor coating my tongue as I bring her to the brink.

"Vlad, I..." She wrenches her mouth from mine, pupils dilated, lips swollen, "There's something happening to me, I..." She looks confused, her mouth parting on a soundless moan as her body starts trembling in my arms.

I hold her even tighter, letting her ride her pleasure as I kiss her neck, my teeth nibbling at her flesh. A power rush like no other—not even killing—washes through me knowing I made her come without even touching her.

"Let it wash over you," I whisper in her hair, slowly trailing my fingers down her back.

She's breathing hard as she leans into my chest. My cock is still painfully hard, but I'd rather suffer with blue balls than force her into something she's not ready for.

For once in my life, I found something good, and I'm not about to let her go. If anything, I'll keep on holding on to her, ready to do anything to keep her looking at me like that—with innocence and wonder in her eyes.

She nuzzles her face in the crook of my neck, her mouth leaving a wet trail of kisses as she works her way up.

"Ah, fuck, Sisi," I groan, her small ministrations only making it harder for me to gain some control of my lower half.

Just then a knock on the window startles us both, and I turn my head to see a police officer shining a light at us.

For the first time, I'm amazed at the fact that I was not aware of anything happening around me. Years of mental training went down the drain in one second.

And there's only one culprit.

Sisi.

She's snuggled against my chest, her eyes wide with confusion, and as she turns those big orbs on me, I can only do my best to shield her.

"A problem, officer?" I ask as I roll down the window.

The cop looks suspiciously between Sisi and me before asking us to step out of the vehicle.

My hand immediately reaches for the gun under my seat, and as Sisi notices my intention, she turns her dazzling smile toward the officer.

"What seems to be the problem, Sir? My husband was

just comforting me after we heard some bad news," she lies, and I watch in wonder how her face changes immediately, her acting top-notch.

"You see, my cat, bless his heart, finally succumbed to death." She releases a sob, taking a napkin from a compartment and dabbing at fake tears.

The officer's expression becomes softer, and he looks almost embarrassed.

"I see, ma'am. I'm sorry for your loss..." he stammers, and as Sisi bats her lashes at him, I swear I see a blush appear on the fucker's face.

"Thank you, officer. But as you can see, my *wife* is going through a hard time. We shouldn't bother her further." I fix my eyes on him, and he swallows uncomfortably. Whatever he's seeing in my expression is making him second-guess his next move.

My smile slowly widens, and his discomfort only increases as he takes in the sharpness of my gaze.

Ah, prey recognizing the predator.

"Yeah... well... I'm sorry for bothering you," he eventually says, taking a few steps away, "you can go," he relents before he all but runs back to his patrol car, hastily driving off.

When he's out of sight, Sisi giggles, punching me softly in the arm.

"Can you stop scaring people off?" she asks, amused.

I grip her jaw, a little more roughly than I'd intended, and I bring her face to mine for a quick kiss.

Sisi is making me realize some new things about myself, the latest being that I don't like when other men look at her.

15
VLAD

With a few hours to spare until dawn, I take her to my compound. The drive only makes me more frustrated as I glance at her luscious form, my balls weeping for relief. It's also sobering enough to make me reconsider my stance.

I'd approached her because of her effect on Vanya, wanting to find out why her presence makes my sister disappear. Instead, I'm just lusting after her like a schoolboy with his first crush.

Okay, maybe I *am* the equivalent of a schoolboy with his first crush, but I need to put a damper on my growing infatuation with her lest it ruin my plans.

Easier said than done, though, when just the sight of her tits makes me hard, countless visions of me palming, licking and sucking them assault me without any warning.

For fuck's sake, I've avoided this particular affliction for close to three decades, and it only takes one almost-nun to make me lose my game. Granted, she does *not* look like a nun, nor does she act like one.

I need to focus.

For a moment, I wish Vanya were here. Maybe she could give me some advice on how to deal with Sisi.

"Are we there yet?" Her voice startles me from my musings, and I glance at her, her hair mussed, and lips swollen.

Fuck!

"Yeah, right around the corner," I answer curtly, steering the car toward an underground garage. I shuffle a little in my seat, adjusting my erection, and mentally grounding myself.

When we get out of the car, I am back to my old self—or as much as can be.

"I'll take you to my room and you can have a nap before I take you home," I tell her, leading her inside.

"What are you going to do?" She frowns.

"I need to pay my friend Petrovic a visit." That is my first order of business, since whoever had paid those men to come for me had to have been quite desperate. Now, to me that only means one thing.

Petrovic knows something.

"Can I come?" she asks, skipping up and down to keep up with my stride.

"No," I answer, my tone not leaving room for discussion.

Whereas at any other time I may have let her, I can't risk it right now. Not with her seeing the state Petrovic must be in, nor with the fact that she might influence him into *not* talking.

When we reach a big steel door, I press my finger to the biometrics pad and it swings open.

"Wow, this looks like a fortress," she notes when she sees the thickness of the metal door.

It is.

I'd had that built a couple of years ago when my blackouts had become more frequent, my level of bloodlust almost doubling. It's to keep me in and to protect the people who work for me from *me*.

What Sisi doesn't realize is that the entire compound is built with one express purpose—to keep me in. Considering my grasp on sanity is questionable at best, I need to make sure that I'm contained—should the day come when I finally lose it.

Inside, the room is bare except for a king-sized bed, a wardrobe and an adjoining bathroom. Not that I need much.

"Make yourself comfortable," I tell her, taking off my blazer and placing it on a hanger. "You can take a shower if you'd like. There are clean towels in the closet." I point toward the wardrobe.

She takes a seat on the bed, testing the softness of the mattress, and I have to wrench my eyes from her, knowing that if I keep on staring I'll only imagine what I'd like to do to her on that bed.

Shaking myself out of my reverie, I leave the room, heading straight for the garden.

When I open the door, I'm instantly greeted by a putrid stench, and I'm happy I didn't let Sisi accompany me.

"Oopsies, he doesn't look so good," Vanya chimes in, startling me with her voice.

"Long time no see, stranger," I add strategically, curious to see if she's going to comment on her absence.

"You missed me?" She preens next to me, coming to hug my midriff.

"Where were you hiding, V?" I ask, but she just smiles at me, shaking her head.

"Wouldn't you want to know?" she says cryptically before dashing off to greet our lovely prisoner.

The bamboo sprouts have already grown, and three of

them have impaled his body. He is writhing in pain as a movement causes the bamboo to shift in its socket.

Two bamboo sprouts have pierced through his upper thighs, and one of them had already made a clean break as the head reached the other side of his leg.

The third one, however, seems to have perforated his anus.

"Lucky bastard," I mutter, amused at the irony.

Blood and feces are pouring down the length of the bamboo, both contributing to the smell that's permeated the entire room.

With his head hung low, he moans in pain as he moves his neck, trying to raise it to look at me.

I am very surprised that he's still holding on, all things considered. But I think I owe some thanks to Maxim, as he must have ensured that Mr. Petrovic did not die of sepsis until now.

"Mr. Petrovic," I drawl, bringing a chair and positioning it in front of him. "It seems we are at an impasse. I have had the pleasure of meeting some of your associates, and it's fair to say they didn't enjoy my welcome."

He raises his head slightly, blinking twice to get some focus in his sight.

"I hope maybe this time you have something for me?" I ask, raising my eyebrows at him.

"You're too easy on him, brother." Vanya pouts from my side, her eyes assessing Petrovic and his impaled ass.

"I'm busy, Vanya," I tell her before turning to my prisoner.

"I can't..." he stutters, sweat clinging to his face.

"We've gone through this before, Mr. Petrovic. You can. You just don't want to. See, there's a difference." I make a disappointed tsk sound, going to the back and taking a small tool set.

"I can't," he breathes again, before uttering two words, "food, water."

I frown, sure that Maxim should have already fed him.

"So you're saying that if I give you food and water you'll talk?" I ask skeptically, and his head moves in a slow bob.

I just shrug. Maybe he wants one last meal before his death, since he won't be living for much longer.

I'm about to message Maxim to bring some food and drink before Vanya stops me, beckoning me to listen to her whispered plan. She sure has an overactive imagination as she details an interesting form of autophagy.

Mr. Petrovic's brows draw together as he looks between Vanya and me, no doubt asking himself if I've gone mad.

The answer is yes.

But if he considers me insane, then he might be more inclined to talk. After all, he'll be the one to withstand my *insane* tactics.

After I text Maxim to bring me the necessary items, I try to talk some more to my lovely prisoner, hoping to dispel some of the boredom he nonetheless must be feeling trapped up there with bamboos sticking up his ass.

"To show you that I'm a good guy," I start, plugging in the electric grill and waiting for it to heat, "I'm going to give you some premium steak. Courtesy of my sister, of course, since she was the mastermind behind this."

His brows furrow as he looks at me in confusion. I can't fault him, since how is it fair that Vanya decides to only show herself to me?

"You see, sometimes she surprises me with savagery. It's like we're twins," I joke, but he doesn't understand.

Vanya, on the other hand, is chuckling by my side, eyeing the grill with curiosity and urging me on.

"Which side?" I ask, and she turns to Mr. Petrovic to analyze him. She goes closer, looking up his mostly collapsed ass, and I groan out loud.

Phantasm or not, Vanya's still a child. She shouldn't be looking up men's asses.

"Vanya." I tap my foot, knowing she'll get my meaning.

Sighing deeply, she slumps her shoulders as she comes back next to me.

"The thigh, right around the hole," she suggests, and I narrow my eyes at her.

"It might be infected. He'll get indigestion," I reply.

"Well, then he does." She shrugs, a mischievous smile playing at her lips.

"Your wish is my command." I feign a bow before taking a knife and stooping low, under Mr. Petrovic's ass.

"Vanya, Vanya, this is all for you," I say in a sing-song voice.

I can't say I haven't missed her, but at the same time it had been liberating to be alone for the first time in decades. And Sisi...

Damn it. I can't allow her to intrude in my thoughts when I'm doling out torture. What kind of mob boss would I be if my mind were fixated on *one* woman twenty-four seven? Once more I have to thrust all thoughts of her from my mind, before my dick decides to take the reins, and the cop incident showed me that I'm not good at *that* type of multitasking.

I scrunch my nose at the stench coming from Mr. Petrovic, quickly getting to work. I use the small knife to cut cubes of flesh from around the wound, slowly enlarging the hole. Mr. Petrovic is so spent he can barely make a noise even though this must hurt like hell. I make sure my cubes have predominantly more meat than skin, so Mr. Petrovic can enjoy a hearty meal before his inevitable demise.

When I've harvested enough meat, I go to the already hot grill and carefully place them on it. Then, going through some of the seasonings Maxim had brought me, I apply some and cook the meat.

The smell wafts through the air and I close my eyes at the aroma. Hard to believe this came from Mr. Petrovic, considering his currently disgusting state.

It's almost... mouthwatering.

"What are you looking at, V? Fancy some meat?" I pick up a piece, wielding it in front of her. She closes her eyes, inhaling.

"I wish I could," she says, her eyes following the steak.

When all the pieces have been cooked, I go in front of Mr. Petrovic, enticing him to try some of his meat.

"Come on, Mr. Petrovic. It's not every day that you get to taste yourself." I pause, chuckling to myself, "Well, not like this anyway. So why don't you open your mouth and I'll even do the honors of feeding you," I tell him, moving the fork with the meat in front of him.

He looks disgusted as he looks between me and the piece of meat, but as his stomach growls, he seems to give up. Opening his mouth, I stuff the piece inside, watching in satisfaction as he chews on his own thigh.

"So? How is it?" My lips stretch in a wide smile as he tries his best to swallow.

"He wasn't as disgusted as you said, V," I say, looking behind to find Vanya gone.

My brows furrowing, I peruse the entire garden for her, but she's nowhere in sight.

And there can only be one explanation.

"Sisi, you can show yourself," I call out, and not even a second later she emerges from behind some bushes in the back.

Her eyes take in Mr. Petrovic's not so stellar state and she scrunches her nose.

Aghh, I didn't want her to smell this...

"What's happening?" Sisi comes forward, dusting the hem of her dress, and I notice that mud is smeared on her clothes from kneeling in the mud.

"I told you to stay in my room." I exhale, thinking of ways to explain this entire fiasco. While bamboo torture is not my usual go-to, it still doesn't look—or smell—great.

She shrugs, coming closer to inspect the meat on the grill.

"You should have known I'd get curious," she replies, her eyes focused on the remaining pieces of meat.

"This smells delicious." She picks up a piece.

"Sisi, don't!" I hurry in front of her just in time to stop her hand.

She turns her face toward me, narrowing her eyes at me.

"It's human meat, isn't it?" she asks, nodding toward Mr. Petrovic.

I feel compelled to nod, pursing my lips and awaiting her condemnation.

How did she even find the garden? I'm going to have some words with Maxim.

"I thought you said you don't eat humans anymore?" She stares me down as she raises her hand, the piece of meat still in her hold.

"I don't," I reply, squaring my shoulders. "It's for him," I point toward Mr. Petrovic.

"You're feeding him his own flesh?" Her eyes widen in surprise.

This is it. This is where she curses me out and leaves.

I nod very slowly, waiting for her outburst. I guess there's a line between seeing me beat up a few men and... this.

"That's genius!" she exclaims. "I don't think I've heard of something like this. How did you think of it?"

"He wanted one last meal," I say, studying her and her unusual reaction.

She takes it even further by chuckling at the joke.

"Ingenious, I like it," she comments right before she pops the piece in her mouth.

I'm momentarily taken aback by her gesture, but as I remember the not-so-great condition of Mr. Petrovic, who is currently moaning for help, I can't in good conscience allow her to eat that. If she wants to try human meat, I'll get her some. Or even better, I'll give her a piece from my own body.

Damn, but wouldn't that be the height of eroticism?

Acting fast, I grab her by the waist and bring her into me, forcing her mouth open with mine, and prying the meat from it.

Wide-eyed, she doesn't struggle as I lay a chaste kiss on her lips, pressing my teeth down to chew on the meat.

"You..." she trails off, looking at me as if I've grown a second head. "Good Lord, Vlad." She bends over, laughing.

"Help..." Mr. Petrovic is still trying to get her attention.

"Shut it." I turn to him at the same time as Sisi. Seeing our matching actions, we both burst out laughing.

"You're insane," she croaks, her lower lip trembling from too much laughter.

"Me? You're the one who tried to eat a piece of my prisoner!" I jokingly accuse.

"Well, don't leave them lying around. Besides, isn't it good manners to offer food to guests?" She raises an eyebrow at me.

"I thought we'd established I *lack* manners," I fire back.

"Hmm, and I think we also established how I'd take care of your... lack of manners," she replies saucily, and not for the first time tonight, I find myself enthralled with her.

"Help," Mr. Petrovic moans again, and we both turn sharply toward him.

"Can't you see that we're talking?" Sisi shakes her head at him, coming to my side and laying her head on my shoulder. "Now care to tell me what this is all about?" she asks, her eyes examining the desolate state of Mr. Petrovic's ass.

"Oh, Hell Girl," I groan, my arm sneaking around her shoulders, "you're not squeamish at all, are you?"

"Well, the meat wasn't that bad, although I only had a taste."

"Next time," I assure her, quickly going over my plans with Petrovic and how I think he might be the missing link to find who took my sister.

"I'm sorry," she whispers after I'm done recounting everything. Weird how not even Bianca, who's been my partner for almost a decade, knows the details of my plans. Yet one evening with Sisi and I'm about to tell her my deepest, darkest secrets.

Hell and damnation!

"But you do realize that especially after *that* he's not likely to talk," she comments, and I sigh deeply.

"I didn't think he'd last this long. The stick up his ass alone must hurt like a bitch..." I purse my lips, admitting for the first time that Mr. Petrovic is showing more resilience than I'd given him credit for.

Sisi purses her lips, stroking her chin with her thumb. Her eyes briefly light up, and she takes me aside, out of Mr. Petrovic's hearing range.

"You said he fears for his family," she whispers, and I nod. "Then threaten him with his family."

"I don't know where they are," I grimly reply. That had been my first thought too, but he's hidden them well.

"Pretend you do," she says, and my ears perk up.

"I have to say, Hell Girl, you continue to surprise me." I chuckle when she suggests we play good cop, bad cop.

"Let's see if it works."

Turning back to the situation, I continue feeding Mr. Petrovic the meat, all the while Sisi is pacing the room, looking extremely anxious.

"He has to speak, Vlad. I know he will. Just please don't harm his family... they're innocent!" Her entire face transforms as she shifts into her role, her eyebrows drawn in concern, her mouth downturned.

"Sisi," I groan, getting into my part, "this is exactly why I didn't want you here. Now you're feeling sorry for him!"

"They're children, Vlad! The eldest is only eight... How can you do that to them?" she yells, tears already gathering at the corner of her eyes.

Damn me, but she's killing this.

"You know what I was doing when I was eight? I was disemboweling my father's guards. He'll be fine." I wave my hand in the air. "A little pain never hurt anyone," I add, and I immediately note Mr. Petrovic's quick intake of air.

"But it's you... you're like the spawn of evil," she says, and I can see a small smile playing at her lips. "He's just an innocent child."

"No one is innocent in this world, Sisi. He may be now, but wait until he grows and wants to avenge his father. Better cut them while they're young," I say, enjoying her scandalized look.

"Wha-what are you talking about?" I hear Mr. Petrovic's low voice.

"Vlad, he's a child!" Sisi screams at me, coming forward

to grab the lapels of my shirt. "Are you so soulless that you would harm a *child?*" she cries, her hands going to my chest as she's punching me.

"Shh now," I say, grabbing her face, "maybe Mr. Petrovic's next meal will be a little fresher. I say, eight-year-old meat..." I trail off, and Sisi's eyes widen. For a moment I fear I've taken it too far, but she continues to play along.

"You wouldn't." She shakes her head, taking a step back, her eyes filled with horror.

"Stop!" Mr. Petrovic finally says, his tone defeated. "I'll tell you just... please... don't let him harm my children." He looks at Sisi as he says this.

"Speak," I prompt him, suddenly anxious to hear what he has to say.

"Project H-Humanitas..." he trails off, taking a deep breath, "I don't know too much, just that your sister was given to Miles, the head of Project Humanitas." He looks between Sisi and me before pleading once more with her, "Please don't harm my family."

Project Humanitas...

"Vlad?" Sisi asks when she sees I'm not responding.

I blink twice, some type of memory resurfacing before it's gone again.

"Vlad!" I feel her hand on my arm as she pinches me, and I finally react.

"I need to go," I mumble, disentangling her fingers from the material of my shirt.

I'm almost in a trance as I leave the garden, heading straight for my room. Vaguely, I realize Sisi is hot on my trail, but I can't seem to care right now.

I'm quick to rip the shirt off my back, discarding my pants and underwear before climbing into the shower. The water is scalding hot on my skin, red in its trail as it cascades down my body.

"Project Humanitas," I whisper to myself, pain assaulting me when I utter the words.

Dazed, I collapse to my knees, holding on to the bathroom stall for support.

"Vanya," I call out, my voice barely above a whisper. "Where are you, Vanya?" I ask, desperate to hear her voice. Why is she not here when I need her the most?

My breath hitches as my body starts trembling uncontrollably, visions of blood and organs, all lying at my feet as I kill and maim.

"Vanya, please," I say on a sob, bringing my head hard against the wall. "Where are you?" I ask again, hitting my head even harder. "Please." My voice is broken as I beseech her to answer me.

I keep banging my head against the wall until bright red mixes with the clear water.

"Vlad?" I think I hear a voice calling my name. I'm barely conscious as Sisi climbs into the shower with me, her arms wide open as she takes me in her embrace.

"You're safe," she whispers in my hair. "You're safe now." Her soft hand caresses me and my body slowly regains its function.

"I..." I start when I regain lucidity, "I'm sorry," I say in a small voice, seeing the situation I find myself in.

"What happened?" Her gaze is gentle as she looks at me, her touch so comforting.

"Project Humanitas..." I barely manage to say the name out loud. "They killed my sister."

"What?" She frowns. "How do you know?"

"Not Katya..." I whisper, "My twin sister, Vanya."

And they made me what I am today.

16
SISI

"Sisi, you don't look too well," Lina mentions when she sees me at breakfast. I give her a tight smile, even though I know I must have pretty bad dark circles, since for the last week I've been sneaking out almost daily to see Vlad. I don't even remember when I last had a full night's sleep.

Still, I wouldn't trade the time spent with Vlad for sleep, not when everything about him is so... fascinating.

True to his word, he's shown me around the city and taken me wherever I wanted. But we spend most of our time at his house, where we talk about everything and nothing.

What I've found about him has just confirmed my first impression. Loneliness clings to him like a second skin, and I can tell that even the small things I do surprise him. It's like he expects me to bolt at any point.

"Are you afraid yet?" he'd ask, almost jokingly, but I can see the truth in his eyes. He's afraid that he's going to do something and scare me.

He's afraid I'm going to leave him.

Frankly, the more I see how his life looks, the more I feel

sorry for him. He barely talks to people outside of his right hand, Maxim. Even with him, he exchanges a few sentences here and there, mostly via text. The rest of the time? He might be planning his revenge or world domination, but he's doing it all by himself.

With his bare room, or the fact that his entire home is underground, it's hard not to feel sad for his bleak existence.

But I can see why. He's not... normal. Hell, he's probably the definition of unhinged. Even knowing that, I can't stay away though. He's just... him.

And in a wicked way, we complement each other. He feeds my need for destruction and I feed his need for sanity.

God!

I fan myself as I find my thoughts heading into R-rated territory. He hasn't kissed me again or asked for me to kiss him, even though it's all I can think about sometimes when I'm near him.

The sensations he'd wrought from my body had been simply otherworldly. There's no other way to describe the way my body had opened up for him, showing me it was capable of great pleasure instead of pain.

Ah, and his kiss... The fact that he's never kissed another woman before had delighted me beyond measure. For the first time, I felt that something was truly mine. No one had been that close to him, and no one will if I have anything to say about it.

Because one week's been enough for me to decide something.

I'm going to keep him—dysfunctional personality included.

He hadn't mentioned the bathroom incident and I hadn't probed. Seeing him so lost, so full of suffering, had done something to my heart. I'd wanted nothing more than to hug him and take away all of his hurt.

"You aren't hungry?" I'm brought down to earth by Lina's voice—again. I've been so absent-minded lately, mostly because all my thoughts revolve around one man—and his wicked lips.

"Oh, sorry, just woolgathering." I smile, helping myself to the food on the table.

My brother and Lina had decided to hire a governess for Claudia, Venezia and me, saying that we would all benefit from having a more formal education. We've already started lessons, but I don't think I need it that much. After all, I have all the information I need at the tips of my fingers.

Vlad had been extremely helpful in showing me how to operate a computer and navigate the internet. Since then, my time is mostly split between him and my laptop. There's just so much to read on, so many things that are part of normal life but had not been accessible during my time at Sacre Coeur.

And he's been more than willing to slowly walk me through everything.

"I know it's hard to get used to life outside Sacre Coeur..." Lina starts, her hand reaching for mine. "I'm having a hard time too, but I wasn't there since birth. For you it's all you've ever known." She takes a deep breath. "Please let me know if there's anything I can do to help. I don't like seeing you so closed off."

"I'm fine, Lina. Seriously. It's just a lot to take in, but I'm getting there." I give her a reassuring smile.

Marcello is watching the interaction between the two of us, his eyes fixed on me.

"Assisi, please see me in my office after breakfast," he

says, pinning me with his gaze for a moment before turning back to his food.

I frown, since Marcello hadn't tried to talk to me until now. Even Lina seems a bit worried, but she squeezes my hand in comfort.

Claudia and Venezia are engaged in playful banter, and suddenly the house seems a bit more like... home.

But for as much as I'd like to believe that, I can't. The more I look around, the more I feel like an outsider.

My place hadn't been at Sacre Coeur, and it clearly isn't here either. Not when I see everyone around me talk with such ease, such familiarity. They make the perfect picture, with me on the sidelines taking it in.

When breakfast is finished, Marcello gives me a nod and I follow behind him as he heads to his office.

My palms itch, the anxiety killing me. Until now I haven't really had the time to have an in-depth conversation with Marcello, and I still have the feeling that I'm an extra in this house.

Closing the door behind me, I watch him go around his desk to take a seat, motioning me to do the same.

I sit down, back straight as I'd been conditioned, the scars too painful to make me bend even a little. My hands in my lap, I'm the model of decorum.

Don't send me back!

The only thing I can think of is that I never want to set foot in Sacre Coeur again. And while inside I'm boiling with curiosity as to what Marcello will say to me, on the outside I look as serene as ever. It sure comes in handy to have perfected a poker face over the years.

"Assisi," Marcello starts, looking intently at me, "how are you getting used to the house? I trust everything is to your liking?"

"Of course," I readily agree, "it's more than I could have asked for. Thank you for this," I add.

He nods almost absentmindedly, and I get the vaguest impression that he wants this meeting to be over as soon as possible. My palms are sweating, but I keep my smile in place.

He seems to be hesitating as he asks, "Was Sacre Coeur okay? Did you have any problems?"

For a second—just a brief second—I consider telling him everything I endured. How my body is riddled with scars from those righteous nuns. For that tiny moment, I want to lay everything on the table and ask him *why*. Why did they have to abandon me there? What did I ever do besides being born?

Over the years, the nuns had enjoyed telling me how I'd been abandoned because of my birthmark and that my family did not want to be saddled with a cursed child. They'd been so delighted in *always* pointing out how no one wanted me.

But as soon as those thoughts resurface, I push them down. Why bring back the past? And most importantly, why ask something I might not like the answer to? What if he tells me exactly what I don't want to hear?

"It was fine," I start, stretching my lips even more. "The nuns were so good to me," I lie, that one untruth burning through me as it leaves my lips. "But they've also helped me understand I'm not suited for the monastic life," I add just to be sure. If he thinks the nuns don't want me, then he can't ship me back there.

"Why?" He raises an eyebrow, and I'm put on the spot. "Why were you not suited for monastic life?"

"I..."

"I'm just trying to understand you better, Assisi,"

Marcello interjects, his eyes boring into me.

Why do I suddenly feel like I'm being interrogated?

"I was too curious," I admit truthfully, "and I was not predisposed to following the dogma. You could say my teachers and I butted heads often over disparate opinions." I choose my words carefully. If only he knew the stunts I pulled at Sacre Coeur...

After years of abuse, I'd just snapped. I didn't care about what happened to me anymore, so I just acted out. Certainly, after Cressida's death, only worse things awaited me. So I just gave in, and for the first time, I stayed true to myself instead of forcing myself to be someone *they* wanted me to be.

And hell if it hasn't been relieving. Like a weight being lifted off my chest, I've finally found a modicum of happiness. Maybe that's also why I'm so drawn to Vlad. He doesn't judge me for who I am. Instead, he cheers me on, both our crazies mixing together.

"I see," Marcello replies.

What do you see?

Why is he so closed off? I can't get a reading on him to know if my answers are satisfactory or not.

"It is good to be curious," he continues. "You should never stop asking questions."

Silence envelops us, and we're just looking at each other, the awkwardness only increasing.

"Right," I say eventually. "If that's all?"

He nods at me, picking up his glasses and putting them on. Shuffling some files around his desk, I can tell I've been dismissed.

And as I leave his office, I can't help but ask myself.

Does he even want me here?

17
SISI

"Why do people need so many profiles?" I ask, watching Vlad help me set up my social media accounts.

He looks up, shrugging.

"I don't use any," he replies, clicking some things on the computer until the profile is done.

"Why?" I tilt my head to study him. I'd read up on social media profiles, and I'd made a list of the ones I wanted him to help me set up. I'd looked into the matter extensively, because according to some people, if you don't have a social media presence then you don't exist.

"I'm not exactly an exemplary citizen," he smirks. "I don't need that type of exposure. Especially since nowadays you can track everything."

"What do you mean?"

"See this?" He shows me a picture I'd awkwardly taken to add to my profile. I nod. "Every picture has metadata that shows when and where it was taken." A few more clicks and he pulls up a new window.

"That's Marcello's address," I say, my mouth hanging open in shock.

"Yes, it is. It only takes someone who is a little skilled with computers to get this. Every picture you post has the potential to give vital information to enemies. There are other tricks too, since everything you do online leaves a signature," he continues to explain, and I'm listening attentively. He seems to know a lot about it and as he's talking, his features show the barest hint of excitement.

"But I don't have enemies."

"You don't. But your brother does. And *I* do." He looks at me intently for a second before turning his gaze back to the computer. "Luckily for you, I'm going to set up everything neatly and install some safety mechanisms as well," he says, already getting to it.

I watch him work his magic, and I mentally go over my rehearsed lines. Since he hasn't tried to kiss me in a while, I feel I may need to push him into it. After all, the articles online had mentioned that men enjoy being the aggressors.

"Done!" he says, handing me back the computer as he scrolls through the different profiles.

"There's one more platform," I add, and he raises an eyebrow, looking at me expectantly. "This." I open the tab for him, all the while surreptitiously watching for his reaction.

"A dating site?" he asks in disbelief, looking back and forth between me and the screen. "Why do you need a dating profile?" he repeats, narrowing his eyes at me.

"Doesn't everyone?"

"No. I don't." He glowers at me.

"But you don't date," I reply with a feigned huff.

"And you won't either!" He quickly exclaims, his eyes widening at his own outburst.

"What? Of course I will. I'm young, I've finally started living, and I need to think about dating at some point," I lie, closely studying his expression.

"No," he decrees, folding his arms over his chest and looking at me defiantly.

"Excuse me?" I ask in faked outrage.

"You can't!" He takes my laptop from me, quickly punching some keys.

"What are you doing?" I frown at his unusual reaction. I'd only wanted to give him a little push to kiss me again.

"There," he hands it back to me, "I blocked all dating sites from your computer," he says smugly.

"Why would you do that?" I push, needing at least an explanation. If he's not going to kiss me just yet, I'll settle for a small admission that he *doesn't* want me to date.

"It's not safe," he quickly answers, a small scowl appearing on his face. "Besides, when would you have time to date? I occupy most of your time," he reasons, looking mightily pleased with himself.

"You do, don't you?" I probe, a smile playing on my lips.

"Exactly," he replies, "why would you need a boyfriend when you have me?"

The reaction is delayed as he realizes what he just said. He blinks twice, his mouth half-open as he undoubtedly must be thinking of ways to correct his mistake.

Instead, he amazes me when he continues. "That's right, I found you first. Finders keepers," he declares proudly, placing the laptop on the table in front of him. Out of nowhere, his arm darts out, his fingers grabbing onto my chin as he tugs me into a bruising kiss.

"There you have it," he speaks against my mouth, "sealed with a kiss."

I can only stare into his eyes, the pupils so big they almost overshadow his irises. He doesn't seem to wait for my approval as he looks at me like a feral animal ready to devour its prey. Out of nowhere, his tongue sneaks out and he licks my lips with a long swipe.

I'm frozen in shock at his actions, because even in my sheltered mind this isn't normal. But the more I look at him, the more I realize that *he* isn't normal. He probably has no idea how to behave with a woman. Lord, I'm surprised he even knows how to behave with other people.

There's a savagery in him that can't be tamed by superficial manners. And no matter how expensive his suits, or how practiced his expressions are, he can't hide what he really is.

A beast.

A smile pulls at my lips, and I return his lick with one of my own.

He might be a beast, but I wouldn't be this drawn to him if he weren't.

His teeth catch my tongue, and he sucks it into his mouth, his palm fitted around my throat as he brings me into him.

"I prepared something for you," he whispers, his teeth nibbling at my lips.

"What?" I ask in a breathless tone. Already visions assault me, of us naked together, limbs tangled, mouths fused... Ah, my thighs clench together just thinking about that.

"The ocean. I'm taking you to the ocean," he says, and he's suddenly off me and righting his clothes.

"That sounds amazing," I answer, trying to keep the disappointment out of my voice. I barely got him to kiss me again, and he didn't waste any time in finding a reason to stop.

For a brief moment, I have to wonder if maybe he's not attracted to me. At his age, it's almost unheard of that he'd never kissed anyone before. I should know since I've spent exorbitant amounts of time researching men and relationships. So what if... he's not into women at all?

The thought makes me still, and when he takes my hand and leads me to the car, I have to force myself to smile.

The drive is quick as we get to Vlad's childhood home, which is only a few steps away from the beach. He's tight-lipped when I ask him more about his family, mainly commenting that they are all dead.

"So there's only Katya left," I remark as we climb out of the car. Vlad is carrying a couple of blankets so we can sit on the sand, and a basket with a few snacks and drinks. I'm actually surprised by the effort he's put into this.

"Yes... if she still lives, that is," he replies, giving me a half-smile.

Not wanting to ruin the moment, I quickly change the topic.

"You do realize this looks an awful lot like a date," I add cheekily as we take our shoes off, walking barefoot in the sand.

He turns to me, and a little pensively he comments, "You're right. It does look like a date."

Without adding anything more, he walks in front of me, setting the basket down and laying the blankets on the sand.

I shake my head at him, realizing he just can't take a hint.

It does look like a date?

Would it have been that hard to agree it *is* a date?

I rub my arms with my hands as the chilly night air brushes against my skin. I didn't realize it would be this cold on a summer night, but I guess it's because of the ocean breeze.

"Done!" he exclaims, sporting a proud expression as he looks down at the little picnic he'd set up.

"Good job," I add drily, and his smile suddenly falls.

"You don't like it," he states, his expression downcast.

"No, I do," I quickly reassure him. "I love that you put so much thought into this," I add, and his face lights up.

"Perfect! I wasn't sure what girls like..." he says, scratching the back of his head. Suddenly I realize I'm not the only one who is confused.

The more I think about it, the more I can't control myself as I burst into laughter. Vlad looks at me like a lost puppy, as if his very life depends on my acceptance.

"Then why..." he trails off, and I want nothing more than to take him into my arms and shower him with kisses.

How is it that this practiced killer can be confident and deadly one moment and then become so timid and unsure of himself the next?

"I just realized that I've been going about everything the wrong way," I tell him, lowering myself to the blanket and patting the seat next to me for him. He sits down, his eyes big and full of curiosity as he glues himself to me.

"What do you mean?"

"I've been second-guessing everything that's been happening between us, thinking that maybe you don't find me attractive or..." I feel my cheeks heat up and for some reason I have a hard time bringing up the fact that I'd thought he wasn't into women, "Or that you didn't necessarily like women," I finally admit.

"You... thought..." A smile pulls at his lips before he also starts laughing. "Oh, Sisi, if you only knew..." he groans, bringing his face next to mine. Our noses are touching, our eyes having their own staring contest.

"I like women," he states bluntly, "one woman specifically," he amends, and my lips twitch in response. "But I admit I'm not the best at dealing with women since you're about the only one I've been around in a very long time."

"I think we've settled that neither of us is great at understanding the opposite sex," I mention jokingly.

His eyes darken and his gaze bores into me. Chills erupt all over my body as I soak in his intensity.

"Make no mistake, however," he whispers, his breath so close to my skin.

"Yes?" I ask breathlessly.

"I find you very attractive, Sisi. So much so that every time you leave I have to take a fucking cold shower. Is that what you want to hear? That just being near you makes me so painfully hard I'd like nothing more than to lift up your skirt." His fingers brush my leg as he takes the hem of my dress up in a tantalizingly slow motion, "And fuck you raw and bloody until we're both spent." His mouth nuzzles at my throat.

"Why don't you?" My voice comes out on a low moan.

"Oh I will, just not yet." He brushes his cheek over the skin right above my collarbone, "This isn't a race to the finish line, it's a marathon. And for the first time in my life, I find that I'd rather have patience." His lips press right above my heart, "And unwrap you bit by bit."

Suddenly, he tears his mouth from my body, standing up and taking his shirt off. My eyes widen as I take in his sculpted torso, the entirety of it a canvas for a myriad of images. There's barely any spot left untouched by ink.

"Wow," I whisper.

The corners of his mouth curl up, and he wastes no time in picking me up off the blanket and taking me into his arms.

"What?"

"I brought you to the ocean to enjoy the *ocean*," he says in my hair as he dashes toward the violent waves.

My arms tighten around his neck as he plunges us both in the cold water.

We go down as he fully submerges us in the water. My hands tighten around him, but he doesn't let go of me, not even for a second.

"What?" I ask, sputtering when we finally come back to the surface. The water is incredibly cold, and I suddenly start shivering. "Why would you do that?" I demand, scandalized.

Vlad has a wicked smile on his face, and it doesn't seem like the cold does much to his body. No, his skin is still incredibly warm as I huddle closer to him.

"I needed a cold shower," he retorts, and I can only stare at him open-mouthed.

"You mean..." I trail off, pointing to his lower half.

He tugs me closer until my front is flush against his, and I can feel the hard outline of him.

God, he's huge!

"How could you think I wasn't attracted to you when you look like hot sin?" His hand trails down my neck, his fingers brushing the sensitive skin. "I only need to glance at your fucking tits and all the blood rushes down to my cock," he rasps, his molten voice the fire I needed to keep warm in the water.

"Then let me help you," I whisper, my hands already going to the front fastening of my gown, untying the knot and slowly slipping the material from my body.

My breasts bounce free from the confines of the bodice, and Vlad's gaze is immediately fixated on my puckered nipples.

"It's cold," I quickly make the excuse, but he cuts me off, shaking his head as he stares at them reverently.

His hand slowly moves lower as he explores the valley of my breasts, his touch hot and exciting.

"Fuck me," he curses under his breath on a whistle. One hand sneaks behind my waist as he prompts me to wrap my legs around him, bringing that hard part of him in contact with my center.

A whimper escapes me at the sensation, and I can't help myself as I keep on rubbing against him.

"Damn it, Hell Girl, you're driving me crazy," he says, bending his head and giving one breast a long lick before wrapping his lips around my nipple, sucking it into his mouth.

The warmth of his mouth contrasts with my cold skin, the effect on my body sublime. He follows the contour of my breast, laying small kisses on the scar right above my heart. At any other moment, I'd feel self-conscious of the many marks on my skin, but as he continues to worship my flesh like it's the eighth wonder of the world, I can't seem to muster the shame.

I tighten my legs around him, urging him on as I keep on grinding against him, his tongue doing marvels to my flesh. He takes turns between both breasts, sucking, teasing and licking.

"I could feast on you forever," he speaks, his hot breath making me gasp. Taking one bud between his teeth, he bites. Hard.

"Vlad," I half-moan, half yell as I feel a shot of lightning go straight to my core. "I'm so close," I barely manage to get the words out, but he seems to know exactly what I need as he continues to lavish the same type of attention on the other nipple, until I'm spasming in his arms. The cold of the water is promptly forgotten as I feel tingles spread through my entire body.

My body spent, my limbs almost numb, I barely realize when he's carrying me out of the water.

He lays me gently on the blanket, his eyes still hungry as he looks at my half-naked body.

Kneeling between my legs, he grabs me by the ankles, dragging me to him, his hands roaming up my calves.

"I'm glad you were hidden at Sacre Coeur until now," he admits, his voice gruff. I tilt my head to get a better look at him, his eyes glazed with desire as his fingers explore my body.

"Why?" I ask languidly, my senses still overwhelmed from the pleasure he'd wracked from my body earlier.

"Because you're for my eyes only." He uses one finger to lift the hem of my dress, pushing it over my thighs. I follow his movements closely, and just when I think I have his trajectory figured out, he surprises me by grabbing onto my dress with both hands and ripping it in the middle. The material falls away immediately, his strength amazing me once more.

The hands of a killer.

A quick intake of breath and I realize there's a change to him. No longer the playful rogue from before, he's now a predator on the prowl.

Why does it excite me even more to know that he has the power to snuff the life out of me? It would be so easy, hands around my throat, a snap of my neck, and he'd end me.

And why do I want just that?

I can almost imagine the way his fingers would dig into my flesh, just under my jaw, tightening his hold until I can barely breathe before letting go, granting me a small respite. There's this hidden part of me that wants him to dominate me until I'm begging for mercy, and it both scares and excites me.

"What are you doing now?" I'm dazed as I look at him, all ink and bulging muscle, his chest rippling with every small exertion. I want to spread my palms over his flesh, feel his hardness under me, and as I try to do just that, he stops me.

He shakes his head, amused.

"The moment you touch me, Hell Girl, I'll combust," he drawls, his fingers still drawing circles over my naked flesh. "I'm barely in control as it is. The moment my cock is out, or you, God forbid, place your hands on it, I'll lose whatever control I have left." His voice is thick and strained, and I can see he's trying to fight himself.

He trails the back of his hand over my damp panties, and my breath catches in my throat as he skims that *extremely* sensitive part of myself.

A part that no one but me has touched before.

A blush envelops my features at that train of thought, but I'd read enough online to know what to expect, and that knowledge only serves to make me even wetter, my pussy leaking out in an attempt to get him to give it the attention it craves.

"You're wet for me, aren't you, Sisi?" he asks, sliding the material aside to push his finger between my drenched folds, feeling exactly what his voice—his very presence—does to me. He moves slowly as he takes some of the moisture, coating his entire finger and lifting it up to his mouth.

I watch hypnotized as he opens his lips—those sensuous lips that should be illegal on a man—placing his finger inside and sucking.

"You make me like this," I answer breathlessly as he uses his tongue to lick every last drop.

What he doesn't know is that from the moment I first saw

him, he made me feel like this. I may have failed to recognize it then, but the second he'd directed those black eyes at me, his hands on my throat as he'd lifted me in the air, I'd been painfully aroused, my entire being tingling from his nearness.

"Fuck, Sisi. You have no idea what those words do to me," he rasps, his eyes half-closed, a pained expression on his face.

18

SISI

He's on his knees between my parted legs, and I move my eyes lower, to his pebbled stomach, the ink only serving to emphasize the tight squares of his abdominals more. His waist tapers down, and I note his wet pants, and the way they mold to his hips and...

I swallow hard as I see the contour of his cock, and I get an idea of what my words do to him.

I'm not ashamed to admit I'd explored the internet in my quest to find out why he makes me feel this way, and I'd read enough to know that *that* isn't the norm. But then again, everything about him is superlative, so I shouldn't be surprised that his cock is an outrageous size too.

And yet, even as my eyes have a hard time believing something *that* big will be able to fit inside of me, I can't help the way I squeeze my walls instinctively, almost able to imagine him sliding in and...

A moan escapes my lips, the image too vivid, my body more awake than ever.

His gaze darkens as he watches the way my pussy slowly contracts, more wetness pouring out of me.

"Damnation, Hell Girl," he growls, palming that monster in his pants. "Your pussy's too fucking perfect," he says, shaking his head as he keeps on staring.

Suddenly, his hands skirt along the edge of my panties and a breath catches in my throat as he slides them down my legs. The action is so tantalizingly slow it's only building up my anticipation—and my frustration.

He chuckles when he sees my impatience, leaning down and teasing my lips with his own.

"I want to wreck you, Sisi," he whispers, his mouth hovering on top of mine. There's an intensity to the way he looks at me, and I truly believe him capable of doing just that. If anything, I'd welcome it.

Maybe even beg him for it.

"I want to tear you apart and put you back together." He trails his tongue down my face and onto my chin, goose-bumps appearing all over my skin. "But in the reconstruction phase, I'd keep something of yours," his teeth scrape along the curve of my neck, "so that you're never whole without me."

"Yes." I find myself agreeing, even though his words should make me run. "Please," I whisper, and his mouth opens wide right at the junction of my neck, his teeth lodging into my skin and breaking the surface.

I gasp at the unexpected pain. He applies suction, and my legs open up, letting him fit himself between them, seeking that close contact.

"For now," he whispers as he raises his head, blood staining his white teeth, "I'll settle for this."

A rough kiss and then he continues his journey along my body, stopping briefly over my stomach and trailing his tongue down. He nestles his head between my legs, and for one brief moment I want to protest.

But as he gives me a long lick my head hits the blanket with a loud moan.

"You're wicked," I breathe out, and I feel him smile against my pussy. He wraps his lips around my clit, sucking it into his mouth.

My hands fist the blanket, my thighs trembling as he continues his ministrations. Bringing his finger to my entrance, he tests my opening, finding me snug around him.

"Christ," he exclaims, his hot breath fanning over my pussy making me squirm, and one hand sneaks behind my waist, holding me flush against him. "You're so tight, I can barely fit a finger, Hell Girl. Fuck me, I can't help but imagine the way you'll bleed all over my cock," he rasps, his words meant to scandalize, but instead they only arouse me further.

I want to bleed all over him.

Lord, but I must be losing my mind.

Thrusting his finger in and out of me, he continues to tease me with his tongue, an ache forming inside of me as my arousal mounts. I writhe beneath him, my thighs bucking, my muscles tensing as he bites down on my clit, the pain mingling with pleasure in an unstoppable crescendo.

At some point, it feels too much, and I try to twist away from him, but he doesn't let me. Holding me even tighter, he thrusts in and out of me, his tongue gliding over my clit.

Suddenly, I start spasming around him, a gush of wetness flowing out of my channel. He continues to lap at me, devouring my release. It's an assault on the senses as he continues to wreak havoc on my body, coaxing more sensations.

When he's finally done with me, I'm boneless.

"What are you doing to me?" I barely find the strength to ask, my eyes droopy, my breathing harsh.

"Bribing you," he drawls, slowly trailing his tongue on my belly. "Giving you so much pleasure, you're going to become addicted to me." He smirks at me.

I almost groan at his arrogance, but the truth is that it would be so easy to become addicted to him. Certainly, his kisses have become my new favorite form of sustenance. Add the orgasms to my new diet and he's near damn indispensable.

But there's more to him than that. Way more.

It's in his darker than black eyes, and the suffering that sometimes leaks through the cracks. It's in his perfectly built facade and the way he presents himself to the world. But more than anything, it's in the way he allows *me* glimpses beneath his mask.

I see the screeching loneliness and the maniac instability, all leaving way to a pure yet misunderstood genius.

And I want it all.

I *crave* it all.

There's no explanation for the things he makes me feel. My own essence calls out to his in a way that sometimes makes me question my own sanity.

But do I really need to be sane when I'm with him?

There's freedom in his brand of insanity—of ruthlessness, violence and brutality. And no matter how much I've tried to rationalize *him*, I simply can't.

He's beyond logic, and even beyond feeling, in a realm of his own where rules don't exist.

He interrupts my train of thought as he moves up my body, taking my mouth in an aggressive kiss and making me lose my head.

Intoxicating.

That's what I'd call his lips when they touch mine.

I'm lost in his embrace and I don't even realize as he rolls us over, until I'm lying on top of him, my naked skin against his.

I release a contented sigh, feeling happier than I've ever been, a sense of belonging slowly beckoning me and letting me know I may have found my place.

Nuzzling my cheek in the crook of his neck, I start tracing his tattoos, noting that many of the figures resemble demons.

"What do they mean?" I ask, glancing up to find him staring at me with an inscrutable look on his face.

"My curse," he answers cryptically, tightening his arms around me.

Taking a deep breath, I just allow myself to enjoy the proximity of his body, the way my skin feels next to his, and as we start talking some more, I find myself confiding in him about my dilemma with my brother.

"I don't think I'm welcome there," I admit, laying out my vulnerability for him.

"Why?" He frowns.

"Marcello is..." I trail off, not knowing how to put it since he is friends with my brother, "He doesn't seem very happy I'm there. Most of the time he ignores me, and when we finally had a conversation he was incredibly awkward." I take a deep breath, trying to dispel the knot forming in my throat.

Vlad is silent for a moment.

"Don't judge him too harshly," he finally says, turning to look me in the eye. His hand caresses my face, tucking a strand behind my ear. "I've known Marcello since we were young. He hasn't had it easy, and considering the circumstances of your birth, I don't fault him for being a little closed off."

"What do you mean?" I ask, blinking rapidly.

What circumstances of my birth?

"I'm not sure how much you know about your birth mother," Vlad continues, his voice unusually soothing, "but she was mentally ill. She was also a religious fanatic who thought the devil was trying to tempt her at every turn. Marcello didn't have an easy childhood because of that. When you were born, she was convinced you had the mark of the devil," he says, his fingers tracing the red mark above my brow.

"Marcello knew he couldn't let you live with her, or with your father, since he was even worse, so he thought it best to send you to Sacre Coeur. I don't think he's ever forgiven himself, though, for sending you away," Vlad mentions.

I take a moment to digest what he's saying.

"Were they that bad?" I ask eventually, because in my mind nothing could be worse than what I'd endured at Sacre Coeur.

"You don't want to know," Vlad replies. "There's bad, and then there are your parents," he says, and I take his word.

If Vlad thinks they were bad, then chances are they *were*.

"Thank you for telling me," I whisper, brushing my lips against his.

This changes things, and it makes me want to put in the effort to know my brother a little better. Maybe I'm not as unwanted as I'd initially thought.

* * *

The following day I have a hard time keeping my eyes open. Vlad had returned me home in the early hours of the morning, and I barely got a wink of sleep. We'd ended up eating, drinking and talking all night, alternating between playing in the water and walking down the beach.

Being the only people there had been liberating, and we'd enjoyed a small break from the humdrum of daily life. I also know that Vlad has become increasingly stressed with finding his sister, and that's all he's doing in the time I'm not with him.

A headache mounting, I make my way to the dining room, ready for family time. Even though Vlad had shed some light on Marcello and his behavior, that doesn't mean I still don't feel like an outsider.

Just as I start down the stairs, I see my brother and Lina kissing in the hallway.

At least someone's happy.

"Sisi?" Lina asks, and I avert my gaze, hiding a smile at witnessing her tender moment with Marcello.

"Sisi, wait!" she calls out as I head toward the dining room.

"What?" I turn to her, frowning.

"What's that?" she inquires, coming to my side and moving my hair aside. She points to something on my neck and it takes me a moment to realize what she's talking about... and how I'd gotten it.

Oh, damn!

"Are you ill?" she continues, obviously worried about me. My heart beating loudly in my chest, I mumble an excuse.

"What? No... something must have bitten me." The lie slips easily, but I can't bring myself to meet her eyes. "I'm hungry, I'll see you in the dining room." I quickly excuse myself and dash out.

That was a close call.

What was Vlad thinking to leave that type of mark on my skin, knowing people would see? More than anything, what was *I* thinking to allow such a thing?

I shake my head at myself. It's like I lose all inhibitions the moment I find myself in his presence.

We're taking increasingly more risks, and I don't want to think of Lina or Marcello's reactions if they found out how I've been spending my nights. Getting to know Vlad a little better has made me aware of something. We might fit perfectly together, but that doesn't mean the outside world will see it as such.

From what Vlad had told me, I'd been able to glean that he isn't much accepted into society. Hell, Marcello, who by all accounts is his friend, doesn't trust him to not go into a murderous rage at any point.

If anyone knew just how much time we spent together, or how much he's started to mean to me, I have no doubt they would try to put a stop to our rendezvous. And because of that, I can't afford to slip, not even a bit.

Yes, Vlad is my little secret, but at this point he's the only thing keeping me sane.

It's later in the evening that I muster the courage to seek Marcello out.

Knocking on the door of his study, I steel myself when I hear his voice calling out, "Come in."

Entering, I hold my head high as I take a seat in front of him.

"Yes?" he says, surprised to see me.

"I wanted to tell you thank you," I start, and his eyebrows shoot up in confusion. "For taking me in, and for offering me this chance to start anew," I explain.

"Sisi, you don't have to thank me for anything," he replies, and for a moment I'm shocked as I hear him use my nickname instead of my full name as he usually does. "This is your home, too. If anything, I should be asking for your forgiveness for not inquiring earlier whether you wanted to stay at Sacre Coeur. I just assumed..." he trails off, looking uncomfortable. "It was wrong of me to think that just because Sacre Coeur was all you've ever known that you wouldn't be curious about the outside world."

"You couldn't have known," I tell him. "For all intents and purposes, I looked right at home at Sacre Coeur."

I sigh deeply. Years of interacting with the same people seem to have stunted my ability to relate to others.

"I'm glad we've sorted this out." I give him a small smile.

"Me too. I would hate for you to think you're unwelcome in your own house. I know you have a very tight relationship with Lina and Claudia, but I'd like if we could get to know each other too. Slowly." He returns my smile with one of his own.

"I'd like that," I nod.

19
VLAD

"I'm surprised to see you here," Enzo mentions, raising an eyebrow at me as he lights up a cigarette.

"Are you?" I ask, taking a seat and making myself comfortable.

Considering our previous enmity, it might seem surprising that I'm visiting Enzo right in his home. But I've recently found some tidbits of information that have changed my perception of him and our situation. The fact that he's not receiving me with a shotgun in my face just confirms what I already know—Enzo Agosti is a crafty son of a bitch.

And I have to begrudgingly admit that my respect for the man has increased.

I'd had my eyes on the Agosti business for a while now, especially since I'd heard some not-so-glamorous rumors through the grapevine. In my desperation, it had been all the impetus I'd needed to put Agosti under the magnifying glass.

And I'd used my former partner, Bianca, to do just that. In a quid pro quo exchange, she'd placed a few bugs in

Enzo's office, and for months now, the insight I'd gained had helped me narrow down my options.

"Get to the point, Kuznetsov," Enzo states, looking already bored.

Ah, but when he hears what I have to say, that boredom will for sure be wiped from his face.

"So impatient. And here *I* was the one with ADHD," I joke, helping myself to his pack of cigarettes uninvited.

He narrows his eyes at me as I light it up, taking a full drag of the cigarette.

"I'm not in the mood for your antics, Vlad." He rolls his eyes at me, clearly hoping to see me gone soon.

"Hmm, and what antics are we talking about?" I feign ignorance.

He raises an eyebrow at me. "Really?" He shakes his head. "Shall I remind you what happened the last time we were in the same room together?" he asks, and I start chuckling.

We've had our differences over the years, and all of them started from his wife, or at least his *current* wife. After the initial debacle, we hadn't had many opportunities to meet. But one time at a summit, we'd once more come to blows when I'd hired a suite of strippers to make their entrance right in the middle of the meeting. I'd even sent them with the personalized message that they were for his wife, since he's not capable of satisfying her.

Enzo had been thoroughly embarrassed, just as I'd wanted, but his reaction had not been as vehement as I'd anticipated.

Now I know why...

Still, the bad blood runs deep, and I doubt this one conversation will magically fix everything. He has something I want, though, so I will bend *a little*.

"Come on, Agosti. Where is your sense of humor? They were top class, too. You have no idea how much they charge per hour." I look him up and down, my lips twitching. "You know, if you ever want to retire, that might be one avenue. You're not bad on the eyes. Certainly, the ladies love you..." I trail off when I see the tick in his jaw.

"I wonder if you have a death wish, Kuznetsov. I've always known you to be reckless, but not entirely suicidal."

"Ahh, Enzo, Enzo," I chuckle, "recklessness is but the desire to die without the actual courage. Maybe I just like to court death, but I'm not quite ready to meet my maker," I say, amused.

"Well, here you are," he replies drily, and I decide to get to the point lest he take out his guns on me. I'd rather not have any holes when I meet Sisi tonight.

"I want information," I tell him, my smile completely gone.

He scoffs at me, and I know I need to bring out the big guns.

"Jimenez," I start, and his attention snaps to me. "I know you've been working with him. Which means that you are currently in possession of some of his businesses."

His mask doesn't drop at my mention, but his ears sure perk up.

"What do you want?" he asks tensely. Ah, I knew Enzo was smart. If he realizes I'm aware of his extracurriculars, then he must understand I know far more than that.

"I told you. Information. I'm looking for a certain Miles, affiliated with Project Humanitas."

He turns his icy stare on me, debating for a minute what to answer.

"Come on, Agosti, it doesn't cost *you* a thing to help a fella out. On the other hand... it could prove very costly to someone living at Sacre Coeur." I stretch in my seat, gleefully watching as my threat sinks in.

He grits his teeth, but he gives me a brisk nod.

"I don't know anything about a Project Humanitas," he says and I'm quick to tsk at him, "*but*," he continues, "there is a Miles that is known in the club scene, especially in Jimenez's territory. I don't know the guy personally, but he has multiple brokers buying for him every month."

"Marvelous," I exclaim, a wide smile on my lips, "where can I find this Miles then?"

"Like I told you, he doesn't show himself. But you can find his brokers," he continues, taking out his computer and punching some keys.

"These are the clubs I know for sure they frequent." He pushes the screen toward me and I lean in to read the list of clubs and their addresses.

"I wasn't aware Papillion was Jimenez's club." I narrow my eyes. The rest I am familiar with as I'd been to all of them in the past in my search for answers. But they are all out of state. Papillion, though, is in NYC, and widely known to be under Agosti.

"No one was," Enzo explains, "but since he wasn't welcomed in New York, he disguised the club. It was the first term I agreed to when I partnered up with him. I'd open a club in my name, and he'd have free rein over it."

"I see," I drawl, "I'm going to need access to the club."

Enzo pauses for a moment.

"I trust your discretion with..."

"You have my word."

He nods, taking out his phone and making a few calls.

"You're going as a VIP. Try not to stand out too much. I may have my name on this, but it's out of my control," he says.

"Don't you worry, Agosti. I'll be a fly on the wall." I give him a dazzling smile, and he closes his eyes, his hands going to his temples.

"That's what I'm worried about," he groans. "I'm serious, Vlad. The people who frequent those places are *not* people you want as enemies. It's best if you draw as little attention as possible."

"Come on, how bad can it be?" I would think it should be the other way around, since my moods are fickle at best.

He doesn't take my bait. Instead, he withdraws a USB, plugging it into his computer and programming a few things on it.

"This will give you access to the feed. You know the drill. The club is a front, the auctions are in the basement. Papillion is mostly known for immigrants," he comments, handing me the USB.

Ah, he wants to get rid of me as quickly as he can. I can only oblige as I stand up, pocketing the USB.

On my way out, however, I feel compelled to add, "A favor for a favor, Agosti. Your secret is safe with me."

I don't look back as I leave his house, realizing I need to plan my next move.

* * *

With a last glance at the bags of clothes I'd bought, I can only hope Sisi will like them. Since our misadventure jumping out the window had not worked so well, we'd improvised and developed a system for her to get out undetected through the staff door in the back of the house.

I've already parked my car off the main road and now I'm just waiting for her to come.

After leaving Enzo's house, I'd spent the entire day

watching the feed from Papillion, making a blueprint of the place and coming up with back-up plans in case our visit might draw unwanted attention.

I'd decided to let Sisi accompany me for three reasons. One... Well, I don't want to miss a day with her. Two, she will help me blend in, and three, she will ensure I stay focused, since Vanya won't be a problem if she's there.

Why, there's just no reason not to bring her with me, especially since I trust myself to keep her safe.

"You're smiling again," Vanya points out, and I give her the eye.

"I'm not," I huff.

"Yes, you are." She crosses her hands over her chest, raising an eyebrow at me. "It's the girl, isn't it?" she asks knowingly.

"Of course not," I answer a little too fast, and she just smirks at me.

"It is the girl," she repeats, and I sigh.

"Okay, *maybe* it is the girl. I'm not saying it is though. I'm saying there is a *possibility*." I skirt around the issue, hoping she would drop the subject.

It's not the first time Vanya's brought this up. In her own words, she's trying to make me realize my feelings for Sisi and that I should wife her up as soon as possible. I mean, technically, what she's saying isn't a bad idea.

If I were to wife her up, then she'd belong solely to me. The feelings part is a little murky since I don't think I have those—factory defect, unfortunately—but I can certainly pretend.

"I knew it!" she exclaims. "You always get that dreamy, star-struck look on your face," she adds and my mouth drops open.

"I do not!" I state vehemently, but she only tsks at me.

"You doth protest too much." She smirks at me before her form disappears into thin air. Raising my gaze, I spot Sisi running toward the car in the distance.

For a moment, I think back to Vanya's observations. I agree that *maybe* I am a schoolboy with a crush. But who wouldn't be? Sisi's not only incredibly attractive, but she's also witty and funny, keeping up with my fucked up sense of humor. She even approves of my less than usual morbid inclinations. If that's not a keeper, then I don't know what is.

Maybe I should wife her up.

The idea isn't so bad. Marcello might try to kill me, but at least we wouldn't be sneaking around all the time. I'd even be able to see her in daylight, a fact which has proven mightily difficult so far. You'd think us vampires with our nocturnal schedules.

But the more time I spend with her, the more I crave her. It's not nearly enough that I get her near, listening to her laughter, tasting her very essence.

"God," I groan out loud, reaching down to adjust my cock. It's a common occurrence now. I only have to think about her and I'm instantly hard. It's that simple.

Hell, the other night at the beach I'd been so crazy for her I'd come in my pants. Awkward, but I'd been able to brush it off by suggesting another dip in the water. Her smell, taste, just the feel of her pussy on my tongue had been an experience unlike any other.

And as someone who'd previously scoffed at the idea of getting *that* up and close to another human being, I find that now I can't get close enough.

For that, I need to do my best not to screw things up. I know I don't have too many things going for me, and that she could do a whole lot better—and more normal—but I have to show her that even with my flaws I'm the best choice.

Good thing I have strong protections on my computer, because it would be embarrassing to look through my browsing history.

What type of trained killer searches tips on how to romance a woman?

Even worse, what type of assassin spends his time on women's forums cataloguing date ideas? I'd be an embarrassment to the entire assassin community, if there even is such a thing.

Would my victims even fear me anymore if they knew I spend hours picking out women's clothes? Or that I now know there are different shades of blue? I must have memorized the entire color palette in my search for something Sisi would love.

Fucking hell!

I'm really losing it this time.

"You're here." She opens the passenger door, climbing up. She's out of breath from running toward the car, but her smile is wide on her face.

"You're here," I repeat numbly, sounding like a broken record.

Sisi doesn't waste any time and leans forward, giving me a quick kiss.

"So, what's on for tonight?" she asks excitedly, and I find myself leaving behind all my apprehensions, seeking instead to soak in her presence.

"Tonight, we go hunting," I tell her, quickly detailing my plan.

Papillion works a bit differently than the Block, another of Jimenez's most famous clubs.

As I'd combed through the footage, I'd marked a pattern.

The club opens up at twelve, operating as a normal strip club until two. Then, insiders are invited to the basement to watch the entertainment of the night and bid on their favorites. Enzo hadn't been kidding when he'd said immigrants were the main attraction.

The club receives requests for different types of people from around the globe, but instead of fulfilling them in a one-time deal, they prefer to make buyers fight for the merchandise, and as such raise their profits. It's all quite ingenious, from a business standpoint, since apparently Papillion's ability to outsource *any* type of human is unparalleled.

I can definitely see why Miles would be a regular in such a place. Now, though, I'm curious to know what personalized requests *he* puts in.

Luckily, from what I'd been able to glean, the host calls out the specifications, thus putting the potential buyer on the spot and ensuring potential competition gets wind of it to drive the prices up.

The entire scheme is brilliant, and I can only imagine the type of money Papillion brings in.

Our plan is pretty straightforward. Sisi and I would go inside, hang around until called for the auction and then be on the lookout for Miles' people.

The outfits I'd gotten us should help us blend in. I'd gone specifically for a style completely unlike my usual one. That way, even if someone might know me, they would be thrown off by two things — Sisi's presence and my clothes.

"Are you serious?" Sisi arches an eyebrow at me as she finishes donning the clothes I'd gotten her.

"Damn," I whistle, admiring the view.

Okay, *maybe* I should have gone for more conservative.

She's wearing a pair of leather pants that accentuate her

legs, the bold contour of her ass making men want to weep. Certainly, my dick approves. My head, though, not so much, since everyone else will be seeing the same thing.

For her top I'd gone for a simple black shirt, this time making sure there's no cleavage showing, since her tits are a one-way ticket to hell for anyone whose eyes stray even a little bit.

"Come on, you can't be serious," she repeats, holding out the leather cut that says *Property of Berserker*.

"It's cute!" I reply, turning my back and pointing to the *Berserker* written on mine, "We match, see?"

She shakes her head at me, but eventually relents and puts it on.

Frankly, I'd had to improvise fast and find a good disguise, especially for that type of club. So I'd gone the easy route—pretend I'm part of some made-up MC chapter named *White Trash*, casually strolling up into *Papillion* with my biker babe to buy some new humans.

Considering my entire body is full of ink, it doesn't seem entirely too farfetched that I'd be part of some nefarious gang. But most of all, it is so polar opposite from how I usually present myself that I should go unnoticed.

To match Sisi's outfit, I'm also wearing a pair of leather pants, a white tank-top and the leather cut with the club's name. If anyone will catch onto the irony of the name remains to be seen, although based on previous experiences, the jab should fall on deaf ears.

I'd also gone to great lengths to temporarily modify my Bratva tattoo, lest someone recognize that one.

"I can't believe I agreed to this," Sisi mutters under her breath.

"We need to go in undetected. Just think of it as a new

adventure. When will you ever have the chance to be a biker babe again?"

"I'm not sure this is my definition of an adventure." She rolls her eyes at me, "But I'll help you."

"Great!" I say, loudly smacking her ass.

"Ouch! Why did you do that?" Her hands go to her ass as she's trying to diffuse the pain.

"Getting into character." I wink at her.

And to top it off, I'd also gotten an old Yamaha that's been gathering dust in my garage. This time when Sisi sees the motorcycle, she doesn't scoff at it. Instead, she's quite enthusiastic at the prospect of riding it.

"Wow," she breathes out as I hand her the helmet. "This is amazing."

"Are you that happy riding bitch?" I joke, and her eyes widen before I get a jab in my ribs. "Joking, joking." I hold my hands up in surrender.

She pouts and I turn to her, taking her mouth in a rough kiss, my teeth catching her lower lip as I bite it.

"Hang on tight," I say against her lips, taking her arms and wrapping them around my waist.

We reach the club just as it opens, and after I show the bouncer that I have Enzo's approval, we're invited inside and told to wait for a staff member to show us to our VIP lounge.

As we step inside the club, I note that it's nothing special. At least compared with some other places I'd seen, this is rather tame.

There are mini stages throughout, all hosting pole dancers and strippers surrounded by horny men. There are a few couches and tables in the back, all busy with men and women in different stages of fucking. From afar, it looks like a banquet worthy of Caligula himself.

"Is that?" Sisi whispers when she sees the show, and for one second I regret bringing her here. I do *not* want her seeing some stranger's dick.

Shielding her eyes with my hand, I divert her attention by steering her to the bar.

"Wow," she continues to say, looking around in awe. "That looks so much fun." She points toward the girls dancing on the poles. "But also hard." She frowns when she sees them do a rather complicated move.

"You need strong muscles to do that." I'm barely looking at the pole, my entire attention held by *her*. Her expressions are so vivid, so mesmerizing, that they have the power to make me forget myself.

"I want to try it," she replies animatedly.

"You what?"

"I want to try that. It looks so interesting," she repeats, releasing a dreamy sigh as she continues to admire the girls' moves.

Shaking my head at her, since clearly that's out of the question, I turn to the bartender and ask for two shots of vodka.

"Here." I hand her one, a little peeved that her attention is wholly on the stage. She doesn't even look at me as she takes the glass out of my hand and downs it, quickly sputtering. Her hand goes to her face as she fans herself, turning toward me with wide eyes as she's asking for help.

"Breathe," I lean in to whisper.

"It's so strong..." She barely gets the words out.

So far, I'd only offered her softer drinks like wine or champagne, wanting to ease her into the exploration of alcohol.

"Whose fault is it that you shot it down like a pro?" I tsk

at her, amused. "Let me show you how it's done," I tell her, my eyes intently on her.

I take my shot glass, downing it in one go. Then, before she can react, my hand shoots out, grabbing her by the jaw, my thumb prying her lips open as I tease her with my mouth. Opening wide, I share the drink with her, licking her lips clean when I'm done.

She's quiet as her eyes rove over me, her arousal clear in the way her pupils dilate. She bites her lips slowly, a come-hither gesture that's instantly making me hard.

So focused am I on her and her seductive little games that I don't realize when another woman plops herself in front of us.

Sisi is the first to move her head, studying the woman with narrowed eyes.

"A lap dance?" the woman asks, placing her hand on my shoulder. "She can watch," she nods toward Sisi. The woman's clad only in a pair of bikini bottoms, all the goods in sight as she's no doubt trying to find clients for the evening.

20

VLAD

I'm about to take her hand off me, but Sisi beats me to it, roughly grabbing her wrist and bending it.

"No, thank you." She fakes a wide smile, getting to her feet and putting herself between me and the woman.

Well, isn't this interesting...

"I didn't ask *you*," the woman replies smugly before turning to me. "I didn't know bitches could talk back," she continues, looking Sisi up and down in distaste, and it takes me a moment to realize that biker babes should be submissive.

Alas, I have failed in choosing this disguise, since Sisi is anything but submissive.

"Oh, this one can," Sisi replies, tightening her hold on the woman's wrist and twisting it. She whimpers in pain, but she doesn't seem to give up as she aims her other hand toward Sisi's hair.

I'm thinking of intervening, but one look from Sisi and I put my hands up, letting her do her thing. So I just lean back and watch the show.

Sisi is quick to parry the woman's hand, wrapping her

fingers around her nape and bringing her head into the bar table. A resounding thud, and everyone suddenly fixates their gazes on the ongoing match.

I watch with pleasure as Sisi continues to bang the woman's head on the table until blood starts pouring out of her face.

Fuck, if this doesn't make me even harder.

It's interesting that no one intervenes to help the woman, considering she's an employee here. No, instead everyone is cheering for Sisi as she's ruining the woman's face.

Her smile twisted at the corners; she's got a look of pure satisfaction as she wreaks even more havoc on the woman's body. It's only when she goes limp in her arms that she lets go, the woman crumbling to the floor, unmoving.

Sisi is unbothered as she steps over her body and comes to my side.

"She was right, you know, you *should* be submissive," I add sarcastically, and before I know it, her punch shoots out, her knuckles grazing my cheek.

"You let her touch you," she hisses at me, and I blink twice, surprised at her outburst.

"I did?" I ask slowly, weirdly turned on by this side of her.

"You let her fucking touch you." She jabs her finger in my chest, aggression rolling off her as she comes onto me.

My eyes move over her body, the way her chest rises and falls rapidly, her throat contracting and forming a hollow just above her collarbone.

"Fuck her! Fuck her! Fuck her!" The chants are getting louder as more people surround us, all interested in the ongoing spectacle. "Fuck her! Fuck her! Fuck her!"

Not one to miss a dramatic exit, I quickly lift Sisi off her feet, throwing her over my shoulder, and signaling an employee to show us to our lounge.

A fly on the wall... Well, mission accomplished.

* * *

The room is small but private, with a round couch and a table in the middle. I nod to the staff and close the door, finally dropping Sisi to the ground.

"You," she seethes at me, and it's the first time I'm seeing her like this.

And I fucking love it.

She wastes no time in pushing me down on the couch, climbing on top of me, her hands fisted in the material of my shirt.

Her outburst amuses and delights me at the same time, so I just lay back and let her dish at me whatever she wants.

"You wanted a lap dance?" she asks, her expression serious and oh, so bloodthirsty. My cock twitches in my pants, the bastard fucking loving this side of her.

"If I remember correctly, I did not even react to her suggestion," I point out, trying to keep a straight face. But she's not having it.

Stepping away from me, she takes the cut and her shirt off, remaining only in her bra. That luscious body of hers is going to give me a heart attack in the future.

"Goddamn," I whisper, my eyes honing in on her tits.

"You'll have a lap dance," she tells me, moving around in a sensuous manner, her tits jiggling as she climbs up on me ever so slowly.

I swallow. Hard.

"Do you even know how to give a lap dance?" I ask her, quirking a smile.

"Can't be that hard," she mumbles under her breath. Her expression immediately changes as she seductively bats her eyelashes at me, brushing her chest against mine as she blows hot air on my neck.

Using her hands, she caresses my arms, undulating her ass until it glides enticingly over my dick. My eyes are already glazed, my focus solely on this temptress in front of me that seems to have a possessive streak.

Snaking my arm around her waist, I bring her flush against my chest, stopping her movements. She looks at me suspiciously as I grab her hand and put it between us.

"Feel this, Hell Girl," I say, pressing her hand on my erection, so she can see just how much she affects me. "This is only for you. I only *ever* get hard for you."

I pull her closer to me, my forehead resting on top of hers.

"Get it through that pretty skull of yours that I'm not going to look at another woman. *Ever*."

"Good. Otherwise, I'd be forced to do something I wouldn't like," she says, her eyes still shooting daggers at me.

"What?" I rasp, the mere feel of her against me driving me insane.

"Kill you," she whispers, her hands caressing my chest until she stops at the waistline of my pants. "I'd cut your dick off, then kill you," she continues, her fingers tracing the outline of my hard cock through my pants.

"Is that so?" I ask, lust simmering in my blood. Fuck me, but why does she have to be so hot while saying she'd cut my dick off?

"Yes, and I'd be very sad." She pouts, her tongue sneaking out and giving my cheek a long lick. "But maybe I'd keep it as a souvenir," she breathes against my face, and I just about combust from that alone.

"It's yours," I groan when she slowly lowers my zipper, her hands moving past the waistline of my boxers.

She's tantalizingly slow, and my breath stops when she puts her hand on me.

By Jove, this is torture.

For a moment, I have to mentally take a break, doing my best not to bust a nut this very second.

"Hmm." She makes a sound deep in her throat, her palm opening over my shaft as she caresses me from tip to base.

My eyes flutter closed, the feel of her small hand over my cock making me shudder.

"I read about big dick energy online," she says, her voice low and husky.

"You did?" I ask with a strangled moan.

I know she did. Hell, I know her entire search history by heart. I even know that my sinful nun has been reading naughty books, and she's clearly been taking notes to please me.

Not that I'm one to talk, since I've been doing the same.

"Mmm." She leans in to lick my ear. "It fits," she whispers as she tightens her hold over me, and I groan out loud.

Her hand is already moving up and down my shaft, her thumb swiping over the head of my cock as she uses the pre-cum to lubricate her movements.

Yes, she's definitely been taking notes.

"You're killing me, Hell Girl," I grab her by the throat, keeping her face glued to mine. "You're fucking killing me."

"Not yet," she replies cheekily.

"Is this what they teach you at the nunnery? How to drive men insane? Because, fuck, you're succeeding." I grit my teeth as she continues to put those dainty hands of hers to use.

Her mouth pulls up in a smile, and she bites her lip in the process.

"Well, technically we are the brides of Christ..." She trails off suggestively, and I just about lose it.

Fuck, am I jealous of a fictional prophet?

But the thought of anyone, even a saint, touching or even looking at Sisi has me going crazy.

I'm barely in control as it is, letting her take the reins and willing myself not to bend her over and fuck her like an animal — fast and dirty until she renounces her religion and proclaims me her new god.

And as her hand continues to torture me, the movements increasingly faster, I can only take her mouth in a bruising kiss, our tongues fighting, our mouths mashing together. I revel in the savageness that seems to mirror my own.

My hand lodged in her scalp, I hold her close to me as I nibble and bite at her, wanting to permanently mark her as mine.

"Fuck," I curse as she continues to stroke me.

Out of nowhere, she shoves my hand aside, getting on her knees and opening her mouth to take my cock inside. Her lips stretch across the head as she licks and kisses it, swirling her tongue on the underside like a fucking pro.

The warmth of her mouth as she envelops more of my cock almost makes me black out, the new sensation exhilarating.

But only because it's her.

She keeps sucking me deep into her mouth, her lips effortlessly gliding over my shaft as she peppers kisses all over it. Her hand is still working me up and down, using her spit to get my entire length nice and wet.

Fuck!

I reach out with my hand and caress her cheek, holding her hair to the side as she sucks my cock like she should have been worshiping Jesus.

"You're such a bad nun," I rasp, my eyes alternating between closed and open.

She smiles with my cock in her mouth, and hell if I've ever seen a prettier picture. Batting her eyelashes at me, she takes me deeper, gagging on my length until she's choking.

The way she's looking at me, with her seductive gaze wrapped in innocence, has me close to the edge.

She palms my balls, slowly massaging them. Lifting my cock with one hand as she licks her way down, enclosing her lips over my balls and sucking them into her mouth.

"Sisi." My voice sounds foreign to my ears as she gently squeezes my balls in her mouth before leaving a trail of spit all over my length.

How is she fucking real?

She's a temptress come down to lure me into sin—not that I wasn't already knee-deep in it. But fuck if I'm not thankful she's been hidden away this whole time. Because otherwise, I would have had to kill my way through the entire city to make her mine.

Someone with Sisi's beauty and intelligence would have attracted all kinds of attention, and she would have had her pick of men.

Shit, but I don't even know if she would have given me the time of day if I hadn't gotten to her first. And that thought makes me still.

I'll never let her go.

She's saddled with me now, and I'm such a possessive bastard that no other man will ever even graze her hand. No, all her touches are strictly reserved for me. All her smiles and her seductive glances.

Everything.

Her hands are stroking me up and down, her mouth sucking on the head, her eyes fixed on me. She swirls her tongue all around the tip, letting more saliva dribble down my length and using it for added friction.

She's so beautiful I can barely breathe. And when she gives me one last suck, those plump lips wrapped around my cock, in what I can only describe as a warm, wet heaven, I know I can't last anymore.

"I'm coming," I warn her, feeling a tingling down my spine as my balls contract. I expect her to pull away, but she doesn't.

She keeps on working my cock until my cum shoots into her waiting mouth. She doesn't stop until I'm wholly spent, swallowing every last bit of my release.

With a wicked smile, she undulates her body as she climbs up again, her legs on both sides of mine as she's straddling me.

"Forgive me, father, for I have sinned," she whispers naughtily in my ear.

"What is your sin?" I find myself asking.

"I've been very, very bad," she sighs.

"How so?" My hand goes to her long hair and I pick up a strand, bringing it to my nose, inhaling deeply.

"I sucked cock... and I liked it," she admits shyly.

"You did? That's very, very bad indeed," I tell her, my hand trailing down her back until I'm palming her ass. "You might be going to hell."

She feigns a horrified expression as her eyes widen, her mouth parting. "Oh, no!" she exclaims.

"But it's okay," she amends saucily. "I'll have company." She winks at me.

Damn it all, but I'm never letting this woman go.

With a quick snap of a button, I have her pants opened, my hand pushing her panties to the side to find her soaking wet.

"You're fire, Hell Girl." I look her in the eye, my fingers already caressing her pussy before settling on her clit. "Why don't you say a prayer so I can take you to heaven?" I nuzzle my face in the crook of her neck, her breathing harsh as she grinds herself on my fingers.

"Can you do that?" I ask, and she gasps when I enter her, using her juices to ease my way in.

"Our father, who art in heaven," she starts, pausing as I thrust into her, burying two fingers to the hilt, "hallowed be..." she moans when I use my thumb to flick her clit, "Thy name." She clears her throat, her walls contracting around me. She's so fucking tight, her pussy greedily grasping onto my fingers as I stroke her deep. "Thy kingdom come..." She trails off on a long whimper as I curl my digits inside of her, finding her G-spot.

"Please make me come," she breathes hard, abandoning the prayer and lowering herself on my hand as she seeks her release.

For a moment I want to keep teasing her, enjoying her little mewling and the way she's putty in my arms. But one look in her eyes and I cannot help myself as I focus my attention on her clit until she's screaming my name.

"I didn't realize what a jealous little thing you were," I comment as she peers at me through her lashes. She's laying on my chest, spent and purring in satisfaction as I move my hand up and down her arms in a light caress.

She gives me a sheepish smile.

"I take my possessions seriously," she adds, yawning slightly.

"Is that what I am for you?" I raise an eyebrow, pretending to be offended.

"Mmm," she burrows her face into my chest, "you're mine," she says, tracing her name on my skin with her fingers.

I've never belonged to anyone before, and the prospect of being hers fills me with an unprecedented warmth.

"I..." I start, but I'm interrupted by a knock on the door.

Quickly helping her dress, I right my own clothes as I open the door.

"The entertainment is about to begin," an employee informs me, and I give him a nod.

"Ready?" I turn toward Sisi, and she comes to my side, lacing her fingers through mine.

"Let's do this," she whispers, kissing my cheek.

The employee scans his finger on a steel door in the back of the club, motioning us to follow him. We're led down a dark corridor until we reach a set of stairs. As we start descending toward the basement, noises begin attacking my ears. The music is blasting, but it's almost drowned out by collective voices yelling, cheering and cursing. For a moment, I am confused, since this is merely supposed to be an auction.

But as we step onto the platform, the entire basement spreading in front of us, I realize why Enzo had said their entertainment is *varied*.

The basement had been turned into a fighting arena. A big stage stretches in the middle of the room, with people surrounding it as they cheer on, some swinging their auction paddles around while yelling exorbitant amounts.

As the employee shows us to a corner, he gives me an

auction paddle with the number sixty-four on it. He doesn't even glance at Sisi as he leaves, and I'm once more reminded that in these places women are little more than chattel.

She doesn't seem to notice the affront, her eyes glued to the stage as one man climbs up, a microphone in his hand.

"Is everyone ready for tonight?" he calls out, people yelling yes at him. Introducing himself as Mauro, he goes on to give a brief introduction of what's up for tonight.

I half-listen to him, my eyes focused on my surroundings as I take in everyone, looking for familiar faces. Off the bat I see people I'd been following for years, all elbows deep in human trafficking.

Now, who could be Miles' broker...

I somehow don't doubt that Mr. Petrovic must have worked for him at some point, or any other influential person, since someone must have sent those people to look for him. I'd looked into their backgrounds trying to tie them to someone in Mr. Petrovic's inner circle, but I hadn't gotten any hits on that. Too bad Mr. Petrovic ended up dead not long after he'd divulged Miles' name, since I have no doubt he had more information than he'd imparted.

"Are they..." Sisi tugs my hand as she nods toward the stage. Two men, looking more like killing machines than anything, walk on the stage.

"On the right we have Seth, hailing straight from the pyramids. With a total of fifty kills under his belt, he is yet undefeated in the ring. He's been without a master for the past two months, so place your bets gentlemen. We're going to have an interesting show."

The host introduces one of the men, a hulking beast of at least seven feet and a half. His entire body is filled with scars, one of his eyes replaced with a glass one.

"Damn, that must be tough," I mutter.

"Why?" Sisi leans into me.

"That's a hell of a disadvantage for a fighter to have. You need your eyes for coordination, but also for peripheral view. If he's managed so many wins with only one eye..." I whistle in admiration.

"Next up is Drew, our resident champion. Mr. Meester has allowed us to borrow him for yet another entertaining evening. Let's give a round of applause to Mr. Meester." The host motions to one of the men at the balconies who waves smugly at the crowd.

"Who is he?" Sisi asks.

"A crime lord, more or less," I say with half a smile.

I had expected to see people I know here, since most of the criminal world has no scruples, certainly not when it comes to the easiest and cheapest form of exploitation— human labor and sexuality. But I certainly had *not* expected to see Petro Meester here.

And now it's imperative he doesn't notice me.

"Let's hope we don't get his attention," I tell Sisi, giving her a quick rundown of my history with the man.

A Ukrainian immigrant, he'd been under my father's wing for a long time before branching out and building his own empire. All had been fine and dandy, until Misha had killed father, and then I'd killed Misha.

Petro had approached me with a potential alliance with his daughter, which I'd promptly refused. He'd taken it personally, and we've butted heads on more than one occasion since then, but mainly in business. I don't know why he'd been so offended by my refusal, but every time I was about to close a deal, he'd intervene to try to stop it.

"His pettiness knows no bounds," I add drily.

I'd never gone out of my way to look into him, but last I knew, he was in the meth trade. Interesting that he's leveled up, and it makes me wonder if he has any connection with Jimenez and the Gallaghers.

"Drew is Mr. Meester's favorite, and he has a total of two hundred fifty-four kills under his belt. Quite a discrepancy, no?" the host asks the public, and everyone is quick to shout their predictions. That Drew will finish Seth off.

"What's the point of all this?" Sisi asks, looking intrigued.

"He's showing off, no doubt," I explain. Knowing Petro's hubris, that's exactly why he would lend his champion to one of these fights. "Other than that, I guess there must be a bidding on the winner, should Seth win instead of Drew."

"What do you think? Who will win?"

I look closely at the two men. Their physiques are closely matched, but logically speaking, Drew has more experience and should be the favored one in this battle.

"Seth," I say, narrowing my eyes at the stage.

"What? Really? Why? He has fifty kills versus two hundred and fifty-four kills. How can he stand a chance?"

"We'll see," I add, curious about the outcome too.

But while the two fighters look evenly matched in physical strength, Seth has something Drew does not — the desire to live. Drew's many victories must have stroked his ego, because I can see the smugness in his gaze as he looks down on Seth.

After a lengthy monologue by the host, the gong is hit, the fight officially starting.

Drew is the first one to advance, immediately taking the offensive. Seth, on the other hand, skirts around the stage, avoiding a direct confrontation. Instead, his good eye is focused on Drew's movements, cataloguing every step and *how* those steps are done.

Interesting.

More dancing around each other, and Drew grows impatient, just like the crowd. And out of that impatience, the first mistake is born. Drew jumps on Seth, throwing his entire weight forward, no doubt counting on tackling Seth to the ground. Instead, Seth stays put until Drew is but a millimeter away from him, after which he promptly moves away with incredible speed for someone his size.

He places his body diagonally, rooting his lower half on the ground while he twists his torso to the right. Holding one foot down, he uses the other to knee his adversary in the gut, the combined momentum of Drew's jump plus the strength behind Seth's kick magnifying the pain. Drew winces, the air knocked out of him, and he takes a second to stabilize himself.

A second too much, because Seth finally unleashes his true potential, barreling into Drew with his fists. He concentrates on his head, landing blow after blow at his temples until Drew can barely stand still.

One more punch, and Drew looks dazedly at the crowd before his knees buckle and he hits the floor.

"Wow..." Sisi breathes, and I share the feeling.

Impressive. Very impressive.

The entire room is silent as they are probably mourning the loss of their bets, and I sneak a glance at Mr. Meester who is looking at the stage as if he can't believe what just happened.

As I predicted, the host blunders through a small speech, eventually putting Seth up for bidding.

"Starting price is determined by Mr. Meester, since it is his loss," the host says, but Mr. Meester is already gone from his balcony, no doubt the disappointment too great for his fragile ego.

My lips pull up in a smile as the host settles on a random

amount, with multiple people already trying to up the previous bid.

"Ten." I raise my paddle, unable to help myself.

It's like everything stops as the host looks at me askance, rolling his eyes no doubt at my current attire.

"I'm sorry Sir, but we're talking millions here, not thousands," he says almost exasperated.

"Ten million," I agree, shrugging.

Sisi is looking at me as if I'd grown a second head, while the entire room seems to be awfully quiet at my pronouncement.

"Right, so... ten million once, ten million twice..." Not a soul challenges the amount, so the host is obligated to declare me the winning bid.

"What are you doing with a fighter?" Sisi asks in shock, "A ten million dollar fighter?"

"What could I do? Make him fight, of course." I give her a brilliant smile.

Seeing his skills firsthand solidified it for me. He's the perfect candidate. Because at some point in the future, he *will* need to fight. Intriguing, though. Seth might just be the warrior drawn on my back manifested into reality.

The one who will save the world from me.

21

SISI

Sometimes I look at Vlad, and I don't know who I am seeing. No matter how much I get to know him, there's just so much hidden, so much he's not saying. He's always giving me the facts. But never more than that. With him, it's always cold, logical facts.

Like now.

I watch stupefied as he bids ten million dollars on a man, and I can't figure out why he would do that.

Once the auction is over, Mauro comes to speak with Vlad, telling him he'll be able to pick up his purchase after the recess, since they have to get Seth ready for his new owner. Vlad grunts in approval, his hand never leaving my waist as he finalizes the details.

"What's the plan?" I ask when the host leaves, and Vlad gives me a weird look.

"No plan. It was merely a spur-of-the-moment decision." He quickly gives me one of his charming smiles, but I can see what he's trying to do.

"You're not fooling me." I narrow my eyes at him. I can

see through the mask he's trying to put on, and I'm sure there must be an ulterior reason for it.

"Sisi, Sisi," he tsks at me, stooping down so that our faces are on the same level, "sometimes your intuition amazes me," he says, the intensity in his eyes making me shiver. "You might be right, but then you might be wrong too," he jokes, his lips pulling up in a lopsided smile.

So many masks, so many faces. When will I ever truly know him?

I shake my head at him, my expression telling him that I'm on to him. But just as I look into his eyes for any sign of vulnerability, his features become grave, his hand catching me by the throat, his fingers massaging my pulse.

"Sometimes," he leans forward, whispering in my ear, "ignorance is bliss, Sisi."

"And knowledge is power," I reply, watching a myriad of emotions filter over his face, eventually settling on fake joviality. His smile widens as his lips brush over mine.

"Knowledge is also damnation," he replies, his voice deep with an underlying hint of threat.

"Aren't we already damned?" I ask, bringing my hand up and caressing his cheek.

He doesn't reply, his eyes pinning me to the spot, his touch making me his prisoner. Even the boisterous sounds surrounding us fade away as we gaze at each other, so close yet so far away.

And just as it started, everything is over. His hands off me, he settles me next to him, turning his attention to the stage and the continued entertainment.

We'd been so in sync not too long ago, and that intimacy we'd just shared had made me think we'd become... more. A first for both of us, I'd really thought that in that moment he was irrevocably mine.

I slip my hand into his, threading our fingers together, and for the first time, the coldness of his skin seems to seep into mine. He's like a marble sculpture looming over mere mortals, his presence imposing and awe-inspiring.

Looking at his profile, I have to wonder if this man can truly belong to one person. He's so raw, so barely contained, that sometimes I feel he might overwhelm me. He's full of wicked charm and sinister intentions—a deadly combination both to my body and my heart.

But why is it that I'm so drawn to him? So taken by this inexplicable darkness that lies just beneath the surface, waiting to engulf me whole? Why do I crave him like an addict craves his next fix? Because I can barely go through the day when he's not with me.

In such a short time, I've become so dependent on his presence, so used to the warmth of his skin on mine, that I don't know what I'd do if he suddenly disappeared.

I want him.

For the first time in my life, I'll let myself be greedy. I want the bad and the good. I want everything.

The noise coming from the stage brings me back to reality, and I shake myself from my musings.

Five almost naked women take the stage just as the music changes from lively to seductive. For a second, I'm confused, since the atmosphere looks identical to the one at the bar. Mauro, though, is quick to explain what's going to happen.

All five girls are available for one round, and each will be bid on individually.

"One round?" I ask, confused at the terminology, and Vlad grimaces.

One after another, the girls are auctioned to someone in the crowd. When the fifth one's been called, all the men who won make their way to the stage, slapping the women around and tearing the clothes off their bodies.

"What." I frown, but it's soon clear what one round meant.

The men are quick to unzip their pants, and that's the last thing I see as Vlad suddenly twists me in front of him, blocking my view of the stage.

"Don't watch," he whispers, holding me tightly.

"Why? Isn't that the whole point of us being here?"

"I don't want you watching naked men." He tips my chin up, ensuring I look into his eyes. "I want you to *only* see me." He smiles. "You're not the only one with the jealous streak," he jokes.

Warmth unfurls inside my body at his pronouncement.

"Is that so?" I let my hands trail up his muscular arms, feeling the tension bubbling under his skin.

He catches my errant hands, bringing them to his mouth, his teeth nibbling at my fingers.

The volume of the music decreases, moans and shrieks resounding in the room.

"I'm the only man you can look at," his tongue does wicked things to my fingers, and my breath hitches every time he sucks the tips into his mouth, "the only one you can touch..." He trails his lips over my wrist, right above the pulse point, "The only one you can fuck."

Words fail me as I become lost in his seductive gaze. How is it that he can be so detached one moment, but so suave the next?

"Will you... keep me?" I ask, my voice small. For the first time, I'm asking what I've wanted to know from the very beginning.

One arm tightens around my waist as he lowers his mouth to my ear.

"Keep you? You're mine, Sisi. You go where I go, in Hell or beyond." I feel him smile against my skin. "Dead or alive," he says and chills spread across my skin. "Even if I have to kill you myself."

"As long as you never abandon me." I lean back so he can see the seriousness in my gaze. "I'm yours. Dead or alive." I must be insane to agree to such a thing, but for him, I'd do just about anything.

"I'm glad we're on the same page." He smirks, toying with a long strand of hair. "Because I'd miss your lovely heartbeat."

"You'd kill me if I left you?"

He doesn't answer, his smile wide.

Only when we hear Mauro's voice announcing the next event does Vlad let me turn around, keeping a possessive arm around me.

As everyone stops at the bar at the other end of the room for refreshments, we're invited by one of the employees to follow him to get to Seth.

I hold on to Vlad as we go down some dimly lit corridor before we stop in front of a row of cages.

"Lord," I whisper when I see eyes glinting in the darkness of the room, all curious and full of pain. I'm momentarily struck by what I'm seeing, and Vlad tugs me forward, shaking his head at me.

The employee opens one of the cages to reveal Seth, already dressed in a clean shirt and pants, his gaze empty and numb as he glances at us.

"This is your controller." The man gives Vlad a tiny device, explaining that Seth has a chip implanted in his brain, and the controller zaps him into obedience.

"I'll leave you to get acquainted. Ten more minutes until

the main event." The man winks. "You don't want to be late for the fun." He laughs as he steps away.

Vlad quietly assesses Seth, moving around in a circle as he studies his form.

"You'll do," he declares, pleased with himself.

So far Seth has not reacted to anything, not even to his own sale. He's just looking blankly in the distance.

Vlad's eyebrows knit together as he notices the same thing — Seth is motionless.

"Well, hello to you too." He waves a hand in front of him.

No reaction.

"Cat got your tongue?" Vlad chuckles, taking out the remote and studying it. "I wonder what would happen if I clicked this button," he intones, his fingers gliding around the smooth surface of the controller.

"You know, I've always had an obsession with buttons. And I've never resisted temptation before," he notes just as he's about to push the button.

Seth's good eye moves toward Vlad in his first reaction since we got here.

"Oh, great. For a moment I thought you were a robot. Good to know you're human." Vlad beams at him, taking two steps until he's in front of Seth.

Taking his hand, he places the controller in it. Seth frowns, daring to look down at the device in his palm.

"Here's how this is going to go. You're free to do as you please. You've more than earned that right. I don't know how you ended up here, or what happened in your past, and frankly I don't really care."

Seth tilts his head at Vlad, narrowing his eyes at him as if he doesn't understand what he's saying.

"Maybe he doesn't speak English," I nudge Vlad.

"He does, don't you boy?"

Seth moves his head to the right, as if he's finally paying attention to Vlad.

"I have an offer for you. I'd like to give you a job. Again, no strings attached. You're free if you want to leave, but I could use someone with your skill. I'll pay you and give you a place to live. You will act as my bodyguard, of sorts. Not too hard, if I do say so myself." Vlad preens, looking at me for confirmation.

I roll my eyes at what can only be the beginning of a dramatic performance.

"I don't require much of your time, and you will be fairly compensated." Vlad goes on about the benefits of working for him, making himself out to be some sort of spoiled prince who needs constant monitoring.

I guess in another life, maybe. A smile pulls at my lips as I watch Vlad try his best to convince Seth to come work for him.

I can't believe he's paid ten million dollars and he's setting him free. A new respect for him blossoms in my chest as I see him try to offer Seth a fair chance at living.

Vlad's speech ends, but there's still no reply from Seth.

"Well." Vlad's shoulders sag for dramatic effect. "I tried," he says with a shrug, grabbing my hand and turning toward the exit.

Out of nowhere, Seth's hand is on Vlad's shoulder as he stops him. Opening his mouth, he points to his tongue... or what's left of it.

"So cat did get your tongue," Vlad jokes, quickly sobering up and handing Seth his phone to type up a reply.

He's quick to write something, and Vlad's expression tells me it's a positive answer.

"What does it say?" I ask, and he just shows me the phone.

Help me get revenge and you have a deal.

"Welcome aboard, Seth." Vlad pats his back, and I'm once more intrigued about Vlad's intentions.

* * *

B ack in the arena, the main event is about to start as Vlad and I resume our places. Everyone is looking at us askance as Seth hulks in the background, situating himself behind us, his good eye scanning the crowd.

Mauro is back on stage, introducing the event as multiple people come to bring different props.

"The moment you've all been waiting for is here." He pauses, looking around to increase anticipation. "No doubt, most of you have submitted requests and are eagerly awaiting to get your hands on the prize. But just like every time, your request will be publicly shared, and everyone will have a chance to bid. The more unusual, the more money you'll have to spend." He chuckles, and the crowd seems incensed.

Still, a few smug people nod their heads, no doubt sure they will be able to secure their order.

"So what is it? Just people?" I lean in to ask Vlad.

He'd given me a rundown of the club, but he hadn't told me any details.

"You heard him. Unusual people," he replies, his gaze intent on the stage.

Mauro introduces the first person up for auction—a virgin Kumari. A young girl dressed in ostentatious clothes and with her face painted in a combination of red and black is ushered in. Four people are carrying her in on a throne, settling her in the middle of the stage.

"Kumari?"

Vlad's jaw is ticking as he looks upon the ongoing auction.

"Kumari is a Nepalese tradition that uses young girls to embody a living goddess. They can only fulfill the role, though, until they reach puberty," he explains and my eyes widen with horror.

"You mean..."

"Yes. Some people probably think they will get some divine powers if they fuck a child." He shakes his head in disgust.

"Can't we do something?" I whisper, looking between him and the stage.

The girl looks dazed as she keeps herself unmoving on the throne, showing absolutely no fear for what will no doubt happen to her.

"We can," Vlad replies, and I breathe in, relieved. "But we won't."

I frown at him. "What do you mean we won't?"

"Sisi," he starts, his eyes still glued on the stage. "There will be more girls like her. More people that need help. We can't possibly save everyone."

"But we can try," I say weakly.

"Hell Girl." He turns to me, the back of his hand tracing my cheek. "I didn't realize you had a heart," he comments ironically, no doubt trying to take my mind off what's happening.

"And I didn't realize you had none," I retort, my gaze accusatory.

"A little too late for that realization." He tsks at me, coming closer to whisper in my ear. "I told you once, Sisi. Don't make me into something I'm not. I'm not kind, nor gentle, and I'm *definitely* not a good guy."

"But Seth..."

"Nothing I do is without a purpose," he interrupts me. "Don't ever misconstrue my actions for kindness. It will only get you hurt," he says, and it's like I don't recognize him anymore.

"Then what about me? What's my purpose?" I ask, suddenly afraid of the change in him. It's funny how he never scares me when he's at his most violent, but when I sense this apathy coming from him, I get the urge to run as far away as I can.

His eyes are emotionless as he studies me, almost put off by my question.

"You're mine," he replies. "That's it."

He promptly ends the conversation as he turns his attention toward the stage where a winning bid had been chosen.

A few more rounds of people with disabilities, or people with a certain rare blood type, and I'm already dreading everything about this.

I know what it's like to be stripped of your freedom. But I can't imagine what these people must be going through, knowing there's simply no way out. Just pain... and abuse.

Vlad explained that a lot of the time, these people are used for organ transplants if they are a match, and most often medical files are hacked and people hunted for this particular reason. It's simply a black market for humans.

The next person is brought in. Dressed entirely in black, it only serves to emphasize the paleness of his skin, the whiteness of his hair.

"What's wrong with him?" I blurt out when I see him stumbling around.

"He has a genetic condition called albinism. His body doesn't produce melanin, so he lacks color," Vlad starts telling me about the biology behind the disorder. "You should look away, Sisi," he tells me, tugging me to his side, ready to shield me.

"Why?"

"It's likely going to get brutal." He purses his lips. "Albino people are usually sought after for one thing," he says, and right at that moment, the man's arm is strapped to a table, another man joining them on the stage and wielding a huge blade.

"Last chance," Vlad whispers, but I shake my head.

I need to see this. I *want* to see just how fucked up this world is. In my naivete, I'd thought I'd endured the worst at Sacre Coeur, but I'm slowly finding out that life outside of the convent's walls isn't any less brutal.

In fact, this is downright atrocious.

His arm around me, I can tell he's trying to comfort me, especially as the blade falls upon the albino's arm, slicing it at the elbow.

A bloodcurdling scream erupts in the air and people are cheering on, everyone already shouting exorbitant amounts.

The hand is taken from the albino and placed in a pot.

"You don't mean they..." I'm shocked as I see them cook the arm on a stove.

"Albino limbs are used in witchcraft. A lot of superstitious people believe that a potion made from albino flesh will give them prosperity," Vlad speaks, and I watch stupefied as they do just that, preparing a live potion for whoever will spend millions on it.

"God," I whisper.

"You should have looked away, Sisi."

"No. This is the reality we live in. I *need* to see."

The first pot is auctioned for two million, with three more pots prepared from the other arm and his two legs. The screams continue as two men cut his legs using a saw. The poor man hasn't even been given anything for the pain, and the crowd seems to cheer at his continued screams. As the bone gives way, blood slowly starts to flow onto the floor, before suddenly gushing in rivulets as they take away the limbs.

His expression is half-closed, the pain too much. I have to wonder how much longer he's going to live.

Looking around, everyone is excited to watch this inhumane handling of a person. Someone even shouts to cut the head too. I suddenly realize just how deep the depravity lies, and that in a way, the outside world functions just like Sacre Coeur.

Eat or be eaten.

There are only two choices. Be the victim, or the assailant.

One glance at Vlad and I see him avert his gaze from the bloody show in front of us. The stage is already red as most of the blood has drained from the man's body. Vlad's shoulders are shaking slightly as he struggles for a modicum of control.

"Are you okay?" I turn to him, noticing the paleness of his features and the strain in his jaw. He's close to snapping. I can feel it.

He gives me a brisk nod, but he looks anything but okay. Grabbing his face in my hands, I raise myself on my tip-toes, turning him away from the bloody spectacle. I lean in until my lips meet his.

22

SISI

H is eyes are unfocused as he holds himself still, and the scene from the restaurant replays in my mind.

"I'm here," I speak against his lips. "Everything is okay," I brush my lips back and forth on him, teasing him with the barest of contact. "I have you."

He slowly starts reacting, parting his lips under mine, allowing me to explore the depths of his mouth.

What starts as a tentative but sensuous kiss soon turns into a hungry and heated one as he brings me flush against his body, his mouth opening on top of mine to devour me. He's already hard, and a thrill goes down my body at being able to awaken this reaction from him.

His mouth leaves my lips as he starts trailing small kisses down my neck, sucking on the skin at the junction between my neck and my collarbone, his teeth scraping the surface.

"I'm here," I repeat as I see him slowly come down from his crisis, his pupils dilated, his entire body full of unreleased tension.

"God, Sisi," he groans, holding me closer to his chest as

he nuzzles his head over my heart. "Thank you," he breathes deeply—in and out. "Thank you," he repeats.

A smile pulls at my lips as I see the color come back into his cheeks.

"I think I know my purpose," I say cheekily, almost lost in those black eyes of his.

"Do you?" he asks, his voice dangerously sinful.

"I ground you," I reply, pleased with the discovery. Because if I do, then he'll never discard me. He'll *always* need me.

A sad smile plays at his lips as he shakes his head. "You don't just ground me, Sisi. You make me fucking human."

I soak in the praise, incredibly happy at the prospect of being indispensable to him.

Once Vlad is under control, we turn our attention back to the stage as more and more weird bids take place. A pair of conjoined twins and some people with incredibly rare disorders are rushed to the stage, paraded in front of everyone and sold for millions.

It's all incredibly eye-opening, and a pattern soon emerges.

Power. Control.

All these people are weaker and therefore easier to control. And they are merely used for sick bastards to get their daily ego boost.

Just as I think I've seen it all, a man holding a monkey on a leash struts onto the stage presenting it to the world.

"Is that..." My mouth is hanging open in shock.

The monkey is completely hairless, wearing a two-piece bikini and a wig, her entire face rouged up in a grotesque painting.

"Why would a monkey..." I trail off, simply speechless.

"It's an ape," Vlad corrects, looking quite uncomfortable,

"an orangutan specifically. And it seems that someone around here is into non-human partners," he adds drily.

"You mean someone wants to fuck an orangutan?" I ask, stupefied.

"Don't be surprised, Sisi. Humans are degenerate beings. And sadly, what you've seen tonight is only the tip of the iceberg. As long as you have money, you can afford anything... and anyone."

"Have you ever..." I inquire tentatively, afraid of the answer.

"Hell no!" His answer is immediate and vehement. "Don't get me wrong, I cater to a different type of vice, but after what happened to my sisters, I could never stomach human trafficking. I'll be honest, it's one of the most lucrative industries, since humans have an almost unlimited capacity for labor and diversity of use. It's really the best resource out there if you want to get rich," he explains, and I sigh in relief.

This is exactly what I love about him.

He's an unapologetic bad guy, but his moral compass is just uniquely skewed. There's no right or wrong for him. But there is fair and unfair.

"You surprise me sometimes."

"Why? Because I don't deal in humans?" he jokes. "Don't worry, I do a lot of other stuff that might be equally as bad *or* worse. Let's not forget that murder is my capital sin." He gives me his signature devilish smile, a small dimple forming in his right cheek.

"You can murder me anytime," I murmur, peering at him seductively from beneath my lashes.

"Hell Girl, you know *just* the way to a man's heart." He smiles, amused, kissing the top of my head and bringing me closer to him.

More people are brought to the stage, with Mauro listing

what makes them special, and I soon start tuning everything out. Vlad seems incredibly bored too as he taps his foot, glancing at his watch every now and then. Seth, on the other hand, has just stayed in the background, already taking his job as Vlad's bodyguard seriously.

Every time someone approached a little too closely, he would put a hand up and guide people to keep a distance. Vlad, of course, could not help but beam at Seth's actions, repeating that he'd made the right call.

"Last but not least, we have a very popular request. We've had multiple people inquire about this, so it's only fair to start the bidding at five million," Mauro speaks into the microphone, and the crowd is getting rowdy, some people saying it's too much for the start, while others are simply curious as to what type of merchandise could possibly be that expensive.

"A rare mutation in the amygdala that results in an unusual form of autism. Most prevalent in twins, you can already guess how hard it is to find this in the wild," Mauro jokes, and I feel Vlad tense next to me.

"But don't you worry. We've secured a pair of twins with these exact specifications. The first one we've found in the last five years," he says and people gasp, "yes gentlemen, it's that rare, and the reason we're starting at five million."

Mauro continues his speech, introducing the five-year-old twins, a brother and sister. They are steered toward the stage, their little faces scrunched up in confusion as they take in the crowd staring at them.

Angelic blond curls, both children look so innocent dressed all in white. They are holding hands as they take the stage, the girl getting shy and trying to hide behind her brother.

"Sweet Jesus and Mother of God," I hear Vlad mumble, for the first time using a religious appellation.

I turn to him to find him staring in awe at the twins, his eyes wide, his mouth agape.

"Vlad?" I call out his name, my hand reaching for his. "What's wrong?" I ask, seeing him so shaken.

"It can't be." He frowns, his brows pinched together as he tilts his head to the side, his eyes rapidly moving around and assessing his surroundings.

"What is it?" I repeat my question, but it's like he's not hearing me. His focus is solely on the stage and on the children trying to escape public scrutiny.

It's almost an eternity later that he finally replies.

"That mutation," he starts, his gaze shrewd, his features sharp. "That's what I have. What my sister and I had."

"Your twin sister?" He nods, releasing my hand and stepping forward in the crowd.

The bidding is already starting, and contrary to the initial disgruntled sounds, people seem quite enthusiastic to bid an entire fortune on the twins.

But why?

"Why?" I catch up with him, grabbing his hand and making him face me. "Why is this mutation so important?"

"Twenty million," someone calls out, and I gasp at the amount.

"Why?" Vlad chuckles, but his face is *not* smiling. "I have the same question. Why would someone pay so much for twins with a random mutation?"

"It doesn't seem random," I remark, since people wouldn't be so keen on acquiring the twins if it was just a fluke. "Does it give you superpowers, or what?" I crack a joke, but I realize my timing is off.

Vlad is *not* in a jovial mood. And as he follows the

bidding closely, he seems to become more tense, his muscles twitching, his fists furling and unfurling.

"Thirty," Mauro calls out. "Thirty once... thirty twice... Sold to number sixteen! Congratulations!" Mauro announces the winner, and I follow Vlad's gaze to a scrawny man lowering the paddle with number sixteen.

"Stay with her," he commands Seth, before he dashes to the crowd, quickly out of sight.

"What..." I whisper, my feet moving of their own accord as I try to follow, but Seth catches my arm, holding me back.

One look at him and he shakes his head, motioning me to stay put.

"For God's sake," I mutter under my breath, annoyed. Even so, I can't help but worry about Vlad. What does he think he's doing? Especially when he's very close to snapping. He's just recovered from a close call and now he's diving headfirst into another.

What if he snaps?

Lord, I don't want to imagine the carnage. And with this many people around, I don't want to think what might happen to Vlad if anyone tried to stop him.

Please come back... Don't do anything stupid.

I can only hope he's going to think this through. Whatever that mutation means and the fact that Vlad has it too must have triggered something in him.

I'm restless as I wait, my arms wrapped around my midriff as I scan the crowd for him. Finally, only when I see him head toward us can I sigh in relief.

"What were you thinking?" I run toward him, my hands wrapped in the material of his shirt.

"I got what we came for," he says, "information." He briefly winks at me before giving a nod to Seth.

"We need to go. Now. I just bribed an employee for the

contact information of whoever bought the twins. Imagine my *not* surprise when it turns out it's our Miles." He scowls, "So we need to act fast and follow his broker."

Taking my hand, we sneak back into the club, leaving through the main entrance to reach the parking spot.

"And now," Vlad says, stroking his chin. "Since we have an additional guest, the motorcycle is out of the question," he muses, his eyes lighting up as they move around the parking lot. "But that," he points to a big car, "is perfect."

He doesn't wait for me to reply, dashing to the car. Taking out his leather cut, he wraps it around his fist before he brings it down on the window, smashing it to pieces.

Recognizing that he's already planned the entire thing, I just wait while he finishes whatever he's doing.

Sneaking his hand inside, he effortlessly opens the door to the car, calling us to hop in.

"You're crazy," I mutter as I climb into the passenger seat, Seth taking the back one.

"We need to be fast, Hell Girl. I can't waste any time," he smirks, kicking the board of the car and grabbing onto the wires underneath.

"Do you know what you're doing?" I ask just as I see someone else exit the club, their eyes fixed on the car we're currently trying to steal.

"Maybe." He scrunches his nose, combing through the wires attentively.

"I think you *should*, because those people don't seem too friendly." I point to the three men who are already unholstering their guns and aiming toward us.

"Almost," Vlad mumbles, flinging the wires together until there's a spark. "There we go," he says, pleased with himself.

But just as the car purrs to life, the bullets start raining on us.

"Down!" Vlad shoves me down, my head hitting his lap. He's maneuvering the car around, putting it in reverse just as the bullets hit one window.

Pushing his foot on the accelerator, he successfully leaves the parking lot.

"What now?" I ask breathlessly when I finally come out for air. Seth is unbothered in the back, his gaze as empty as before.

Vlad, on the other hand, has a manic smile on his face as he speeds down the street.

"Now, we go to the back entrance and wait for the broker to leave with the twins," he answers, his voice full of enthusiasm.

"Then we just follow?"

He nods, his eyes gleaming as he steers the car toward a hidden spot a few blocks down. Parking just off the entrance, he stops the engine and we wait.

"Can you tell me more about this mutation?" I muster the courage to ask since he hadn't seemed very receptive the first time.

He leans back in his seat, his eyes on me.

"I don't know much about it, only that in my case it causes my emotions to be muted," he starts. "There's not much research on it, but the one doctor I've spoken to has noted that generally it affects areas of emotions and social interactions."

"Your emotions are muted?" I ask, blinking rapidly as I'm trying to digest the information.

Does that mean he has no feelings?

"Indeed." His lips widen in a smile that doesn't quite

reach his eyes. I'm just staring at him, every moment of our acquaintance replaying in my mind.

His learned behaviors and the social masks he dons. The wicked smile that he plasters on his face, so that everything he says is taken as a joke, even when it's the furthest thing from one. The way his words seem to amuse, but they *always* hide a double meaning unknown to anyone but him. The emptiness in his gaze that I notice in the rare unguarded moment, or the way his eyes rove around the room like a predator stalking his prey.

It all makes sense... And yet it doesn't.

Everything about him is so carefully crafted, so minutely sourced to portray only a certain image. But what about the real him? How many layers do I have to peel before I meet the real Vlad?

"Then *what* do you feel?" I don't want to know, yet I can't *not* know.

"The truth?" His mouth curves up and I nod.

"Nothing."

Nothing.

The word echoes in my brain, a sudden dizziness overtaking me.

"Nothing," I repeat numbly, the words sinking in and making my heart beat loudly in my chest, a small pain reverberating at the core of my being.

"I do get hungry, and thirsty, and," sparing a glance to Seth, he leans to whisper, "horny," before resuming his position, "but that's about it. I do feel want, but my desires are more egotistical than most."

"What do you mean?"

"I want something, I take it. Regardless of the consequences." He shrugs. "I've just learned how to play the system so that it doesn't seem that way."

"Is that right..." I try to work up a smile, but my entire body is rebelling.

"Of course, over the years I've managed to study social interactions, and I've perfected my approach to people. I'm not exactly a savage," he continues, not catching the way I'm just mechanically nodding. "I do have an honorary system of right and wrong that I've developed, and I always repay my dues in kind. See, I'm not that complicated. In fact, one might argue that having no emotions is freeing."

"I see," I reply vaguely, and he doesn't seem to notice the sudden change in my behavior.

Because with one word, he dashed all of my hopes.

"There he is," Vlad mentions, getting the car ready.

The man is leading the twins to a car, loading them in the back with two guards before getting behind the wheel.

When he drives off, Vlad follows.

My hands folded in my lap, I look out the window, blocking everything out.

He can't feel.

I've always wanted one thing. To be loved. Just once I wanted to be the most important person to someone, and just when I thought I might have found that, it's brutally taken from me.

God, how is any of this fair?

Maybe I should have second-guessed everything from the beginning. He is, after all, a remorseless killer. How could someone like that have any tender feelings? Or any feelings at all?

But I'd seen the way he treated me, the way he cared for me... like I was precious. It was the first time someone had given me that much consideration in my life and so I'd let myself believe that, maybe, he felt something for me.

He can't feel.

Tears burn behind my eyes as every fantasy I'd built in my mind is simply shattered.

We continue to follow the car for what seems like an eternity, Vlad taking the necessary measures, so that they don't see we are behind them. They pull into the back of an abandoned factory, and Vlad slows the car, parking it off the road.

"Odd," he notes, looking around the area, "I could have sworn these buildings were up for redevelopment."

Unbuckling his seat belt, he gets out of the car. I do the same, but when I try to open the door, Vlad stops me, pushing his hand against it.

"You stay here," he says, glancing at Seth, "it's not safe."

"It's not safe for you either," I protest, pushing against the door. "And you're not leaving Seth with me." I speak before he has the chance. "He can help you too, if anything happened inside," I point out.

"Yes, but I don't want *you* in danger," he sounds exasperated as he tries to keep me inside the car.

"I'm not letting you go alone. So decide quickly, because either way, I'm coming after you," I declare, folding my arms across my chest.

He might have no feelings, but I have plenty enough—for him.

He ponders it for a moment before he relents with a sigh, opening the door for me and helping me out.

"You stay next to me at all times," he whispers in my ear, his hand in mine.

It's in moments like this that I feel he might care. Why else would he be so careful with my safety?

Knowing I need my wits about me, I push my disappointment out of my mind, focusing instead on the situation at hand.

Seth trailing behind us, we enter the warehouse, finding the first level completely empty and dilapidated.

"Where could they have gone?" I ask, looking around bewildered at the unoccupied space.

"There must be something around here," Vlad muses out loud, scanning the surroundings. He walks around the walls, checking every crevice.

"They couldn't have just vanished," he murmurs as his hands feel for the concrete of the walls. "See this," he knocks on one side before moving a few feet to tap on another. "This is empty," he says, knocking again, a hollow sound answering back. "There must be an opening." He talks to himself as he feels around the surface of the wall.

Seth and I stay back, leaving Vlad to do his thing, since clearly he's got this.

"Here." He moves a stone, and a fissure appears around the wall as a piece of it is dislodged, protruding on the outside. Grabbing on to it, Vlad yanks it toward him to reveal a door.

"Interesting," he mutters, waving us over.

Grabbing my hand once more, we walk inside the tunnel.

It doesn't take us long to reach another room, light filtering into the tunnel and confirming that the factory is in fact used by someone.

"Shh," Vlad raises his hand to his lips as he takes a step forward, voices resounding from the other room.

"We need to keep this under wraps for as long as we can," one man says.

"He needs the kids pronto," another replies, "the other ones are already done for. The boy died and the girl is broken. He doesn't think he can salvage anything, and the bitch can't get pregnant anymore."

"What do you expect, Glen? He's been using her as a

broodmare for too long. I'm surprised she's lasted until now." He sighs, and I can hear someone pacing around.

"You know how rare this is. He's spent decades looking for more subjects and he can barely find some every few years. Not even then. We're talking about revolutionizing warfare, Patrick. It's hard now, but in a few years when his research is complete, countries will clamor for his studies."

"I don't like this. He's taking too many risks."

"Your job isn't to like this. Just do your tasks. I need a full physical on the twins, and let me know if there's anything salvageable from the others. Sometimes he likes to keep the organs," Glen says, and it's clear he's the one in charge.

"All right," Patrick relents, and then we hear more shuffling.

Vlad is tense as he follows the conversation closely. He turns toward me, placing my hand on the knife he'd hidden in the back of my trousers. I nod at him, and watch as he takes out his own knives, offering some to Seth. He firmly shakes his head, pointing to his arms and fists.

Vlad raises an eyebrow at him, but eventually shrugs it off with a smile.

Putting three fingers up, he slowly lowers each, giving us the signal when to go inside the room. He's the first to burst inside, immediately immobilizing one man, while nodding to Seth to do the same to the other.

I look between the two of them, noticing one is dressed in a white gown, while the other has a gray suit on.

"I'm guessing you're Patrick." Vlad points to the man in white that's currently struggling in Seth's hold. "And you're Glen." He gives him a nudge, his knees buckling and hitting the floor.

"Who... who are you?" Glen cries out in distress, looking between Vlad and Seth.

"Depending on your answers..." Vlad trails off, smiling from ear to ear before adding, "The devil or..." He purses his lips, looking undecided, "The devil."

"I didn't do anything!" Patrick is quick to profess his innocence. "They're paying me. I'm just doing my job. Please... I have a family..."

Vlad tsks at him. "And I don't care. Save your breath." He rolls his eyes at him before turning to Glen. "Now, where are the twins?"

He's trembling from head to toe, and it only seems to get worse as Vlad's patience is nearing its end.

"You can't take them," he whines, trying to move out of his hold. Vlad has a bored expression on his face as he takes out one knife, playing with it along Glen's throat.

"And you're out of your depth here, *Glen*," Vlad starts, trailing the knife toward his face. "Let me tell you how this is going to go. You tell me where the twins are, and then you answer my questions about your boss, Miles."

Glen pales when he hears Miles' name, and Vlad merely smiles at him. "If you cooperate, I will kill you fast. If you don't, then I'll just have to take out a body part at a time."

Looking up, he addresses Patrick. "You're a doc, aren't you?" The man slowly nods, or as much as he can, given Seth's firm grip. "Good. Why don't you tell my pal, Glen, how painful puncturing the eardrum is." Vlad chuckles as he places the tip of the knife right over Glen's ear. "I don't hear you," he speaks in a sing-song voice when Patrick doesn't immediately reply.

"It's very... very," he gulps down, "painful."

"There you have it, Glen! A professional opinion."

"I can't tell you!" he exclaims. "He'll kill me," he cries out, tears gathering at the corners of his eyes.

"Glen, Glen." Vlad shakes his head at him. "A little weak,

aren't we?" With a disappointed sigh, Vlad jabs the sharp point of the knife into Glen's ear. His eyes widen, his mouth open in shock as a shrill escapes his lips.

"I'll tell you! I'll tell you!" he yells just as blood pours out of his ear. "They're in the exam room. Last... last door," he breathes out, his entire body racked by tremors.

"Sisi, can you grab the twins?" Vlad asks and I nod, quickly moving in the direction Glen had indicated and leaving Vlad to interrogate them further.

I spot the door, and as I walk toward it I hear more screams, evidence that Glen and Patrick might not have been too forthcoming with the rest of their answers.

And as I enter the room, I realize that nothing Vlad could do to those men could make up for the horror I'm seeing.

The twins are huddled together in a corner, holding on to each other for warmth. In the middle of the room there are two surgical beds, each with an inhabitant on them.

Dead.

I tentatively near the beds, and I have to take a deep breath at the sight. Two children, both of them cut from neck to pelvis, their chest cavities exposed, their organs placed in some containers next to them. It seems to be an autopsy room of sorts, and my heart breaks even further when I hear a small voice.

"Don't look."

Turning back, I see the little boy shielding his sister, thrusting her behind him as he addresses me.

"Hi," I offer tentatively, not knowing how to comfort them or get them to trust me.

The boy looks at me suspiciously.

"Who are you?" He narrows his eyes at me, one arm spread out to keep his sister in the back.

"I'm here to take you home," I say, watching him scrunch

his nose at me, assessing me from head to toe. "Do you want to go home?"

For a moment, there's no reply. But then, I hear the soft voice of a girl as she utters a single "Yes."

"Let me take you home." I take a step toward them. "I promise I'll get you home." I crouch down in front of them when I'm about a step away, giving them a tremulous smile and hoping they will feel comfortable trusting me.

"You promise?" the girl asks again, and her brother pushes her back.

"Stop, Leila," he hisses at her.

"It's okay. It's fine to be suspicious, especially after what happened to you. But my friend and I were there, and we saw you get taken. We followed you here and we want to help you get back to your families." I do my best to explain.

"Please, Leo," the girl speaks, pinching her brother, "let's go home."

Leo seems unsure as he gazes between me and his sister, but seeing Leila's sad expression seems to make him reconsider his stance.

"Fine." He takes a step toward me, still keeping his sister behind.

I reach out to take his hand, surprised when he allows that.

"It's going to be okay," I repeat, hoping my promise won't be in vain.

We walk back to where Vlad and Seth are, and Glen is already dead, his skull half opened, his brain visible through bone cracks.

I keep the kids behind, so they don't see the slaughter, but given the abundance of blood now coating the floor, I can't help myself as I check up on Vlad.

"Are you okay?" I call out, and he whips his head up

suddenly, as if he hadn't been aware of my presence before. He gives me a brisk nod, his foot shooting out to kick Glen's corpse to the ground before focusing on Patrick.

"Seth, why don't you take the kids to the car," Vlad says absentmindedly as he grabs onto Patrick, flinging him down to the floor.

Seth immediately complies, coming to my side and swiftly taking one kid in each arm. The twins are too in awe of Seth's size and appearance to protest, looking at him as if they'd never seen a human before.

He gives me a nod before heading back out with the kids.

"There were two children's bodies in the room. Autopsies," I tell Vlad as I join his side.

"Doc's work, no wonder," he comments, his eyes fixed on Patrick.

"You should have let me take the kids to the car. If they get restless or ask questions, Seth can't answer them."

"I should have," he answers vaguely, "but you stick by my side. Always."

Grabbing Patrick by the nape, he drags him toward the autopsy room. "Now, let's evaluate your skill, doc," he says, signaling me to follow him.

Vlad kicks the door open, throwing Patrick in the middle of the room as he assesses his surroundings.

"Talk!" he commands him, and I can tell he's no longer in the mood for jokes.

His lip curls up in distaste as he surveys the carcasses of the children, and his arm shoots out, choking Patrick and lifting him in the air.

"I said talk," Vlad enunciates again, slamming him onto one of the tables. His hand shifts to his nape as he pushes his head down in the open chest cavity of one child.

"See, this is your brilliant work. How does it look up

close and personal?" he asks, and Patrick makes choking sounds, his arms flailing around.

I'm so sickened by what they're doing to children, that I can only hope Vlad will give him his due. My eyes trail over the utensils, taking some and placing them next to Vlad.

"He should feel it on his own skin," I nod toward Patrick, a sick desire taking shape inside of me. I want to see him suffer for what he's done. Even more than Glen, I want to see him beg for his life while Vlad opens him up like a lab rat.

"A girl after my own taste." Vlad smiles at me, sending me an airy kiss before suddenly becoming serious again, yanking Patrick out of the cavity. He breathes hard, gasping for air, his eyes wide with horror as he looks between us.

"Talk or..."

"I just do what I'm paid to do!" he exclaims, close to tears.

"And that is?"

"They bring me people... kids... and I do physical exams on them, if they are alive. If they are dead..." he trails off, looking at the corpses on the table, "I perform autopsies."

"Why? What is Miles looking for?"

"Failure," Patrick says in a low voice.

"Failure?" I repeat out loud, frowning at his choice of words.

"He wants to know why his experiments failed," Patrick explains.

"What experiments?"

"I can't..." he says, moving wildly in Vlad's arms. He's becoming even more anxious the more Vlad probes about Miles.

Out of nowhere, he pushes his feet on a bed, briefly escaping Vlad's hold. Instead of running, though, he reaches for the instruments, taking a scalpel and holding it to his neck.

"My family..." He shakes his head, taking a few steps back until he hits a counter. One hand on the scalpel, the other searches under the table for something. "I'm sorry," he mouths right before plunging the scalpel into his own neck, blood gushing freely, his eyes blank and lifeless as he hits the floor.

At the same time, an alarm sounds in the building, accompanied by a robotic voice doing a countdown.

Vlad's eyes widen and he immediately reaches for me, taking me in his arms as he starts running.

"Hold tight," he whispers in my hair as he runs for the tunnel, barely reaching it before a huge explosion propels us both forward.

Cradling me to his chest, he tries to take the brunt of the fall, but somehow I feel a pain in my temple before everything fades away.

23
VLAD

"Sisi," I groan as I roll over, taking her with me in my arms.

Fucking Patrick. I hadn't pegged him for a loyal one. In fact, I'd have thought he would be the weakest link between the two. I certainly hadn't thought the lab would have a self-destruct mode either. And now that makes me even more curious about what they're hiding.

I get into a sitting position, annoyed at the destruction around us.

At least we got out in time.

"Sisi." I shake her, but she's not reacting.

Frowning, I drag her to my lap, using my hands to check her body for wounds.

"Sisi, it's not funny," I add, just in case she thought to prank me.

Just then, my hand brushes across her forehead, and a small rivulet of blood starts flowing down her temple, coating my fingers in the process.

My eyes become fixated on the shade of red, of her blood,

my lids flutter closed as I bring my fingers to my mouth, tasting it.

Fuck.

I already feel myself slipping, the allure of the blood almost too much.

More...

My hands ball into fists as I try to resist, focusing instead on the still breathing human in my arms.

Focus.

"Sisi?" My voice trembles as I shake her, trying to get her to react.

Because if I lose it, she's the only one who can bring me back... the only one.

I attempt to regulate my breath, all the while feeling her body for more injuries. A head wound could prove dangerous. Information filters into my brain, and I focus on that. Facts are safe, science is safe.

Another deep breath.

Quickly taking my phone from my pocket, I activate the flash. Then I lift one lid, placing the light into her eye and watching it constrict when it meets the light. For the first time, as if bothered by the insistent light, she starts moving in my arms, a low moan escaping her lips.

I sigh in relief.

She's fine.

"Sisi," I use a gentler tone as I bring my fingers to her face, stroking her cheek and avoiding staring at the enticing blood staining her pale features.

God, but it's like a feast for a starving man.

"What..." she whispers, whimpering in pain as she brings her face to my shirt.

I don't waste any time in tugging her to my chest, holding the entire weight of her body as I stand up. I'm a little shaky, probably from the adrenaline overload, but right now the most important thing is to get Sisi back to my house and get her the care she needs.

I all but sprint to the car, where Seth is already outside, waiting. Seeing Sisi in my arms, he looks at me questioningly.

"She'll be fine," I tell him, refusing to believe she will be anything but okay.

The kids are quiet in the back as I load Sisi next to them, both looking at her with worry in their eyes. Considering they share the same condition as Vanya and I, they certainly look more empathetic than we'd ever been.

Seth buckled in the seat next to me, I'm ready to go.

I drive back to the compound in record time, ordering Maxim to get Seth settled in and handing the kids over to his wife, who is the only female living here and who might know how to behave with children.

When everyone has something to do, I call Sasha, our resident doctor, to look at Sisi's injury.

Getting to my room, I take off her clothes, dressing her in one of my shirts, so that she's more comfortable. Laying her on the bed, I quickly get a wet towel from the bathroom and wash her wound.

"Can you hear me, Hell Girl?" I ask, gently wiping the blood off her face.

"Mmm," She releases a sound low in her throat, turning around in bed as if she can't find a comfortable position. "What happened?" She yawns, slowly opening her eyes to peer at me.

I've always marveled at the color of her eyes, a light amber that swirls with dark specks. They are simply fascinating, and sometimes I find myself lost in them, almost as if I were lost in the redness of blood. The world falls away as she turns her gaze to me, batting those pretty eyelashes and making me lose my mind.

Literally.

As someone who prides himself on his keen intellect, the fact that I can so easily become mindless in her presence is a little disturbing.

"There was an explosion," I explain what happened, and that we are currently in my room.

She's a little disoriented as she looks around, raising herself to her elbows to have a sip of water.

Luckily, Sasha is right on time as he comes in and performs a checkup, assuring me her wound is nothing serious and that I should just let her rest, but monitor her throughout the night. Thanking him, I turn back to Sisi, who is frowning in confusion.

"I need to get home," she mumbles, scrambling out of bed and walking toward the door.

"No, you don't." I stop her, placing my hands on her shoulders to steady her.

"But..." She frowns, still looking out of it.

"I'll handle it," I tell her, already brainstorming ways to ensure no one will find out she's missing. "You know you can trust me, Hell Girl." I wink at her, attempting some light-heartedness.

"Okay." She nods, swaying a little on her feet.

"I got you." I swoop her up into my arms, returning her to bed and drawing the blanket up over her body.

"The kids?" she asks as she turns to her side, placing her hands under her head.

"They are fine. Seth too," I reply, brushing her hair off her face.

Sasha had applied a band-aid over the gash above her temple.

"Does it hurt?" I ask as I graze my hand over the gauze. She shakes her head slightly, letting out a big yawn.

"I feel tired," she whispers, looking worn out.

"Rest," I say, caressing her forehead, "I'll watch over you."

"Can you..." She trails off, and I swear I detect a blush creep up her cheeks. "Can you," she clears her throat, "get in bed with me?"

"You want me to get in bed with you?" A smile spreads over my face. "It must be my magnetic charisma that charms even the convalescent," I barely finish the phrase as her hands swat me.

"Fine, then don't." She pouts at me, moving to turn with her back to me.

"No, no," I call out, quickly shedding my clothes and getting into bed with her. "You're not getting rid of me, Hell Girl," I say as I move closer to her.

Her lips pull up into a smile as she swings an arm over my midriff, placing her head on my shoulder and giving me a quick kiss.

"Did you find what you wanted today?" she asks.

Putting my arm around her back, I tug her into me, resting my chin on top of her head.

"I don't know," I admit truthfully.

Certainly, I'd found out *something*. But it had only confused me more. I'll need more time to put all the pieces together to get the full picture.

"One thing is for sure. These people are more powerful than I previously gave them credit for. At least now I know the truth about why Vanya and I were taken when we were little."

"Your condition," Sisi adds, and I nod.

"If only I could remember what happened in those years... I'd have more insight into how these people operate, because it's clear that they perform experiments on people."

"Do you..." She starts, grimacing, "Do you think they did that to you too?"

"If they did, I don't remember. Maybe it was too horrific and I just blocked it all out," I joke, but Sisi doesn't find it funny.

"Don't..." She raises her head to look me in the eye. "It's not funny that they might have..." She trails off as she traces the raised ridges on my stomach.

"God," she whispers, getting into a sitting position and spreading her hands over my chest. "This is why you have so many tattoos, isn't it?" She whips her head up, her gaze accusatory. "My God, there are so many..." She shakes her head as she keeps on bumping into scar after scar.

Long, jagged lines that feel like surgeon's sutures mar my entire torso. Before I covered them in ink, I'd looked like a Frankensteinian monster, body parts sewn together to give the appearance of something human, when intrinsically it was anything but. I still remember the glances of pity that would nevertheless transform to horror as people turned away from me in disgust.

Freak.

Misha's appellation might have been appropriate, since I wasn't just wrong on the inside. I was wrong on the outside, too.

I bring my hand over hers, stopping her.

"You're too smart for your own good, Hell Girl," I say, staring intently at her.

I don't want her to know that part of my life, just like I don't want her to look at me differently. I've always known what I am, but the prospect of her truly knowing too is unusually distressing.

And how she's managed to connect what she saw in that factory to the scars on my body is beyond me.

"It's true, isn't it?" she continues, her features filled with worry.

"Might be." I shrug. "I don't remember."

It's technically true, but for the first time, I find myself uncomfortable in my own skin. No one's ever seen or touched my scars besides Vanya. But seeing that she's just a figment of my imagination, I don't think she counts.

"Vlad, that's awful," she whispers, tears accumulating at the corners of her eyes.

I freeze, stunned as I see one tear make its way down her cheek.

"You..." I blink twice, unsure of what's happening. "You're crying," I say numbly, "for me..."

"Of course, you fool." She brings her fist down on my chest in a light punch. "How can I not when I just have to close my eyes and see the child you were and the things they must have done to you." She sniffles, and more tears fall down her cheeks.

"Sisi," I say her name, speechless for the first time.

No one's ever cried for me. No one's cared enough to.

I slowly bring my hands up, swiping her tears with my thumbs, simply floored that someone would cry for me.

"Don't, Sisi," I gruff out, "I'm not worth your tears," I tell her, tenderly stroking her cheeks.

Sometimes I'm more animal than human, and animals certainly don't deserve her misplaced emotions. They don't deserve anything.

"You." Her mouth opens in shock, her eyes wide with pain. "What are you talking about?" She shakes her head at me, covering my hand with hers and bringing it to her mouth.

"You are worth it." She lays a kiss onto my open palm. "You're worth it to me," she continues, and I can only stare at her, unable to cope with the responses she's coaxing out of me.

I wish I came with an instruction manual. Then I'd know how to react when this exquisite being decides to waste her energy on someone like me.

"You're worth it," she repeats, leaning forward to touch her lips to mine, brushing them back and forth over my skin. I can taste the saltiness of her tears, and they are imbued with a strange aroma, causing a tingling in my body.

Uncomfortable. It's out of my comfort zone.

"Sisi," I groan, but she just continues her ministrations, kissing my neck before going lower, to my chest. "What are you doing?"

"Showing you that you *are* worthy," she speaks against my skin, licking it once before blowing hot air and making me shiver.

She takes her time as she traces each scar, her lips the cure I didn't know I needed. And as they slide lower and lower, covering every inch of my skin, I can't ignore the way my entire being is responding to her.

She's pushing me into an unfamiliar corner, and for a second I feel trapped and overwhelmed by thousands of things all at once.

I can't do this.

Instead of dwelling on the other things she's making me feel, I simply focus on my body's response to hers, and the way only *she* can make me react.

"Not like this." I don't know where I find the strength to say it. Not when all my instincts are telling me to take her. Turn her on her back and fuck her until she's screaming bloody murder. Pump my cum into her and mark her as mine forever.

But I can't. Not yet.

"You deserve better than a simple roll in the hay," I tell her honestly, amazed at myself and the control I'm displaying. "When I finally fuck you, I want you to be at full capacity," I nibble at her lower lip, "so I can destroy you myself."

"Damn it, Vlad," she half-moans, wedging her wet pussy right on top of the head of my cock. I close my eyes, at war with myself. There's just some piece of fabric separating us, and the thought makes me groan out loud once more.

Who told me to be so fucking noble?

But the truth is that I know it would end me if I did something wrong and she'd never forgive me for it.

There's this urge inside of me to take her like an animal, mount her and fuck her like a beast. But if I give in... I'm scared she might turn away from me. Finally realize just how unnatural my desires and I are and leave me.

I can't risk that. I can't ever risk her shunning me. And if I have to deny myself, then so be it.

"So you're just going to leave me like this?" she whines, her hands splayed on my chest as she's moving up and down my shaft.

"How could I?" I smirk, trailing my hands down her body until I reach her panties. They're so thin, so fragile, that they give way with one snap of the fabric. When I find myself with unfettered access to her pussy, I simply can't help myself.

I lower my boxer briefs, releasing my stiff cock into Sisi's waiting hands as she strokes me, her thumb playing with the head. I'm already leaking, as I always do when she's so close to me. She swipes some of the moisture from my cock and brings it to her mouth, licking her fingers clean.

She's certainly lively for someone who was moaning in pain just a short while ago.

"I love your taste," she says enticingly, flicking her tongue over my lips in a brazen move. I open my mouth, catching it and sucking on it.

"My dirty little nun likes cock." I bite onto her tongue until I feel blood spurt into my mouth. Sisi doesn't pull away, her eyes glazed with arousal as she gives me a come-hither look, daring me to consume her. She glides her tongue over my teeth, luring me into deepening the kiss. And when I do, she returns the favor, taking my tongue and biting it down until my own blood fills her mouth.

"Yes," she breathes out, moaning into my mouth. "I'm your dirty little nun." She leans back to watch me with hooded eyes, the corner of her mouth stained with our combined blood, and for the first time, the red liquid makes me want to fuck, not kill.

"And what does that make me?" I ask cheekily, entranced by the way her features react to every touch.

"God," she replies, her eyes half-closed, "*my* God," she continues, her arms winding around my neck as she gives me full control over her mouth.

Ah, but how can I refuse that?

Holding her close, I devour her, exchanging blood in a dangerous kiss that has me teetering on the precipice. I reach for her ass and guide her over my shaft, her pussy lips spread to accommodate my length.

"And what do you do for your God, my dirty little nun?"

My hands on her ass cheeks, I knead them as she moves in circular motions over my erection, the head brushing over her entrance, the greedy bastard pushing forward as it tries to get past her barrier. She's so fucking wet that her pussy's sliding effortlessly over my cock. It would be so easy to slip inside...

"Pray," she cries out just as my cock glides over her clit, "worship, obey." Her words make me even harder, and it takes everything in me to stop myself from coming or fucking her until she's screaming my name.

Or both.

"Fuck yes." I move my lips lower over her throat, sucking on the pulse point. "Pray to me," I rasp, wanting to hear her soft voice beguiling me, asking me to fuck her into eternity and beyond.

And ah, but I would. I'd make a deal with the devil himself if I could tie her to me forever.

"Oh my dear God," she starts, a saucy grin on her face as she peers at me, "please suck on my breasts."

"You want me to suck on these pretty titties?" I ask, my hand coming up to cup them through the material of her shirt.

"Yes, please." She bats her eyelashes at me, the minx knowing fully well that I can't resist that trick.

I tug her shirt down, her breasts bouncing free and into my face. Leaning forward, I take a nipple into my mouth while my hand plays with the other.

"Vlad," she moans my name, increasing the friction as she takes her pleasure. I bite down on her nipple, and her orgasm hits, her entire body trembling, her pussy soaking my cock even more.

Her hands are clawing at my back, her nails already digging into my skin as she's tensing, her muscles spasming as she's riding her climax.

Taking advantage of her dazed state, I turn her on her back, her legs wide open, her pretty pussy greeting me nice and sated. Pushing her knees apart, I lean down, giving her a long swipe as I taste her release, sucking her clit in my mouth and making her come again.

Hands in my hair, she's tugging at my scalp as her thighs close around my head, her voice loud as she's screaming my name.

"Vlad," she whimpers, grabbing at my shoulders and dragging me up her body for a kiss, her hands reaching for my cock.

At this point, I'm so hard I'm almost bursting. I line my cock to her pussy, thrusting against her lips as I move my length up and down, her warm juices coating my shaft and making me groan at the sensation.

Skirting by her hole, I'm almost tempted to throw caution to the wind and just take her, but for the first time, I don't want to allow my selfish desires to ruin this experience for her.

Even though I'd give anything to have just the tip of my cock nestled inside her tight body...

"Fuck," I curse out, closing my eyes to regain some control over myself.

"Let me," she whispers, wrapping her hands around my cock as she jerks me off, moving up and down, her grip firm and tight. Her fingers work their magic as I simply close my eyes, giving in to the pleasure that only she can give me. My cum shoots in hot spurts on her stomach, my release unending as I struggle to find my breath.

"Hell Girl..." My eyes snap open to see her swirl my cum around on her stomach, coating her fingers in a thick layer before dipping them lower to her pussy. She plays with herself, her fingers brushing past her clit as she spreads my cum around her lips. Two digits go lower, pushing at her entrance as she presses my seed all the way inside.

"My greedy little nun," I rasp, unable to take my eyes off

the way her pussy is eating my cum, the white perfect against her glistening pink. Taking my fingers, she prompts me to do the same.

"I like yours better; they're bigger." She blushes, and I can only oblige.

Using two fingers, I press all my cum inside of her, swiping at her walls, the velvety feel of her channel only making my cock weep with envy. Slowly moving my fingers in and out, Sisi is soon moaning again, lifting her hips and widening her legs so I can fuck her better.

"That's... right there," she cries out as I stroke her deep inside, her walls immediately contracting around my fingers. "Yes, God!"

I collapse next to her, and she burrows closer, snuggling in the crook of my arm. Her fingers are back to tracing the surface of my chest, and my discomfort from earlier resurfaces. She's making my skin tingle with an awareness that wasn't there before, and I don't know if I like it. As she continues with her caresses, my breathing hitches, my mind going into overdrive. I start thinking of all the possibilities, all the things that *could* happen but *should not*.

"I'm going to take a shower," I blurt out, taking her hands off me and rising from the bed. "After that, I'll take you home," I say, not waiting for her reply as I head to the bathroom.

I spend some time under the shower, the water ice cold to calm my errant heart and bring some clarity into my turbulent mind. I don't like feeling like this... It's just like being on the cusp of an attack that never comes, my body primed for fight, my mind ready to slip.

But it doesn't.

I'm breaking down. There's no other explanation for it. My expiration date is nearing. I'd known for a long time that

I wasn't going to live forever, not with the way both body and mind betray me.

My limbs start trembling, from cold or residual adrenaline I don't know. I just recognize my own failing body as it seeks an equilibrium.

Human biology is so mind-blowing; it can immediately recognize foreign bodies and expel them, ensuring continuation of life. The entire purpose of one's body is to protect itself from the outside.

But what if the danger comes from the inside?

I am the foreign entity in my own body, and I can feel it trying to rebel against my presence, wrestling with my own conscience to throw me out.

I'm running out of time.

The realization is both sobering and, for the first time, saddening.

I need to get to Katya before anything happens to me. I need to punish Vanya's killer. And more than anything, I need more time with Sisi before I lose myself.

24

VLAD

I'm having problems concentrating throughout the day, my thoughts drifting back to Sisi. I'd managed to get her home before noon, and luckily no one had realized she was not in her room. She'd proceeded to tell me that Marcello and Catalina had been giving her a wide berth since they think she's having a hard time accommodating to life outside Sacre Coeur, so they've mostly left her to her own devices.

While her explanation had been satisfactory, I couldn't help but notice that she'd become slightly closed off, not meeting my eyes and not even offering to kiss me when I'd dropped her off.

She'd just looked at me blankly and said her goodbye, effectively kicking me out.

Did I do something?

I've been racking my brain the entire day, thinking that maybe I'd offended her somehow. I'd gone through every single interaction, cataloguing my replies and her reactions, and I'd found all to be satisfactory. Why, I'd made her come at least four times, and she'd looked perfectly sated.

Until she suddenly wasn't...

Maybe it's because I told her I'd get her home? Did she want to sleep with me in my bed? But she'd been the one to want to get home before anyone noticed her absence, so I really don't understand what I could have done to make her behave like this.

Sighing deeply, I close my computer and massage my temples. Since I'm unable to get any work done today, I might as well focus my efforts elsewhere.

A while later, I find myself at Marcello's house, paying him a short visit. He certainly seems surprised to see me, as he narrows his eyes at me, reluctantly inviting me into his office.

Ah, but I know exactly why he's giving me such a *warm* welcome. He thinks I'm a danger in his house, especially now that he has something to lose.

"Stop worrying that pretty head of yours," I drawl as I take a seat, "I'm not going to go on a killing spree anytime soon."

"Better safe than sorry," he mutters under his breath, and I roll my eyes.

"Marcello, Marcello, you wouldn't say we've been friends for more than two decades," I tsk at him.

"Friends?" He scoffs at me. "Is that what you call friends? Oh, sorry, you don't have any."

"Ah, 'cello," I bring my hand to my heart, "you wound me. You know how popular I am. I have to fend off wannabe friends with the end of my knife." I smile, and I notice his lips curling up too.

"And that's exactly why you have none. They all end up dead."

"Enough of that." I wave my hand. "I didn't come here to

squabble with you, no matter how fun it might be," I add, seeing his face relax slightly.

Marcello hasn't been the same in the last decade, and it might be odd, but sometimes I miss our times together in the past.

"What did you come here for? Do you have more information on the shipment?"

Some time back we'd both suffered some losses when some unknown culprit had decided to be smart and attack our shipments. Although I'd been rather angry that someone had dared that, and thereby ruining my mood, I'd quickly pushed it out of my mind since I had more important things to take care of. Marcello, though, is perpetually on guard since he thinks someone is targeting him and his wife.

"I might," I smirk, "but I'll need something from you," I add.

He regards me suspiciously, as he always does, even though over the years he's asked for my help on numerous occasions. For all his efforts to lead a life away from crime, he'd always find his way back to me, asking me to break the law for him.

"What is it?" he asks tersely.

"Nothing too much, old pal, I'm not about to ask for your firstborn," I watch his features draw up in pain, "but maybe I'll settle for your sister. She's quite a looker," I add, wanting to rile him a little.

"Stay away from my sister." He grits his teeth. "I mean it, Vlad. You don't go near Venezia or Assisi, or we'll have problems."

"Wow, big bro making an appearance. A little too late, don't you think?"

"Vlad." His nostrils flare, and I can tell I'm one step from going too far.

But who am I to resist?

"Marcello, really," I groan, "imagine us being a big happy family," I continue, but one look at Marcello's expression and I know I've taken it *slightly* too far.

"I'm serious, Vlad. Stay away from my sisters, or God help me, I *will* kill you." He clenches his jaw.

"You and your God," I sigh, resisting the urge to tell him his sister calls *me* her God. "Fine, I'll drop it. For now." I give him a smile, even though this just confirmed what I thought.

Marcello would never let me near Sisi. And that makes things a little complicated. Especially since I plan on tying her to me—one way or another. Alas, if I have to make another enemy in the interim, then so be it.

"Do you still have Valentino's things?" I finally get to the reason I'm here.

"What do you need?" He frowns.

"You may remember that twenty-something years ago Valentino was looking into a human trafficking ring when they came across me, or rather what was left of me." I give him a rueful smile. "I want to know if he had more information about that ring, and about a Project Humanitas."

"Project Humanitas?" He raises an eyebrow at me, getting up and heading to his file cabinet. "I remember seeing that name, let me see. But I should warn you, Tino left his affairs in a dissolute state. I doubt there's anything that might help in here. As for twenty years ago..." He trails off, looking pensive. "My father would have still been around, so he must have had most of the information."

He starts skimming through the files, intently looking through the documents.

Marcello's father had been an interesting figure. A little too sadistic for my taste (ironic, I know), he was the definition of mental.

"Here," he says, pulling out a file and handing it to me. "It's not much, but it's the only mention of Project Humanitas I remember seeing." He resumes his seat. "Why are you looking into this now?" he asks, but I'm busy studying the file in my hands.

"Did you know your father wanted to invest with a Dr. Miles Holloway?"

The file contains a business proposal submitted by Dr. Miles Holloway to Marcello's father, asking for forty million dollars. The proposal paints Project Humanitas as a rehabilitation program designed to create the perfect soldiers by erasing their notion of right and wrong and making them susceptible to blindly following orders—the perfect killing machines. The proposal, however, only mentions behavioral therapy and not any type of physical experiments.

"No, what is it?"

"He wanted your father to pay him forty million for access to his research." I smirk, suddenly making sense of Valentino's presence at the laboratory when I'd been found. "I'm guessing your father wanted to see for himself what he was going to pour his money into, so he sent your brother to check the project—incognito, of course."

"And he found you," Marcello says, his expression grave. I nod.

"You know, Tino never told me the specifics of how he ended up in that place. Thinking back, it does seem unusual that he would miraculously find you when your father hadn't been able to for years."

"Exactly. Your father never shared his knowledge about Project Humanitas, and now I have to wonder if somehow he wasn't involved."

He would have had many opportunities to tell my father

who had kidnapped Vanya and me and why, but he'd never done it. Maybe he just didn't want to incriminate himself.

"Can you look into your father's finances around that time?" I ask Marcello, hoping I can find a paper trail at least.

"Will do." He gives me a brisk nod, and I rise to leave.

"What happened to you there?" he asks as I'm on my way to the door. "Why do you want to find them *now*?"

I turn slightly, shrugging. "Things that happen to helpless children," I add, not wanting to get into details. I may not remember what happened, but my body is another story. "Miles and another person were the ones who poisoned Misha against my father and our family, promising him the leadership if he helped them. And Miles is the one who took Katya."

"I see," Marcello replies, his hands in his pockets. "I'll look into it."

"Thanks." I give him a mock salute, leaving.

Behavioral therapy.

Besides the experiments, they also performed behavioral therapy. Then... What if my crises are a result of that therapy? And what if they have a cure?

I don't get to dwell on that as another thought intrudes in my mind, and I find myself surreptitiously sneaking upstairs, finding Sisi's room with ease.

"I told you I'm not in the mood," I hear her voice as I slowly open the door.

"You." She furrows her brows when she sees me come inside her room, locking the door behind me. "What are you doing here?" she asks, narrowing her eyes at me.

For a second, my entire mood is shattered as I realize I'm *not* welcome.

"I was visiting your brother and thought I'd drop by." I feign a smile.

"You're taking too many risks." She scowls at me, getting up from her bed and coming toward me. "We just saw each other too."

"So what if I wanted to see you again?" I give her my most charming smile as my arm sneaks around her waist, bringing her into me. "Tell me you didn't miss me." I inhale the scent of her freshly washed hair, and for the first time today, I feel at peace.

"We just saw each other," she sighs, "when would I have had the time to miss you?" She raises an eyebrow at me, seeking to disentangle my hands from her body.

"You should go before anyone finds you here," she repeats, and I feel completely blindsided.

What happened? What did I do wrong?

"Are you feeling okay?" I ask, suddenly worried about her injury. My hand grazes her forehead, but she stops me, flinging it away.

"Yes, don't worry. I'm just tired and I want to sleep." She turns her back to me, returning to the bed and getting under her blanket.

"You should. You're not sleeping enough," I tell her, worried I've been keeping her up too late at night. Taking a seat by the bed, I place my hand over hers.

"Yeah..." she agrees, but something in her expression bothers me. "Maybe we should stop seeing each other for a few days," she suggests, her words throwing me off completely.

"What do you mean?"

"So I can rest a little." She yawns, snuggling deeper under her blanket.

I'm about to protest, but seeing her so tired makes me reconsider my stance. *I have been keeping her up too late.* Even though I'm loath to, since I know it's going to be painful to be without her, I need to let her rest a little.

"Okay," I reply, schooling my features. I don't want her to note the disappointment in my gaze.

She seems surprised by my easy acquiescence, so she just nods.

"I'll see you on Monday?" I ask, thinking that two days should be enough for her to recover her strength.

Her eyes widen. "Monday? Why?"

"Well, I know Marcello has a thing for Sundays and he will expect you to be present. So that leaves Monday. You should be rested by then."

"Right..." she murmurs, and I find myself thrown off by her expression again.

What's happening?

"Perfect. I'll text you the details." I lean in to give her a quick kiss on the forehead before leaving her room, stealthily making my way back down and out of the house.

I guess I'm lucky that Marcello isn't the best at choosing his guards, since I've managed to slip some of my own men inside. It's one of the reasons why Sisi's managed to sneak out successfully for so long.

And now I have to wait until Monday....

I groan out loud at the thought. What can I do until then to take my mind off things?

I'm out of the house and heading to the parking lot, my mind still on Sisi's odd behavior when I get inside my car.

Monday...

Something is niggling at my conscience, and I can't put my finger on it. I feel like I'm missing something.

It's only when I get back home and I check Sisi's file that I realize what I've been missing and the reason she's been behaving like this.

Monday is her birthday.

Damn it! She probably thinks I forgot, or that I won't remember and that's why she's cross with me.

Not one to panic, I remind myself that I have two more days to plan something to blow her mind. She'll be so impressed with me that she will bat those pretty eyelashes at me and beg me to kiss her.

* * *

S atisfied with what I'd prepared, I shoot Sisi a text to meet me at the edge of her brother's property. I'd arranged a candlelit dinner for her birthday, complete with a full course meal and one hundred candles spelling "Happy Birthday."

I'd scoured the internet for ideas that would make her see that I'd put a lot of effort into this and that I had not forgotten. I'd even hired a chef to cook the perfect dinner, and I'd chosen all of her favorite foods.

For her gift, I'd decided to give her the giant teddy bear I'd seen her admire at the shopping center, as well as a custom Cartier necklace with her name on it. That one had been a little trickier to get, since I'd had only two days at my disposal, so I'd settled on threatening the jeweler with a gun to his temple, while he'd worked on the necklace.

I'd been quite impressed that his hands had not trembled while he'd worked on the necklace. Not even when he'd encrusted the diamonds in the letters. Indeed, I could see why their stuff was so pricey.

Now I can only hope that she will like it too and that she will forgive me for whatever I did. I'd spent the entire weekend thinking what I could have done to offend her, and

I'd concluded that anything was possible. After all, I'm not the best when it comes to dealing with women.

Not even the advice columns on the internet had been able to provide me with a straight answer. I'd even joined a forum and asked for advice, but another man had replied that women are inherently an enigma, and that I shouldn't take it to heart. He'd recommended flowers, so of course I'd added that to the dinner ensemble as well.

Again, it hadn't been that easy to get a thousand roses to strew around on the ground, but a little intimidation does wonders.

Still, I've learned my lesson. From now on I'll never forget when her birthday is and I will make sure to have everything prepared in advance.

Sparing a glance at my clock, I realize that she's late. I wait another five minutes, and still, no sign of her, so I try to call her.

Nothing.

Is she... ignoring me? The prospect is distressing so I keep ringing her phone.

Another ten minutes, and a hell of a lot of missed calls later, I abandon the site of the dinner and I decide to confront her in her own home. Surely if I confront her directly she will be able to tell me what I've done wrong and why she's been so cross with me.

Even during the weekend, she'd been very terse in her replies, and while that had been worrying, I'd bet everything on this dinner and on wooing her with my marvelous planning.

What the fuck...

I'm already restless as I imagine countless scenarios coming to play as I confront her, the worst being her saying she never wants to see me again, or that she thinks I'm too much for her.

Fuck... What if she thinks she can do much better?

I mean, technically she can, but that doesn't mean I'm about to let her do that.

As I'm walking—okay more like sprinting—toward the house, I can't help the way my brain is pushing forward the worst possible scenarios.

Whatever may be the case, I will ask for her forgiveness, and then we'll be able to move on. Surely, she can't be that upset at me, right?

Even as I scale the walls to her room, I'm still plagued by visions of her saying she hates me now, and I realize that I should probably ban the word hate from her vocabulary, just to be safe in the future.

Propping the window open, I push myself inside, about to call her name when I realize the room is empty.

Her phone is thrown in the middle of the bed, but there is no sign of her.

And as I watch the play of shadows on the wall, I realize that for the first time, I feel truly and utterly lost.

What if she decided that I'm not worthy after all?

25
SISI

I roll over in bed, and for the second day in a row, I can't fall asleep. I sigh in frustration.

It's all because of him.

Even now, when I remember his words—that he feels nothing—a deep chasm forms in my heart, and I have to stop myself from sobbing out loud. I'd already done that enough.

How am I supposed to continue being with him knowing that my own feelings for him deepen every day? It's a recipe for heartbreak, no matter how I look at it.

The more I thought about it, the more I realized I have to detach myself somehow. Especially since we've seen each other almost every day for a while now. How can I stop myself from falling for someone who treats me like a princess? Who respects me and showers me with attention, always showing me that I *matter*?

How can anyone resist *that*?

Barring his murderous side and his lack of emotions, Vlad is pretty perfect.

As someone who's never been made to feel important, he

certainly made me feel like I was the *only* one for him. And I'd hopelessly fallen down the rabbit hole knowing that he was *only* mine, too.

But he isn't. Not really. Because he can never be. How can he truly be mine when he cannot offer me the one thing I want the most?

I'd rationalized everything. Lord, I'd thought about him day and night, trying to come to terms with my emotions and what is to be done to protect my heart. I've had enough people snubbing me in the past, and I *never* want to see him do that.

It would break me.

And yet knowing he can never give me what I most desire, why is it that I can't let go? He's on my mind twenty-four-seven. Logically, I know I should stay away, but I can't help myself when my thoughts stray to him... to his scars and his bad attacks. How can I leave him alone when I know there's no one there to care for him? To help him through his crises? To show him that he matters too?

It seems that for the first time, my mind is at war with my heart.

I go through the motions the rest of the day. Funny how I thought I'd get some sleep these days, but my restless thoughts simply won't let me.

I miss him...

Shaking myself, I focus on the current conversation with Claudia.

"She told me I could skip to the more advanced stuff," she says proudly, a small smile appearing on her face.

"I'm so happy for you." I squeeze her hand.

Marcello had hired a governess for Claudia and Venezia and had suggested I attend some of the lessons too, to complement the (not so great) education I'd received at Sacre Coeur.

For Claudia, this is the perfect arrangement, as she's starting to come more into herself, no longer held back by dogmatic old hags. Suddenly, she can tap into her full potential and study to her heart's content.

As for me... it would have been great if I'd been able to focus. But seeing that my mind is on a certain someone at all times, it's a little difficult to concentrate on the lessons.

Claudia continues to tell me about her studies, being extremely lively as she describes everything the new governess had given her to read. I nod and try to listen attentively, until out of nowhere, she jumps into my arms, kissing my cheek.

"Happy Birthday, Aunt Sisi," she whispers, a blush appearing on her cheeks.

"Thank you," I answer, a little shocked that she'd remembered. I return her hug, my arms wrapping around her.

"I'm not supposed to say anything," she starts, her voice low, "but *Mamma* said she has something prepared for you."

"For me?" My eyes widen in surprise.

She nods, a sheepish smile on her face.

Now that she's sown the seed in my head, I can't help but look forward to whatever Lina has prepared for me, the prospect of someone remembering and trying to do something special for me exciting me to no end.

It's only later in the evening that Lina comes to get me, telling me to get dressed and that we're going somewhere. Already inferring this might be the surprise, I'm entirely too giddy as I choose a dress to wear.

Coming down in the foyer, I see everyone already dressed, including Marcello and Venezia.

"Where are we going?" I ask as Lina takes my arm, a secretive smile on her face.

"You'll see," she whispers in my ear.

We split ourselves among two cars, and as I look out the window, I realize we're going into the city.

The journey takes about thirty minutes, the car stopping in front of a fancy restaurant.

Getting out of the car, we all gather at the entrance before being ushered inside by a staff member.

"Surprise!" Lina says when we get to the back of the restaurant, where a big sign spells Happy Birthday, balloons and gifts everywhere.

I still, my eyes greedily roaming about the room, unable to believe this is for me.

"For me?" I croak in disbelief, needing verbal confirmation that this is indeed for me.

There are balloons in every color suspended from the ceiling and hanging around the walls. In a corner, next to the main table, neatly packaged gifts are placed one on top of the other.

"Happy Birthday!" everyone calls out, individually coming to congratulate me.

"I don't know what to say..." I feel a little out of my depth as I look around, taking in everything they'd prepared specifically for me.

God, but I'm getting teary.

I dab at my eyes, feeling incredibly overwhelmed.

"Sisi," Lina takes me in her arms, "don't cry," she pats my back.

"We wanted to," Marcello coughs, "do something special for your birthday. Lina's told me that you couldn't do much at Sacre Coeur. I hope you like this," he says, looking a little out of his depth.

"I love it," I immediately assure him. "Thank you so much!"

"Do you want to open the gifts now, or after dinner?" Lina asks.

"You didn't have to get me anything... this is already so much," I sniffle, and more tears fall down my cheeks. "Thank you," I repeat.

"Sisi..."

"Open the gifts!" Claudia says, and Venezia nods.

A little unsure, I go to the back, opening one gift after another. They'd thought about everything, from books to clothes, even to some makeup. And as I look at the personal notes attached to each gift, I can't help but feel a warmth in my heart.

So this is what it feels like to have a family.

"Thank you. You have no idea how much this means to me," I add after I've managed to gain some control over my tears.

"I'm glad you like it, Sisi," Marcello replies, looking a little uncomfortable.

We sit down at the table, and two waiters come around to serve us. I'm placed between Claudia and Venezia, with Lina and Marcello sitting next to each other.

It doesn't escape me the glances they share, or the hidden touches under the table. I may not have been as present in the house, but it's clear that Lina and my brother are getting along just fine.

More than fine.

Marcello looks at Lina as if the world begins and ends with her, a tenderness so unlike the man I'd gotten to know. And Lina doesn't seem immune either, if her blushes are any indication.

"Your mother seems happy," I whisper conspiratorially to Claudia, and she gives me a wide smile.

"She does, doesn't she? I like Marcello too. He's nice to me."

"I'm happy," I say, ruffling her hair.

While Marcello doesn't necessarily seem inclined to emotive displays, at least he *has* emotions. Unlike a certain someone...

Not going there.

"He's been helping me with my studies too," Claudia says, and for the first time I note a hint of happiness on her features.

I'm so glad she got out of Sacre Coeur before they did any lasting damage to her, like they did to me. Lina has pushed very hard to get her professional help after the Father Guerra incident, and looking at her carefree expression, it has definitely paid off.

More chatter, and the conversation flows comfortably, everyone contributing to the overall atmosphere of the table. Even Venezia, who is usually closed off, participates and even banters with Claudia.

"Have you thought about what you want to do, Sisi?" Marcello asks, and I blink rapidly, his question taking me by surprise.

"Marcello! It's her birthday! Sometimes you're too tactless." Lina lightly punches his shoulder, shaking her head at him. He grimaces, quickly amending that it wasn't his intention to make me uncomfortable.

"I'm curious if you have any interests you'd like exploring. We can arrange for you to go to college if that's something you'd like," he continues, and I get a little awkward at being put on the spot.

Truth be told, I hadn't given much thought to what I

want to do. Back at Sacre Coeur, I'd had a million ideas, dreaming up countless scenarios of what I'd do if I could. But now that I actually *can*, none of them seem even remotely appealing.

It's all his fault.

"I like investigative work," I finally say.

Accompanying Vlad everywhere while he'd been looking for clues for his sisters had been exhilarating. Finding clues and putting them together to get a big picture is oddly satisfying and I wouldn't mind doing that in the future too.

"Really?" Marcello smiles. "What did you have in mind?" he asks, taking a sip of his wine.

"Maybe detective work," I shrug. "I've been reading up on the FBI," I continue, and Marcello chokes on his wine.

"Detective work," he repeats, giving Lina a side glance. "Lina, have you explained to Sisi what our family does?"

Lina nods. "Yes, she knows."

"Then don't you think it would be... a conflict of interests so to say?" he asks, forcing a smile.

I hold myself still, trying not to laugh at the euphemism.

"You were a lawyer," I point out.

"Yes, but lawyers can be..." He trails off, glancing uncomfortably between Claudia and Venezia, "On the other side of the law too."

"Well, can't detectives be on the other side of the law, too?" I retort cheekily, watching Marcello try to find a reply, especially as he seems to be concerned about Venezia and Claudia hearing his answer.

I'd watched Vlad's interactions with the law enough to know there are dirty cops everywhere. Why, he even has a game he plays with NYPD, as he'd happily recounted to me. Every time there's a new detective in town, Vlad likes to taunt them and test their loyalties, offering them temptation and waiting to see if they crack. More than half the time, they do, which speaks volumes to people's integrity when incentives are involved.

"You'd like to be a detective on the *other* side of the law?" Marcello raises an eyebrow at me.

I look at him intently, not knowing how much to reveal.

"I don't particularly care which side I'm on," I admit. "It's still investigative work. Truthfully, I am interested in murders," I add tentatively, "and seeing that both good *and* bad people die, does it really matter what side I'm on?"

"Interesting approach. Does any of this have to do with what happened at Sacre Coeur?" He continues, and Lina purses her lips, giving him a look that says *drop it.*

"Partly," I reply. This is the first real conversation I've had with Marcello, and while he *is* putting me on the spot, I can't help but be happy that he's at least treating me like an adult. "It's certainly awakened my interest," I say, taking a sip of water.

"If you're serious about it, then I can point you in the right direction. Adrian, my best friend, has experience on the force," he comments just as the next course arrives.

As we're about to dig in, the sound of someone clapping draws our attention to the entrance.

"What a big *happy* family." Vlad claps his hands, slowly nearing the table.

My hands still on my cutlery, my expression one of shock as I see the one person I did *not* expect here tonight.

"Vlad," Marcello mutters, his jaw clenched, his entire body stiff with tension.

"A party," he whistles, reading the birthday wish on the wall, "and you didn't think to invite me? 'Cello, 'Cello, you ought to read up on friendship etiquette," he tsks at my brother, looking around the room disinterestedly. "And whose birthday are we celebrating?" He smiles, plopping himself on a chair at the table, right next to Marcello.

"It's Sisi's birthday," Lina replies, her hand on Marcello's arm.

"Is that so..." He narrows his eyes, his gaze sweeping around the table until it finds mine. "Happy birthday." He takes a glass, pouring himself some red wine. Holding it forward in a toast, he gives me a smile as he downs it, his eyes never leaving mine. "I have to say, my dear Marcello, you have spared no expense. Vintage, 1996. Not bad."

"Since when are you such a wine expert?" Marcello snorts at him.

"It's red." Vlad shrugs, barely taking his eyes off me as he's talking with my brother. "Like blood."

"Vlad." Marcello doesn't look too happy to have Vlad here, and suddenly I worry about a potential conflict.

"Why don't we eat?" I interject, hoping this would give everyone something to do.

A waiter comes to bring Vlad a plate, and for a moment everyone is quiet as they start eating.

"How did you find us here?" Marcello asks, his fist on the table.

"The same way I can find you anywhere." Vlad winks at him. "Haven't you told them that we used to be soulmates?" Vlad asks, an innocent expression on his face. I narrow my eyes at him, not understanding the purpose of his visit.

Did he come here just to ruin my birthday dinner?

"Soulmates?" Lina asks curiously. "What do you mean?"

"Ahh, good question! You see, Marcello and I go way back. What is it, twenty years?"

"Vlad, enough." Marcello grits his teeth, looking at Vlad as if he'd like nothing more than to shoot him.

"Come on, old pal, you've forgotten our golden days?"

"Wow, you've known Marcello for that long?" Catalina doesn't seem to pick up on the tension between the two, her usual good-natured disposition shining through as she tries to include Vlad in the conversation. "What can you tell me about him?" She smiles, oblivious to the undercurrent as she laces her fingers through Marcello's.

"What can I, indeed." Vlad's face erupts into a wide, charming smile. He knows he has an in through Lina and he's taking full advantage of it. "We were closer than siblings, weren't we, Marcello?" He raises an eyebrow.

"Was he as brooding then as he is now?" Lina is quick to ask, leaning over the table, her face full of curiosity.

"Oh, even more. I could barely coax a word out of him. Sometimes I had to ask a question and answer it too." Vlad laughs and everyone joins in, since Marcello is not the most talkative individual. "But he had a gift."

"A gift?" It's Venezia who asks.

Somehow Vlad's managed to entrance the entire table and make everyone invested in his story.

"Yes, a gift for art. Why, he's a wonderful sculptor. You should have seen his art pieces." Vlad shakes his head, pursing his lips and releasing a mournful sound. "Too bad he's given it up."

"Vlad, stop," Marcello's voice is low and I detect a tinge of threat.

"Art? Really? Oh, Marcello, you have to show me," Lina says excitedly.

"Maybe some other time," my brother mutters.

"Yes, he needs very specific materials." Vlad leans back in his seat, a look of satisfaction on his face.

"What do you mean?" Lina asks, a frown appearing on her face as she looks between Vlad and Marcello.

"Hmm, what indeed, Marcello?" He tilts his head to the

side, pushing his chin up as if daring my brother to answer. "The tongue of a traitor, the skin of a deceiver, the d..."

"That's enough!" Marcello's hand hits the table, and everyone is suddenly quiet.

"Tongue of a traitor?" Claudia asks, her eyes wide.

"Vlad, so God help me, I *will* do what I promised," Marcello speaks, the threat unmistakable.

"See, this is what I'm talking about. You and your God..." Vlad shakes his head, sighing deeply. "Is that who you left me for? See, I don't get this God business. Imaginary friends aren't as much fun as you'd think."

"There are children at this table, Vlad. Censor yourself," Marcello tells him, Lina's touch the only tether to keep him from snapping.

"Children are children, until they are not," Vlad replies vaguely, his lips stained with red from the wine.

My eyes hone in on that, and I find it increasingly harder to pretend I don't know him, or that I'm not aware of his presence in this room. I only have to look at his broad shoulders, the way his throat contracts when he swallows, his Adam's apple bobbing slightly, or how the hollow of his neck makes me want to swirl my tongue around it, dripping wine inside and licking him clean.

Damn, why do I have to be so wanton?

I don't know what his game is, and why he's intentionally riling my brother up, since it's clear he has a death wish. And looking at Marcello, I know it's just a matter of time before he snaps.

Vlad's gaze moves around the table until it settles on me.

"And how old is our birthday girl now?"

"Twenty-one," I answer, narrowing my eyes at him. He knows fully well how old I am.

"That means she can *legally* drink alcohol, can she not?"

He stands up, taking the bottle and two glasses with him. He places one in front of me, filling it to the brim, before doing the same with his.

"Happy Birthday!" He clinks the glasses before taking a sip of his, his eyes never leaving mine.

I take my own glass, lifting it to my mouth. But just as the liquid is about to hit my lips, a hand stops me.

"You don't have to drink, Sisi," Marcello says, already asking Claudia and Venezia to go sit by Lina. "Vlad is leaving."

"She's legal now, Marcello. It's her prerogative to drink or not." He smirks, his tongue peeking out to lick his lips.

I swallow.

The devil.

He knows exactly what he's doing.

"You need to leave, Vlad," Marcello tells him. "I get that you're bored, and friendless, and whatever, but I won't tell you again. Stay away from my family." He grits his teeth, taking the glass from me and slapping it on the table, the liquid teetering on the edge and spilling on the white cloth covering the table.

"Damn, 'Cello, you've gone all big bad wolf on me. Are you afraid I'm going to pluck this flower?" He lays his hand on my shoulder, and I hear someone gasp at the table.

Everything happens in slow motion.

A waiter is coming in, bringing a huge birthday cake on a trolley. The hand on my shoulder disappears just as Marcello twists Vlad around, flinging him from me, and punching him in the face.

Lina's hands are on Claudia's eyes, while Venezia looks oddly intrigued.

Vlad doesn't even react or fight back as he accepts the punch, his body being flung back and into my cake.

My mouth opens on a silent sound as I see half of Vlad's face land on the cake, ruining everything.

Marcello has a smug expression as he looks at Vlad, and for the first time, I've had it with them both.

"Stop!" I stand up, putting myself between them before the conflict escalates. "This is *my* birthday dinner, and you are both ruining it," I speak, my voice serious. "You, stop hitting people." I point at Marcello. "And you," I turn to Vlad, "stop asking to be hit!"

"Me? Asking to be hit?" Vlad rights himself, the upper part of his suit full of cake as more falls from his cheek.

"Stop!" Both Marcello and I speak at the same time.

I can barely contain a smile as I see the cream on Vlad's face, and I just shake my head at him.

"Here's how this is going to go," I say, looking at everyone. "You are going to calm down," I address Marcello, "and you are going to come with me to clean up. After that, *everyone* will behave, and we'll eat what's left of the cake in peace. Think you can do this?" I look at Vlad.

I'm almost at my wits' end and there's only one reason for it.

"You're not going anywhere with him." Marcello stops me. I turn to him, giving him my most no-nonsense expression.

"I'll be fine," I say, "if he tries anything I'll just give him more cake," my lips twitch, "seems to shut him up just fine."

"Hey, I'm here," he interjects, but before he can insult my brother further, I grab him by the arm and take him to the bathroom, locking the door behind us so we're undisturbed.

"What is wrong with you?" I hiss at him when we're finally alone.

"You stood me up," he answers quietly, hands in his pockets.

"What do you mean?" I frown.

"We were supposed to meet. An hour ago to be more exact," he says, showing me his phone and the messages he's sent me—quite a lot of them.

"I don't have my phone with me, and we never planned anything."

He mutters something under his breath that I can't understand, but with his half-caked face, I can't even take him seriously.

"Is that why you came here so ready to wage war?" I ask, swiping my finger over his face and tasting some of the cream.

"You stood me up." Is all he says. Like a sullen boy, he pouts, looking anywhere but at me.

"I didn't stand you up. I didn't even know we were supposed to meet," I breathe out, a little exasperated with current circumstances.

Why does he have to be so reckless? He could have blown the entire thing, and I have no doubt that Marcello would have killed him—and me.

"Fine..." he agrees, but he doesn't seem any happier.

Shaking my head at him, I tug him to the sink, wetting a napkin and cleaning the cake from his face and clothes. All the while he's watching me with an odd expression on his face, as if he can't quite understand me.

His lips are slightly parted, his breath labored as I swipe the cloth over his face. My own skin is covered in goose-bumps, awareness of his presence—so close by—prickling from head to toe. My cheeks feel heated, my palms sweaty.

Out of nowhere, his hand shoots out and grabs my wrist, lowering it. Still holding my gaze, he backs me into a corner, his body crowding me until he's fitted to my front.

He's hard.

It's the first thing I feel when he presses himself into me, my own thighs clenching in response.

His fingers brush across my neck, before he grips me in a painful hold, bringing my face close to his.

"You don't stand me up," he rasps, his breath on my lips.

"I don't?" I blink twice, the change in his behavior throwing me off. One moment he looks like a lost puppy, the next he's throwing me against the wall ready to ravish me.

"You're mine, Hell Girl. That means you're only mine." His lips trail over my jaw. "You promised me," he says, his thumb moving up over my lips, parting them.

"I did," I answer, the intensity in his eyes hypnotizing me.

"Say it," he whispers, lightly kissing me on the lips. "Say it."

"I'm yours," I say and he lets out a big breath, as if relieved.

"I'm never letting you go," he rasps, the sound barely audible.

"Did you really have to be so mean with Marcello?" I raise my hand to palm his cheek, my annoyance with him already melting away.

"You're mine," he repeats, leaning down to deepen the kiss before suddenly turning me around, making me brace my hands on the wall.

"Vlad?" I ask, uncertain of what he's about to do.

His hands are skirting around the hem of my dress as he drags it up over my ass.

"We don't have time," I whisper, even though all I want is for him to go on. "He'll come looking for us."

"Just a moment," he says, his voice low and anguished. "I need to know you're mine."

His hand moves past the band of my underwear and between my legs, his fingers dipping low between my lips as he circles my clit. My breath catches in my throat, my eyes closing as I focus on the sensations he's wringing from my body.

"You're so wet, Hell Girl. And all for me," he rasps, his mouth nibbling at my ear.

"Yes," I reply, grinding myself against his hand.

He starts moving faster, his fingers working their magic on my pussy while his mouth is slowly massaging the column of my neck, alternating between sucking, licking and teasing.

In no time, I'm coming, barely holding back my voice as I push my ass into his erection. I sag against him, my body turning to jelly as I ride the last of the orgasm.

"Happy birthday," he whispers.

Turning, I steady myself against the wall, watching as he takes his fingers and licks them clean.

"Better than the cake." His voice sends shivers down my spine, his black eyes holding me captive.

I'm barely aware of what's happening as he shoves his hands in his pockets, removing a small box and thrusting it in my face.

"What's this?" I ask, taking it in my hand.

"Your present," he says, suddenly not meeting my gaze.

Curious, and a little surprised he'd gotten me something, I open the box to find a necklace with my name, diamonds encrusted in the letters.

"For me?" I stare at the beautiful object, unable to believe he'd gotten it for me.

"Let me," he says, taking it out of the box and placing it around my neck.

"Beautiful jewelry for a beautiful lady," he remarks, and as I look into the mirror, feeling the cold metal against my skin, I can't help but sigh in satisfaction.

"Thank you." I tug him closer, giving him a resounding kiss. "It's amazing."

For the first time, I see a genuine smile on his face as he nuzzles his cheek into the crook of my neck.

Finishing up in the bathroom, we return to the table.

Marcello looks between the two of us suspiciously.

"Took you long enough," he mutters.

"I didn't know he was afraid of water," I shrug, taking a seat.

"I am not!" Vlad protests, grabbing the chair next to me. With Claudia and Venezia seated next to Lina, he can finally sit closer to me.

"Sure." I shrug, amused. "That's why he kept saying he was going to melt if water touched his skin."

"What can I say," he bats his eyes innocently at everyone, "it's not my fault I'm related to the wicked witch. We can't choose our parents," he says, turning his attention to Marcello, "you of all people should know."

Marcello doesn't reply, but the tension in his jaw tells me the jab is personal.

"Anyone want cake?" I ask out loud, already tired of playing pacifier.

"Yes!" Claudia replies.

"Me too," Venezia responds.

Cake is served, and for the first time, no one wants to kill anyone. And to reward Vlad for his behavior, I grab his hand under the table.

He looks mildly surprised, but he squeezes my hand, holding tight.

I guess this is what it feels like to have a family...

26
SISI

Getting out of bed, I walk sleepily to the bathroom, quickly taking a shower and brushing my teeth. I'm still so tired I can barely see straight.

Wrapping a towel around my body, I head back to bed. Checking my phone, though, I realize what time it is.

Fuck!

"Wake up!" I push at Vlad's shoulders, trying to shake him awake. "It's late, you need to leave," I tell him, but he doesn't seem to hear anything as he mumbles something in his sleep.

"Vlad!" I continue shaking him. Out of nowhere, his eyes snap open, and he's staring intently at me. "You need to leave before the guards do their rounds." I soften my voice.

His gaze is still on me, his hand grabbing onto my towel, unraveling it. "Vlad!" I exclaim, scandalized.

He's quick to turn me on my back, looming over me as he breathes in my scent.

"Not yet," he whispers against my skin, his lips brushing over one nipple.

"What..." I drift off when he wraps his lips around it, sucking it into his mouth. My legs automatically fall open, inviting him to nestle inside.

He's still wearing his underwear, but I can feel the unmistakable hardness of his erection as he grinds it against me.

"I need one last taste," he rasps against my skin, his mouth open over my stomach as he trails his tongue down, "to last me until later."

"It's late." I try one last excuse, but as he catches my clit between his lips, biting and sucking, I forget why he needs to leave.

Hands in his hair, I urge him on, his masterful tongue doing wonderful things to my pussy and making me moan in pleasure.

"Sisi?" I hear Lina's voice outside my door as she knocks softly.

My eyes widen, and out of pure instinct, I throw the blanket over Vlad, covering myself to my chin.

"Be quiet," I whisper, but he doesn't reply. No, he continues to assault me with his tongue, my toes curling as I try to pretend I'm not having the best time of my life with my secret lover.

"Yes?" I cough to clear my voice.

"Sorry to come in so early, but I was thinking that we could have an afternoon to ourselves?" she asks, a smile on her face.

"Of course!" I immediately agree, one hand in Vlad's hair as he doesn't seem to be able to stop himself. It takes everything in me not to react to his devilish tongue, or the way he's pushing it inside me, fucking me with it.

Lina beams at my response, enumerating a few activities she has in mind. I listen with half an ear, nodding until she makes to leave.

God!

A small sound escapes my lips as Vlad inserts two fingers inside me, his tongue back to sucking on my clit.

"Are you... okay?" Lina stops, turning to ask.

"Yeah, of course." My voice comes out weird, and I have the hardest time schooling my features to not show the way my eyes want to roll to the back of my head, my climax imminent.

"You look a little red. And sweaty. Aren't you hot?" She points to the thick blanket on top of my body.

"No, no. I'm very cold at night," I lie, and just at that moment Vlad increases the speed of his fingers. I bite my lip. Hard. It's all that's keeping me from screaming out loud. My legs are quivering, my entire body racked by small tremors as he wrings an orgasm out of me.

"If you're sure..." She's still in the doorway, looking unconvinced.

"Yes," I breathe out roughly. "I'll see you later," I say, sweat coursing all over my body.

She eventually nods, finally leaving the room.

I yank the covers to see Vlad's mischievous smile as he gives me yet another long lick of his tongue.

"You're wicked," I accuse, shaking my head at him.

Why is it that he's becoming more and more reckless by the day? This is proof enough that he doesn't seem to care that we might get caught at some point.

Where I once decided to distance myself from him for fear I may get my heart broken, it seems it's easier said than done. No, make that a hell of a lot harder to do.

After he'd popped in uninvited at my birthday party, he'd become relentless, finding a reason to spend time with me *every day*. Since he was unstoppable in his resolve, I'd started letting him sleep over, thinking that this way I'd get my rest, and he'd get his fill of me. Of course, I'd get my fill of him too, since there's hardly a day when I don't want him by my side. After all, him pursuing me with such ardor had only made me realize that I want *anything* he can give me.

So what if he doesn't have emotions? I don't believe that he doesn't care for me. And as long as I'm his, and he is mine, that is enough for me.

For now...

"What if we get caught? You know what Marcello thinks of you even being in the same room as me," I tell him, pursing my lips.

After the birthday debacle, Marcello had taken me aside and had warned me against Vlad, telling me he might seem charming, but that it's nothing but a facade. Of course, he'd gone on to name all of Vlad's flaws, not counting on my finding them appealing.

I'd nodded, feigned understanding, and we'd closed that discussion.

"He won't be able to do anything when I marry you," he whispers against my throat as he takes me into his arms.

"I don't remember you proposing," I retort.

It's not the first time he's said that he will marry me, and while I'd accept it in the blink of an eye, I want him to work for it. I won't settle for anything less than the perfect proposal. Besides, he should hurry if he ever wants to have sex, since for some purely idiotic reason, he'd gotten it into his head that he's only going to sleep with me when we're married.

"It's what you deserve," he'd try to convince me, even when his cock was one thrust away from claiming me.

We'd tried to do it a few times before, but he just couldn't fit inside—a terrible combination of me being too small and him having an abnormally large dick. When he'd notice that he was hurting me too much, he would promptly stop, concerned.

The most he'd gotten in had been the head, and while it had hurt, it had also felt heavenly. I would have taken all the pain if he would just shove it in and be done with it. But no, he'd reacted like he was the one hurting.

For someone who claims he doesn't have feelings, he'd sure shown more consideration than a lot of people would have.

I sigh just thinking about it.

"Soon," he whispers, suddenly rising up to dress.

I watch him with interest, thinking it wouldn't be bad at all to have this every day.

"Soon..." I repeat, a little disappointed.

It's later when I emerge from my room that Marcello calls me to his study, a grave expression on his face.

For a moment, I fear he knows about Vlad, and I'm ready to deny everything to my dying breath. After all, I don't want any blood spilled, as I have no doubt that would happen if he knew what we were really up to.

I don't really understand how their relationship works. Both claim to be friends, but Marcello would rather keep Vlad at arm's length, certainly far away from the family. And seeing how a so-called friend treats him, I can't help but feel sorry for Vlad. Why is it that no one tries to understand his side too?

"Sisi," Marcello rises up, "I have something I need to talk to you about, and I need your discretion."

"Yes, of course," I reply, frowning a little at his request.

"You know the situation with Lina and Sacre Coeur," he goes on to tell me that he suspects another mob family,

Guerra, might have had something to do with the death of the nun.

"As retaliation for Father Guerra, you mean," I add, and he nods.

"Father Guerra was the nephew of Benedicto, the current capo. It stands to reason they would want some type of revenge. However, in my interactions with Benedicto, I have not been able to gauge any hidden grudges. On the contrary, he's been very enthusiastic about working together and..." He trails off, looking a little uncomfortable.

"And?"

Marcello grimaces. "He's been particularly vocal about introducing you to his son."

"His son?" I ask numbly, not sure I understand where this is going.

"His son, Rafaelo, is around your age and..." He seems mightily uncomfortable.

"Out with it, Marcello. What is it with his son?"

He takes a deep breath. "He's hoping there might be a match between the two of you."

My eyes widen in disbelief, and I'm ready to make up an excuse, anything to not have to deal with that. But Marcello quickly amends his words.

"Of course, I told him it could only be your choice, but he wants a meeting at least. To see if you suit."

"I see," I reply, a little unenthusiastically.

"I know it's a lot to ask, but can you at least pretend to spend some time with him? I'm still not sure about Guerra's intentions, and it would be a good way to observe them."

"But I don't have to marry him, right?" I need to make sure that's *not* on the table.

"No. Unless you want to, that is." He gives me a tight smile. "I should warn you that his son has some... problems."

He continues to tell me about his stutter and his shy personality.

Seeing that he's not in a hurry to marry me off, I agree to his plan, promising to entertain Rafaelo when the time comes.

Well, to my everlasting surprise, the time comes way sooner than I would have anticipated, with Benedicto, his wife and Rafaelo coming for a surprise visit.

We're all gathered in the drawing room, before Benedicto and Marcello retire to the study to talk business.

Lina and I are left with his wife, Cosima, and Rafaelo. Cosima looks to be about forty, her features clear, her style elegant and put together. She also seems to be quite the talker as she starts parroting about this and that, her voice already grating on my nerves.

Rafaelo, on the other hand, is quietly sitting by his mother's side, shoulders slumped, head bent forward as if he doesn't even dare meet our eyes. In fact, he barely manages to say his greetings without passing out in a swoon.

Do men even swoon?

Rafaelo is certainly prone to it, as he sways on his feet, a deep blush on his features.

"Assisi, what a lovely name you have." Cosima tries to involve me in their conversation, her eyes looking me up and down, no doubt judging me.

"Thank you," I reply drily, but still try to keep a poker face.

"Now, tell me, what are your thoughts on marriage?" Cosima jumps right in, and I have to struggle not to laugh in her face at her lack of tact.

"M—M—mother," Raf interjects, trying his best to form some words. "S... stop."

"Nonsense, Raf!" She shuts her son down, returning her gaze to me.

"I haven't thought about it since I was supposed to take my vows before I left Sacre Coeur." I give her a neutral enough answer, trying not to show how much I'm starting to dislike her.

"There's enough time for that, dear," she casually says. "Why don't you two go over there and get to know each other better." She's not even trying to mask her intentions as she dismisses us.

I mutter a curse under my breath, but keep a smile on my face as I move couches with Rafaelo.

For the longest time, he just sits next to me, his gaze on the ground. Certainly, he doesn't even seem to acknowledge my presence. He's slumping down, almost as if there's something interesting on the floor that has his rapt attention.

I take a moment to study him and I note that he wouldn't be unattractive if not for his awful body language. It almost seems forced with how tense his shoulders seem as he tries to maintain his posture.

"This is boring, isn't it?" I try to break the ice, the silence even more unnerving.

He slowly turns his head toward me, his eyes still downcast as he looks anywhere but at me.

"I don't bite," I feel the need to add, "or judge." I shrug, leaning back in my seat. "We're going to be here for a while, so we might as well get to know each other."

Something about his presence is awfully pitiful, and it's not his stutter. No, there's an aura of perpetual sadness lingering around him.

"W-w-why?" he asks, his face tilted toward me.

"Why talk? I don't know. It's what humans do?" I try to

crack a joke, and for a split second, I fear I may have offended him, since he *doesn't* talk very well.

But then the hint of a smile appears on his face.

"Th-they d-do, d-d-don't th-they?" he asks, his stutter slightly more pronounced.

I frown a little, something niggling at my mind as I start studying him more.

"So talk away. Tell me about yourself," I prompt him, wanting to test a hypothesis.

God, I sound like Vlad now.

Too much time in his presence and already my brain is syncing with his. I'm becoming paranoid about everything and everyone.

On that thought, though, I need to ensure Vlad doesn't get wind of Guerra or their intentions toward me. I don't think I'd want their blood on my hands, all things considered. It would just bring about a mob Armageddon, as Vlad likes to call it.

Damn it, I need to stop thinking about him for a second. Or think like him...

Turning my attention to Raf, I watch the play of emotions on his face as he's trying to find his words.

"I l-like rocks," he eventually says. "I s-tudy rocks a-t university," he continues, lifting his eyes to meet mine for the first time.

Damn, but I wasn't prepared for that.

His eyes are the lightest shade of blue I've ever seen, his blond hair only bringing out their unusual hue.

"Cool," I reply, my knowledge of rocks pretty limited. "Why do you like rocks?"

"They d-don't talk."

I stare at him for a second before bursting out into laughter. Realizing it might be misconstrued as me making fun of him, I immediately stop. But one look at his face and he seems more relaxed than before.

"You're funny," I add, stifling a smile.

He's slow, but his mouth tugs up in one too.

"I've n-never been c-called funny b-before," he says, and again, I note a strange pattern with his speech.

"Probably because you don't talk much?" I raise an eyebrow at him. Instead of being offended, he just shrugs, but there's amusement on his face.

"You're n-not what I-I imagined," he tells me, leaning back onto the couch and making himself more comfortable. His posture opens up a little, his spine no longer so hunchbacked.

"And what did you imagine?" I ask, curious about it, but also needing to hear him talk more.

"I d-d-on't know... A n-nun?" he asks, cracking a joke for the first time.

"Fair enough," I reply, and we continue to make some small talk. He still speaks in short sentences, almost as if he is afraid of saying too much at once.

I note Cosima watching us intently from the other end of the room, no doubt assessing the situation and her son's prospects.

But the more I engage Rafaelo in conversation, the more I notice things. It's in the way everything is manufactured, from his posture to his voice, and then there's his speech.

"You don't really have speech issues, do you?" I lean forward, whispering in his ear.

"Wh-what d-d-o y-you m-mean?" he asks, and I feel my lips stretch into a smile at the silent confirmation.

"You stutter only the second word in a sentence when you're relaxed, as if it's a taught pattern, but you stutter the entire sentence when you want to prove a point." I shrug, this observation being one of many I've drawn over our rather short acquaintance.

More than anything, I see the way his body reacts to outside stimuli, as if he's making a conscious effort to close himself in and coordinate his movements.

"I-I d-don't k-know wh-what y-you m-mean..." he tries to defend himself, but I note his rigid posture. If I'd been wrong, he would have been upset, maybe drawing himself back and away from me. Instead, he's holding himself tight, tension coiled in his muscles. It's more like an animal ready to pounce than one on the verge of running away.

When you spend years running away from people who mean you harm, you start learning some patterns. The body never lies, even when the mouth does.

"Raf, dear! It's time to go!" Cosima's voice rings in the room, and there's a hint of relief on Rafaelo's face.

He rises from the couch, resuming his slouched posture as he makes to stagger to his mother's side.

"Don't worry." I stop him, my hand on his shoulder. "Your secret is safe with me." I wink at him.

I don't know why he'd present himself in such a negative light, but that's his business.

Everyone has secrets.

We get back to Lina and Cosima. They are still engaged in conversation as Raf takes his spot by his mother's side.

Hand in his pocket, he draws it quickly, something small falling to the ground. We both lean down to pick it up, and I realize it's a tiny brown rock.

He pushes it toward me, his gaze clear as it meets mine for the first time.

"Thank you," he whispers, no trace of the previous stutter.

I pick up the rock, playing with it in my hands as I watch them leave.

Interesting.

* * *

Humming a soft melody to myself, I pull the thread through, satisfied at the design starting to take shape. Lina and I have been hanging out a lot more lately, and she started teaching me how to embroider.

Since I'd seen that Vlad always carries a handkerchief with him, I'd decided to make him a personalized one—with my name, of course. That way he can always carry me with him around, and other women can see he is taken too.

I smile to myself as I add a tiny red heart next to my name.

"I see someone's been busy," Lina remarks as she takes a seat next to me, her eyes on my work.

For a second I'm tempted to hide it, but when she continues to talk, I breathe out, relieved, realizing she thinks it's for someone else.

"I can't believe you and Raf are so close," she says suggestively.

"Yes, we've become friends," I reply.

It's technically true. After the initial visit, he'd dropped by a few more times, and he'd slowly confided in me the reason for his behavior.

"When people deem you as weak, they don't see you as competition," he'd said, implying that he was trying to go as undetected as possible.

But as he'd told me about his brother and his thirst for power, it had become clear why he'd try to go under the radar.

In the time I'd gotten to know Raf, I'd realized he's a very gentle soul who'd like nothing more than to be left in peace. He certainly has no aspirations for power or money, regardless of how much his father might want him to take the reins of the Guerra family in the future.

"You're the first one who's managed to notice," he'd told me at some point, amazed that I'd seen past his mask.

Little did he know that I have a knack for seeing behind masks.

"And you didn't have to confirm my suspicions, so why did you?" I'd fired back. Certainly, he could have continued to deny my accusations. Instead, he'd ended up confiding in me.

"You're not like them," he'd shrugged off, although he hadn't explained who *them* refers to.

And so a pleasant friendship had developed. So pleasant that he'd even asked me to marry him, to my great chagrin. For a moment I'd worried that maybe I'd given him the wrong signals, but he'd quickly assured me that he only sees me as a friend, and because he is so comfortable with me, it wouldn't be a bad idea if we married, since his father keeps pushing him toward it.

I'd gently declined, explaining my own circumstances and that I already have someone. He'd been very happy for me when I'd told him more about Vlad, and he'd even suggested using him as a cover if needed.

Safe to say, a partnership had bloomed from the unlikeliest of places.

"He'll definitely enjoy that." She points to the heart with a knowing smile, and I instinctively blush.

Oh, yes. Vlad *will* enjoy it. After the effort I put into this thing, he better *never* take it out of his pocket.

"I'm so happy for you, Sisi," she continues, releasing a

dreamy sigh. "After the incident with your birthday I was worried for a moment."

"What do you mean?" I frown.

"I'm sure Marcello's already told you about Vlad. He's not... someone you should interact with."

"Why?" I ask a little vehemently.

Why is everyone so against him? What did he ever do to them?

From what I've seen, he's always helped everyone when needed, and yet, not even Marcello, who's known him the longest, can offer him the tiniest of consideration.

"He's not a good man, Sisi. I know you're new to this world, but there's bad... and then there's *very* bad." She purses her lips, looking at me with concern in her eyes.

"How is he so bad?" I'm getting heated, the need to defend him gnawing at me. I know all she's saying is coming from a good place, but I'm getting tired of everyone crucifying him without even trying to understand him.

"He kills people, Sisi," she starts, and I resist the urge to roll my eyes, "he's a cold-blooded killer."

Debatable, I'd say he's rather hot.

"He simply has no moral compass." She shakes her head, as if she's not married to the same ilk.

"What about my brother?" I shoot back and she frowns.

"There's a world of difference between Vlad and your brother," she adds, almost horrified I'd imply such a thing.

"See, I think you're wrong, Lina. It's just a matter of perspective." I shrug.

"Sisi..."

"Your villain might just be my hero, Lina. Is there really such a thing as black and white? Or moral and amoral?"

"Sisi... I hope you're not sympathizing with him!" She sounds scandalized, and I realize I'm treading on thin ice.

"Of course not," I reply, "I'm just trying to say that you

can't really know a person until you've walked a mile in their shoes." I shrug.

She's quiet for a moment as she regards me pensively.

"You've become quite the philosopher." She finally smiles.

My lips stretch up as I return it.

One has to when one's lover is the villain in everyone's story.

But mine.

27
VLAD

"This should work until we get you a new prosthetic tongue." I hand Seth his new device. "It's text to speech. You can even choose your voice," I explain, "but please don't choose a woman's voice. I don't think I could reconcile that with—" I wave at his massive body.

He grunts, quickly typing a reply.

"Not my kink," a robotic male voice replies.

"Good," I nod, "not that I would have judged. I'm *very* open-minded." I give him a big smile.

He doesn't return it as he takes a seat in front of me, furiously typing on the device.

"Are the kids safe?"

"Yes. They've been successfully returned to their parents. I've offered to relocate them in case those people look for them again. Sometimes I amaze myself." I sigh deeply. I'm losing my mojo if now I'm helping people instead of harming them.

And where's the fun in that?

Seth nods at me, back to typing.

"Regarding your promise," he starts, and I motion for him to continue. "I want to end Arsen Aliyev."

"The Azerbaijani mogul?" I raise an eyebrow, surprised he'd be the target of his revenge. "Why?"

There's a flash of pain in his eyes.

"He made me who I am," he pauses, closing his eyes briefly, "and he stole what I loved the most," he says cryptically, but I can read between the lines.

"Fine by me. I've only met him a couple of times, but I don't think we've exchanged more than a few words." I shrug. I'd promised him revenge, and I shall deliver. "All my resources are at your disposal, and everything you need."

He narrows his eyes at me.

"Why?" he asks, his features drawn in suspicion. "Aliyev is a powerful man. Why would you risk it?"

Opening the drawer of my study, I pick up a pack of gum, popping it in my mouth.

"Because there are very few people I have *not* upset so far. What's one more? Besides, I have a more important job for you."

"What job?"

Opening my computer, I turn it to him.

"I think you've noticed that this compound is a little differently structured."

He nods, studying the layout.

"There's a reason for it." I lean back in my chair, not relishing the fact that I have to make my weakness public. "I have some episodes... crises if you will, and I become extremely unpredictable."

He raises an eyebrow questioningly.

A few buttons and I replay one of my episodes from last year, when I'd finished off half the staff. Not my greatest moment, but the attack had been so sudden, I hadn't been able to see it coming, least of all control it.

Seth watches attentively, studying my movements. I already know what he's seeing. A creature wearing the skin of a man, but that is neither. I'd watched the tape enough times to know just how much damage I'd caused as I'd cut everyone to pieces.

I hear screams in the video and I know it must be the moment I start washing the hallway walls in blood, breaking absolutely everything in my path.

Seth is silent when the video ends, slowly raising his head to meet my gaze.

"As you can see, I'm not exactly a walk in the park. In fact, it usually takes about ten people's efforts to immobilize me, and even that is not without casualties. You, on the other hand, have the skill I need."

"You want me to kill you?" he asks and I shrug.

"If it comes to that. I certainly want you to stop me before it gets too far. Usually I recover after a while but..." I trail off. "For some time now my episodes have been worse and worse, some lasting for days. If I don't come out of one..."

"I understand," he states.

"I must warn you, though. For all your skill, which is great by the way, awesome match," I praise him with a smile, trying to alleviate some of the doom in the air, "I won't go down easy. How long have you trained for?"

"Fourteen years," he replies.

"I have more than two decades of experience," I simply state so he can see what he's getting into.

"But you're..." He frowns at me, since we're about the same age.

"Yes. The earliest kill that I remember was when I was

eight. Might have killed before then." I shrug, almost certain I'd killed before.

No one suddenly wakes up with a thirst for blood without having been conditioned to it. And I'm becoming increasingly sure that whatever Miles did to me must have damaged something inside of me.

"So you see, I'm not going to be that easy to take down. Which is why I'd like to train you until you become familiar with my moves."

Seth nods, intrigued.

"There is one more thing," I add, "and probably the most important one. *Never*, and I mean *never* let me harm Sisi. I'd rather you kill me before I even set my sights on her."

She might be able to ground me for now, but I never want to take any risks with her safety. I'd rather be dead than know I'd done anything to her in one of my rages. Because knowing the usual results, I can only imagine the state I'd leave her in.

"Your girlfriend?" Seth asks, and my lips pull up in a smile.

"Yes, my girlfriend. You are to protect her at all times. *She* is your charge. I come second."

He tilts his head, looking at me intently before typing something.

"Does she know that?"

"No, she does not. And we'll keep it like that." I smile ruefully.

Sisi might hate me, but for the first time I find that I'd rather preserve someone's life than take it.

I spend some time going over everything with Seth, wanting to make sure things will be perfect in case something happens.

By the end of the evening, I am already tired.

I've been getting more and more tired.

Weary might be a better word for this tiredness that seems to seep into my bones and strip everything from me.

It's funny how a few months ago I would have been fine just going through life like I've always done, recklessly and carelessly, even the rush of killing fading over time.

Now there's her...

And her presence in my life has just shown me how pathetic I've been before. The thought that I may not have too much longer would have delighted me in the past. After all, why would anyone want to live if nothing ever brought joy, with the simple act of living being a burden? Now, for the first time, dying makes me scared. Because then she'd be gone.

I wouldn't see, touch, or smell her.

"Maxim," I dial his number, "find me the best psychiatrist in the city."

I'm grasping at straws, but I have to try it.

For her.

My last resort is Miles, but it's taken me nine years to get here. Who knows when I'll find him? And with how fast my condition is advancing, I'm afraid I won't make it.

"Don't be sad." Vanya's lips are down-turned as she takes me in. "I don't like it when you're sad," she says, swinging her feet off the bed and coming to my side.

"I'm not sad, V. I *can't* be sad, remember?" I attempt a smile for her benefit.

"You are. I can feel it." She takes my hand and brings it to her chest. Her gesture is endearing, so I allow it for a moment.

But as I blink, I see my hand lodged into her chest cavity, blood pouring down my knuckles.

"What..." I draw back as if burned.

There's a gaping hole in Vanya's chest, her heart missing as blood keeps gushing out.

"Help me," she whispers, her eye dangling in its socket. "Help..."

I take a step back, all the while shaking my head.

It's not real. It's never real.

My back hits the wall and I fall down. Vanya's form keeps on approaching, even more blood pooling at her feet.

"Help me, brother. Don't let me die," she keeps muttering, her voice a haunting melody that sounds like a screech in my ears.

I shut my eyes, counting to ten, imagining the soft sound of a pendulum as it calms my mind. I do it until there's no more sound.

Taking a deep breath, I open my eyes to come face to face with Vanya. She's right in front of me, her features distorted, her flesh rotten.

"You failed me," she whispers, the iris of the dangling eye moving as she gazes around. "You failed me," she continues to say until she starts yelling in my ear.

"No..." I whisper, "I didn't."

But she doesn't stop. The sound is deafening as I feel myself slipping. Without even thinking, I fish my phone from my pocket, quickly calling *her*.

"Vlad?" she answers on the first ring, and I breathe out, relieved. *"Are you there?"* she asks, her voice the cure I needed.

I watch in awe as Vanya's receding form becomes smaller and smaller until she disappears, as if in thin air.

Hell, if I were more superstitious I'd say she's a ghost and Sisi's holiness is driving her away.

As it stands, I'm well aware that the disease is in my

brain. My mind is the one infected with whatever's been plaguing me.

"Sisi," I breathe out, my body trembling with unreleased tension.

"How come you called? I wasn't expecting you until midnight," she says and I soak in her voice, closing my eyes and imagining she's next to me.

"Can't I miss you?" I ask in an amused tone, not wanting to betray the state I'm in.

She might know *some* of my secrets, but she's not prepared for all of them.

"Are you bored? Is that why you're calling?"

"Sisiiii," I groan.

"I'll see you tonight," she tells me in a soft voice, *"I miss you too, but I have to go."*

She hangs up.

I hold the phone to my ear just a little longer, wishing I could put her voice on a loop. The demons are coming again, and this time they won't settle for anything less than my sanity.

* * *

The appointment with the psychiatrist set, I don't tell Sisi about my intentions, not wanting to give her any hope where there is none.

Over the years I'd gone to different specialists, and I'd allowed them to probe and prod until it had gotten to a point where I hadn't cared anymore. I'd been reconciled with my rather fast-approaching mortality, and I was fine with it.

Sure, I regretted the knowledge I would never manage to acquire, the experiments I'd never run, and simply the world I wasn't going to experience. But it had been pretty simple to convince myself that with my already muted senses, there wasn't really any joy in it anyway. Interesting was the most feeling I could muster, but even that was an overestimation.

But more than anything, I knew that no one would miss me. Maybe Bianca would put an epitaph on my tombstone, but she's not any more capable of deeper emotion than I am.

In the end, no one would mourn.

Promptly forgotten.

Never loved.

Lately I've noticed a melancholy getting to me. For the first time I'm actually pondering things of a spiritual nature, wondering if maybe it's not too late for me.

It is too late.

I'm a fool for even hoping things might be different. I guess Sisi's arrival in my life has done a number on me. Feeling something other than boredom can wake even a dead man from his slumber.

And I've certainly been awoken. Now I just have to figure out a way to stay awake.

Looking at my watch, I realize it's time for the showdown.

I tighten the tie around my neck and head to the meeting room.

With so many things about Miles and Project Humanitas coming to light, I'd started thinking more in-depth about it, and a few glaring issues had arisen.

Most importantly, how is it that Miles and his partner had been able to approach both Misha and Giovanni Lastra? And they had earned their trust, too. So I'd started mapping out all the events, particularly leading up to Misha's coup.

I remember father had put him in charge of the New Jersey travel routes, and he'd been commuting between states to attend meetings and settle with providers. Was it during one of those trips that he met Miles?

The missing piece is the unknown partner. Without him, it's simply an endless puzzle, since he could have easily been the liaison between them.

But since now I have Miles' full name, I plan to set a small trap. I'd summoned all seconds-in-command tonight for a short meeting, hoping to summon a syndicate summit soon.

Not that I've been on good terms with any of the other pakhans, but they need me more than I need them. After all, New York is one of the biggest hubs on the East Coast. Knowing that, all evidence is pointing toward someone who'd stand to gain something from Misha's leadership, and so every pakhan on the East Coast falls under suspicion.

Now I'll just need to get them talking, and what better way than to hold a summit? I just need everyone together in the same place. I'll provide them with everything they desire —alcohol, drugs and women—and I'm just going to hope their tongues loosen up enough.

I'd try torture, but even *I* am not that reckless to get the entire East Coast on my back. Well... half maybe, just not *all* of them.

And since everyone has a bone to pick with me, I'll have to be inventive with this invitation.

Exiting the room, I meet Seth.

"Ready?"

He nods, swinging the big backpack on his back. He's carrying a few interesting items that should make this party merrier.

"Then let the show begin." I wink at him.

About ten men are all waiting for me in the conference room, all gathered around the round table.

"Gentlemen," I greet them with open arms.

Seth takes his spot in the back as I walk around, shaking hands with everyone and kissing their cheeks.

One last kiss. Who said I'm not generous?

As I'm taking my seat at the top of the table, Maxim gives me a nod, closing the doors and locking us inside.

The men don't even notice that small detail, their attention focused wholly on me now.

"Say, Kuznetsov, why did you call us here?" One asks, and I have to squint my eyes at him, his name escaping me for the moment.

"Sorry, but who are you?" I ask, relishing the way outrage spreads over his features.

"What?" he sputters, looking offended.

Some of the other men are stifling laughter. Alas, a name is just a name, just like a grave is a grave.

I tilt my head to the right and make a small motion to Seth. Opening the bag, he hands it to me to make my choice.

Pursing my lips, I browse the items, ultimately settling on a machete. As soon as I draw it out of the bag, I hear the gasps behind me, the men no doubt scrambling for their weapons.

Alas, their guns have been confiscated, so they likely only have some puny knives.

Turning toward them, I test the sharpness of the blade against my finger, blood pouring instantly.

Bringing it to my mouth, I smile as I lick the red liquid.

"So, gentlemen, where was I?" I beam at them, jumping on the table and carefully choosing the first target.

The man who'd spoken first is also the first one to fly for the door. Ah, of course the loudest are the loudest for a reason.

Two big steps and I jump right in front of him, swinging

the machete to an angle, his head falling effortlessly to the ground.

"Damn, but it's sharp," I note just when someone tries to tackle me from behind.

I duck, his small knife hitting the air just as I roll on the floor, nabbing his knee. He falls down just as two more come toward me. Not wasting any time, I cut his head in one swift motion, turning around to deal with the newcomers.

A cut here, a cut there and two more heads are rolling on the floor. Adrenaline is rushing through my veins, my blood pumping hard as my pupils dilate at the sight of blood.

Oh, it's on.

The rest is a blur of movements, body parts and guts spilled on the floor, the entire room painted in red as blood flows freely.

The machete becomes an extended arm as I cut and wade through the dead bodies, enjoying the feel of the flesh giving in to my sharp blade.

When all the heads have fallen, I can't help myself as I start tearing the bodies apart, using the machete to cut them into tiny pieces.

Blood. More blood. So much blood until I'm drowning in it, laughter bubbling in my throat as my hands grab at the viscous liquid, draping it over my body like a sheet. I feel it coating my skin, flowing down my limbs until it's covering me like an armor.

From blood to blood.

Until it ends.

I don't know how much later I open my eyes, clarity returning to my gaze. I'm lying on my back on the table, my clothes shredded, blood everywhere. Moving around a little, I realize nothing hurts, so it's not my blood.

"Are you okay?" Seth's robotic voice asks from the corner.

He's relatively clean considering the mess around.

"Now, yes," I groan, getting up and taking in my work of art. "Did I damage any of the heads?" I ask, hoping at least those would be intact.

"No. I managed to collect them while you were busy," he replies with a straight face, pointing under the table where all ten heads are lined up in a row.

"Clean cut." I whistle, amazed at the skill I'd displayed.

Calling Maxim inside, I tell him to catalogue the heads and send them as gifts to their respective bosses.

With the invitations done, I only need to wait for my guests to come.

Ah, who said letting loose every now and then wasn't fun?

* * *

"Tell me more about your childhood," Dr. Reese prompts me and I'm almost tempted to roll my eyes at him. But I'd promised myself I'd make an effort.

"I thought I told you, doc. Bloody," I joke, "lots of blood."

He sighs, placing his notepad down.

"Vlad, this isn't helping either of us. You came here with a problem, and you're not going to solve it if you're not going to be honest with me. I'm here to help you," he says in his fatherly voice.

"This was a mistake," I mutter, rising from my seat and heading for the door.

"Maybe you don't want help," he comments and I stop, my hand on the handle.

My mind conjures up Sisi's face, the thought of having more time with her making me still.

I do want this.

"I don't remember my childhood. Or much of it." I turn back, casually sitting on the couch.

"Good, that's a start. What is the first thing you remember?"

Killing a doctor.

"I was kidnapped when I was three with my twin sister. I don't remember any of the years spent in captivity," I start, detaching myself. "My sister, Vanya, died there," I say, watching her huddled in a corner, her eyes tear-streaked. "I didn't." I shrug.

"Do you think your sister's death might have something to do with you blocking out the memories?" he asks in a gentle voice.

"I don't know," I answer truthfully. "Maybe. I still..." I take a deep breath, gazing down at the seat next to me where Vanya suddenly appears. "I still see her," I admit, and her face scrunches up in horror, her mouth opening to yell in my ear. It takes everything in me not to cover my ears, or wince every time she hits a higher note.

"Is she here? Now?"

I slowly turn my head toward the doctor and I nod.

"Interesting. You were probably very traumatized by her death since she was your twin."

I nod. "I spent years thinking she was still alive. And when I found out..."

"What happened?"

"It triggered something in me. I wasn't fine before either, but it exacerbated whatever was in my brain. I started having blackouts... very violent blackouts."

Dr. Reese nods thoughtfully, jotting things down on his notepad.

"It could be a symptom of PTSD. Do you have any idea what happened to you during those years in captivity?"

I stare at him for a moment, debating whether I should show him or not. In the end, I stand up, unbuttoning my shirt and prying it open, so he can see my chest.

"Impressive," he chuckles at the sight of my tattoos.

"Look closer," I say. He leans forward, his glasses on, his mouth opening as he realizes what the tattoos are hiding.

"Can I?" he asks as he raises his hand. I nod, and using his fingertips he traces some of the scars, frowning. "These are surgical," he states.

"Yes. I'd wager a guess that *this* happened to me in captivity," I add drily. "Doctors did full exams on me and they couldn't find any issues."

I spend some more time going over my blackouts, keeping out the murderous details, but giving him enough to know I am dangerous.

"And your girlfriend..."

"She calms me. But..." I take a deep breath to explain wherein lies the issue, "They've been getting worse and worse. I fear that when a bad one hits even her presence won't be enough. And I'll hurt her."

"I see." He purses his lips. "Have you ever tried to remember those years? They may be the key to understanding your current symptoms."

"That's why I'm here."

"You realize that this isn't an exact science. I can't assure you *anything* is going to give you your memories back," he warns, but I wave my hand dismissively.

"I know. And yet I am here trying it as a last resort."

I'll be the first one to protest that it's not even a science, as it doesn't have the core characteristic of replicability for it to be deemed a proper science. But a desperate man would do anything.

And I find myself increasingly desperate.

Who knows, tomorrow I may kneel in front of a weeping icon.

Weirder things have happened.

"I'm glad you understand it. I'd like to suggest an age regression for your issue, and after that we'll assess and move forward accordingly."

Dr. Reese goes through the procedure, detailing everything that will happen. I just nod, still a little skeptical, but pushing through at this point.

He instructs me to settle down in a relaxed position, and use his voice as a guide.

Closing my eyes, I do what he says, letting my mind relax and follow his words.

"Deep breaths," I think I hear him say as he instructs me to regulate my breathing, his words having a soporific effect on me.

A blackness paints itself in my mind, everything else falling away. My body slows down, its functions almost on standby.

"Move backwards." His voice sounds like an echo in the distance. "You are now seven years old."

He speaks some more, the blackness in front of me distorting as light pushes through cracks. I shield my eyes, and it's like the ceiling is disintegrating, pieces of black glass falling on me.

And then I fall.

28

VLAD

M y back hits a solid surface, my eyes snapping open as I take in my surroundings.

"Scalpel," I hear someone say as my pupils adjust to the light directed on me. Moving my head to the side, I see a man. His face is hidden by the shadows, but he's wearing scrubs, his gloved hands holding a scalpel as he leans over my body.

For the first time, I dare to look down, my eyes widening as I note my chest wide open, my ribs in full view. The doctor takes the scalpel, cutting tissue away, and yet I barely feel any pain.

"See," I hear a voice. "He's awake and not a sound. I think it's working."

"This is..." another voice joins in, and I see another figure on the sidelines as he walks around the surgical bed, looking at me in wonder.

"Tell me, my little miracle, does it hurt?" the doctor cutting asks me, his hand tenderly brushing across my cheek. My eyes are unblinking as I stare at him, slowly forming out a *no*.

"See, my little wonder is already miles ahead of the others," he speaks, his hand still working inside my body.

"I understand now why you won't let us touch him," the other grunts, clearly displeased.

"Of course." The doctor scowls. "Where would I find another perfect specimen like him?" He turns abruptly toward the other.

I'm still dazed, the entire situation seemingly surreal as I feel an emptiness inside of me that's spreading all over my body.

"Fuck you, Miles. You know what you promised us..." The words become a buzzing in my ear.

"You have enough to choose from, for fuck's sake. This is revolutionary! You can always get your dick wet but this..." He points toward me. "His ability to withstand pain is unheard of. Why, he's the only one capable of this out of the batch. His sister is not even close, and they're twins." He shakes his head. "I don't know what it is about him but..."

I blink once and the entire scene changes. I don't know how old I am, but I feel old beyond my age...

I'm in a cell, and Vanya is huddled by my side, her entire body quivering as she tries to hold on to me for some heat.

"I'm hungry," she whispers, her lips almost turning blue from the cold.

"You know you can't eat anything solid after the test." I stroke her hair, wishing I could take away her pain.

The door to the cell opens, and two guards come in. Something about their eyes doesn't sit well with me.

One of them takes Vanya by the nape, making her kneel in the middle of the floor, while the other secures my hands behind my back, holding me still.

There's a panic within me, but I don't know why. What I

do *know* is that this isn't the first time something like this has happened.

"Please, not today. You'll tear her stitches." I hear myself speak, struggling against the man holding me.

"Shut up!" he snickers behind me, placing his hand over my mouth, stifling my sounds.

I watch in horror as Vanya kneels on the floor, her hands around her midriff as she's trying to hold on to her stitches.

The guard looks down at her, his meaty fingers grabbing her jaw as he raises it to look her in the eyes.

"Miss me, sweetness?" he asks, his dirty hand daring to touch her.

I'm breathing heavily as something within me grows to a painful extent. It's a strange feeling, as if I know what's to come and I'm primed for battle.

His hands caress her cheeks, and there is a vacant look in her eyes as she just stares forward, her body sagging as if sapped of strength.

The guard lowers the zipper to his jumpsuit, taking his erect dick out and thrusting it into her face.

"Swallow, and today I'll be gentle," he tells her, spitting into his palm and moving his hand up and down his erection.

I can't watch this.

My limbs start bucking and I do whatever I can to escape the hold of the guard.

I need to help Vanya!

But it's all in vain.

With a kick, he pushes me face down on the floor, his entire body weight on me as he keeps me motionless.

My eyes are still glued to my sister—my twin, and my eyes tear up as I see her open her mouth to suck on the bastard's dick. How his pudgy fingers fondle her nonexistent breasts, or how he tears at her clothes to reach between her legs.

A sound that won't come out forms in my mind, my entire being assaulted by a pain unlike any other.

"This little shit won't stop moving," the man holding me comments, the other guard's grunts filling the room as my sister sucks his dick like she's done this a million times in the past.

Vanya...

"Careful with him, he's the special one." The guard chuckles, his hand pushing my sister's head forward until she's choking on his dick, her eyes moist with unshed tears.

"Special my ass," the man behind me says, and one hand starts pawing at me, going lower and lower...

"Yo, Yosuf, we can't touch him," he groans, but Yosuf doesn't seem to hear him as he starts tugging my pants down.

"I won't tell if you don't," he laughs, snorting in the process as if it's the most amusing thing.

"Only if I get a turn after." He winks at Yosuf.

At some point, my body and my mind separate. I still feel everything though. The weight on my body, his hands moving my legs apart, his dick entering my body and tearing me in two.

And it continues, his breath on my nape as he thrusts in and out of me, his sweat transferring on my back as he increases his movements, and then his seed as he spends himself inside of me.

But I don't react.

My body is immobile, my gaze fixed on Vanya's as we lose ourselves in each other, taking comfort where there is none.

Her eyes tell me everything I need to know.

You're not alone.

We'll get through this.

Together.

I gasp for air, my eyes snapping open, my hand shooting out as I reach for something.

I'm drowning.

There's no other explanation for it, as I struggle for my breath all the while my fingers are snuffing it from someone else.

Dr. Reese's body crumbles lifeless at my feet. I barely react as I stumble out of the cabinet, my entire being in shreds, my wounds bleeding where there's no blood.

It's only when I round the building that I call Maxim, realizing he needs to clean up my mess. After that, I just wander... aimlessly walking the busy city streets, drowning in the noise, drowning in myself.

Sisi.

I need her more than I need my next breath, and yet I feel too tainted to reach out.

Walking around the city, I don't know how many hours I spend just drifting about, not really rationalizing anything that's happening around me. But even so, I cannot stop my feet from taking me to my one source of comfort.

Climbing her window, my heart plummets in my chest when I realize her room is empty. Pure desperation claws at me as I go inside the house, stealthily moving around, yet courting danger at every turn.

And then I hear her, chatting and laughing with someone —a man that is not me. I barely control myself, feeling my increasingly volatile temper rising and seeking to take over. It takes everything in me not to barge into the room, blood spilling to assuage my rage, a warning that *no one* can have her.

I hover on the staircase, a direct view into the drawing room as my eyes focus on Sisi, sitting so comfortably in the presence of another man.

She's laughing at something he said before she raises her gaze, her eyes widening as she notices me.

A few words and she's already flying toward me, tugging me by my hand and dragging me to her room.

"What are you doing here? God, Vlad, that was so reckless of you." She keeps talking while closing the door behind her and locking it.

My breathing becomes labored, a red haze covering my gaze as I grab her by the throat, pushing her into the wall, my face buried in the crook of her neck.

"Who is he?" I rasp, barely recognizing my own voice. "Who were you smiling for?"

"Vlad, calm down!" Her hands go to my shoulders, rubbing them down in tender motions. "He's just a friend. Nothing else."

"Who. Is. He?" I hiss, needing to know the name of my future victim. Because he won't get away with his life. Not after what I saw.

"He's my friend. Really, Vlad, there's nothing going on. Please." That one word has the power to tear down all my walls. One hand reaches out to touch my arm, her expression so lovely, so full of warmth.

My knees buckle and I fall, wrapping my arms around her for support. I press my head against her stomach, breathing harshly as I hold on to her for dear life.

"Sisi." An anguished sound escapes me. For the first time, I feel my old self coming back, her presence the balm I needed to heal.

"Dear God, what happened?" she whispers, taking my

face between her hands and lowering herself to her knees to be on the same level as me.

"Sisi." I can't even articulate my thoughts properly as I look her in the eyes, her expression filled with worry. "For me..." I murmur, my fingers tracing her features.

"Talk to me," she says as she places her lips on top of mine. I open up to let her in, tasting the saltiness of tears, humbled that she would cry for me.

But as I open my eyes, I belatedly realize *I* am the one crying, my tears flowing down my cheeks uncontrollably.

She doesn't say anything. She just brings me to her chest, rocking with me as she tells me that everything will be okay.

"Tell me you're mine," I rasp, my body almost convulsing from accumulated pain. "Please," I implore her, seeking the assurance that she's never going to leave me. That I am hers and she is mine.

"I'm yours," she says, "always and forever." Her fingers caress my hair, her chin resting on top of my head. "Just like you are mine," she continues, her arms tightening around me.

I soak in her presence. I let it permeate every atom of my being as I seek to stabilize myself.

Wrapped in each other, we stay like that for what feels like hours, my body melting into hers, our scents melding into one. I hold on to her so tightly that I forget where I begin and where she ends.

It's just us.

"What happened, Vlad?" she asks after some time.

"I went to a psychiatrist," I tell her, briefly recounting what had happened, but leaving out the details of the rape. I don't even want to think about her expression when she realizes just how broken I am.

"Vlad." Her brows knit together in concern as she opens

my shirt, tracing my scars with her hands before leaning in to kiss them. "Always come to me." She raises her head to look me in the eye, "Always."

"Yes," I say, "always."

"Come." She takes me by the hand, leading me into the bathroom and slowly undressing me before doing the same for herself. Nudging me gently, she takes me into the shower, the hot water falling on my skin, my eyes closing on a sigh as it makes contact with my body.

She takes a sponge, lathering it with soap as she brings it down my chest, cleaning me.

I watch through hooded eyes the way she's caring for me, and my heart squeezes painfully in my already shattered chest.

"You're safe with me," she whispers as I tug her closer, skin flush to skin, coldness next to warmth. I let her heat seep through me, her soft body cushioning mine.

"You're my home," I tell her, sweeping her hair aside so I have access to her neck. "You're where I want to lay my head for eternity." I brush my cheek against her delicate skin, inhaling the scent that's solely hers.

"You're mine too. You have no idea how much you mean to me." Her words touch me in a way I'd never thought possible. I wrap my arms around her back, her breasts pressed against my chest, and yet none of my thoughts are of a sexual nature.

She's Sisi. Brave, beautiful and kind. She's the warmth I didn't know I needed, the ray of sunlight in my perpetually dark life.

And she's mine.

Turning the faucet off, she takes a towel and dries my skin. She's thorough yet gentle with me, as if I were the most precious thing. Her actions alone make me want to weep, the care she's giving me more than I could have ever imagined someone like me deserved.

Leading me to the bed, she settles the pillows, lifting the covers for me to get in.

She nestles close to me, naked skin against naked skin, her eyes gazing into mine.

"I made you something," she whispers, the back of her hand caressing my cheek. She turns briefly to open a drawer, taking out a square piece of cloth.

"I embroidered it for you. So that I'm always with you." She shows me the letters spelling out her name next to which she'd drawn a little heart.

"Sisi..." I don't even know what to say as I look at the precious material. "Thank you." I turn to her, placing my lips on hers.

She opens up, her tongue meeting mine as her arms wrap around my neck. I pour everything she means to me into this kiss, wanting her to know that only when I'm with her am I truly whole. A slow kiss that tortures me with its sweetness.

And I'm finally at peace.

* * *

I snuggle closer to her, the feeling of waking up with her next to me better than a thousand kills. Nuzzling my nose in her hair, I bring her ass flush against my cock, nestling it between her ass cheeks.

"Morning," she whispers, stretching next to me and gifting me with a wide smile.

"You're the most beautiful thing I've ever seen," I tell her, taking in her fresh face and the way her eyes sparkle with mischief.

"Is that so?" She bats her lashes at me, turning to lay on my chest.

"That's why you better tell me who that man was. Don't think I forgot about it." I raise an eyebrow at her.

"Spoilsport," she mutters, pouting.

"I'm listening." I grab her by the nape, bringing her face in front of mine, my lips nibbling at her chin. "And you're not leaving this bed until you tell me." My expression turns from playful to serious.

We can joke about this all day, but I won't have anyone sniffing around her.

"He's just a friend," she sighs but proceeds to tell me all about her new friend Raf. The simple fact that she has a nickname for him makes me curl my lip in disgust.

"And you're sure he has no designs on you?" I ask, still unconvinced.

"Of course not!" She rolls her eyes at me. "He knows everything about you." She points out, poking my chest, "And he's even agreed to help with a cover should I ever need it." She smiles at me and I know I can't stay mad at her.

"I don't like it," I mutter. The more people she'll meet, the more she will realize that she's better off without me, and that *cannot* happen.

Ever.

"Please promise me you're not going to kill him," she murmurs, and I smile sheepishly. She'd guessed just the direction of my thoughts.

"Nope, can't do that." I shake my head, turning around.

"Please..." She continues, peppering kisses on my neck before going lower.

"Nope," I repeat, resolute in my decision.

Since I take my promises seriously, I can't commit to something I *know* I will do.

"Please." She doesn't stop, batting those long lashes at me as she goes lower on my body, gripping my cock in her hand, her tongue licking it from base to tip.

"Fuck," I groan, "you're not playing fair, Hell Girl," I say just as she takes me between her lips, her eyes on me as she lowers her mouth on my cock until it hits the back of her throat. Spit dribbles down her chin as she gags on my length, trying to take me as deep as she can, but only managing half.

My hand in her hair, I urge her on as she sucks me, the sight of those beautiful lips of hers stretched around my cock making me shudder in pleasure.

Hot sin. She's fucking hot sin, all for my taking.

"Please." She licks the underside, focusing on the spot she knows I like, all the while looking at me with those doe-like eyes of hers.

"Christ woman." My head hits the pillow as she pumps me vigorously, her mouth a hot welcoming heaven as I come. Her lips close over me, sucking me dry.

She rises slowly, undulating her body in a sinful dance as she moves toward me, her mouth open, my cum on her tongue.

"Please?" she asks again, playing with my cum in her mouth and showing me how she swallows like the good nun she is. Absolutely hypnotized by her, I ultimately relent, giving her my promise.

She crawls on top of me, giving my cheek a resounding kiss. Turning her on her back, I'm about to return the favor when my phone rings.

"Your brother." I mouth to her to keep quiet. She giggles, and I have to place my hand over her mouth to keep her quiet.

"Marcello, fancy hearing from you," I drawl, truly surprised he'd reach out.

"Yeah, right," he answers drily. *"I thought you'd want to know that Valentino rescued another boy back then,"* he adds and I still.

"What do you mean?" I frown.

Sisi sees my expression and she snatches the phone from my hand, putting it on speaker.

"Funnily enough he ended up with Agosti. I don't know how, but he's now working for Enzo. Maybe you can arrange for a meeting," he says, clearly in a hurry to end the conversation.

"What's his name?" I ask, and Sisi looks at me with worry in her eyes.

"Nero. He's around your age. Talk to Agosti." He doesn't even wait for me to reply as he hangs up.

"Marcello's still holding a grudge," Sisi comments, and I have to agree. He's still sulking from last time, but I know he's going to come around. He always does.

"Maybe this Nero will know more," I add, a little optimistic for the first time.

After the flashbacks I had of what happened to Vanya and me there, I know I'll rain hell on everyone involved. They should really find their God fast and pray, because nothing will stop me from making their lives a living nightmare.

My plan set for the day, I only leave when my girl is purring with satisfaction.

A short while later and I'd managed to schedule an appointment with Nero at Enzo's house. I'd called Agosti, and I'd explained the circumstances—or as much as he needs to know—and he'd been rather accommodating in helping me meet with Nero.

I arrive at his house a little after noon, and I'm invited to his study. From the first moment I look at Nero, I can see a familiarity.

I don't know if I've met him before, but his eyes have the same quality as mine — both soulless. It's further confirmed when he moves, a robotic stiffness that I'm somewhat familiar with. In my case, though, I'd spent years trying to fight it, observing how people around me behaved and emulating those behaviors.

"Vlad." I smile at him as I stretch my arm to greet him.

His eyes are blank as he just gives me a nod, going to the couch and taking a seat.

Damn, but he's even ruder than me.

I take a seat next to him, continuing my observation.

His back is straight, not touching the couch, his hands on his knees as his spine makes a ninety-degree angle. He's like a soldier on a drill. His eyes are facing forward, as if I'm not in the room, but I can see small movements at the corner—he's assessing his surroundings.

"I assume you're curious about why I wanted to talk to you since we've never met before," I start, keeping my tone jovial.

He still doesn't answer, merely facing forward. For a moment I have to wonder if he's like Seth and the cat got his tongue too.

"Project Humanitas," I get to the point, and his jaw twitches, a sign that the name means something to him.

"What do you know about Project Humanitas?" he asks, and I get to hear his voice for the first time. It's raw and scratchy, as if he'd been exposed to smoke for prolonged periods of time, his vocal cords damaged.

"I was there." I shrug, waiting for him to give me more than a facial twitch.

Slowly, his face turns toward me, his eyes narrowing.

"I'm told we were both taken out at the same time. By Valentino Lastra," I add, happy that he reacts to the name.

He's silent for a while before asking.

"What did they do to you?" He blinks slowly, almost mechanically.

I guess it doesn't hurt to show him, since I'm making an educated guess that he's been through similar things as me. Opening my shirt, I show him the ridges from the surgical scars, and he nods.

Surprisingly, he does the same, showing me a large scar on his back, running from his neck to his pelvis.

"I'm surprised you lived," I comment, noticing the extensive scarring.

"Ditto," he replies, putting back his clothes.

"What do you remember?" I ask, telling him that a lot of my memories from captivity are gone.

"You're lucky," he says quietly. "There's not a day that I don't remember what they did to me... what they tried," he chuckles.

"What do you mean?"

"You're aware they were trying to build the perfect soldier," he starts and I nod, "and for that they needed children who had a certain defect from birth that made them unlikely to care about right or wrong. Think a psychopath of a sort."

"The mutation in the amygdala. You have it too?"

"Yes. Everyone who was there had it. That was the baseline. After that, they tried to condition us to become killing machines, taking out the humanity from us and replacing it with bloodthirst. But they also needed something else..." he trails off, lifting his sleeve and folding the end of his shirt and trousers to show me a bionic arm and leg. "Physical prowess. They wanted someone invincible, so they were trying to eliminate pain, and to turn our bodies into weapons."

"They did *that* to you?" My eyes widen, and he just shrugs.

"They implanted metal in my spine. It connects to the arm and leg. It was bad after I was rescued since I needed to have them resized, and there aren't that many engineers out there who could do it," he comments casually.

Fuck, he is half-robot.

Now that explains his posture.

"Were you also a twin?" I ask, and for the first time I see a flash of pain in his eyes.

"Yes. Although he is long gone."

"Mine too," I add, and we have a short moment of understanding.

"Why are you asking about them now? It's been over twenty years." He frowns, tilting his head and regarding me curiously.

"I've been made aware that my younger sister was sold to Miles from Project Humanitas around nine years ago."

"Why? Did *she* have the mutation?"

"No. But I think he needed her for something else." Some things are becoming clearer, and while I won't stop until Project Humanitas is in the ground, I do hope to find Katya dead. Because the alternative is way more gruesome.

"Isolating the gene somehow," he shrewdly notes, and I grimly nod.

"He'd assume it runs in the family," I add.

"It would make sense. It is my understanding that it is quite rare. If Miles had an in-house factory, things would be much easier for him."

I grunt. I'd thought about it, but I hadn't wanted to admit to myself that my sister could have been used as a lab rat all these years, subjected to countless horrors. Hell, now that I know a fraction of what happened to Vanya and me, I can wager a guess as to what they would do to her, too.

Patrick's words in particular had led me to that reasoning, as he'd mentioned someone giving birth repeatedly.

I can only hope it's not Katya...

"I'd like to ask if you can remember anything that might be of use for me to find them," I tell Nero, surprised when he offers to send me a detailed account.

"Just let me know if you do find them. They need to pay for what they did to my brother."

"Of course," I readily agree, ready to leave.

"No, Enzo, I can't," I hear Catalina's raised voice as I make to leave. "Please get Claudia settled... I need a moment," she says, dashing up the stairs.

Odd.

Yet her presence here, distressed, must only mean one thing.

She knows.

Damn. I wonder how Marcello's doing. For a moment I'm tempted to call and ask, but I know it wouldn't be welcome. Especially at this time.

So I just hop in my car and drive home, anxious to hear back from Nero.

The pieces are coming together, and I'm not sure if I like the image I'm getting.

"I remember him," Vanya says, sitting in the passenger seat.

"You do?" I raise an eyebrow skeptically at her.

"Yes. He was the boy with the dimple. He was nice," she says with a dreamy sigh.

"You had a crush on him!" I tease, and she blushes from head to toe.

"Maybe," she whispers, going silent as she gazes out the window.

The memory I'd seen resurfaces, and I have to wonder just what type of life we had there.

I'm almost home when my phone rings. Seeing that it's one of the guards from Marcello's house, I immediately answer, afraid something might have happened.

"Yes?"

He's quick to tell me that Sisi found Marcello covered in blood and they are now on their way to the hospital.

Damn!

Maybe Marcello did need a friend after all. Too bad it's never me...

29
SISI

"I'm worried, Vlad. I told the doctor he wouldn't try to kill himself, but what if he did?" I pace outside Marcello's salon. The nurses needed to sedate him after he'd woken up, begging Vlad to kill him right in the lobby of the hospital.

"He's going to be okay," Vlad says, taking my arm and tugging me to his side. "I don't think he was *really* trying to kill himself. But I suspect Catalina's abrupt departure from the house must have had something to do with it."

"How did you know?" I frown, leaning back to look at him.

"I spotted her at Agosti's. And she didn't look much better than your brother," Vlad purses his lips.

"What could have happened..." I mutter, confused.

How come everything happened all at once? Lina had left the house in such a hurry, taking Claudia with her and not answering any of my calls. For the first time, she'd truly shut me out, and I don't know what to do about it.

"It's for them to figure out, Hell Girl. We can only make sure that your brother gets out of this unscathed."

"Can you stay over? There's no one at the house and..." I trail off. I don't know why the prospect of an empty house scares me so much. Maybe because I'm still a little afraid of dark and lonely places.

"You don't even have to ask," he tells me, and I'm immediately more at ease. "I wouldn't dream of leaving you alone. Especially if rumors of Marcello's absence were to circulate."

I nod. I hadn't thought about that, but it makes sense that we'd be seen as easy targets. I'd learned a thing or two about the mob since leaving Sacre Coeur, and family is always the weakness most exploited.

"God, when will the misfortunes stop?" I groan out loud, sagging against Vlad's body.

"I trust your brother will figure things out," he sighs, "and as soon as he gets his shit sorted, I'm telling him about us. Including that I want to marry you," he declares, and my eyes widen at his words.

Pulling back, I look suspiciously at him, studying him from head to toe.

"What brought this on?" I ask. He'd casually said he was going to marry me before, but I hadn't taken it to heart, since Vlad has a flair for the dramatic. That and his dry sense of humor make for a deadly combination, ensuring that I rarely take his words seriously. But now? He seems pretty serious to me.

"I'm tired of hiding, and I'm tired of walking on eggshells around him. But mostly I don't want to be apart from you anymore," he tells me, a defeated look on his face.

I quickly sober up, knowing there must be more to this. Especially considering how he'd behaved last night, desperation clinging to him as I'd tried to comfort him in my arms. The pure shock I'd felt when I realized tears were flowing down his cheeks... Whatever he'd found out during his visit to the psychiatrist must have affected him more than he'd let on.

Even now, with his body against mine, I can feel the tension radiating off him, his usual smile gone as if keeping up the ruse of joviality is too much for him.

I know he's not telling me everything, and it's killing me inside to see him like this.

"Why?" I throw the question at him, doubt niggling at me.

His eye twitches as he forces a smile on his face.

"I told you, Sisi. You keep the demons at bay." Is all he says as he pulls me into him, his lips on mine.

I let myself enjoy the kiss, but a foreign thought invades my mind.

He's never told me what demons.

Hell, the most I know about his problems is that he has bad episodes. But besides that, he's still an enigma. I know his history, I know his quest, I know all the facts. But why do I feel like I'm missing the biggest piece of the puzzle?

The truth is that I'm too far gone to consider what that might mean for me or for our relationship. I already love him too much to ever consider leaving him, regardless of what he's dealing with. I'll just do my best to help him through it.

I know that as long as I'm useful to him he'll never leave me, so I'll just have to make sure I'm indispensable to him.

"Okay," I agree in a soft voice. "Never let me go and I'm yours. That's my only condition, Vlad." I take a deep breath, "I know who you are, and what you are capable of." I raise my hand to caress his cheek, his eyes pinning me with their intense stare, "And I accept all of you as you are." I brush my thumb against his lips, "The bad and the good. Just don't *ever* leave me." My own lips tremble as I utter the words, baring my soul and my one weakness to him.

"I don't think I can imagine a world where you're not, Sisi. Not anymore," he confesses and my lips tug upwards.

"Good." I give him a full smile.

Because I don't think I can imagine a world without you either.

It wouldn't be fair to say I'm not scared of the future, especially since Vlad is so... volatile. But I knew the moment I realized my feelings for him that loving him would never be easy. It will always be a battle with myself *and* him. With myself because I don't think I'll ever stop yearning for his love, even while knowing he's *not* capable of it. And with him because there might come a day when his logical mind will tell him I'm a liability, and of no further use.

As long as he never lets go, I will never let go.

"I love you." I lay my head on his chest, whispering the words so softly he can't hear them, because he wouldn't even know what to do with them. No, they're for my benefit only as I'm trying to materialize this love I feel so deep in my chest.

"What was that?" He frowns, but I just shake my head and smile.

"Nothing," I say, taking refuge in the warmth of his arms, the only type of warmth he's capable of giving me.

* * *

A couple of days in the hospital and Marcello is discharged to come home. For all his protests that he hadn't tried to kill himself, the doctor in charge asks me to supervise him so that he doesn't try anything again.

Vlad has been spending all his free time with me while

I've been alone at the house, even though I know he has some outstanding matters to attend to as well. His gesture has been sweet, and we've found ways to entertain ourselves.

He's definitely been overly enthusiastic to share his favorite movies with me, even though I did *not* find them romantic in the least. Why, I should have known that with a title like *Human Centipede*, I wasn't bound to find anything remotely sappy inside—other than a lot of freely flowing bodily fluids.

Considering it was one of the rare times I'd seen him so immersed in something, I tried to share his enthusiasm, especially as he delved into the science part, gushing about the creativity of the scenes.

"Maybe you should try this next time you torture someone," I'd joked, and he'd turned to me wide-eyed, giving me a big smooch as he told me I was a genius.

"Why didn't I think about it before? Fucking hell, this is exactly what I need for my next experiment, and there doesn't have to be too much blood either." He'd become so excited and I'd listened patiently as he started designing the experiment, using some pointers from the movie, but putting his own spin on it.

But two days and I've been spoiled by his presence, and now that Marcello's back we need to be more careful. At least until things settle down.

I am still skeptical about whether Marcello is suicidal or not, and because of that I want to be extra careful with Vlad, already anticipating how Marcello's going to react to the news.

"Do you need anything?" I ask my brother as I help him to his room. The mere fact that he's allowing my touch when he'd been a beast to the nurses is astounding. I'd gotten some details from Vlad about his aversion to touch, but nothing concrete.

"No." He sounds surly as he answers, hopping to his bed and resting his leg on it.

"Marcello..." I start, but he doesn't even let me continue as he asks me to step out.

Sighing, I do, but that doesn't stop me from visiting him every few hours, just to make sure he doesn't do anything stupid.

"He's not very cooperative," I tell Vlad on the phone after I've said good night to Marcello. "I don't know what could have made him behave like this..."

"Don't worry that pretty head of yours, Hell Girl. It's between him and his wife, and they should solve it at some point."

"You're right but," I lower my voice to a whisper, "I think I heard him cry, Vlad. I don't think he's doing fine at all. I'm worried." I bite my lip, my forehead creasing.

"Sisi," Vlad groans, *"it's complicated."*

"So you know what happened," I fire at him.

"Of course I do," he replies, almost offended, *"I wouldn't be me if I didn't,"* he jokes, and I can already see his satisfied smile behind the phone.

"Well, spill. What happened?"

"I may know the circumstances, but it's not my story to share, Sisi. Your brother fucked up, but I can't say he was wholly guilty," he says cryptically, avoiding answering any of my questions on the subject.

"Fine, I'll figure it out," I mutter, hanging up.

I don't understand all the secrecy. Marcello is surly, Vlad knows what happened but won't tell me, and Lina won't even answer my calls. I'm one minute away from going to her brother's house and demanding a meeting.

"Sisi?" Venezia knocks on my door.

"Yes, come in." I give her a welcoming smile. If I'm in the dark, I can't imagine how Venezia feels.

She walks inside slowly, almost uncertain of herself.

"Sit." I pat the bed next to me.

"Do you think Lina and Claudia are ever coming back?" she asks in a small voice, her tone telling me that she doesn't think they will.

"They will," I try to reassure her, "they have to." I take her hand, squeezing it gently.

She gives me a tremulous smile, leaning forward to place her head on my shoulder. I tug her into my arms, giving her a hug.

"They will," I repeat, though even I'm not sure of that either.

But I can see my younger self in Venezia, and how the only thing I'd ever hoped for had been acceptance — somewhere to belong. For the first time she'd had a semblance of a family, and it had quickly disintegrated.

"I'm glad you're here with us," she whispers, her eyes damp with unshed tears. "I like having a sister."

"Me too," I reply, kissing the top of her head. "Me too."

The situation doesn't improve. With each passing day, Marcello becomes even more withdrawn, spending all his time locked away in his study. The few times I'd tried to reach out he'd made it clear that I'm not welcome and that I should mind my own business.

When a week's gone by and all my attempts at drawing him out of his shell are in vain, I resort to calling Vlad—the self-confessed thorn in his backside.

"You're hurting me, Hell Girl," Vlad complains on the phone when I tell him my idea.

"You know it's true. So go do your best and annoy Marcello into joining the world of the living again."

"Fineeee." He relents, even though I can tell that inside he's giddy at the prospect of messing a little with my brother. They certainly have a weird dynamic going on.

A while later, I can tell that Vlad's worked his magic, but not in a good way.

"Stay away from him, Sisi. I mean it. I made it clear to him that he's not to interact with either you or Venezia, but he can't seem to help himself." Marcello pulls me aside after his meeting with Vlad, looking pissed off.

"Marcello, I don't understand why you're so against him. You're friends, aren't you?" I raise an eyebrow at him.

"Friends..." He gives a dry laugh. "Vlad doesn't have friends. He only has people he uses. So don't try to feel sorry for him."

"What do you mean? What did he ever do to you?" I'm tired of Marcello warning me off Vlad but never telling me anything more.

"He isn't like other people, Sisi. Don't try to find anything good about him because there's none. Yeah, he's damned smart, and he makes sure to use that brain of his to manipulate everyone around him," he continues, and I stifle the urge to roll my eyes.

"You're still not telling me why you dislike him so much."

Marcello sighs. "I don't dislike him per se, but I know to be wary of him. He's... unpredictable. He has his interests and he doesn't care who he harms as long as he reaches his goals. Why, he might as well have been the one who put the gun in Valentino's hand," he mutters, and I still.

"What do you mean?"

"It's complicated, Sisi. I told you, he's not what he seems, and I need you to trust me that no good will come from you being anywhere near him. Only death comes to those who get tangled with him."

"Fine," I lie to placate him, even though he still hasn't told me why he's so wary of Vlad.

On the bright side, at least Marcello's speaking to me again.

As I'm starting to hope that harmony will return to our house, Marcello gets himself into trouble again. Granted, this time it's for saving Lina, but after what he's done to her it's the least he could do.

I don't realize how bad his situation is, though, until I get to the hospital. Vlad and Adrian are already there, and they tell me that Marcello's had a narrow encounter with death. Lina had gotten away with a few bruises only, and Enzo had managed to convince her to go home and rest.

"At least there's no more danger, right?" I ask Vlad when we're finally alone. Marcello's been moved to a private salon, but the anesthetic hasn't worn off so we can't see him yet.

"Yes. I killed Nicolo myself. In fact, I have his body in the trunk of my car and I should probably get rid of it soon." He scratches the back of his head, feigning an innocent look.

"Damn." I swat him. "That's reckless," I say, narrowing my eyes at him, and he looks bashfully away. "You do realize I'm not marrying you in prison," I add, watching a sheepish smile spread on his face.

"And miss the conjugal visits?" One finger trails down the front of my dress, lightly caressing my nipple.

"Get your head out of the gutter, mister." I catch his finger, pushing it away. "We need to get rid of that body while my brother is still out of it."

"I forgot you're not the squeamish type, Hell Girl," he drawls, caging me against the wall. One look around and I realize we're in full view of the entire hospital.

"People are watching." I raise my eyes to find him gazing at me with an amused expression on his face.

"Let them watch." He lowers his mouth to my ear, his voice making the hairs on my body stand up. "You know how my cock reacts every time you're talking murder," he whispers, his tongue sneaking out to lick the lobe of my ear.

"The murder has already occurred," I mention, trying to steer the conversation to a more serious order of business. "We need to do the clean-up."

"Doesn't matter, it involves a body. A dead body," he continues, twirling his tongue around my cheek, "you know I love it when you talk corpse to me," he says and I can't stop myself from giggling.

"Is that so? You love it when I talk corpse to you?" I grab him by the lapels, bringing him into me.

"Hell Girl, you have no idea how hard you made me the first time I saw you push your hand into that nun's guts. Fuck if it wasn't the hottest sight I've ever seen," he rasps against my flesh.

"Mmm, since it's confession time," I start, watching his pupils dilate with arousal, his nostrils flaring as he pushes himself into me, rubbing his erection against my stomach, "I was dripping wet when you choked me in the church."

"Sisi," he groans, his shoulders sagging. "You shouldn't say something like that."

"Why?"

"It makes me want to do more. Things that would make you scream in pleasure and in pain."

"Do it," I dare him, wanting everything he has to offer.

"Fuuuuck!" He takes a deep breath. "Let's get rid of the body."

A smile pulls at my lips at his obviously frustrated expression, and as we get to the parking lot, he opens the trunk to give me a sneak peek of Nicolo—or what's left of him.

"You couldn't have made this cleaner?" I shake my head at him. The entirety of Nicolo's skull had been blown to pieces.

"Well," he grimaces, "I got too into it." He shrugs.

"When do you *not* get too into it?" I mutter under my breath, amused. "Okay, now what's the next step?"

"Hmm," he strokes his chin pensively, "depends on what you want to do with it. We can burn him, chop him up and throw him at the bottom of the ocean, or even better chop him up and scatter him across the city. Like a treasure hunt." His face lights up.

"And the evidence? Wouldn't that be courting danger?"

"Isn't that the beauty of it?" He tilts his head back, smiling. "Why would anyone kill without the thrill of being caught? It's like a drug." He takes a deep breath, controlling his excitement.

"Is that what you normally do?" I raise an eyebrow at him.

Vlad might be volatile, but he's also smart enough to cover his tracks every time.

"Sometimes," he shrugs, "when I want to play with the cops. I leave them a crumb here, or there. It's awfully fun to watch them take the bait and follow fake leads," he explains, a wide smile on his face as he reminisces about some of his encounters with the FBI.

"One time, I was even brought in as a witness, if you can believe it," he chuckles. "I had to put on the best act of my life as I tried to look distressed. I might have even shed a tear," he recounts, proud of himself.

While he might find these events funny, I find them rather sad. Is that what he does because he has no friends to *play* with? It certainly looks like a lonely boy trying to get some attention any way he could—even if it was from the police.

"Right," I reply drily, "let's do bottom of the ocean. I don't think we need any scrutiny right now."

Especially with my brother in the hospital, the last thing we need is the police knocking on our doors.

"You're no fun," he complains, but he does get in the driver's seat, putting the car into gear and leaving the parking lot.

"Okay, we need to drop by your place and cut off the recognizable parts," I add, having read up a little on the subject.

Vlad might enjoy the thrill of being chased by the police, but I like the thrill of knowing that a dead body stays *dead* and *unsearchable*.

"Hell Girl, your knowledge astounds me," he praises, bringing my hand up to his lips for a kiss. "I might even let you do the honors."

"Why, Vlad, that might be the most romantic thing you've ever said to me." I bat my lashes at him, playing his game.

"Only for you," he murmurs softly, and I get a tingling in my lower region, the thought of him taking me on top of the car's trunk while my uncle's dead body lies beneath us, making me incredibly hot.

We're soon back to the compound, the moon high up in the sky as Maxim takes out Nicolo from the trunk, bringing him into one of Vlad's science rooms and laying him onto a table.

"What first?" I ask as Vlad starts the drain, the blood pooling under the table and into a system specifically built to get rid of bodily fluids.

"Hands?" He pulls on a pair of gloves, giving me one too.

"Come." He takes me into his arms, his back to my front.

His cock is wedged right between my ass cheeks as he wraps my fingers around a blade.

His breath on my neck, he guides me as I push the sharp end of the knife into the dead flesh. His hand on top of mine, he supplements the strength needed for the blade to puncture the skin.

My breath hitches when he lifts my hand, bringing it down with so much force against the bone, cutting through it, pieces shattering around us.

"Yes," he whispers, "just like that," he rasps against my ear, and I instinctively push my ass into him.

"Yes," I repeat after him, entranced by the way my uncle's body gives way to the pressure, more splintered bone flying through the air, the flesh breaking, but little blood pouring out of the open cuts.

"It turns you on, doesn't it?" Vlad murmurs, his open mouth trailing up my neck. "Death, destruction, devastation... it makes you wet, doesn't it?"

I whimper, unable to respond as my legs part of their own accord. Vlad is quick to tug his gloves off his hands, his bare fingers trailing the inside of my thigh. I'm almost bent over the dead body, my back arched as the tips of his fingers light the fire in my veins.

"Cut," he commands, handing me the butcher knife, while he picks up another skinnier one.

I comply as I push the blade into soft flesh, a gasp escaping me when I feel him part my ass cheeks, a foreign object sneaking between my folds.

"So fucking wet," he groans, pushing the hilt of the knife against me. "Imagine this is my dick fucking you, pressing into you." His words are only making me wetter as the top of the knife probes at my entrance, easily sliding inside. It's almost the same size as two of his fingers, but the forbidden feeling of being fucked by a knife has me almost coming on the spot.

"Vlad..." I moan at the sensation as the knife slowly moves in and out of me.

"Next time it's something bigger, and bigger," he rasps, pushing it deeper inside of me, "until you're ready to take my big cock into your tight little body." He brushes my hair aside, peppering kisses over my exposed back.

"Cut!" His voice booms into my ear as he continues to thrust into me, and I have to force myself to obey, bringing the blade over my uncle's body, the pleasure so intense I don't even know where I'm cutting anymore.

I'm just swinging the blade around, slashing haphazardly as Vlad fucks me with his knife.

"God," I moan when he increases the speed, and I feel a warm liquid coat the hilt of the knife as it enters me, lubricating the walls of my pussy even more.

"Come," he demands, one finger playing with my clit until he brings me over the edge, my voice ringing into the room as I tighten my hands over my own knife, hitting with as much force as I can, nabbing my uncle's chest as the blade lodges into his sternum.

Sagging against him, he slowly removes the knife from my pussy, bringing it up to his mouth and sucking in the mix of my juices and blood.

My eyes widen as I take in the blood dripping from the blade, but then I realize where it's coming from. Vlad's hand is wrapped around the sharp part of the knife, his skin broken and bleeding.

"What..." I grab the knife out of his hand, turning his palm up so I can see the damage. "Why did you..." I trail off, noting his intense stare, the darkness of his pupils as they engulf his eyes.

"I wanted to pour myself into you," he whispers, his palm sliding up my neck and smearing his blood on my skin.

I'm enthralled by his presence, even though I can feel he's teetering on the precipice as his gaze narrows on the red on my body.

Bringing his hand to my mouth, I suck on each finger, my eyes on his as I let my tongue lap at his open wound.

"Hell Girl, you're my fucking kryptonite," he says before he brings me roughly against him, our teeth clashing as his mouth opens over mine, kissing me with an unexpected ferocity.

I can taste myself on his tongue, as well as the metallic taste of his blood. Knowing he pumped his blood in my pussy somehow makes me even hotter, and I proceed to show him just how much by worshipping his cock with my mouth.

In the end, Nicolo gets thrown into a furnace, his body burned and turned to ash. Vlad's excuse, though, is that he wanted to see my savage side as I desecrated my own uncle's body.

I'd be mad at him if it hadn't been the height of eroticism, once more confirming that there's nothing Vlad could do that would turn me away from him—not even him fucking me on top of a dead body. In fact, one might argue that's his allure.

"I won't be able to come by tomorrow," he tells me as he drops me off at home, stopping the car across the street from my house. "I have a meeting and it might take the entire day," he sighs.

"What meeting?" I ask, hearing about this for the first time.

"I'm inviting the syndicate bosses from the East Coast for

a small fête," he replies, not sounding in the least enthusiastic. "I want to see if they know anything about Miles." He explains why he thinks they might have some information, recounting how his brother had been a liaison with the other states and he thinks he might have met Miles or at least his partner through some of the other bosses.

"And you really think they'll talk?"

"No," he smiles ruefully, "but I aim to gently coax them into talking."

"You're joking." I raise an eyebrow at him when he tells me about his grand plan of organizing an all-out debauchery full of naked women, drugs, and alcohol.

"I can't just kill them," he pouts, "I'd become public enemy number one. Not that I'm *not* already. But I'm trying not to become everyone's target." He sighs, as if it's the hardest thing he's ever done—not killing someone.

"I'm with you on that account." I cross my arms over my chest, "Until the naked women part."

"Jealous?" He wiggles his eyebrows at me, a smile playing on his lips.

"If you want your dick to remain where it is—attached to your body." I lean into him, my fingers brushing against the front of his pants as I grab him. "You better be deaf and blind to anything that goes on there."

"Damn it, Sisi," he breathes harshly, maneuvering me on top of him, "how can I bear to leave you alone when you say something like that?" He nuzzles his face in my hair, "You know I love it when you threaten me."

"You're weird," I joke.

"And you're the only one for me. I thought we'd established that." He looks me in the eye, his expression serious. "Now run along before I decide to cuff you to my side."

"Tempting," I drawl, dragging my nails down his chest.

"But not productive. At least for now." He gives me an intoxicating smile. "Maybe later," he whispers against my lips as he gives me one last kiss.

Reluctantly, I leave him as I make my way back to my room, the exhaustion of the day finally catching up with me.

But as I go to bed, I can only dream about how sweet the future will be.

30
SISI

"I'll see you later, Venezia." I give her a hug as I rummage through my bag, making sure I have everything with me. With how hectic things are around here, I have to catch a taxi to take me to the hospital.

I'd talked with Adrian in the morning, and he'd assured me that Marcello is doing fine, having just woken up from his surgery. Hearing the wonderful news, I couldn't help myself as I'd promised to meet him at the hospital to visit my brother.

Too bad there's still no news of Lina, and to some extent I am worried that her conflict with Marcello will extend to us, too. After all, she hadn't returned any of my calls yet.

Trying to think of a way to get her to talk to me, I don't even notice when a van pulls over right in front of the gates of the house. My reaction is entirely too delayed as I turn around, feeling a sharp pain in my neck before I tumble to the ground. My eyes heavy, I have the vague impression that someone is carrying me toward the van.

The sound of a moving car makes my ears prickle, and I'm jolted awake by a sudden stop.

"*Krasivaya*," I hear a man murmur in my ear, his hands pawing around my rib cage. I start fidgeting, trying to shake him off, but I realize there's rope all around my upper body, holding me in place. My feet, too, are tied around the ankles.

"No, shto eta?" the same man asks, brushing my bangs aside to reveal my forehead.

"Don't touch me!" I hiss, moving my head to the side.

"Vasily," another man whistles, "the kitten has claws," he laughs derisively.

I take a moment to look around, noting there are five men inside the van. Four of them are around forty or fifty years old while the one next to me seems to be the youngest at around thirty.

"Kuznetsov doesn't have bad taste," one of the elders says in an accented voice, and it finally dawns on me why I'm here.

Vlad.

"I thought he was gay," the younger one laughs.

"Maybe she's his beard."

"Let's hope not, or the plan won't work," the elder says, turning his attention to me.

"Tell me, little bird, are you his beard?"

I narrow my eyes at him, not entirely sure of the question but not willing to show them any weakness.

"Last I checked he was clean shaven." I smirk down at him.

He stares at me for a second before bursting into laughter.

"Oh, she's a feisty one. Maybe not his beard, after all. God knows, a meek one wouldn't stand a chance."

"Here we are," one of the men in the back signals, "bag her up," he says and I frown, not understanding his meaning.

Out of nowhere, a gag is placed in my mouth and a huge bag is thrown over my head as one of the men drapes me over his shoulder, exiting the van.

It seems that Vlad's really pissed some people off this time. I know I should be scared, but for some reason I trust that Vlad won't let anything happen to me.

These guys, on the other hand... I feel bad for them, and I would have told them as much had they not put this blasted gag over my mouth. They might think they know Vlad, but they're in for a pretty big surprise when they realize just how dangerous he can be.

"Gentlemen, you're early!" I hear Vlad's voice as he greets the men. There's an echo resounding, so I'm guessing it's a large room.

Some shuffling and I'm thrown to the ground.

"Oh and you brought a present too?" he asks in that amused voice of his.

I wiggle my feet, hoping he'll notice my shoes, but it's in vain as the men continue to address him.

"We couldn't resist after we got your gifts," one speaks, "especially given that Ilya was my brother-in-law." I can hear the tension in his voice and for some reason I'm sure Vlad's gifts had not had any good intentions attached to them.

"Well, it brought you here, did it not?" he asks, moving around the room. "You'll have to excuse the lack of entertainment. I wasn't expecting you until..." He trails off, and I can just imagine him checking his wristwatch, "Two hours from now. The girls I hired for tonight don't start their shift until midnight." He sighs audibly and I smile against the gag, his theatrics never failing to amuse me.

"Good thing we brought something, too. We can use her in the meantime," the younger one whose voice I have memorized by now says, yanking the bag from my body.

I blink twice, trying to accommodate my eyes to the light as I notice we're in a warehouse. A huge warehouse. There are two rows of tables around, all adorned with food and drink, an altar of sorts at the end of the space, a huge, gilded icon of the Virgin Mary gracing the wall. Everything seems almost regal, from gold cutlery and plates to silver and gold chalices, it looks like the feast of a tsar.

Vlad is standing maybe a few feet away from me, his eyes looking at me intently before he turns to the others, smiling.

"Wonderful," he says, not betraying any emotion.

Besides the five men from earlier, there's no one else in the vicinity, and for a moment I fear that Vlad may be outnumbered. Even Seth, who should have been here protecting Vlad, is nowhere to be seen.

But then I remember his acrobatics from the restaurant and I realize I shouldn't worry too much.

"You don't recognize her?" one man asks, mildly peeved at Vlad's reaction.

Vlad walks toward me, looking at me from head to toe.

"Nope. Should I?" He shrugs, gazing up at the men. His act is so flawless, even they start doubting whether they got the right person or not.

"Then why don't I start?" Vasily drawls, coming next to me and placing his hand on my breast.

Vlad's gaze darkens, and a sinister smile appears on his face.

"Yes, why don't you?" His voice is low, but you'd have to be deaf not to hear the unmistakable danger reverberating from it.

Vasily unties the rope around my torso, freeing my arms. But I don't get to enjoy my newly found freedom as he rips the bodice of my dress, the entire front tearing along the seams, my breasts exposed.

I still, my eyes widening as I'm unable to react to the sudden assault.

"Sisi, move back!" Vlad yells at me, his entire body stiff and on the verge of erupting. I make to move, but Vasily has me firmly in his grasp, his greedy eyes fixed on me as he glances at my exposed chest.

He doesn't get to touch me again as a knife embeds itself in his throat, his expression shocked as he clutches at the bleeding wound with his hands.

I scurry to the back, managing to avoid another man as I run to where Vlad directed me.

"So she does matter. Kuznetsov, we'll have so much fun with her once we've dealt with you," an older man says, not reacting in the least at the bleeding Vasily, or the fact that Vlad had barely moved a finger to mortally wound him. "Maybe we'll keep you alive so you can watch," he continues.

A loud noise erupts in the warehouse as Vlad starts laughing, bending low to grab his stomach as more and more laughter spills out of him.

"You?" he asks, pointing at the four men still standing. "You?" he asks again, barely containing his laughter.

The men are already in position, raising their guns to aim at Vlad, an entire arsenal at their disposal. For the first time, I'm scared.

Because yes, Vlad is a wonderful fighter and could theo- retically take those four old men. But he's also defenseless, and for all his claims to the contrary... he's just a man.

"Sisi, get behind the altar," he commands, the switch in his voice immediate.

With shaky fingers, I try to untie the rope around my feet, frustrated when it doesn't give way immediately.

"Now, Sisi," Vlad yells. The rope untied, I hurry behind the altar, my back hitting the frame of the gilded icon.

"Do you really think you can take all of us, Kuznetsov?"

"Ah, gentlemen." Vlad walks casually around, picking up a golden goblet of wine. "Who taught you to poke the sleeping dragon?" he asks, donning a mask of amusement once more.

"You think you can kill our men and we'll come in peace?" another man chimes in. I sneak my head around the small altar, watching the scene unfold.

"I rather thought you'd thank me," Vlad replies daringly, "after all, what good does it do to have useless men around you? I did you a favor." He shrugs, a smug smile on his face.

"You..." An elder steps forward, his mouth in a scowl, but another man stops him.

"I've never quite liked you, boy. You think you can order everyone around to do your bidding? We've long decided you needed to be taught a lesson. This just happened to be the perfect occasion," he spits out, his gun pointed at Vlad.

"See, gentlemen, I really wanted to be a gracious host today. You can see I've spared no expense. Why, even the gold is real." He lifts up his goblet, the light hitting the metal and making it glint. "And you have to come into my own home and disrespect me as such?" He shakes his head, making a tsking sound.

"I would have let you leave with your lives intact too, but you really had to go there. You just had to mess with my property." He purses his lips, a frown on his forehead.

His property? I'm his property?

We'll need to have some words about that after he's done with these people.

"Look at him," one man laughs, swinging his gun around, "he's behaving as if he's already won."

"Oh." Vlad smiles, the goblet falling to the ground with a thud. "But I have," he says just as he ducks, the noise of gunshots permeating the air.

"Missed," his voice rings out as he rolls to the ground, taking with him the tablecloth, all the cutlery, plates and food falling to the ground in a deafening noise. More gunshots, with the occasional "missed," from Vlad as he moves around like a ghost, his movements insanely fast as he avoids all incoming bullets.

He can't be real.

I rub at my eyes, thinking I'm seeing things, but Vlad's movements are just insane by any standards, and even the men going against him have a hard time believing what they're seeing.

He's playing with them as he ducks, rolls, moving his body like a trained gymnast. He's not even trying to go on the offensive. Rather, he's relishing letting them chase, their frustration seemingly increasing his enjoyment.

The gunshot sounds keep on going until they suddenly stop. There are some stilted sounds as the men keep on pushing the trigger of their guns, entirely out of ammo.

"Well, I guess now we can talk like civilized people?" Vlad emerges from a corner, casually moving around as if they haven't emptied four guns chasing him around the room.

"Fuck you!" one yells, throwing himself at Vlad. One look at his face and I can see him rolling his eyes.

Vlad merely moves a few steps to the right, his foot shooting out as he trips the man. Falling to the ground, he groans in pain. Vlad's foot presses down on his back, holding him to the ground.

"Didn't I tell you it was useless?" He shakes his head at them, a knife in his hand as he plays with the blade.

The men aren't deterred as they all tackle Vlad, grabbing knives from the ground and trying to get a hit.

Vlad sighs deeply, maneuvering his own knife as he throws it at the first man, hitting him right in the eye. With inherent ease, he waltzes around, avoiding any direct hit, his hand reaching out to dislodge the knife before pushing it into another man.

The scene continues as he uses just one knife to stab all three men, leaving them all bleeding on the ground.

When he sees that they're all out of commission, he comes over to me, taking me into his arms.

"I'm sorry," he whispers, "Did they..." He trails off and I quickly shake my head, watching relief flood into his features. "I didn't expect they'd go for you, which was an oversight on my part," he confesses—one of the rare moments I've seen Vlad admitting he was wrong.

"I knew you'd take care of them," I tell him. My faith in him had not wavered even for a second.

"Damned right. No one touches you and lives." He smiles at me, and I finally allow myself to relax.

But it's too early as we turn around, alerted by the screeching tires of another car stopping in front of the warehouse.

There's a split of a second where Vlad pushes me back behind the altar, his body on top of mine as more gunshots ring out—this time the noise more powerful than before.

"Shit. They brought out the big guns," he mutters, his hands opening a cabinet behind the altar table and taking out a few weapons of his own.

"Where is Seth? Or Maxim?" I ask, worried he might truly be outnumbered this time.

"Don't curse me out, Hell Girl, but I actually sent Seth to watch over your house. They must have grabbed you right before he arrived," he explains, a little exasperated. "Afraid it's just me for now."

"You better not get yourself killed. Or me, for that matter," I mutter as more shots are aimed toward the warehouse doors, the entire thing riddled with bullet holes.

"Never." He stares at me intently before brushing his lips ever so lightly against mine. "Stay hidden," he whispers before arming himself to the hilt and going out to greet his guests.

It's only as I look around at the already fallen men that I realize his chasing game had been all about *not* drawing blood. And as more armed men burst into the warehouse, I know it's only a matter of time before he truly snaps.

And everyone will be sorry to have woken the beast.

The playfulness starts to recede as he jumps in front of one man, moving his weapon out of his reach before knocking him out and turning the gun on the others around. It's a massacre as he shoots like a madman, a smile of pure bliss on his face as five men drop to the ground.

For a moment, I have to wonder just how many more are coming, as more and more trickle inside the warehouse.

Vlad continues the shooting, ducking and hiding when the fire is directed toward him, using the tables as shields.

No one stood a chance.

It's as clear as day as he rains chaos on them, his glee audible as he kills man after man. Bullets are flying through the air, the icon behind me becoming riddled with holes, the sounds deafening.

"Drop your weapon," I hear someone yell. Sneaking my head around the altar table, I see Vlad in the middle of the warehouse, breathing hard.

There are four more men in front of him, all of them pointing their guns at him.

"Interesting to see you all working together," Vlad jokes, walking around slowly, "do you even have any more bullets in that rifle of yours?" He nods toward one man's gun.

"You're dead," the man hisses at him.

"Am I?" he asks, feigning surprise. "Let me tell you how it's going to go, old chap. That rifle in your hands holds at most thirty rounds." His eyes rove over the other men, a smirk on his face as he zones in on their weapons. "Someone hasn't been counting," he chuckles.

"What..."

"Come on, shoot me if you can," Vlad says, spreading his arms like an eagle waiting to be poached. "You can't, can you?" He shrugs, amused.

I smile too, realizing he'd been baiting them to shoot all their rounds, counting the bullets.

Damn, that's impressive.

"Don't move." I feel a breath on my neck as a hand sneaks over my mouth, forcing me to move from behind the altar. The barrel of a gun is jabbed against my temple, his words sending shivers down my back as he takes delight in telling me just what he'll do to me after killing Vlad.

"You're not the only one with an ace in your hand, Kuznetsov," the man behind me speaks out, pushing me forward as I almost stumble to my feet, the gun still menacingly at my head.

Vlad turns slowly, dangerously slow, his gaze clouded as he takes in the man behind me. The smile is completely gone as he takes a few steps toward us.

"So this was your marvelous plan," he adds drily, "band together on *one* man."

"You've been upsetting some pretty important people,

Kuznetsov. We're merely delivering the message." His hands tighten over me, and my gaze flies to Vlad's, worried about what will happen next.

He looks between the two of us, suddenly a bored expression on his face.

"Let's count, shall we? I see at least fifteen men on the floor. Five more to go. What do you think the odds are?" he asks, his hand lowering ever so slowly with the tilt of his head, his gaze back on me.

My eyes widen as I realize what he's trying to communicate, and I give him a slow nod.

One hand on a rifle, the other is resting by his side, his fingers slowly unfurling in a count.

One.

Two.

Three.

When I see the third finger, I drop my head low, gathering momentum and pushing myself back with as much force as I can muster before dropping low again.

In a split of a second, Vlad's gun is up, his finger on the trigger, the bullet whizzing past the top of my head and lodging itself into the man's forehead.

He drops to the floor with a thump, Vlad's languid steps taking him next to me.

"Hide," he whispers, and I waste no time in obeying.

He crouches low next to the fallen man, taking out a long blade and planting it deep into the man's chest.

The other men are at the back, just watching, their raised weapons for show as they no longer have any ammo to use.

I bet they never thought they'd need that many bullets for just one man.

Vlad's blade cuts through the skin, using the butt of the

gun to smash through the ribcage until he has clear access to the heart.

No...

One hand wraps itself around the heart, yanking it out of the man's chest. The bleeding organ is still seeping blood, a trail developing as Vlad strolls along the warehouse, pumping the heart with his own hands.

"You thought to come into *my* home, and threaten what's *mine*?" His voice rings out—it's different.

There's an ominous quality to it, and even I react to the pure evil behind his mask. He's gone, or at least almost gone.

But as he brings the heart to his mouth, biting a big chunk of it, blood trailing down his mouth and horrified gasps echoing in the warehouse, I have my confirmation.

He's gone...

Dear God, but I don't know what's going to happen now. He's fought so much to keep himself under control, playing with the assailants to avoid a face-to-face confrontation that would result in bloodshed.

And now...

I watch in horror as his mouth widens into a malefic smile, his entire countenance changed. Sinister intentions ooze off him as he catches one man by the throat, raising him in the air with ease before bringing his head to the ground, smashing the skull with so much force the entire cavity breaks, brain matter leaking out.

He doesn't stop.

He keeps on smashing until there's little left than a mass of mangled brain and bone, both barely hanging to the body around the neck.

The other men try to flee when they see his true nature, their hands moving rapidly in the sign of the cross as they say prayers.

In vain.

One after another, Vlad chases them around. Masterfully wielding his blade, he cuts one man's arms, blood leaking down, a horrified expression on the victim's face. But Vlad's smile only widens as he uses the man's own palms to slap him around until he becomes bored, his victim already bled out.

Gathering his long blade, he stalks his next prey, cutting the man at the waist in such a smooth line, the torso immediately becomes separated from the lower part of the body, organs spilling out on the floor.

Vlad's laughter fills the room as he smears his face with the blood and entrails of the dead man.

I guess he wasn't kidding that he bathes in entrails.

Two more men are still up for grabs, both hiding around the room and trying to avoid Vlad's detection.

They may think they're safe, but Vlad finds them with ease behind a table, his hands grabbing onto their napes as he drags them toward the center of the room.

Already the floor is red with blood, more and more flowing from all the victims—the slaughtered and the shot ones. It's like an ocean of red as he dumps the two cowering men right in the middle of it.

They fall down, the blood splashing around, their expressions of horror as they try to get away from Vlad. They pick up whatever's close to them, flinging it at him, but to no avail.

Blade swinging high, he effortlessly cuts their heads, both falling to the floor and rolling on the ground. But he doesn't stop just at that. He keeps smashing, bringing the blade into their bodies and destroying what's left of them.

Flesh hanging, blood pouring, bone shattered.

There's only destruction in his path as he continues to

wreck all the other bodies too, cutting them to pieces—the only thing that's mildly satisfying him.

The walls are splattered with organic matter, the entire warehouse almost fully painted red.

I'm still behind the altar, unsure of my next steps.

Vlad seems even more feral as he rips his shirt at the seams, tearing his clothes off until he's standing naked in the middle of the blood bath.

He's swinging the liquid reverently around, using his hands to paint himself from head to toe in blood.

Like a pagan god, he's standing there among his sacrifices, blood both his armor and his weakness.

I'm at a loss for words as I watch him in awe, the stark red against his inked skin, the look of pure rapture on his face.

How is he human?

A low sound escapes him as he falls to his knees, blood splashing around him and staining his skin further.

I need to help him.

How is it that even in this form I'm not afraid of him? I see him as the devil he is, and while his skills never cease to amaze me, I can't help but be turned on by him in all his bloody splendor.

Mustering the courage to leave my hiding spot, I tread carefully, moving toward him slowly. His head snaps back, his gaze unfocused as he looks at me, like an animal ready to pounce at any moment. His ears prickle with awareness with every step I make, the sound reverberating in the room.

He turns fully toward me, his eyes watching me closely but without a hint of recognition.

"Vlad," I whisper when I'm almost at his side, kneeling in front of him. He tilts his head to the side, watching me.

Slowly, my hands reach out to touch his face. He flinches

at the contact but doesn't pull away, looking at me with a mix of curiosity and want. Leaning into him, I press my lips to his bloody ones, happy when he doesn't push me away.

But he's not kissing me back, either.

Knowing it takes a while for him to come back to himself, I gently coax him with my lips, applying the barest hint of pressure as I move closer to him.

31
SISI

He's looking down at me, his eyes almost blank as he tries to make sense of what's happening. My tongue sneaks out, and I lick his lips, seeking entrance into his mouth. His lips part slightly, allowing me in. I'm careful as I wind my arms around his neck, bringing him flush against my chest as I deepen the kiss.

He still holds himself stiff, his open eyes following my every movement.

Breathing hard, I lean back, blood seeping from the ground and into the material of my dress. I take a moment to observe him, looking for any clues he might be closer to reacting. As my gaze trails down his body, I realize he's fully erect.

Without giving it much thought, I quickly undo the zipper of my dress, flinging it off my body until I'm as naked as he is, standing in front of him like an offering.

Oh, but I am one.

Taking his hand, I bring it to my mouth, sucking his finger in. His gaze is sharp as it follows my every movement.

Tantalizingly slow, I bring his hand down my neck and onto my breasts, urging him to touch me.

His other hand comes up of its own accord, his palm fitting itself around my breast as he feels his way around my flesh.

I lower his hand even more, pushing it between my legs to find me dripping wet for him.

He blinks rapidly, his fingers brushing against my clit in a slow motion. I release a whimper at the sudden touch, watching his rapt expression as he explores my pussy, one finger playing with my entrance before dipping in.

But his hand is soon gone as he brings his fingers to his nose, inhaling my scent before placing them in his mouth and sucking them.

There's still no recognition in his eyes, but as he becomes more reactive, I become bolder, trailing my hands down his chest until I reach his erection.

Pupils dilated, his lips part as I circle my fingers around his girth, stroking him.

"Come back to me, Vlad," I whisper. His head whips back at my words, his hand shooting forward and wrapping itself around my neck. In less than a second, I'm on my back, his body looming over me as he settles between my legs, his cock twitching against my stomach.

His nostrils flare as he lowers his head to my face, breathing in deeply. A growl escapes him, his teeth bared as he licks my skin. He continues to explore the flesh just beneath my jaw, his nose nuzzling, his wet tongue trailing behind. Like an animal, he's trying to determine my identity by smell and taste.

Blood clings to my hair and my body as he pushes me further into the floor, the liquid staining my skin and making it sticky as I move around.

"Come back to me." I continue to lull him back with my voice, my hand caressing his hair as he continues the exploration with his mouth.

Out of nowhere, his big hands grab my ass, spreading my legs further to accommodate his hips.

I don't even get to speak as he dives forward, impaling me on his cock in one smooth slide. All the resistance falls away in the face of his assault, my pussy stretching around him in what could possibly be the worst pain I've ever experienced.

Eyes wide, my mouth opens on a scream, my voice echoing inside the room.

It hurts.

He's fully seated inside of me, the pain so intense my eyes are tearing up uncontrollably. But he doesn't notice. He doesn't even seem to register my scream of distress. His hands on my ass, he forces himself inside me even deeper, my pussy meeting the base of his cock before he's suddenly out again, slapping back inside me with a force that makes me see stars.

It's like he's tearing me apart in two.

God...

His fingers dig into the skin right above my hip bones, his movements hurried as he thrusts in and out of me, the agony so intense I feel myself slipping.

But I can't!

I need to do this for him, bear it until he comes back to me.

Even though it kills me inside, the stinging pain so blinding I'm almost passing out, I wrap my legs around him, moving my pelvis up slightly to help his motion.

"Come back to me," I whisper on a sob, my throat

clogged from the burn his cock leaves behind as it pushes forward and retreats.

His thrusts are so powerful, his thick cock stretching me beyond belief as he touches me deep inside. Despite the pain, it's like I can feel him in my very soul.

"I love you," I confess. "So very much," I whimper as he keeps on wrecking my body, my words barely coherent as I gasp every time he slides in.

This was supposed to be such a beautiful act. The culmination of all our stolen moments, of all the time we'd spent learning each other's bodies. It was supposed to be a unique experience as we fully gave ourselves to the other for the first time.

But now? It takes everything inside of me not to black out, my soul's pain as intense as my body's, watching this special moment being wrenched away from us.

"I love you," I repeat, anchoring myself in the unconditional love I have for him. An emotion so all-encompassing it's the only thing making me hold on.

He pauses, his head snapping up, his eyes on me, yet he still looks feral, as if he can't understand human language.

A big swipe of his tongue down my collarbone and his mouth latches onto my breast, biting so hard around my nipple I'm sure he's drawn blood.

"No!" I yell, my breath coming in short spurts. My hands hit at his back, the combined pain of the bite and the burn I still feel at the entrance of my pussy making me squirm against him, trying to get him to slow down.

"Please," I whisper, my voice ragged from screaming, my sight foggy from tears. What I'm asking him, though, I don't know.

I just know I'd do anything for him, including letting him break my body apart if that's what's going to bring him back.

He lets go of my breast, his tongue lapping at the blood flowing from my wound before moving again to my neck.

His movements are increasingly violent, like an animal in the throes of mating, his fingers bruising my flesh, his cock pistoning in and out of me at unnatural speed.

At this point, I can only hope he's close, and so I clench my walls around him, hoping to make him reach his climax faster.

His teeth nibble at my neck, his body flush against me so I have no breathing room. And then he bites—again.

But this time he breaks the skin in one go, and I feel his sharp teeth as they reach my muscle, blood pooling out of the wound and all around his mouth. He holds on to my skin so tightly that I feel the rip in my very soul.

"Vlad," a feeble sound escapes me, the pain so intense I'm almost losing consciousness. He's latched on to my throat, like a dog going for the jugular, his teeth lodged inside, his tongue swirling at the broken flesh.

Fear pools in my stomach as I realize he might very well kill me.

I need to get away.

I kick at him, using my hands to push him off of me. I manage to take him by surprise, his eyes unfocused as I shove him to the side, flesh and blood at his mouth.

My flesh and blood.

I feel for the wound, noting there's a gaping hole where my shoulder meets my neck. Panic bubbles inside of me, and I can only scramble back, somehow managing to get to my feet before running.

I don't get far though, a hand in my hair pulling me backward, and I fall on my ass, my scalp burning from his assault.

"Vlad, don't." I try to extricate myself from his grasp, but his eyes are just soulless, watching me as I struggle, his mouth pulling up as if he's enjoying my pain. "Please," I add again, attempting to disentangle his fingers from my hair.

Instead of loosening his hold, it only makes him tighten his hands over my scalp, dragging me backward, the blood on the floor only making it easier for my body to slide against the concrete.

"Vlad, you're hurting me." I keep talking, still not losing hope. Knowing that somehow I'll be able to reach the side of him that's mine and mine alone. "Vlad, please."

Flinging me forward, my back hits the cold, barren floor, and more pain erupts in my joints. I don't even get to react though, both his hands wrapping around my throat as he raises me up on the altar, the edge of the table hitting my ass as he spreads me on its surface.

"Vlad..." I struggle to speak, but he doesn't care. He tilts his head, looking at me through narrowed eyes, his hands tightening around my neck as he enters me again.

My arousal is long gone. The only lubricant somewhat easing his way in is the blood from my ruptured hymen. His hips move in and out of me, fucking me so roughly I'm barely holding on. I feel even more blood gush out of my pussy as he pushes his cock inside me with such ferocity, I'm not sure I'll ever be whole again.

His thrusts gain speed, his hands applying even more force on my throat. I try to push at his shoulders, my breath increasingly more shallow. I feel lightheaded, my limbs losing most of their strength.

He's choking the life out of me.

My arms fall, the fight in me all but dying. My lips are probably purple, every breath I take bringing me closer to my last.

And then it happens.

I feel his muscles tense, his cock jerking inside me as he comes, his warm release shooting up in spurts and flooding my insides. His thrusts slow down as he fills me up with even more cum, his hands becoming slack, his entire body racked by tremors.

His eyes widen for a second before he falls on top of me, completely out of it. I can only stare at the high ceiling, tears dried down my cheeks, wounds still bleeding.

It takes me a while to regain my breath, and when I feel some of my strength coming back, I push him off of me. His back connects with the table, his cock slipping out of me and leaving a burning trail in its wake.

On shaky legs, I almost fall down as I get off the altar table. A mixture of blood and cum flows out of me, slowly dripping down my inner thigh. I don't even dare touch myself in the area, sore and tender from the ravage he wreaked on my body.

There's still a lingering pulsating pain, and I find that I can't even sit down. I just take a few deep breaths, trying to pull myself together, ignoring how everything else hurts like hell.

Skirting around the room, I ignore the carnage around me as I grab a tablecloth, fashioning it around me into a gown. Tearing some more material, I hold it against my neck wound, the bleeding still going strong.

I don't even want to imagine how it looks, the feel of it alone almost making me want to die. I'm pretty sure he ripped skin and muscle from my neck when he bit into it.

I groan out loud, barely holding myself together as I search for something to drink. Finding an unopened bottle of water, I drink greedily, trying to regain some focus.

Damn, Vlad. You almost killed me.

Laughter bubbles inside my chest at the thought. My

entire body is beaten and battered, but I can't help myself as I think of the hilarity of the situation.

He'd wanted so much to avoid hurting me, and he'd ended up destroying me entirely.

It's a while later that he finally comes to.

"Sisi?" I hear his rough voice calling out to me.

I'm barely able to move as I make my way toward him. He's disoriented as he takes in the bloodbath around him, his own body painted in red.

"Sisi?" he repeats, coming toward me.

"You're back," I whisper, relieved.

"What..." He studies me, his brows knitting together.

Coming closer to me, he wrenches the cloth from my body, his gaze horrified as he takes in my bruised flesh.

"It's okay." I'm quick to assure him.

"I did that?" His voice is low and grave, his hand reaching forward to touch me. Without even thinking, I flinch back, my body having a mind of its own—the pain still embedded in its memory. He looks as if I'd struck him when he sees me avoid his touch. "I did that," he states blankly.

"It's not that bad," I say meekly, even though the mere action of speaking takes so much out of me.

"It's not that bad..." he repeats, horrified.

Turning his back to me, he walks numbly back to the altar, resting his arms on the table.

"Vlad?" I walk toward him, placing a hand on his back. I feel his breathing, his chest rising and falling.

"Don't." He turns around, catching my hand. His eyes, while back to normal, are icy cold, a shiver going down my spine at their scrutiny.

"What? Why?" I ask, confused.

"You should go," he says quietly, and it's like I don't recognize him anymore.

"What do you mean I should go?"

His hand unravels the cloth around my neck, a muscle twitching in his jaw as he sees the evidence of his savagery.

"It's fine, it doesn't hurt that much," I lie, my hand going to my neck to cover the wound.

"It doesn't hurt?" He raises an eyebrow, and my eyes search for a crinkling around his eyes, or any type of amusement that would denote *my* Vlad is back. Instead, I find none.

And that scares me more than any physical pain.

He brushes past me as he goes to retrieve his own clothes, slowly putting them back on. Looking around, he finds a phone, calling Maxim and ordering him to come here.

"Vlad?" I ask, unsure about anything.

Why is he so cold?

I don't mind the pain as long as I can have his arms around me, his voice telling me everything's going to be okay. I just want *my* Vlad back.

"Maxim will take you home," he says curtly, yet nonchalantly.

"Vlad... don't shut me out," I plead with him, afraid of this change in him.

"Why would I shut you out when there's nowhere to take you in?" He shrugs.

"What... what do you mean?" I stammer, physical pain and mental confusion getting to me.

"This isn't working, Sisi. Clearly." He smirks, nodding toward the spilled blood on the floor, the corpses littering the entire hall. "You should just go."

"I don't understand," I say honestly. "What isn't working?"

"This." He motions between the two of us, his voice almost robotic. "I kept you around because I thought you could help me with my episodes, but clearly, it's not working."

He's shutting me out.

I can't let him do that. Not now...

"You're not getting rid of me that easily, Vlad. Yes, this was an unfortunate event, but we'll move past it."

"Don't you get it?" He comes closer to me, his breath on my face as he sets his emotionless eyes on me. "You're useless to me now."

I blink. Once. Twice. I keep blinking, thinking I didn't hear him right.

"What... what did you say?"

"You're useless to me now," he repeats, a cruel smile on his face, his fingers wrapped in my hair as he twirls a strand. "I kept you around for one reason, and one reason only. I thought you were the exception to the rule." The corner of his mouth pulls up. "But you're just as ordinary as the others," he states, and my hearing dims, my heart thumping fiercely in my chest.

"Stop," I whisper. "Stop before you say something you'll regret," I beg him.

"Why would I regret it?" He shrugs, looking at me as if I were insignificant.

How did it get here? How?

My throat feels heavy, tears burning behind my eyes at his words.

"I love you, Vlad. You have to know that, I..."

"You love me?" He laughs, the sound painful to my ears. "Sisi, Sisi, you really went and did it, didn't you?" He shakes his head at me derisively. "You know I don't feel *anything*. You knew from the beginning that the most I could offer you were a few orgasms. Nothing more, nothing less."

"Stop." I close my eyes, wanting him to stop talking. It's already hurting too much without him twisting the knife even further.

Because he's just breaking my heart, and I'm already physically broken, I don't need him to deliver the last blow too.

"I should have realized you'd confuse my interest for feelings." He purses his lips, looking at me in disgust. "Fuck, I should have realized someone as unwanted as you would latch on to the first person who gave you attention. But love? Wherever did you get that idea?" he asks, amused.

"You're being cruel." My words are barely above a whisper, a tear falling down my cheek.

"I'm being real. You knew fully well who I was, and what I was capable of. I warned you, didn't I? I warned you not to make me into something I'm not."

"But..."

"We should stop seeing each other," he states, looking at me intently, "after all, it's clear that you're no longer of use to me," he says flippantly.

I stare at him dumbfounded, wondering how everything I cared about could go to hell in the span of a few hours.

He has his emotionless mask on and I can't get a proper read on him.

Honestly, all I want to do is beg him to reconsider, tell him I'll do better, that I'll do whatever he wants me to do and be whoever he wants me to be. *Just don't leave me.*

But the more I look at him, so confident in his decision, so nonchalant about throwing me away, I realize that why should I?

One thing I'd asked of him. Just one.

Never abandon me...

I don't care how much he abuses me, or my body, or how much shit he throws my way. I was ready to accept *every* facet of him—the killer, the animal and the lover. But there's no lover, is there? There's only an emotionless machine wearing the guise of a human.

And suddenly I see how futile everything is.

He's smug as he regards me, probably waiting for me to get to my knees and beg him not to abandon me. After all, that's what someone as *unwanted* as me would do, no?

But I can't... I don't know if he means the words he said or not, but said them he did.

And they hurt.

Worse than the pain in my shoulder, or the one between my legs. They hurt in ways I don't think are healable.

I love him, even when he is not lovable. I love him, but I can't go against myself, forsaking everything I've built for myself just for some fake love.

"I see," I answer slowly.

And for the love I bear him, I'm willing to give him *one* more chance.

"Stop pushing me away, Vlad. I'm still here. And I will still be here if you want me to. You don't have to lie to hurt me..." I trail off when he starts laughing.

The moment my heart breaks... irrevocably.

"Lie? To hurt you? God, Sisi, who do you think you are?" He keeps laughing, pinning me down with those deadly eyes of his.

Empty.

"You're not the only woman on this earth, for fuck's sake," he chuckles. "Fair enough, I tried to see if you could help me, and now that you've failed I just don't need you anymore. It's as simple as that."

"I see," I answer bleakly. "You've made your choice." I nod at him, holding myself straight in spite of the pain, in spite of the way my entire soul fractures under the weight of his words.

"Choice," he shakes his head, "don't be so dramatic. It was a simple matter of trial and error. And well," he smiles, "it seems this was an error."

Grabbing the nearest knife I spot, I tighten my fingers around it, noting a slight reaction in his eyes.

"And now I make mine," I tell him before grasping onto the length of my hair, pulling it forward and cutting through it with the blade.

Once my dearest possession, now it's just a pile of crap.

Strands fall to the floor, becoming soaked in blood. His gaze doesn't stray from me as I keep cutting until the entire length has been severed.

Flinging it to his feet, I do my best to be strong.

"If you can throw me away, then so can I. But make no mistake, from this moment onward you are *dead* to me." How I'm not sobbing my eyes out right now, I don't know.

But as I look at my hair, dead and gathered at his feet, I know it's just a matter of time before I break. And I don't want to give him the satisfaction of watching what's left of my heart shatter to even tinier pieces.

"I told you once, Vlad, I would take anything you dish out at me—anything, as long as you never abandoned me." I take a deep breath, the knife falling to the floor. "From this moment on, we are strangers," I declare, for his benefit and for mine, too.

He doesn't react, like I knew he wouldn't. He just shrugs,

not even looking at my hair as he moves past me, leaving me behind.

I will survive.

I've survived for so long, there's nothing that can really kill me now.

But as I watch his retreating figure, I realize some part of me did die today.

A part I may never get back.

TO BE CONTINUED
Vlad and Sisi's story concludes in *His Hell Girl*.
Join Veronica's reader group!